For Your
Heart Only

Also by Debra White Smith
in Large Print:

Second Chances
A Shelter in the Storm
The Awakening
To Rome with Love

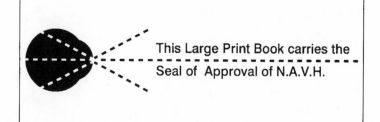

For Your Heart Only

Debra White Smith

Thorndike Press • Waterville, Maine

Published in 2005 by arrangement with Harvest House
Publishers.

Thorndike Press® Large Print Christian Fiction.

The tree indicium is a trademark of Thorndike Press.

The text of this Large Print edition is unabridged.
Other aspects of the book may vary from the original edition.

Set in 16 pt. Plantin by Liana M. Walker.

Printed in the United States on permanent paper.

Library of Congress Cataloging-in-Publication Data

Smith, Debra White.
    For your heart only / by Debra White Smith.
        p. cm. — (Thorndike Press large print Christian fiction)
    ISBN 0-7862-7255-4 (lg. print : hc : alk. paper)
    1. Large type books. I. Title. II. Thorndike Press large
print Christian fiction series.
PS3569.M5178 F67 2005
  813′.54—dc22   2004024840

To my childcare provider, Molly Smith. Molly is always there for me at the drop of a hat. At times I go weeks without needing her, then I call and she's always cheerful and willing to help out. More than once I've called and said, "Uh, Molly, I'm getting on an airplane tomorrow, would you be available to pick up my kids from school?" She always says, "Sure!" What a wonderful woman of God. Thanks, Molly, for always being there and for all you do!

As the Founder/CEO of NAVH, the only national health agency solely devoted to those who, although not totally blind, have an eye disease which could lead to serious visual impairment, I am pleased to recognize Thorndike Press★ as one of the leading publishers in the large print field.

Founded in 1954 in San Francisco to prepare large print textbooks for partially seeing children, NAVH became the pioneer and standard setting agency in the preparation of large type.

Today, those publishers who meet our standards carry the prestigious "Seal of Approval" indicating high quality large print. We are delighted that Thorndike Press is one of the publishers whose titles meet these standards. We are also pleased to recognize the significant contribution Thorndike Press is making in this important and growing field.

Lorraine H. Marchi, L.H.D.
Founder/CEO
NAVH

★ Thorndike Press encompasses the following imprints: Thorndike, Wheeler, Walker and Large Pr int Press.

The Seven Sisters

Jacquelyn Lightfoot: An expert in martial arts, private detective Jac is "married" to her career and lives in Denver.

Kim Lan Lowery O'Donnel: Tall, lithe, and half Vietnamese/half Caucasian, Kim is a much-sought-after supermodel who lives in New York City. Mick, her husband, is a missions coordinator.

Marilyn Douglas Langham: Joshua and Marilyn, along with Marilyn's daughter, Brooke, live in Arkansas. Marilyn works as an office manager for a veterinarian.

Melissa Moore Franklin: After an exciting Mediterranean cruise, Dr. Moore recently married Kinkaide Franklin and moved to Nashville.

Sammie Jones: The star reporter for *Romantic Living* magazine, Sammie is an expert on Victorian houses, art, and finding the perfect romantic getaway. She and her husband live in Dallas.

Sonsee LeBlanc Delaney: A passionate veterinarian known for her wit, Sonsee grew up in a southern mansion outside of New Orleans. Now married to her lifelong friend, Taylor Delaney, Sonsee is expecting her first child. They own a ranch in Texas.

Victoria Roberts: A charming, soft-spoken domestic "genius" who loves to cook, work on crafts, and sew, Victoria is married and lives in Destin, Florida.

FOR YOUR HEART ONLY Cast

Adam Jones: Sammie's husband.

Austin Sellers: Pastor in Ouray, Colorado.

Brett Jones: Sammie's three-year-old rambunctious son.

The Butlers: R.J.'s parents and Sammie's friends. The Butlers own the Dallas-based magazine *Romantic Living*.

Donna Yarbrough: Jac Lightfoot's faithful secretary.

Fuat Rantomi: The leader of the infamous Rantomi family.

Kinkaide Franklin: A nationally recognized Christian pianist, Kinkaide resides in Nashville with his wife, Melissa Moore.

Kinkaide Franklin Sr.: Lawton & Kinkaide's father. He and Rosa reside in Oklahoma City.

Lawton Franklin: A computer whiz, Lawton travels all over the United States helping blind people gain financial and personal independence through computer proficiency. Blind since birth, Lawton is Kinkaide's younger brother.

Maurice Stein: Former policeman who works for Fuat Rantomi.

Norman Green: FBI agent.

R.J. Butler: Sammie Jones' first love and former fiancé. R.J. is an avid motorcyclist.

Rosa Franklin: Lawton and Kinkaide's mother. She resides with her husband in Oklahoma City.

One

❧

"If you don't tell me where they are, you'll regret it!" a bear-like voice growled.

"I already told you!" a weasely voice rasped. "I don't have them! I didn't find them anywhere!"

"Maybe you didn't understand me," the bear snarled.

A trunk lid slammed. A car door clicked opened. An ominous pause sent a chill up Lawton Franklin's spine.

"In case you haven't noticed, this area is deserted right now. Nobody's watching. You better . . ."

Lawton strained to hear the rest of a conversation that diminished in volume as the animosity increased. The faint smell of vehicle exhaust mixed with the humid Dallas midnight as Lawton stepped from behind a concrete pillar, gripped the handle of his laptop computer, and crept forward. His other piece of luggage could wait.

Lawton had spent a lifetime overcoming the darkness that was forever his companion. Tonight's predicament made him resent the darkness more than he had in years. As he moved forward, he adjusted his dark glasses and tried to hear any trace of the heated exchange. He debated whether to yell for a clerk, but the gruff-voiced man had just said there was no one around. If he caused enough commotion, perhaps someone inside would hear, but if he called out and no one came, the scoundrel would undoubtedly get away. As he trudged forward, his sensory perception validated that the airport's curbside was presently deserted.

"I wouldn't put it past you to keep them for yourself!" the bear accused.

"Do you think I would have flown back here if I'd kept them?" the weasel demanded. "I just knocked off two people and searched a house. If I had intended to keep them, I wouldn't have returned. Listen to me — I'm telling the truth!"

"Get into the limo," the bear demanded, "and shut up before somebody hears you."

The voice isn't more than six feet away, Lawton figured. As he headed forward, every crunch of his own loafers against concrete sounded as if it were magnified a thousandfold. The skin across his shoulders prickled. He paused, raised his head, and debated his options. Every muscle tensed while he teetered on the precipice of indecision. The distant hiss of an approaching airport shuttle suggested safety. He stumbled, but caught himself as he relived the events of the last hour.

Lawton had insisted that the friendly airport clerk leave him at the deserted curbside where he was supposed to meet his new trainee and his father. Usually, Lawton's contacts located him as he disembarked the plane. But this time the client called Lawton's cell phone just as he exited the late flight. They were running behind schedule. Lawton had assured his client that he'd procure the assistance of an airport employee and await them at curbside. He had successfully done exactly that so many times he'd lost count. All his nationwide travel had been so uneventful that he never even suspected there would be a hitch.

The nearing presence proved he should have never assumed his trips would always be trouble free. With a plea for help rising in his throat, Lawton stumbled farther away from the approaching man. The rumble of the shuttle's engine grew closer. Lawton's palms produced a thin film of sweat. A viselike hand clenched his forearm and yanked him forward.

"Help!" Lawton roared and flailed his free fist. The smack of knuckles on nose coincided with the bear's surprised grunt. Lawton's stinging fist affirmed that his aim had been true.

"What are you doing?" the weasel called.

"Shut up and help me!" the bear yelled.

"But he's blind! Just leave him —"

"He heard us!"

Lawton tried to dig his heels into the concrete and scrambled to break the bear's hold. As the struggle increased, the oaf yanked Lawton's business jacket half off. In an attempt at freedom, Lawton shrugged out of the jacket and it dropped at his feet. Yet the bear anticipated the move, and his fingers ate into Lawton's arm. Clenching his teeth, Lawton increased his grip on the computer case and slammed it toward the vicinity of the man's head. The crunch of high technology against skull left the bear bellowing and Lawton wincing. Even in this most dire of situations, he hated wielding his prized computer as a weapon.

A fierce blow to Lawton's temple annihilated the fleeting regret, and a biting pain consumed his head. The fog of unconsciousness seeped through the pain, and Lawton toppled forward. As he was shoved into the fragrant folds of leather seats, the airport shuttle's roar reverberated against the portico. The bear and weasel clambered in atop him. The car door slammed. The car jerked forward. Lawton's throbbing skull bade the ebony fog to immerse him, and he slipped into the dark beyond.

Detective Jacquelyn Lightfoot plopped into her office chair and dragged the brown lunch bag from her aging desk's bottom drawer. She opened the sack and peered at a package of whole-wheat crackers, a high-impact salad, replete with bean sprouts, lean turkey, and almonds, and an apple. She turned down the corners of her mouth and grimaced. Normally her simple yet strict diet sufficiently satisfied. Her martial arts training usually left little room for veering from a disciplined eating regime. But a whole month had lapsed since she had veered from her lean diet and cooked up an array of Mexican food to die for. And today she dreamed about a supreme pizza — heavy on the supreme. Jac peered at the phone that doubled as an intercom. Her secretary, Donna Yarbrough, would no doubt agree to sharing an Italian pie. Jac had dedicated today to the sole task of finally preparing her income tax figures for the accountant, and such a task demanded pizza.

"I'm stuck in here all day," Jac mumbled, glancing around the austere office. Her gaze rested on the bookcase lining the far wall. Her vision blurred. In place of the books, a steaming supreme appeared.

"It's a matter of life and death," she rationalized as she punched the intercom button that buzzed Donna's phone.

"I've already ordered it," Donna said before Jac could utter a word. "Thick crust. Extra olives."

Jac chuckled. "You're an angel. Now, if I could just get you to sort through all this income tax stuff."

"Can't do it," Donna said. "Some things you just gotta do for yourself."

"Excuses, excuses."

"Oops, there's the phone again." The phone's intermittent buzz floated over the line. "Don't think that pizza is just for you. This morning has been 'national phone

16

your local detective day.' "

"Thanks for everything. I'd be up a creek without you." Jac released the intercom button, glared at the mound of receipts in the desktop's center, and sighed. She reached down and coaxed open the desk's heavy bottom drawer. Jac slam-dunked the brown bag special inside, and a lone daisy, flat and dry, plopped near the bag. The daisy had originally been accompanied by two dozen just like it. Jac, caught in a sentimental moment of weakness, had preserved one of the blooms. She picked up the dried blossom and held it to her nose. The musty remembrance of an exotic cruise, an intriguing man, and spring's fresh promise met her senses as the stiff petals tickled her nose.

I love the stars. I love them, a voice taunted from the recesses of her mind. Jac compressed her lips, dropped the daisy into the half-empty drawer, and shoved it shut. She rubbed her hands down her jeans-clad thighs, stood, stretched, and trudged toward the corner refrigerator. A cold bottle of water would hit the spot and hopefully dash aside the dead-end memories that threatened to barge upon her day.

The telephone's ring stopped the pint-sized detective in her tracks. Jacquelyn had told Donna not to put through any calls that weren't dire emergencies. She frowned, and her fingers curled into themselves.

The door opened and Donna stepped inside. Her forever present blonde bun and ancient double-knit made the 50-year-old look at least 65. She removed her reading glasses and shrugged. "Sorry. This sounds really urgent," she said over the third ring.

As the phone rang for the fourth time, a black pall draped itself over Jac, and something deep within whispered that this call might very well deliver news that would alter her life. As Donna discreetly exited, Jacquelyn stepped back to her desk and sat down. The cordless receiver shook in her hand as she delivered a reedy, "Lightfoot."

"Jac. It's Sammie."

"Hi, Sam!" The knot in her stomach relaxed, and she leaned against the oak desk, scarred by time. "Whaz-up?"

"I was just on the phone with M–Melissa. She asked me to call all the sisters about an urgent, *urgent* prayer request — and she said I should call you first."

"Oh?" Jac stood.

"It's about Lawton Franklin, Kinkaide's brother."

Jac drew in a quick breath and bit her bottom lip. "Yes?"

A haunting image floated through her mind. An image of a man with mahogany hair and dark glasses and a confident grin that belied any hint of handicap. A man who had the tenacity of six warriors in his little fingertip. A man who had momentarily stirred Jac's latent longings for marriage.

As Sammie's silence stretched, Jac expected the worst. The greater her suspicions grew, the less success she had at shoving Lawton's crestfallen face from her mind. Last spring, one of her six college "sisters," Melissa Moore, had talked Jac into a much-needed vacation. Lawton had likewise accompanied his brother, Kinkaide. The Mediterranean cruise had been all that the brochures had promised, replete with more romance than Jac ever planned to invite into her life. By the time the party arrived in Rome, Jacquelyn knew that Lawton had more on his mind than just a passing friendship. They had been at the base of the Spanish Steps when she coldheartedly delivered her bitter news. Jacquelyn bluntly informed Lawton that she was in no way interested in even friendship. Lawton had remained silent — silent and dispirited. But Jacquelyn knew, even then, that her words stemmed from her terror. Terror and agony. Agony and shame.

Now Jac suffocated amid a fathomless sea of remorse. *If Lawton were dead . . .*

"What's the matter?" she prodded, able to stand the silence no longer.

"He's missing," Sammie said as if she knew full well the implications this news would have on Jacquelyn. The seven-sister grapevine never failed. What one knew about a sister's affections, they usually all knew.

"Missing?" Jac repeated as her viselike grip on the phone relaxed a fraction. "You mean he's not — not d–d–"

"They don't know. All they know is that he was supposed to be picked up last night at the Dallas/Ft. Worth airport. The client and his father showed up but couldn't find Lawton. They spent some time at the airport and had security search any likely places. According to an airport employee, Lawton arrived at the designated meeting spot as planned, but he wasn't there when the father arrived. One of his pieces of luggage was there, but no Lawton. Apparently nobody saw what happened, either."

Jac walked toward the picture window and blindly stared toward the Colorado Rockies that blurred into a blue mist on the horizon. This time the peaked mountains topped in snow did little to ease her tension. She paused but a second then turned to pace back toward her desk.

"Have they reported this to the police?" she snapped.

"Yes, of course. But you know as well as I do that —"

"They won't do much until he's been gone 24 hours."

"Right."

"And when exactly will that be?"

"I guess midnight tonight," Sammie returned.

"I'm flying to Dallas," Jac stated. Not once did she question her decision. She only knew that Lawton was missing . . . that Lawton needed her. Or rather, Melissa needed her. *Yes, Melissa. He's* her *brother-in-law.* She *needs me.*

Jac cast a cursory look at the mound of receipts on her desk and stifled a groan. "Today. I'm coming today. I'll get Donna to book me on the next flight to Dallas." She checked her stainless-steel watch. "If I'm not mistaken, there's a 4:10 from Denver to Dallas. It's just after 12 here. I've got time to make it. If a seat's available, I'll head to the airport as soon as I take care of some details and throw some clothes into a suitcase."

"Good. I think Melissa was hoping for that. She and Kinkaide are flying in from Tennessee. Needless to say, Lawton's parents are beside themselves."

"I can only imagine." Jac rubbed the frown line between her brows. "Can I stay at your place a few days?"

"Uh . . ." Sammie hedged, "sure."

Jacquelyn hesitated and imagined the redhead's characteristic grimace that usually accompanied her uncertainty. Something in the writer's voice didn't ring true, but Jacquelyn didn't have time right now to ponder the cause.

"Thanks."

"Well, I need to call the other four sisters," Sammie continued. "Do you want me to meet you at the airport?"

"No. Don't worry about that. I'll take a taxi. You just get busy calling everyone else. We need all the prayer we can get," Jac finished on a grim note.

Two

~

As she hung up, Jacquelyn plopped into her chair and tapped her finger against the desk's edge. The seconds slipped by. The tapping increased. Jac pressed the intercom button and awaited Donna's answer.

"Something's really wrong, isn't it?" Donna queried before Jac had time to say a thing.

"The woman must be psychic," Jacquelyn muttered under her breath, then increased her volume. "Yes. It's about a friend of a friend . . ." She eyed the potted palm in the corner of the room. The thing looked like it was ready to gasp its last breath. She wondered if Lawton were in equally dire straits. "He's missing."

"Oh, I'm so sorry."

"Can you book me on the next flight to

Dallas? I think that will be the 4:10." She tugged on the front of her oversized denim shirt.

"Sure. I'll see what I can do," Donna said. "Anything else?"

"Yes. I've lost my appetite. Pay for the pizza out of petty cash and enjoy it as a gift from me." The very mention of the spicy food sent Jac's stomach into a queasy lurch.

"Sure thing," Donna said a bit dubiously.

And she had reason to be dubious. Once Jac ordered a supreme, she never turned it down. Absolutely never.

Jac's stomach cramped again, and she released the button. She rolled her chair backward. It squeaked as she stood. Rushing to the small refrigerator, she whipped open the door and grabbed the lone cola that sat behind a collection of bottled water. Jac popped the top and slowly drank several swallows. The effervescent liquid tingled all the way down and eased her nausea.

Rubbing a hand down the back of her silky, bobbed hair, Jacquelyn gripped the base of her neck and squeezed, as if by brute strength she could abate the memories. Yet the dulcet echo of Lawton's voice, sonorous and charming, lured her soul, beckoned her mind.

She rushed to the window and peered at the collection of peaks that hovered over Denver like so many snow-crested sentinels. But even the regal mountains against a snatch of sapphire blue sky did nothing to blot out the rush that promised to torment. Torment and ensnare. Ensnare and mock. Her legs trembling, the memories swooped upon her like the line of clouds swiftly approaching the Rockies. And her traitorous mind dragged her into the past . . . into Lawton's presence . . . to that unforgettable evening on the cruise ship on the lucent waters of the Aegean Sea. . . .

Jac and Lawton settled at a table for two on the Brazil Coffee Verandah. The Olympic Countess, humming beneath them, sliced through the night. The cool breeze both refreshed and teased the senses. The luminous disk, rising upon an intangible canvass of night, whispered of fantasies and bathed the dimly lighted deck in a soft aura. The smell of the sea mingled with the mellow aroma of coffee and seemed to fuse as one with the moonlight.

A thin, swarthy waiter holding a tray

stopped by their table. "Would you care to order?" he asked, his words laced with a French accent.

"I'd like some decaf coffee," Lawton said.

"Me, too," Jac supplied.

"Do you have amaretto?" Lawton asked.

"Yes, of course," the waiter said. "Will that be two?"

Jac nodded and the waiter whisked away.

"Tell me what you see." Lawton placed an elbow on the table and leaned forward.

Jac pressed her back into the chair. Lawton's dark glasses, like the lustrous sea, reflected the moonlight and suggested the depths of this man with a heart the size of the sky. Jac, her pulse gently pounding, wondered how she managed to land herself in this situation.

Endearing. Mel had said that Lawton was endearing. Jac swallowed. *Mel was right. But I don't need endearing. Not now. Not ever.*

What if he tries to kiss me? the thought raced upon her, and Jac's palms moistened. But then she evaluated what she knew of Lawton so far and dismissed the illogical notion. They hadn't known each other nearly long enough, and Lawton didn't seem the type to push himself on a woman. Her stiff spine relaxed a bit.

"Cat got your tongue?" Lawton asked, and his lips tilted into a jocose grin. "Or have you silently deserted me and I'm talking to myself?"

"No, I–I'm still here," Jac said, then gazed toward the ocean. "The moon is full. The sea is slick — like a mirror. And the moonlight is seeping into the water. It's like there's this glow across the water — almost like phosphorous — as if the water is a sponge, soaking up the light."

"Ooo. And the detective is poetic. Do go on."

Jac's hands tightened in her lap and her breath caught as a disturbing realization overtook her. She liked this man before her. She liked him a lot. Her heart hammered, and she was hurled into a whirlwind of conflicting emotions. On one level, she didn't want him to so much as hold her hand. On another level, she longed to step into his arms and relish the warmth of his ardor.

"Hel-low," Lawton said.

"Well, there's not much more to tell. We have an umbrella over us."

"I figured that one."

"I guess there are the stars." Jac tilted

her head toward the heavenly bodies and
scanned the unending pinpoints of light.

"Ah, the stars," he said. His voice, like
a furtive nuance of the night, blended
with the lapping of water along the ship's
sides.

Yes, I love the stars. I love them.
I love the way they shine for the
    hand that created them.
I love their jewel-like magic, dia-
    monds that dreams are made of.
I love their unfathomable number,
    forever on fire to always inspire.
Yes, I love the stars. I love them.
Come with me. Come with me.
    We'll fly to the stars.
We'll embrace them and soak up
    their splendor.
We'll embrace them and forever
    blaze with His love.
Yes, I love the stars. I love them.
We are stars. We are stars.
We are the carriers of light. The
    light of the universe.
We twinkle forth with a message the
    world longs to hear.
Yes, He loves you. He loves all.
Come with me. Come with me. Em-
    brace this Giver of Light.

His jewel-like flame will transform
    dark night.
Yes, I love the stars. I love them.

His words flowed over Jacquelyn like honey. Even bound by darkness, Lawton still basked in God's light. "That was beautiful," she said. "Is it yours?"

"Yes." The word fell between them with a hint of reserve.

"What possessed you to go into computers when you can compose like that?"

"Well, I like to eat, for starters. The last I heard, the word 'starving' often prefixed 'poet.' Besides, I get a lot of reward out of empowering other blind people by helping them use their computers. I also love the travel. And I can still write poetry here and there."

An amazed smile began in Jac's soul and draped itself upon her countenance. The man in front of her had overcome a handicap with a success that few could boast. On top of that, he wrote poetry to die for. The esteem that began a slow burn on the flight to Munich flared. "You know, it's amazing that you travel all over the United States, and you don't even have a dog." The warmth in Jac's voice spoke her approval.

"And the lady does know how to smile," he teased.

Jac's smile faltered. She intertwined her fingers and examined the cluster of people two tables over.

"Actually, I went to mobility school in my younger years. That experience gave me the freedom to choose a dog or not. I decided a dog is a lot of trouble," Lawton said as if they hadn't skipped a beat in their conversation. "Besides, if I had a dog, think of all the adventures I'd miss. Last hotel I stayed at in Mobile, Alabama, I went downstairs to the restaurant and wound up knocking over a sign right smack on top of a waitress." With a chuckle, he shook his head. "Actually, it was the restaurant's fault, not mine. The sign was placed right where I'd walked that morning."

"But aren't you ever scared when you're traveling?" The admiration that refused stifling seeped into her voice.

"What's to be scared of?" Lawton leaned back and crossed his arms. "My mom usually takes me to the airport and makes certain I get on the right plane."

"I guess that's always a plus," Jac interjected with a laugh.

He snorted. "You got that one right. Nothing like getting on a plane to Indiana, only to find out you just landed in Montreal." The breeze ruffled his hair onto his forehead, and Jac figured he hadn't seen a barber in several months.

"Have you ever flown to the wrong place?"

"Not yet. Usually I'm nicely kept track of. The people I'm working for on each particular job are always waiting at the point of destination. And on the flight, the airline employees bend over backward to assist me. Then on the way home, Mom or Dad, or even sometimes my ornery brother, do the honors of seeing me to my apartment."

"So you live alone?" Jac asked, her amazement escalating.

"Don't most 33-year-old men live on their own?" A defensive edge entered his voice.

"Sorry. I guess . . . I'm sorry," Jac repeated. "I guess I've insulted you."

He sighed and scrubbed his fingers through the dark hair that touched his jacket collar. "No, I'm sorry," he said. "You didn't mean any harm."

"Actually, your whole life fascinates me." The admission sprang from Jacquelyn before she realized her intent. The last thing she needed to do was encourage Lawton. He seemed interested in something deeper than mere friendship, and she was not. *Period.*

"I understand." And a veil of satisfaction settled upon his face, as if he read far more into Jac's comments than she ever wished him to. "It's just that — I guess I'm a little touchy at times. You know, I'm no different than any other man, and well, there are times when people treat me like a child. It gets really irritating, especially when that sort of treatment comes from the opposite sex."

The waiter arrived with their coffee, and Jac welcomed the interruption as much as the gourmet aroma. "Do you like cream or sugar in yours?" she asked and prepared to scoot the complimentary packets near his hand.

"No. I'm a *real* man," he teased. "I take mine straight."

"Then I must be a real man, too!" Jac shot back.

"Ha!" Lawton threw back his head as his unrestrained laughter echoed across the night.

"You know, if you haven't already figured it out, you really intrigue me." Lawton leaned back and nodded his head.

"Oh?"

"Mmm," he said and turned his face into the breeze. "And for once, I'm enjoying the chase." He flashed a daredevil grin toward her that revealed an even row of shiny teeth.

Jacquelyn stood and squelched the urge to bolt. "I'm not available for the catch," she stated, the edge back in her voice.

"So why'd you agree to come up here with me?" He waved his hand to encompass the verandah.

"I have no earthly idea," Jac muttered. "Temporary insanity," she added under her breath.

"Ha!" He threw back his head. "I love it!"

"You're nuts," Jac barked.

"Ah, no I'm not," he said. "And you know it. You're just scared, that's all."

"Scared of *what?*" She narrowed her eyes. "I'm not scared of a thing." Her voice held the thread of steel that had long since won the respect of male peers twice her size.

"I know, I know," Lawton said as if he were trying to soothe an overwrought child. "I know."

He stood, and Jacquelyn resisted the urge to walk away and leave him to find his own way back to his room. *I'm not scared!* she wanted to scream. *Except of that dragon.* The thought rushed upon her from nowhere and her stomach cringed. The last few weeks had proven that not only was she frightened of the dragon, she was also terrified that she was of no value. None. She was just a piece of trash that some man had trampled like worthless refuse. What would a man with values like Lawton Franklin even want with her once he found out her body had been squandered before she was old enough to understand the implications?

"I'm ready to go back to my cabin," she said, her voice lifeless. "Is there someplace you'd like me to take you?"

"No." Lawton shook his head and settled back in his chair. "That's fine. I'm going to sit here for awhile."

"Okay, fine." Jacquelyn didn't doubt that the man was tenacious enough to find his way out of a cavern on the back side of Scandinavia. Without a backward glance she strode away. Yet she'd only taken two steps when his imploring voice mingled with the swish of the sea, "Come with me. Come with me. We'll fly to the stars."

Jacquelyn ducked her head and gritted

her teeth. Her eyes blurred, and she hunched her shoulders. Stars weren't in her future. Not now. Not ever. They weren't even in her past. And she wouldn't know how to embrace one if it fell into her lap. She paused beside the elevators. With her fists clenched, she verbalized a fervid vow — "I won't exchange another word with that man," she whispered. "Not *one* word."

The Rockies came back into focus as a tendril of regret plagued Jac's soul. She had tried her dead-level best to live up to her vow. By the trip's end, she could count on one hand the number of stilted exchanges she and Lawton had shared. The last one had taken place at the base of the Spanish Steps when she essentially told him to get lost.

Jac gulped another mouthful of soda and forced it down her tightened throat. Closing her eyes, she imagined the taste and bouquet of amaretto coffee. Lawton's obvious desire for more than friendship had done nothing short of terrify her. And despite her rebuttal, a tiny voice in the back of her mind insisted that she could call him anytime. Her close acquaintance with his sister-in-law, Melissa, presented a forever-present avenue through which Jac could renew communication.

But now he's missing. He's gone. Perhaps dead. Jacquelyn's lips trembled. With a growl, she marched back to her desk, plopped the soda on the edge, and shoved the telephone across the surface. The phone responded with an accusing ring. Jacquelyn blinked as if it had verbalized a protest. Donna had sent through yet another emergency call. Dreading more bad news, she snatched the receiver from its cradle.

"Lightfoot," she barked, and the steel edge in her voice belied her churning emotions.

"Jac? It's — it's me. Lawton. I'm in — I'm in t–trouble," his terrified voice rasped into the line.

Three

~

Lawton, his tongue sticking to the roof of his mouth, stirred against the cool sheets. "Jac?" he whispered, and the corner of his mouth protested in pain. "Are you — are you still there?"

"Yes. Yes, I'm here." She produced several sniffles.

Lawton wrinkled his brow and tried to concentrate. He had awakened only half an hour ago. At first, he was completely disoriented and couldn't figure out why he was in a strange bed . . . why his shoulder was wrapped tightly . . . why his left hand had wires attached to it. But soon the beep of monitors, the ache in his shoulder, and the smell of antiseptic gave him sufficient clues to pinpoint his locale.

"Where are you?" her unsteady voice revealed an emotion Lawton hadn't expected. "There are people looking for you."

"I — I d–don't know," he whispered. "I'm in a hospital s–somewhere." He took a deep breath and his right shoulder protested even the slightest movement.

The weasel's voice permeated Lawton's consciousness: "What are we going to do with him?"

"We're going to shoot him," the bear proclaimed.

"I'm sick of all this killing," the weasel spat.

"Then I'll kill you!"

An ominous silence shrouded the car, and the distinctive odor of Cuban cigars laced the threat.

"Empty his pockets — now," the bear commanded.

Lawton, sprawling from floorboard to seat, tried to fend the man off, but his body refused to obey his brain's promptings.

"Now dump him out your door," the bear demanded.

"Lawton?" Jacquelyn prompted. "Melissa and Kinkaide and your mom and dad are really worried about you. Can you tell me where you are?" her voice slowed as if she were speaking to a foreigner who didn't understand English. "Lawton?"

"The b–best I can — can figure, I've been un–unconscious and they've — they've ad–admitted me." He wheezed, coughed, groaned, and fingered the bandage on the top of his right shoulder. "I just woke up n–not long ago and got . . . got my b–bearings enough to call you." He clutched the sheet. "I–I've b–been shot."

Silence permeated the line.

"Lawton, listen to me," Jac rushed. "Call for a nurse. Ask her where you are."

"N–no!"

"This is not a time to be pigheaded!" the detective ground out.

"I'm — I'm not," Lawton put as much grit into his voice as he could muster, yet he still sounded like a whimpering pup. "Don't you under–understand? I'm scared! The people who sh–shot me. They — they must think I'm d–dead. This h–hospital . . ." He waved his left hand, and the IV tubing protested. "They — the man who shot m–me took all — all my in–dent . . . identification."

"So the hospital doesn't know who you are?"

"I seriously d–doubt it. They don't even know I'm a–awake. What if the wrong person finds me?"

"Do you have any idea how you were admitted?"

"No!" Lawton grimaced and stifled the irritation. The woman was starting to sound like an interrogator.

"So why are you calling me? Why didn't you call your parents? They're going crazy with worry."

"I–I want you to–to come sneak me h-home. I don't . . ." He swallowed and wished for a cold sip of water. "I don't want the men to–to find, find out I–I'm still alive. I'm — I'm sc–scared, Jac. So . . . so scared." Lawton groaned as a wave of anxiety burned over his body, raced down his arms, and left a cold film of sweat across his forehead.

"This is not getting easier. You said it would!" the weasel croaked. "Even after . . . years I hate this. I hate all the killing . . . had two children asleep in their rooms and while they slept I — I can't do this again. Do . . . hear me?"

The bear's hot body stretched across Lawton. The door handle clicked. The car door sighed open, and the humid night attacked Lawton's face. "Shove him out . . . shoot him . . . or be next!"

Hard hands shoved against Lawton. His head slammed into a rock; the hard earth ate into his face and filled his mouth with grit. As unconsciousness threatened once more, Lawton tried to scream. He tried . . . He tried. But his mouth refused to cooperate. *Help! Oh dear Jesus, help me!*

Lawton curled his toes in an attempt to stay the overwhelming urge to rip the IV from his hand and bolt for his life. Jac's voice demanded his concentration. He gasped for air and forced himself to focus on her words.

"How am I supposed to find you? I don't even know where you are. You could be in another state!"

"You're a d–detective. F–find me."

"And until I do?"

"I'm — I'm an unidentified bl–blind m–man . . . in a coma." Lawton's breathing grew more shallow with his every word, and the dark beyond beckoned him once more.

"You must know my number from memory," she blurted as if the thought struck her all at once.

"Of course." Lawton produced an aching smile. Amid the fog in his mind, he recalled the Brazil Coffee Verandah . . . a sea that soaked up the moon like phosphorous . . . a Mediterranean breeze that whispered sweet nothings . . . and an enchanting lady who charmed him beyond all sense of reason.

Yet in the middle of the enthralling mist of the past, reality reared its ugly head. "P–please call — call my p–parents. And Kin . . ."

"Kinkaide and Mel. Yes . . . yes, I'll call them. I'm heading to Dallas on the 4:10 flight. I know Mel and Kinkaide are flying there as well. I don't know if your parents are driving down from Oklahoma or not."

"I . . . I really think . . . I've got to be — to be in D–Dallas . . . in one . . ." He clamped his teeth together and forbade himself to fall into the velvety darkness. "In — in a D–Dallas hos–hospital," he finished.

Lawton's head roared and the darkness tugged him ever closer to nothingness. With the taste of dry earth filling his mouth, he held his breath as the weasel hesitated then uttered a stream of oaths. The gun exploded. The bullet seared an unforgiving path across the top of Lawton's right shoulder. The car door slammed. The engine revved. Screaming tires hurled gravel that stung innumerable pinpoints into his face. And the blackness, all soft and peaceful and irresistible, enveloped him once more.

"Lawton? Are you still there?" Jacquelyn prompted.

The painful smile posed itself once more. "Yes. St–still here. J–just so . . . so t–tired . . ."

"I'm coming, Lawton," Jacquelyn assured. "I'll find you. I'll be there. I promise."

Jac dragged the black suitcase from beneath her bed and plopped it atop the paisley comforter. Within ten minutes she had invaded her dresser, closet, and functional bathroom then hurled the sufficient necessities into her suitcase. Jacquelyn checked her watch for the fifth time in ten minutes and forced herself to realize that she still had more than two hours before her flight departed.

"What's the rush?" she chided then zipped the case, deposited it onto the floor, and extended the handle. The handle's accompanying clicks seemed to check off every item on Jac's to-do list. With a sigh, she lowered herself onto the bed, covered her face, and contemplated the events of the day. After Lawton's surprise phone call, Jacquelyn had phoned his relatives, who professed enormous relief that Lawton was alive. Then she placed a strategic call to a former Dallas colleague who owed her. He, in turn, discovered Lawton at the Dallas Regional Hospital.

She knew Lawton wouldn't be thrilled that she ultimately blew his identity, but the dear man had obviously been too groggy to think clearly. There was no way she would sneak him from the hospital — not in the shape he was in. Furthermore, there was always the chance that the police were the ones who had found Lawton and arranged for him to be admitted.

And in the middle of all this mess he's in, he remembered my number. Jacquelyn raised her face from her hands, smiled a bit, and shook her head. She had passed him a business card during that Mediterranean cruise. He said he scanned all such material into his computer and his special software read it to him. Undoubtedly, he had scanned her card and, in that steel-trap mind of his, had somehow remembered her number. She didn't doubt for a minute that he also remembered every word they exchanged during the whole trip.

She blankly stared toward the family photo on her dresser. Across the edge of the frame hung a platinum bracelet with three stars on it. A bracelet Lawton had bought for her on the Isle of Rhodes. A bracelet his brother, Kinkaide, gave to her in Lawton's stead. Jacquelyn had been helping Melissa pack for her move to Nashville where Kinkaide lived. When Kinkaide handed Jac the bracelet, she almost left it sitting on Melissa's dresser. For some reason she couldn't explain even now, Jac had kept the bracelet.

She stood and approached the piece of jewelry that seemed the only bright spot in the otherwise Spartan bedroom. Unlike her six sisters, the pint-sized detective spent as little as possible on home decor. She glanced in the mirror and noted her easy-swing bobbed hair and lack of makeup. Jac sighed. The carefully crafted bracelet seemed as out of place on her wrist as in her bedroom. Nonetheless, the glistening stars suited her love of beauty. Rubbing one of the platinum stars between forefinger and thumb, she picked up the family photo where the bracelet had resided for the last two months.

"They would like Lawton," she muttered as she gazed upon the photo taken in her parents' home in Livingston, Texas.

Last Christmas she, her two brothers, her mom and dad had gathered in front of the fireplace while her sister-in-law took the picture. Her mother's African American heritage had mixed beautifully with her father's Native American genes to produce two offspring who had hair like black satin, skin of polished bronze, and eyes that spoke of an ebony summer night. Jacquelyn and her next younger brother, Joe, both took after her parents. The third and youngest brother, Jake, was another story. His fair hair, lighter skin, and blue eyes came from their maternal grandfather's Caucasian genes.

Jac tucked her hair behind her ear. "Yes, they'd like Lawton," she repeated. She thought about calling her mother and telling her she was heading for Dallas, but then dismissed the thought. Her mom would only want to know all the details — details Jac didn't want to divulge, even to her mom. She and Mel often joked that their mothers should become secret agents, but in reality, Jac's mother wasn't half as controlling as Mel's. Nevertheless, there were barriers in their relationship that Jac wasn't sure she understood.

She swallowed against the lump in her throat as Lawton's predicament took precedence over familial relationships. His recent words formed a rhythmic tattoo in her mind: "I'm — I'm sc–scared, J–Jac. So . . . so sc–scared . . ."

"You're not the only one," Jac whispered as she set the photo back on her dresser. The bracelet seemed to warm in her hand, and she stared at the stars until they blurred into a silvery mist. A mist that whispered Lawton's poem. A poem forever etched upon her mind.

Yes, I love the stars. I love them. . . . Come with me. Come with me. We'll fly to the stars. . . . Come with me. Come with me. Embrace this Giver of Light. His jewel-like flame will transform dark night. Yes, I love the stars. I love them.

A sentimental whim urged Jac to keep the bracelet and cherish it as a gift from a phenomenal man. Yet a more practical voice suggested that this contact with Lawton would be the perfect chance to return it. Pressing her lips into a grim line, Jac rummaged through her top drawer, past the jumble of correspondence, and gripped the white leather box that had shuffled to the bottom. She flipped up the hinged lid, deposited the bracelet against snowy velvet, and snapped the top shut. Without further deliberation, she stuffed the bracelet into her worn leather back-pack, grabbed her suitcase, and rolled it toward the door.

Jacquelyn's childhood wounds, still gaping and inflamed, would never allow her to develop a healthy marriage. The very thought of a husband's intimate touches repulsed her — even if he were Lawton. She frowned as she paused by the bedroom door and poised her finger over the light switch. Before she flipped the switch, her gaze rested upon her quilted bedspread, rumpled from her packing venture. In that bed, the dragon of her past had chased her until she was so sleep-deprived she had taken a two-month leave of absence and spent time in Oklahoma City with Melissa. During that leave, she had at last acknowledged that she had been sexually abused as a child. But even now, she still didn't know who the man had been. Her mind refused to reveal that fact.

"Or perhaps I just don't want to know," Jacquelyn muttered. The dreadful dragon in her nightmares loomed unnamed. Unnamed but not unloved. For Jac sensed that he might have been closer to her than she really wanted to know. Close. Very close. And highly trusted. Perhaps even alive today. Maybe present at family functions. Scowling, she snapped off the light and hastened toward her apartment's door.

This was not a time to think about the dragon.

Lawton needs me. Or rather, Melissa needs me. Yes, Melissa. Lawton is her brother-in-law. Not mine. He's nothing to me. Nothing. And he never will be.

Four

~

Maurice Stein paced the elegant hotel suite like a wild animal out of its element. The thick-piled carpet sprang beneath his bare feet as he passed the overstuffed sofa, tread toward the window, paused, and gazed upon the Dallas high-rises and congested traffic. He whirled from the window, trudged back toward the couch, and plopped onto the pliant leather.

Pinching his lower lip, he gazed upon the murder headline of the *Dallas Morning News*, sprawled across the mahogany coffee table. A crucifix stood near the paper. A crucifix surrounded by flickering votives. Maurice's crucifix. Maurice's candles. He always carried them. Always.

Maurice sat erect, touched his index finger to his forehead, to his chest, and then each shoulder. "Forgive me, Father, for I have sinned," he mumbled, his face contorting with every word. "Oh, Jesus, Lamb of God, remove this stain from my heart. Remove this blood from my hands."

He went through the same ritual after every murder. Over and over and over. Night after night, morning after morning, he pled for forgiveness until the memory faded in the face of the next job.

"I hate this!" He snatched a slender Cuban cigar from a polished silver box. Leaning forward, Maurice placed the tip in one of the flickering flames and puffed deeply, all the while squinting against the smoke, mesmerized by the half-closed eyes of the suffering servant hanging on the crucifix. The acrid smell filled the room but did precious little to ease his nerves. He tore his focus from Christ, placed his elbows on his knees and stared at the carpet, the color of new peaches. Eyeing his tailormade slacks and shirt, he cursed his lot in life and exhaled a long stream of smoke. Fuat wouldn't be back for a couple of days. Not until the headlines cooled. Not until all coasts cleared.

"Meanwhile, I get to stay cooped up in this forsaken place." He waved his hand toward a corner cabinet, laden with fine crystal. Never had opulence tasted so bitter.

He puffed his cigar and snatched the newspaper from the table. The front page bore the photo of Gary Sellers, noted real-estate entrepreneur, and his wife, Rhonda. Their mysterious murder had snared the focus of more than one reputable paper. Their angelic children, asleep in the next room, had done more than catch Maurice's interest. The kids had driven a dagger into his heart.

"So much like my own . . ." Snatches of the past bore upon him. A past filled with loss. Loss and heartache. Heartache and loneliness. Maurice had convinced himself he could never feel that deeply again. Then he saw the Sellers' children, their raven-black hair as dark as midnight, as dark as his own children's once had been. Children who never lived to adolescence.

Gritting his teeth, Maurice slammed the paper back onto the table and stabbed the glowing cigar into the center of Sellers' smiling face. The paper smoldered around the cigar as tendrils of smoke twisted upward like dancing serpents. He clamped the cigar between his teeth and began his pacing once again.

Fuat Rantomi had no idea that the

Sellerses were Maurice's last job. "The very last. I don't care what I have to do to get out of this, I'm not going to kill another soul." He paused and stared at the crucifix. "Not another soul." Yet a jaded voice suggested that he had made this exact vow before then promptly broke it when the next murder proved necessary. If he ever stuck to his vow, his rebellion would result in his own demise. The reality of his mortality pressed upon Maurice until he could see nothing but his own body in a casket. And no one — no one attended the funeral. Not even Fuat.

Maurice's thoughts, panicked and disoriented, churned in numerous directions. Eventually he forced himself to analyze his situation and form a plan.

Jacquelyn settled into the airplane's seat and shoved her laptop under the seat in front of her. The flight wasn't booked up, and she enjoyed the added space of having two seats to herself. She retrieved her backpack and small handbag from the seat next to her and prepared to plop them beside her laptop. As the flight attendant announced the discontinuance of all electronic devices, Jac decided to double check her cell phone. She opened her backpack and dug through the jumble until she came to the tiny phone. As she had predicted, the power was on. Jacquelyn pulled it out and turned it off. She dropped the phone back into the leather carryall, and it landed atop a white, leather-covered box.

Glancing at her right wrist, Jac wondered how the platinum stars would look against her skin. She had yet to actually wear the piece, and an unexpected whim seized her. *Before I return it, maybe I should at least see what it looks like on.* Until now she had admired the stars from afar. At first she'd hid the bracelet box in the bottom of a dresser drawer. Then she occasionally snapped the box open and stroked the links, nestled against white velvet. Finally, she had draped the bracelet across the family photo, where it stayed until today.

As the plane taxied to the runway, Jac snatched the white box and opened the top. The platinum stars radiated in the plane's dim light. Before she second guessed her motives, Jac removed the bracelet and placed it upon her wrist. An unexpected temptation sprang upon her. A temptation to keep the bracelet. As the plane sliced into the air, Jac leaned her head against the window and watched the mountains and trees recede into toy-like proportions.

Jac bit into a dry piece of skin along her lower lip and wondered if she were crazy to have ever agreed to that night on the Brazil Coffee Verandah. Something inside her hadn't been the same since that enchanted evening. And she wondered, as she had wondered a thousand times, if Lawton Franklin had fallen in love with her — the real kind of love that lasts through the years.

She furrowed her brows and struggled between the notion that she should be honored and the gut feeling that she should reiterate her lack of interest. But telling Lawton she didn't care would be a lie. She was anything but indifferent. Lawton understood that. She knew he understood that. The assured tilt of his head when the Mediterranean trip was over suggested that their stilted goodbyes were actually "see you soons." And his assumption had been correct. Jac would indeed see him soon.

She closed her eyes and rested her left hand upon the bracelet. The polished surface slipped along her fingertips like satin, and Jac recalled the feel of Lawton's hand covering hers. Her mind raced with the implications of this visit, and she wondered if she had lost her mind to fly all the way from Denver to see him. *He would think . . .*

Jac dropped the star and forced herself to think of something else. Anything would be better than this unending conjecturing that could only lead to heartache. Soon the flight attendant passed out bottled water and pretzels, and Jac plunged her mind into the pile of paperwork that still claimed her desk. The income taxes wouldn't wait much longer. She sipped the final drops of water, stuffed the empty pretzel bag in to the miniature cup, then deposited it on the tray in front of her. As she tried to count off the needed steps to income tax completion, her eyes drooped and her thoughts gradually disconnected with reality. Soon the hum of the plane collaborated with her work-worn mind, and she fell into a fitful doze that submerged her into the heart of a tangled forest. . . .

Jacquelyn, pigtails flailing, ran through the dank woods. Her bare feet slammed against the forest floor, and with each step the angry briers snaked out to snare her tender flesh in their unforgiving grasp. Jac whimpered, clawed at the unrelenting foliage, and pushed forward. Footfalls, heavy and near, crashed behind her. She dashed a frantic glance over her shoulder, but the dense forest concealed any signs of the beast. Every breath erupted from her lungs with a painful burst. Every step brought her closer . . . closer . . . ever closer to the blinding beams that penetrated the edge of the forest. Every second empowered the dragon to come nearer . . . nearer . . . ever nearer to his cringing prey. His impatient roar echoed through the forest, and a cackling vulture, twice Jacquelyn's size, swooped down to trap her in his bony talons. She clamped childish hands over her ears and emitted a scream that exploded from the rends in her soul. The dragon's fiery breath crackled through the trees and scorched Jac's back. The smell of singed hair hovered overhead like a cloud of doom while the vulture discharged a triumphant squawk. Jac hunkered down, gritted her teeth, and braced herself for the consumption of her tender flesh.

Yet the light on the forest's edge bid her step into its revealing rays. Jacquelyn, salty tears christening her lips, pushed forward and placed one cautious foot into the glow. The vulture screeched. His talons slipped from her hair. His wings pulsated in a panicked tattoo. The faintest of glistening beams shot up Jacquelyn's leg and penetrated her soul. A soul ravaged by bloody wounds. Wounds and heartache. Heartache and devastation. Jacquelyn lunged back into the forest's shadows, back toward the monster, back through the thorny arms. The internal pain eased. As long as she couldn't see the wounds, the agony diminished to a dull ache.

"No, no, no," she muttered as the vulture descended upon her shoulder then nibbled her ear. "No. Not the light. Anything but the light. I don't want to know. I don't want to know."

The dragon's feet hammered ever closer. His labored breathing raled in and out of oversized nostrils, and he halted behind her. The beast and the vulture merged into one being, and Jacquelyn covered her eyes. His warmth penetrated her back. His foul breath brushed the top of her head. He chuckled over her, as if savoring the moments before he gorged himself. Jacquelyn's skin prickled with gooseflesh. Her stomach roiled with nausea. Sweat trickled down her spine.

Somewhere she had met the dragon.

She had spoken with the dragon. She had embraced the dragon.

An explosion of fairy-like tinkles, rolling ever nearer, bade Jacquelyn to open her eyes. The ethereal beams on the forest's edge exploded with sparkles. They swirled like a thousand tiny stars released from the corridors of heaven. Each sparkle called her name in a voice laden with love. A path, amid clouds of gold dust, opened before her. The dragon's claw raked across her back. Jac jolted toward the light, but the glow illuminated her soul's gaping wounds. With the illumination, the bloody ulcers pulsed, as if the light fueled their agony.

"No, no, no! I don't want to know. I don't. I don't. Don't make me remember. Don't. Don't. Please, please, don't."

The dragon's scaly palm settled across her shoulder. Jacquelyn stiffened. Then a scream, garbled and soulful, erupted from the core of her being.

"Ma'am . . . Ma'am. Wake up. Wake up!" Firm hands gripped Jac's shoulders and shook.

Jac's eyes slid open. Heaving for breath, she stared into the face of the golden-skinned, almond-eyed flight attendant.

59

The plane's engine purred as they sliced through the atmosphere, heading straight for Dallas. And Jac knew the stares of some of the passengers were focused on her.

"Are you okay?" the attendant asked.

With a groan, Jacquelyn rubbed her hand over her damp forehead. *What a place to have that awful dream!* "I'm okay, I–I think," she croaked. "May I — may I go to the lavatory?"

"Yes." The flight attendant straightened, and her dark eyes stirred. "But be quick. We'll be landing soon."

Without a glance at the other people, Jacquelyn unfastened her seat belt and strode back toward the restroom. Once inside the tiny facility, she rested her hands on either side of the stainless steel sink and stared into the mirror. Inky eyes stared back at her like the haunted orbs of an injured owl.

"I hate you," she whispered. "I don't know who you are or even if you're still alive, but I hate you for what you did to me. I hate you, do you hear me!" Jacquelyn's lips trembled and she gulped for air. Leaning against the shift of the plane, she fidgeted with the water levers until she had enough water in the sink to splash her face. The cold dash tingled her heated skin and helped her regain a semblance of composure.

"Hello," the pilot's voice crackled over the intercom. "Just want everyone to know we'll be landing in about 15 minutes. I would like to thank everyone for choosing American and, as always, we hope you enjoyed your flight."

The flight attendant continued announcing gate assignments, and Jacquelyn snatched a couple of paper towels then scrubbed her face. The platinum stars decorating her wrist slightly twisted, and Jac stared at the bracelet as if it had crawled out of her backpack and fastened itself upon her wrist. The stars, sprinkled with droplets of water, gleamed against her bronze-toned skin as if they were created especially for her.

Yet the contrast of dark and light reminded Jac of the difference between her tainted past and the hope she sensed in Lawton. She was better off to return the bracelet and leave no questions in Lawton's mind. She would rather keep him out altogether than open herself up for potential rejection. Many godly men still wanted their wives to be virgins on their wedding nights. Even though the subject had never arisen between Jac and Lawton, some sixth sense told her that Lawton would ask nothing of his wife that he himself hadn't lived up to. That same intuition also suggested that perhaps her lack of virginity would certainly abate his interest in her. *And, well, Mr. Franklin, I can't take the pain of a rejection right now. I just can't.*

With a steadying breath, she increased her resolve to remain aloof, placed the used towels in the receptacle, strode back up the narrow aisle, plopped into her seat, and fastened her safety belt. The surrounding passengers seemed to have lost interest in her plight, but her torment continued. Like a heaving, capped volcano, the agony bulged against her soul. The only time the pain spewed forth unchecked was during her dreams — and she had no control over that. *None.* However, as time rocked on, the pressure from the past grew more relentless. She had hoped that the two months away from her office last spring would deliver her from the encroaching pain. While those days at Melissa's home and in the Mediterranean had indeed delivered a measure of solace, Jac was far from exploring the complete depths of her despair. Admitting that she had indeed been sexually abused had left her in a sobbing heap. But there was so much more to the story. So much more. And as the potential explosion of truth intensified, the pall of depression remained poised to swoop down and drag her spirit into a bottomless abyss.

As the plane coasted in a smooth landing, Jac pressed aside her thoughts in preference for the after-flight juggle of retrieving the carryons, stepping aside for other passengers, producing the polite yet empty smiles, and trudging up the aisle and along the covered walkway.

After she retrieved her luggage, Jac's next mission was to hire a taxi to take her to Sammie's. From there, she'd go straight to the hospital. Straight to Lawton. *To Melissa,* Jac corrected herself. *Yes, Melissa. She's the one who needs me.* The platinum stars, still claiming her arm, mocked her denial.

Jac stepped from the covered passage and into the airport hubbub. She paused near the boarding desk and glanced at the gate signs to gain her bearings. The neon restaurant banners and various shops seemed as impersonal as the multitude of people scurrying here and there, most wearing a determined expression that suggested they were on a mission. The smells of fat pretzels and hamburgers floated from a brightly lit food court, and she stifled the urge to stop and eat. There'd be time for that later.

Jac adjusted her leather backpack, small handbag, and laptop, then stepped into the steady stream of pedestrians. A certain loneliness seeped into her soul as she mingled with the crowd yet again. While flying from one port to another in search of a missing person or certain town that held the exact clue that would seal a criminal's doom, Jac had seen the country. She had seen the country, but she wasn't sure she had ever seen herself, *really seen herself.*

"No time for that," she mumbled. "Focus on the task at hand." That unwavering focus is exactly what had enabled Jac to bury her pain and continue to bury her pain.

"Jacquelyn . . . Jac!" the emphatic female voice pierced through the prerecorded message cautioning against accepting packages from strangers.

With a slight smile, Jac paused and turned to glance behind her as several people cast casual looks her way. She recognized not only Melissa, but also her new husband, Kinkaide. Tall. Dark hair. Ready smile. So much like his brother, except

Lawton was several pounds lighter. Lawton also didn't have a beard like Kinkaide, although he often sported a five o'clock shadow. The younger brother's outlandish sense of humor added a dash of charm that appealed to Jac in a way Kinkaide never would.

"Hey you two!" Jac called. "Whaz-up?"

"We called your office about three, and your secretary said you'd already left," Melissa said as the couple neared. "She gave us your arrival time, and we decided to come back to the airport and meet you. Our flight landed at one o'clock." The brunette stopped beside Jac and gave her girl-next-door smile. The sparkle in her and Kinkaide's eyes attested that the honeymoon was still vibrant. The six sisters had doubted whether Mel would ever marry Kinkaide after he had jilted her six years before. But through a lot of communication and prayer, coupled with a romantic voyage to Italy, the two had tied the knot in Rome last spring.

"We've been with Lawton most of the afternoon," Kinkaide said, resting his arm across Mel's shoulders.

"He seems to be perking up, and we're so relieved." Mel waved her hand in a familiar gesture.

"Is he going to be okay?"

"Yes." Mel nodded. "He suffered a slight concussion and whoever shot him took a chunk of flesh out of the top of his shoulder, but it looks like he's going to be fine."

"He might not be speaking to me," Jac said. "He wanted me to keep his location top secret and come sneak him home." She rolled her eyes and shook her head. "Must have been the effects of the concussion and medication. There's no way that would ever work."

"Sounds like a plan to me," Kinkaide drawled. "Being kidnapped can be the answer to a man's dreams." He draped his arm around Mel and aimed a saucy wink in her direction.

"Oh, you." Mel punched him in the ribs, then turned toward Jac and snagged the laptop. "Let me help!"

"Thanks." Jac released her burden to her friend. "Have the police questioned Lawton yet?" She asked as the three of them fell in line to walk toward the luggage claim area.

"Yep," Kinkaide said, "but he's still really unclear on a lot. All he remembers is overhearing a conversation about a murder, but he can't recall any names right now. The next thing he knew, he was knocked partially unconscious, crammed into a large car, hauled off somewhere, shot, and left to die. The cops also returned Lawton's jacket, luggage, and laptop. He always keeps his billfold in his laptop case, so the only thing he lost was his keys and some change."

"How did he get to the hospital? Did the police find him?" Jac asked.

"No." Mel shook her head. "This afternoon we learned that an anonymous caller dialed 911 and detailed Lawton's location."

Squinting, Jac slowed. "Now that's odd."

"We're just glad he's alive," Kinkaide stated and stroked his beard.

Jac slowed as they neared the escalator, chose her descending step, and boarded it.

"Are they saying when he'll get to go home?" Jacquelyn toyed with her jeans belt loop as Kinkaide and Mel stepped onto the moving stairs.

"Probably in a day or two," Mel said.

Jac absently eyed the boisterous crowd below, but already her mind was turning stones. Lawton had stumbled into something really nasty — something that wouldn't just go away.

"Meanwhile, he's driving us nuts about

you," Kinkaide said from behind. "That's part of the reason we decided to come and pick you up. Every time he wakes up, he asks if you've arrived yet."

"Oh?" Jacquelyn said, trying her best to feign disinterest.

"My parents drove down from Oklahoma City and have been with him. They're really anxious to meet you," Kinkaide said. "I don't know if they'll be there when we arrive or not. They were talking about finding a hotel room when we left."

Jac squelched her curiosity about Lawton's parents. Admittedly, the man intrigued her, and she would be interested in meeting the people who were able to instill such a sense of adventure within him.

"Why *did* you come?" Mel queried. Jac resisted the urge to look over her shoulder and into Mel's penetrating gaze. All the sisters had long since dubbed Mel "the mouth of the South"; she never failed to live up to her name. Once again she refused to shrink from asking the wrong question at the wrong time.

Staring straight ahead, Jacquelyn prepared to disembark the escalator. "Sammie said you'd be glad I decided to come," she shot over her shoulder as she stepped off.

"Of course we are. But that still doesn't answer my question," Mel said, her voice thick with humor.

Jac forged ahead and pretended she didn't hear. But she did hear. She heard much more than Mel's comments. She heard the cries of her own heart. Cries she couldn't ignore.

Five

~

As Lawton emerged from sleep, the first thing he detected were the smells of clean sheets and antiseptic. The antiseptic reminded him that his well-laid plans to begin teaching a new client had gone awry; instead, he had landed in the hospital. With a mild groan, he stirred against the cool linens, yawned, and wondered how long he'd been asleep. After his parents left, he had determined not to doze, and he lambasted himself for giving into physical weakness.

According to the doctor's latest report, Lawton was already showing amazing signs of recovery. Nonetheless, the rebound wasn't quick enough for him. He ran his left hand along the cool side rail, smoothed his palm across the sheets, then pressed the button on his digital watch. A rigid voice announced that it was 8:20.

"Where is she?" he whispered, and the steady purr of the IV pump was his only answer.

From the minute Kinkaide and Mel left to go get Jacquelyn, Lawton had anticipated her arrival. Before he phoned her today, the last full conversation they exchanged had taken place at the base of the Spanish Steps when Jac gave him the "Dear John" write-off. Even then Lawton suspected that she liked him more than she would admit. Her flying all the way from Denver certainly was significant.

His imagination transported him back to Rome — back to the moments when Jac's voice flowed like rhythmic ocean waves, lapping against sand as fine as silk . . . her laugh spilled forth like a melodic summer breeze dancing amid a bamboo wind chime. He smiled with the indulgence of a smitten schoolboy as he contemplated her aura of strength that embodied a silent challenge.

I love a challenge, Lawton thought, *I always have*. A faint beep from down the hall punctuated his claim. No man alive would ever push Jac around. As he considered her black belt in tae kwon do his smile increased, and prickly pinpoints assaulted his wounded face. Knowing Jacquelyn, she didn't have the time to waste on mothering a man. *Nope. Jacquelyn Lightfoot would allow her man to be himself, to be her equal — and expect the same from him.*

Lawton rubbed his face, and two-day's worth of stubble needled his lean fingers. If he were in any shape to shave, he would.

"I think Kinkaide and I are going to get a bite to eat," Mel's voice mingled with the sigh of the hospital door. "That will give you and Lawton some time to visit."

Jac broke in. "Well, just wait and I'll go with —"

"No, no. That's fine. We'll bring you something back," Mel countered.

Lawton smiled as Jacquelyn's voice stirred his memories of a verandah . . . of a phosphorous sea that soaked up moonlight . . . of an entrancing lady who admired him despite her restraint. A surge of adrenaline rushed upon Lawton, and he reveled in the momentary high.

"Hey! Get me something to eat, too, will ya?" he called. "I'm starved!"

The shuffle of nearing feet accompanied Mel's voice. "What do you want?"

"Pizza!" Lawton said as he pinched the sheet between tense fingers.

Jac is here! She's here! She flew all the way

from Denver just because I called her!

"As in double pepperoni!" he continued, and the enthusiasm in his voice far exceeded his love for pizza. "Thick crust. Lots of pepperoni. All they have. Make that two larges!"

"My, my, my, aren't *we* in a festive spirit," Mel said, and the rustle of her sleeves attested to her crossing her arms.

"This has nothing to do with spirit." *Jac is here! She's actually here!* "And everything to do with hospital food. That stuff would kill a robot."

Jac's snickers fluttered around the room and filled the emptiness with delight and joy and charm.

"Okay. We'll do our best," Mel said to the accompaniment of Kinkaide's measured gait as he entered the room.

"Hey, you old goat," Lawton called in the direction of the doorway. "Time's wasting. The pizza is waiting! Get *outta* here."

"Sounds like you're back to your normal self," Kinkaide drawled. "Too bad that gunshot didn't hit you in the head. It would have just ricocheted off, and you'd have walked away."

"Are you implying I'm hardheaded?" Lawton tried to sit up, but his shoulder protested and he stifled a faint gasp.

"Not so fast," Mel threatened in her "doctor" voice as she pressed him back into the comforting folds.

"Who me?" Kinkaide retorted. "I wouldn't dare imply you were hardheaded. Actually, you go *way* beyond that. You've got a skull of steel —"

"Ah, shut up and go get my pizza!" *Jac is here! She's here! Yes!*

"What if I'm not in a pizza mood?" Kinkaide parried.

"Pizza transcends all moods. It's culinary art. It's the stuff that dreams are made of. It's an institution!"

The tap of leather soles against tile, the brush of slacks, the faint scent of floral talc, the gentle plop into the nearby chair confirmed that someone had sat down. *That's gotta be her,* Lawton thought, and his blunt fingernails pressed into his palm.

"Hi, Jac," he said in her direction.

"Hi," she responded without the slightest hint of inflection.

"How was the flight?"

"Fine."

"Anything exciting happen?"

"No. Just the usual. Ate some pretzels. Sipped some bottled water." Her voice's rhythmic cadence floated across Lawton and twined its way right into his heart.

He smiled. *Yes! She flew all the way from Denver! All the way from Denver!* "Ah . . . the pretzels and water treatment. They must really think you're special."

"Yeah . . . or bored."

"So . . ." A daredevil drive spurred him forward. "Are you bored now?" He strained to detect her slightest response, and the taut silence screamed that her reticence was as loaded as his question.

The room door clicked shut, and Lawton realized he had failed to notice Mel and Kinkaide's departure. His mind was too occupied with other options to have heeded those two. But he could only imagine what they were thinking. Knowing Melissa, his dear, nosy sister-in-law, she had probably already given Jacquelyn the fifth degree and planned to interrogate him by sunup.

A stifled yawn escaped Jac. "Sorry. I'm a bit jet-lagged," she mumbled.

"Or maybe you really *are* bored." No sooner had the words tumbled out than a yawn descended upon Lawton, and he covered his mouth with his IV-laden hand. His momentary surge of energy had taken its toll.

"Maybe *you're* the one who's bored,"

Jacquelyn said, her voice laced with a wry smile.

"Not on your life." Lawton lifted his chin, and the starched pillowcase crumpled with his every movement. "If I'd known getting shot would have brought you for a visit, I would have arranged this weeks ago." He raised his left hand for emphasis and winced. "These IV tubes . . ." Lawton paused as his mind took a notion to wander.

"You know, you don't look so hot." Jac stood and neared.

"Thanks. All compliments are welcomed," Lawton quipped and adjusted his position in bed. A telltale stab of pain radiated from his shoulder and down his arm.

"Seriously, you might be talking too much. Earlier today when we talked, you didn't sound like you could barely think. Now —"

"I was really out of it when we talked. I've had a couple of meals since then and been awake awhile." Lawton's final words slurred, and he suppressed another yawn. He flinched against a sharp pain that shot from his wound.

"Sounds like maybe you've been awake too long."

"I think the pain medicine is wearing off."

"Want me to beep the desk for another round?"

"No. The stuff just makes me — makes me sleepy. You didn't fly all the way from Denver to watch me sleep, did ya?"

"Not exactly."

Lawton paused and imagined her standing about four feet away. He had relentlessly tormented Kinkaide about every inch of her appearance until his brother finally declared that enough was enough. According to Kinkaide, Jac was about five one and probably didn't weigh 110 pounds soaking wet. That was fine with Lawton. While Kinkaide usually preferred more rounded women, like Melissa, Lawton had always enjoyed the petite variety. Jac was also supposed to have short black hair that swung around her face like satin, and her skin was a glorious shade of bronze. Kinkaide said she wore no makeup. And in Lawton's estimation, that perfectly fit her no-nonsense personality. Jac was Jac. No frills. No games. Just Jac. And Lawton liked her. Liked her a lot. Liked her too much for his own peace of mind.

Shamelessly, he wondered how he could get her to move closer. And perhaps, just perhaps, if he pushed his luck a bit and was able to stay awake another 15 minutes, Jac might let him feel her facial features. Lawton would really enjoy getting a better image of her in his mind. Even Kinkaide couldn't communicate to Lawton what his sensitive fingertips could impart.

"You know, I *could* use a drink of water," he claimed and swallowed against his dry mouth. *At least I'm being honest in my strategy,* he thought with an unexpressed chuckle.

"Sure thing." The clean smell of her floral talc wafted toward Lawton once more as the sounds of light footfalls and graceful movements accompanied the clink of ice and water hitting a disposable cup.

As she leaned toward him, Lawton raised his head and reached for the cup.

"Here. I've got it," she said, and he would have vowed her soft voice held an endearing nuance. "There's a straw." The straw brushed against his parched lips. "Just relax against the bed. You don't need to be moving around so much."

"Okay." *Being shot certainly has its advantages,* he thought and began brainstorming about ways to keep her close.

He leisurely sipped the water as the suspicions that started in Rome continued to gain credence. Jacquelyn Lightfoot might very well be the answer to his prayers for a friend . . . for a mate . . . for a woman to share his dreams. Only plenty of time and more prayer would tell. There had been a long stream of feminine acquaintances in his past. Women who were intrigued by Lawton; women who would have been glad to take their friendship deeper. But for Lawton, they were acquaintances only. To date, there had not been another woman who had snatched his fancy like Jacquelyn. Part of the fun was that she wasn't quite available. For some reason, Jac continued to keep him at arm's length. But the Franklin men seldom remained thwarted when they set their sights on a goal.

Let the chase begin, Lawton mused. *And how I will enjoy it!* He had spent serious money on the bracelet he'd bought at Rhodes, trusting that the piece of jewelry would speak his hopes. When she had pushed him away at the Spanish Steps, he had feared she would reject the gift outright if he tried to give it to her. So he passed the platinum stars onto his brother to deliver to Jac. Kinkaide said she had reluctantly taken it. As far as Lawton was concerned, her accepting the bracelet added fervor to his expectations. While the chase was far from being over, Lawton wondered if Jac might be running slower.

He continued to swallow tiny sips of the cold water as thoughts of the bracelet ushered in a question that he couldn't deny answering. His fingers trailed from resting on the cup's rim to exploring her right wrist. As his lips broke away from the straw, his fingers traced the outline of three platinum stars against skin as smooth as satin. Jac stiffened, and Lawton toyed with the links that encircled her wrist.

"Nice bracelet," he said through a smile that started in his heart and sprawled across his face.

Jacquelyn stared at the bracelet. A hot rush of panic started in her gut and spread to her cheeks. She peered at Lawton, then toward the bracelet, then back to Lawton. For the first time, she had seen him without his dark glasses. While his cloudy eyes, forever in motion, verified his lack of physical sight, his heightened insight would daunt even the most observant. Jacquelyn felt as if Lawton could read her mind. As his sensitive fingers trifled with the stars then gently stroked her wrist, her skin betrayed her with pleasurable tingles.

And Jac wondered if she were crazy. *Yes, I'm crazy! I'm a raging idiot for having even considered flying here. What was I thinking?*

"Come with me. Come with me. We'll fly to the stars," Lawton crooned. "We'll embrace them and soak up their splendor."

"I want to return the bracelet," Jac blurted.

Lawton's fingers stilled. "No," he gasped as if she had just announced the death of his dearest friend.

She backed away and pulled her wrist from his touch. "Yes. I — I didn't intend to leave it on. Today on the plane is th–the first time I ever even put it on. And —"

"You don't like it?" he asked, his voice dripping with disappointment.

Jac stared at the bracelet. Only the dull click of the IV monitor interrupted the silence. The stars glimmered under the overhead lights as if they were beckoning her to keep them. Keep them and treasure them. Treasure them and cherish the man before her.

"Ah, Jac," he drawled, "it's not like I'm asking you to marry me or anything."

Jacquelyn bolted farther away and deposited the cup on the bedside table amid a clatter of ice cubes and a slosh of water. She walked to the window, crossed her arms, and stared upon the city's myriad glittering lights. The whirring air conditioner beneath her blew a steady stream of chilled air against her bare arms. The icy blast might as well have come from the corridors of her heart.

Of course you aren't asking me to marry you, she thought with frigid reality. *And you probably never would, once you found out. What man of your caliber would want me? I'm damaged goods, Lawton.*

Instead of voicing these thoughts, Jac spoke the next thing that entered her mind. "I'll be glad when the pizza gets here." The words came out flat and cold.

"You mean, you'll be glad when Mel and Kinkaide get back, don't you?" Lawton asked. "Then you won't be cooped up with me all by yourself."

"Lawton —"

"Oh, come on, Jac!" he burst forth. "I'm not going to bite."

She spun from the window and narrowed her eyes. The sight of his pale, drawn features reawakened the concern that had momentarily faded. They shouldn't be having this loaded conversation. Not now. Not when he was still in the throes of the aftermath of being shot.

"Whatever has you so scared . . ." His

legs shifted. "You know, sometimes in life you just need to get over it!"

"You do have a way with words," she spit out as her hands curled into tight fists.

"So, who was he, Jacquelyn Lightfoot?" Lawton paused and lifted his chin in that customary manner that was growing so familiar. "Did he rip your heart out and leave you afraid of all men from now on or what?"

Jac forced herself to draw a slow, steady breath. "Lawton, I recommend that you —"

"You know, you can't stay bound in fear your whole life, for pity's sake!"

"You think you have all the answers, don't you?" she said in a voice that was low and full of steel. She reached for her handbag.

"Don't you dare leave." He waved his left hand then winced. "Not like this."

"I'll leave when I want."

"Not until you get it out in the open. I want to know why you keep doing this to me. You move in close, and I think I'm making progress. Then you shut me out. It's the same thing you did on the trip. This is going to get really old really fast. It's already old, and I want some answers. What happened to you to make you so —"

"Listen . . ." Jac stepped forward, then

glowered within inches of his face before realizing the effect was totally lost on him. "It's none of your stinkin' business. Got it?"

He never flinched. "When you jumped the first flight to Dallas, you *made* it my business." His hand rose to caress the bracelet. "And when you wore this —"

Jac jerked away and stopped herself short of spinning on her heel and stomping out. Instead, she eyed the door and deliberated her options. Even in the midst of her ire, she didn't like the idea of leaving him alone, especially not after someone had tried to kill him.

"I jumped the first flight because I wanted to get to the bottom of who tried to kill you. You're the brother-in-law of one of my dearest friends, and she needed the kind of help I can offer. End of discussion. And as far as the bracelet . . . I should have never put it on." With a flip of her fingers, she clicked open the clasp and dropped the bracelet against his palm.

Without a word, Lawton turned his face toward the wall as his fingers clutched the platinum links. "You are the most infuriating woman I have ever met," he said through clenched teeth before chucking the glistening stars over the handrail. With a protesting clink, the bracelet crashed into the wall above the sink then slipped behind the water spout. Wincing, Lawton gingerly lowered his hand to the top of the covers.

"I was crazy for even *thinking* about coming here."

"I must have been crazy for calling you. I guess I'm just a glutton for punishment." The contorted twist of his lips drove an arrow of guilt straight through Jac's heart. "Go on . . . do what you want to do and just — just leave." He rubbed his jaw, dark with stubble.

A cold knot formed in Jac's stomach.

"Kinkaide and Mel will be back soon enough. I'll be fine. I'm sure the police will eventually find the men who did this to me. Don't feel obligated to do a thing." He closed his eyes and pressed his lips together.

I'm sorry, Jac thought. *I never meant to hurt you . . . or anger you . . . or . . . I'm sorry,* she repeated in her mind. But instead of voicing her thoughts, she uttered a simple "okay" and walked out the door. But as it clicked behind her, she leaned against the wall, closed her eyes, and took a trembling breath. She relived the minutes following the phone call from Sammie. Minutes when she feared that Lawton might be dead. Minutes when she regretted that glacial conversation at the base of the Spanish Steps. Already another layer of regret drifted over her soul. But she couldn't do anything to erase their heated encounter. Nor could she wipe out her past or that nightmare beast.

"I hate you," she whispered. "I hate you for what you did. I hate you because . . . because . . ." she swallowed. "Because I've finally met a wonderful man, and I can't have one conversation with him without your stinkin' breath ruining everything."

Jacquelyn clenched her jaw, opened her eyes, and waited. She wouldn't leave Lawton. She couldn't. She would stay until Mel and Kinkaide returned. Then maybe tomorrow she and Lawton could start over. *Yes, tomorrow.* Jac had come to Dallas to solve a case. She would solve it. *Period.*

Six

"Knock-knock!" Kinkaide called as he entered Lawton's room a few minutes later.

The smell of the long-awaited pizza did little to tempt Lawton. He flexed his left hand and sighed. *What a mess,* he thought. *I don't even know how or why all that blew up like it did.*

"Look and see if you can find that platinum bracelet I gave Jac," he said without preamble as he pointed to the left. "It landed somewhere over there."

A cardboard box brushed against a table. Kinkaide's shoes clicked across the room then halted. The faint jingle of platinum links attested to his picking up the bracelet. "So," Kinkaide mused, "you struck out?"

"I'd rather not talk about it," Lawton

mumbled. "Would you please beep the nurse's desk so I can get my medicine? I think I need some sleep."

"Or maybe you need to read a few more of those Christian romance novels you claim are so informative." Kinkaide's satisfied chuckle increased the exasperation in Lawton's drooping spirit.

"This is not funny," he snapped.

"Oh, so now the tables are turned and you don't like it," Kinkaide prodded. "I recall your mocking me before the trip to Rome because I couldn't get Melissa to so much as talk to me. Let's see . . . if I remember correctly, you told me that the heroes in the romance novels you'd been reading from that client of yours had a few things on me," he said with pontifical nuance.

Lawton gritted his teeth. "Cut it out, Kinkaide," he snarled. "This ain't funny!"

The room fell into an immediate and intense silence only broken by the creaking of a hospital cart in the hallway.

"Well, I guess you really *did* bomb," Kinkaide said on a contrite note. "Sorry ol' man." The scrape of cardboard preceded the aroma of a culinary masterpiece. "Want some pizza?"

"I really blew it. You're right," Lawton

said, ignoring Kinkaide's offer. "I'm just not really sure how!" His wound ached as he shook his head. Every inch of the bed tortured him. The pillow had slipped too low. The sheets were twined around his feet. The head of the bed was too high . . . or maybe too low. The rails . . . *these stupid rails are drivin' me nuts!* Lawton resisted the urge to pound them.

"So, did she throw the bracelet across the room or what?"

"*I* threw the bracelet," Lawton said testily.

"I thought since she flew all the way from Denver —"

"Me, too! I thought that about a hundred times, give or take!" Lawton scratched at his stubble. *Somebody needs to give me a shave, or I'm going to rip out this stuff by the roots!*

"Want me to shave you?" Kinkaide offered.

"Please. And forget the pizza. And ask for my pain pills. And take that bracelet and put it somewhere safe. If I lived on Rhodes, I'd take the blasted thing back!" Lawton vaguely sensed that he was bordering on being obnoxious, but he possessed no means to stop himself.

"Sure thing," Kinkaide said in an unusually compliant voice.

"I told her to get over it — to get over whatever it is that's bothering her, and she went *ballistic* on me."

"You told her to just get over it?" Kinkaide queried as he rounded the bed then stopped.

"Yes! I mean, she keeps moving in like she's interested, then when I reach for her, she shuts me out cold. I don't like playing some stupid games —"

"You told her to just get over it?" Kinkaide repeated as if Lawton had spoken German.

"What's the matter? Didn't you hear me the first time?"

"Man, oh man," Kinkaide breathed. "You just acted about 18 different kinds of stupid."

"Now that's really encouraging!" Lawton said, then snorted. "And *do* something about my pain medication! My shoulder is *killing* me!"

The click of a button preceded a receptionist's sterile voice. "Would you please see if Lawton Franklin can have more pain medicine now?" Kinkaide snapped, and Lawton sensed he had gone too far.

"Sorry," he mumbled as an ominous silence descended upon them. "I just don't handle pain well. You know I never have. I get —"

"You get downright mean. That's what you get," Kinkaide groused. "Now, do you want this pizza I chased down for you or not?"

"Do you know what she's so uptight about?" Lawton asked.

"Can't say."

"What do you mean you can't say?" Lawton raised his head as far as his shoulder permitted then plopped back against the confining bed.

"I mean it's all confidential stuff that I promised Mel I wouldn't tell."

"So, you know why Jacquelyn is so . . . so . . ." Lawton's mind meandered off and left him grappling for the rest of his thought. "So . . ."

"Yes I know, *but I can't say,*" he repeated as if Lawton were daft.

Lawton inserted the tip of his tongue between his teeth and bit until he could tolerate the pain no longer. Once again, he forced himself not to attack the bed rails.

"All I can say is that the last thing that woman needs to hear from you is 'get over it.' That was really stupid, if I must say so myself."

"Yes, I've heard that rumor. Thanks for

repeating it!" Lawton bellowed. "I know I wasn't exactly Don Juan here, but the last thing *I* need is —"

"Do you want a piece of pizza or not?"

"I want you to tell me what you know."

"Not on your life. I promised Mel."

Lawton's stomach surprised him with a grumble.

"You really need to concentrate on getting better so you can get out of here," Kinkaide said in a slightly patronizing voice.

"Nice try, but it *ain't* gonna work. I want to know —"

"I'm not going to tell you. Stop pushing!" Kinkaide erupted. "It would mean betraying my word to Mel!"

Lawton closed his eyes and bit back another retort. Whatever Jac was covering up, something told him it was dark and ugly and that it had completely gotten the best of her.

"She wasn't a prostitute or anything was she?" he asked, voicing the worst scenario his imagination could conjure. His flippant tone belied his seriousness. Lawton knew that Jacquelyn Lightfoot wouldn't allow herself to be used in that manner.

"No," Kinkaide said as if Lawton had just voiced the most ridiculous suggestion possible. "I will tell you that it isn't that. But . . ." Kinkaide hesitated. "Would that matter to you? I mean, if she had —"

"Can't really say," Lawton replied. "You know I've always said that I wanted a woman who had, well, lived by the standards I've lived by."

"That's honorable and right. And I'm glad Mel did," Kinkaide said. "But as you know, due to my own stroll down Asinine Avenue, I can't claim the same. Now, what kind of fix would I be in if Mel weren't willing to forgive me for my past?"

Lawton grimaced. "I'm tired of thinking so much." He yawned. "My shoulder hurts."

"Yes, I know. And I want you back home — safe and sound. I don't know who shot you, but he might still be in the area. Why don't you just eat some pizza, take some medicine, and work on getting better. Jac can wait. And, well . . ." Kinkaide's voice softened, "you might not be in the doghouse as much as you think. She waited outside your door until Mel and I got here."

"She did?"

"Yep. She said she didn't feel comfortable leaving you on your own."

"So are they still here — her and Mel?" Lawton queried.

"No. They've gone to their friend's place — Sammie Jones'. She lives in Dallas. I think Jacquelyn is planning on staying with her while she's visiting."

"So I guess I'm stuck with you tonight?" Lawton asked as he furrowed his brow. That pain medicine couldn't come soon enough.

"Yes, and I hope I'm dead and gone if they *ever* have to put you in a nursing home," Kinkaide drawled.

"Ah, shut up." Lawton produced a twisted grin. "They won't even *put* you in a nursing home. You're so mean they'll probably just shut you up in that grand piano of yours and let you sit —"

"Hey, don't start it with the piano business. It's a tough job, but —"

"Somebody's gotta do it," the two finished in unison.

"So, do you want to talk about it or are you going to stay sullen the rest of the evening?" Mel asked Jac as she pulled the rental car into Sammie's driveway.

"I really don't want to talk about it, but thanks for the offer. And please, Mel, don't say anything to the sisters that will start one of those famous teasing sessions. I don't think I can handle it tonight. I *really* don't."

As Mel put the car in park, the vehicle's new smell made Jac wish for her recently purchased Jeep, parked at the Denver airport. Melissa turned off the engine. As a questioning silence descended upon them, Jac admitted the truth. She not only wanted her own Jeep, she wanted her own bed. She wanted to be far away from Lawton Franklin and the threat he posed — the threat to her heart.

I don't ever want to be hurt as deeply as I've been hurt, Lawton, she thought. *And despite the fact that you are wonderful — yes, I'll admit that you're a spectacular man — despite all that, I will not take the chance. I'm fine like I am. Just me. Just Jac. I'm fine.*

Jac gripped the door release and peered toward Sammie's modest brick home ablaze with welcoming lights. Mel had called from her cell phone when they left the hospital, and Sammie had most likely run to the nearest deli to snatch up some cookies or muffins. While their other friend, Victoria, would have baked mounds of earth-shaking cookies, Sammie usually wasn't together enough to think that far in advance.

With a sigh, Jac dreaded the conference

call with her college friends. Facing Sammie was going to be interesting enough. So far, Mel had miraculously refrained from her usual interrogation tactics. Perhaps Jacquelyn's grave expression and tense silence had convinced her to back off. Maybe the same approach would stifle any overt interest from her other five friends.

Twice a year, the seven "sisters" got together for a girlfriend reunion. Since their college days at the University of Texas, the seven had maintained their deep friendship and considered themselves siblings. The intermittent conference calls and e-mail helped them keep in touch between reunions. Even though the seven sisters were from different walks of life, they loved each other with the bond of equality that had sealed their friendship in the first place.

"Well," Mel finally said, and Jacquelyn cringed, "they're all going to want to know about you and Lawton. I mean, after all, you flew all the way here to be with him."

"Just tell them I wanted to help crack the case. It's the truth. I'm going to do the best I can, but more likely than not, we probably won't find the people behind this. He was obviously at the wrong place at the wrong time. As much as I hate to admit it, real life isn't always like the movies. Every case isn't always solved, and every criminal isn't always tracked down." Despite her words, a renewed urge surged . . . an impatience to find that jerk who shot Lawton and nail him. There wasn't a finer man in the world than Lawton Franklin, and he didn't even remotely deserve what he got.

"Lawton will most likely go home," she continued, forcing all traces of fervency from her voice. "I figure he'll recuperate and go back to his job without another incident."

"So, you're going to drop it just like that?" Mel snapped her fingers, and the click was like a sword in Jac's midsection. "You're going to let whatever happened back there overshadow justice, is that it?"

"I didn't say that," Jac protested. "I'm going to try to get to the bottom of it. That's what I came here to do. I'm just trying to tell you that it might not all fall into place like — like Perry Mason." Jacquelyn peered through the shadows and into her friend's candid eyes.

"Okay, okay," Mel said.

Jac glanced away. No new words came. None. Only Lawton's form. His pale face. His disappointment because she returned the bracelet. His frustration. No words at all. Only images that beckoned Jac to dare hope that Lawton might not hold her past against her. Jacquelyn opened the door, and the sounds of distant Dallas traffic seemed to echo Mel's next question.

"Did you and Lawton get a chance to discuss the case at all?"

"Nope. Not in the least." Jac stepped onto the concrete driveway and snapped the car door shut. The Texas humidity wrapped around her like a hot, damp sponge, and she longed for the cool breezes off the Rockies.

"Hey, girlfriends," Sammie's southern twang resounded from the front door. Jac smiled as the fiery redhead strode barefoot across the lawn with her little boy trotting beside her. Brett's three-year-old legs produced two steps for every one of Sammie's.

"Howdy, pardner," Mel called with a fake southern accent. "Been roundin' up any dogies lately?"

The three laughed together as Sammie hugged first Jac and then Mel. When Melissa bent to greet Brett, he latched onto her neck, and she lifted him into her arms. "Howdy to you, too." Mel mussed his hair, that was just as straight and bright as his mother's.

"I've got a cowboy set," Brett said.

"You do?" Mel asked, her eyes big.

"Yes. With a hat and a holster. Come on! I'll show you!" He squirmed for freedom, and Mel deposited him back onto the lawn, only to have him lean toward the door and tug her hand.

"Just a minute, Brett," Sammie snapped as if the child had committed the most heinous of crimes. "We've got to help Jac get her luggage."

"He's okay, really," Mel soothed through the shadows. Placing a hand on Sammie's shoulder, she shot Jac a speculative glance.

Without response Jacquelyn opened the back door and retrieved her suitcase and backpack. Something was up with Sammie. She didn't know what, but it was something significantly weighty. Right now, Jac wasn't sure she even wanted to know. Too much was already up with her — too much that involved Lawton Franklin.

Seven

∽

"And the morning and the evening were the first day," Maurice Stein quoted as he leaned against the hotel window. The Dallas skyscrapers blazed like glowing titans standing in a sea of flitting fireflies. An airplane, lights blinking as it floated past the towering buildings, beckoned Maurice to bolt . . . To hire a taxi, go to the airport, and take the next flight out of the States, away from the evil that pulled him ever deeper into the cavern of culpability.

In his mind, he listed some of the countries that he could enter without a visa. Maurice stopped on Thailand and smiled. *Yes. Thailand would be nice.* The women were beautiful. Bangkok was inviting. The chances of his getting caught were slim. The city beckoned and Maurice, trapped in the web of silence, savored the possibilities. He had but a few hours to make his decision. A few hours before Fuat would phone with the time of his next flight. A flight that would most likely take him back to the New York headquarters.

"But just suppose . . ." Maurice pinched his bottom lip as his mind hurled him into the land of risks. *Just suppose I were to go back and finish the search for the Sellers' cache. I could sell it quickly then head to Bangkok and relax for life. I wouldn't ever have to worry about money again . . . or about killing . . .*

The phone's accusatory peal sent a jolt through Maurice, and he jumped. He glanced at the digital clock on the nightstand and noted that the call was coming early this time. Maurice's knees locked as the third ring reverberated around the room. As planned, the day had slid by like so many other post-job days he had spent in various hotel rooms all over the U.S. No one had called. No one. Not one significant interruption to his solitary confinement. None except for the arrival of room service.

Now the call was coming through. At last. His isolation would be over. But Maurice wasn't certain he wanted to talk.

Not now. Not while he was still planning. On the eighth ring, he picked up the receiver and waited for Fuat to snap out the accusation.

"What took you so long?" the boss growled.

"I was in the bathroom," Maurice lied, and his shoulders stiffened as the ensuing pause hinted at Fuat's skepticism. Fuat never believed much of what anyone said. Maurice had long since figured that was because Fuat did his share of lying. Certainly he had lied to Maurice on numerous occasions. He had probably lied about the current job when he promised Maurice a cut. As the silence stretched, Maurice narrowed his eyes. Fuat would do whatever it took to get what he wanted. And he'd wanted this for more than 30 years. If he ever found out just how seriously Maurice had shrank from completing the Sellers' job, Fuat would probably shoot him on the spot.

"The blind man is still alive. Did you know that?" Fuat demanded. Maurice's fingers gripped the receiver.

"No," he lied again and sat in the desk chair.

The stony hush screamed that Fuat didn't believe Maurice. And Fuat's unspoken suspicions weren't without merit. Maurice had purposefully shot to wound, not to kill. As soon as he was alone, he had anonymously called an ambulance to report Lawton Franklin's location.

"How did you find out?" Maurice asked and traced the pleat in his slacks with the tip of his index finger.

"I've got my sources."

"The police," Maurice said with finality.

"Of course. As you know, it only takes one bad apple to keep me privy to important tidbits. And, well, looks like there's a few more bad apples out there besides you."

Maurice stifled a retort.

"Money talks. No matter what the badge says. Don't you know you can't get anything past me? I thought by now you would have figured that out. And you should already know that if you don't follow orders, you don't live!"

Maurice's finger hovered along the pleat then quivered. "I tried my best to do what you told me to do," he claimed.

"I don't believe you!" Fuat hissed.

"You were right there with me when I shot him!"

"Yes. I was stupid enough not to double check your work. You've been lying to me since you picked up the phone." Maurice imagined Fuat's narrowed dark eyes, cunning as a demon at midnight. "You never miss when you really want to kill. You're one of the best. If you missed, it's because you *meant* to miss. What is the matter with you? Are you going soft on me?"

"No!" Maurice answered forcefully, and his fist pounded against his knee.

"And if you're hiding the Sellers' findings —"

Maurice stood. The suite seemed to swirl in a hideous contortion of opulence and malice. "I already told you at the airport. I don't have them!"

"You better not! Because if you do . . ."

Maurice's jaw clenched as his face heated. The time had come to break free. Free . . . Bangkok's beckon increased.

"Listen, you have one chance to do what I told you to do. *One.* Do you understand?" Fuat growled. "Sometime in the next 24 hours, I want that blind man dead!"

"But there's no reason to —"

"Yes! There's an excellent reason," Fuat spewed. "Because I told you to do it. I pay you to do what I say. I don't pay you to think!"

Maurice clamped down on the end of his

tongue until he tasted blood.

"And if you don't kill him . . ." Fuat's voice seemed to transcend the receiver and echo off the room's walls — walls that gradually closed in on Maurice. "I will find you and I will kill you."

Pressing his lips together, Maurice stiffened. Fuat Rantomi never spoke idly. Maurice had put bullets behind Rantomi's threats more than he wanted to remember. Once again images of his own form in a lone casket overtook him.

"Got it?" Fuat snarled.

"Yes," Maurice agreed and wrapped his fingers around the ebony pencil lying beside the phone. "I understand."

The phone clicked, and Maurice stabbed the pencil's lead against the table. The pencil broke. The wood cracked against his fingers, and his palm stung with the impact of splinters. Maurice slammed the receiver into the cradle and cursed.

He eyed the crucifix, still sitting in the center of the coffee table, and blasted the day he had ever aligned himself with the likes of Fuat Rantomi. Maurice had needed the money at the time. Nursing homes were expensive. And during those early days after the fire had gobbled his children and left his wife a vegetable,

Maurice had been so numb that he hadn't felt the first murder. Or the second. Or the third. The fourth blurred into another and another. Now he looked back upon the last five years through a haze of irony, amazed that he had ended innumerable lives in order to preserve the life of his spouse. A mate who never spoke to him after the night of the fire. A lover who finally slipped into eternity a mere ten months ago.

He walked to the bathroom, turned on the cold water, leaned over the sink, and dashed water against his features. His nose and eyes tingled with the chill, a chill so like the ice that had long ago frosted his heart. Maurice splashed his face again, and this time his fingers, lean and searching, lingered on his forehead. Beneath his knowing touch, the skin felt like melted wax, forever hardened into a maze of swirls and bumps. He raised his face and looked in the mirror at a man nearly 40. A man with dark hair, hardened eyes as green as marble, and skin that bore the marks of adolescent acne. And then there were the scars. The scars that his well-placed bangs always covered. The scars that Gloria bore over her whole body.

"Gloria . . . oh, Gloria," he breathed as

droplets of water plopped from his eye-lashes. "You would never forgive me if you knew what I've become." The sound of the rushing water conjured up images of Gary Sellers' children . . . images of his own children. "Oh, God," he whispered, "I'm sick of this killing."

He turned off the water and grabbed a towel while Fuat's threat swooped upon him and grabbed him by the throat. Maurice swallowed. He swallowed hard. *I could probably leave for Bangkok tomorrow,* he thought. Yet the Sellers' cache loomed before him. If he went ahead and followed Fuat's orders this one last time, Maurice could dupe Fuat into believing that he was still with him and could buy himself enough time to go back to Ouray, Colorado. Once there, he might be able to break through that boundary that had stopped him in his tracks and ended all attempts at completing the search for the loot.

Maurice's eyes glistened. Bangkok beckoned . . . but the city would be far more enjoyable if he had several million in the bank. Images of the blind man rushed upon him. The horror of killing Lawton Franklin stormed him once more yet diminished in the face of potential freedom and financial independence.

"Isn't that the way it's always been with you?" he mumbled at his reflection, despising the form before him.

You have sworn off of killing before, haven't you? a sinister voice mocked. *But the lure of money always snares your rotten soul.* This time, the monetary gain made his former payments look like pennies.

He paced toward the crucifix, snatched it up, and neared the black suitcase sitting atop the luggage rack. Maurice whipped up the lid, shoved aside the clothing, and plopped the cross on the bottom. He tumbled the clothing over it and slammed down the luggage lid. Once again Maurice Stein would do what he had to do.

Sammie Jones glanced at the antique clock majestically perched on the rustic mantel as if it reigned over the whole premise. Ten o'clock would chime in a few seconds, and Sammie's phone would ring. Then she and her six college friends would interact as they had more times than she could remember. Mel and Jac were waiting in the home office, where they would share the phone. Sammie's gaze listlessly drifted around the latest in Southwest decor covered in clutter, and she tried to remember how long she had been hiding the truth from her best friends. Oh, she had hinted that her marriage wasn't exactly heaven on earth, but she wondered if any of them suspected how it had deteriorated during the last year.

Oh, God, she prayed as she wadded the end of her oversized oxford shirt, *don't let him come home tonight. Not tonight.* Yet another side of her hoped Adam would come home. If he did arrive, drunk and dangerous, then maybe Jacquelyn would help her find a way out.

If you leave me I'll kill you! And if you tell anyone I'll kill you! Adam had said those words so many times over the last year that they had poisoned her spirit with enough terror to keep her silently rooted in the relationship. Breaking free was dangerous.

But maybe I'm ready for the risk, she encouraged herself. *All I need is Jackie's support.* A tendril of guilt mingled with her resolve. Jacquelyn didn't even know that her presence might serve Sammie's hidden purpose. *I'll tell her,* she resolved, *just as soon as the sister phone call is over.*

Sammie shifted in her chair and stood to peer into the gold-framed mirror hanging behind the brass lamp. The young woman looking back at her hadn't changed much since college. Sammie's red, straight hair hung just past her shoulders. She had been told that the freckles that dotted her nose and cheeks lent her a certain fresh and wholesome appeal. Wispy bangs framed eyes the color of bluebonnets; eyes once inviting and kind, now clouded with disillusionment. Disillusionment and heartache. Heartache and hopelessness. On the edges of the hopelessness rested a bruise.

Sammie leaned forward to scrutinize the bluish blur she had tried to cover with pancake makeup before Jac and Mel arrived. Despite her efforts, the shadow remained. With a grimace, Sammie reached inside her purse, lying open on the end table. She dragged out the foundation compact, touched her finger to the cream, and smeared a new layer over the bruise.

Behind her ice hit the bottom of a glass, and Sammie's face tightened. She took a deep breath and snapped the compact shut. A glance in the mirror reflected the open kitchen behind her. *Adam isn't home,* she reminded herself. *It's Jackie. Not Adam.* Sammie bit her bottom lip and released a trembling breath.

She nonchalantly dropped the compact back into her purse and meandered toward the kitchen. The yellow-and-blue decor merrily implied that nothing but joy ever transpired in this bright alcove. The drying bouquet of roses sitting on the counter proclaimed that Sam's husband loved her. Yet Sammie couldn't remember the last time true happiness was present, or the last time Adam's bouquets weren't presented in the aftermath of violence.

The sound of running water accompanied Jac's question, "I guess it's okay if I help myself?"

"Of course," Sammie replied. "Make yourself at home."

Water spilled over the brim of Jacquelyn's plastic tumbler. She turned off the water, drained off the excess, then lifted the cup to her lips. Over the top of the glass, her dark gaze held Sammie's. A silent communication flashed between them. Sammie understood at once that she was hiding precious little from Jac Lightfoot. Her sharp detective's brain hadn't ever missed much — and it still didn't. But unlike Mel, Jacquelyn wouldn't say a word until Sammie confided.

The phone rang, and Sammie jumped. "Oh, that's the sisters," she said, covering her heart with her hand. "Scared me there for a minute."

Jacquelyn took another slow drink of the

icy water and eyed the stack of magazines sitting on the breakfast bar. Magazines that featured Sammie's regular column. *Sammie Jones, star reporter for* Romantic Times *magazine,* Jac thought with a twist of irony. *Noted romance novelist . . . battered wife.*

As Sammie picked up the receiver and spoke her greeting, Jacquelyn wondered how long she had been living in the shadows of abuse. Adam, a respected schoolteacher, had seemed the charming sort, yet he had never interacted much with the sisters. When Jac saw Sam a month ago she had seemed a bit nervous, but Jac had assumed she was under a lot of stress. *Who isn't?* In retrospect, Jac figured Sammie had been hiding the injustice for quite some time.

Adam Jones, like every other wife abuser, probably convinced Sammie that if she told anyone or left him, he would kill her. Those threats weren't usually empty. Jac had worked more than one missing person case that involved an abusive husband who killed his wife after she sought refuge. And then there was the case last year when the abusive wife killed her husband.

The very contemplation that one human being thought he or she had the right to misuse another opened a door within Jac's heart. A door where relentless rage incessantly blazed. The fury poured forth like glowing lava and splashed into every cavity of Jac's heart until she felt as if she were drowning in the heat of her wrath. As a child, Jacquelyn had been in a situation like Sammie's. Taken advantage of. Stepped on. Misused. Treated like trash. And there was nothing she could do about it then. She had been a helpless victim in the hands of selfish lust. And she had been terrified that if she told she would surely be killed.

Now, this is a special secret just between you and me. Do you understand? a masculine voice from Jac's past barged in upon her and plunged her to a time when she was nine. Nine and frightened. Frightened and manipulated.

Yes, sir. She responded with "sir" because her mother always taught her that she must respect him. She must, she must.

And if you ever do tell, your mother will think you're awful, and I will have to kill you. Do you understand? the voice said.

Jacquelyn's throat grew tight. *Yes, sir. I understand,* she squeaked out.

As Sammie embarked upon her amiable chatter, the ethereal beams on the nightmare forest's edge penetrated the haze from the past and bade her to run to the light, to embrace the next dimension of the truth. As in her dream, a path amid clouds of swirling gold dust opened before her. The unrelenting glow threatened to reveal the man behind the voice. But as the beams plunged deeper into her memory, Jacquelyn stumbled backward.

Oh, please, God, she begged, *I don't want to know. I can't — can't handle it. Oh dear Lord, what if it was my own father?*

Images of her Native American father swam before her eyes. He had often taken his children to visit the Alabama–Coushatta Indian Reservation where he grew up. Even though they never lived on the reservation near Livingston, Texas, Jac had spent nights under the stars, watching the mystical dancing, mesmerized by the cavorting shadows and the spark and hiss of the flames. During those enchanting Texas nights, she had snuggled closely to her father and savored the essence of his strength. A strength rooted in his relationship with Jesus Christ. For years he carried a burden for placing the message of Christ within the context of his own cultural heritage. A concept that won the hearts of many of his tribe of origin.

Jacquelyn decided right then that she would rather not know the identity of the molester than discover that he had been her dad. She had trusted him with the abandon that only a child can bestow. She had been robbed of every other childhood innocence. *I couldn't bear losing that one,* she whimpered.

As she focused on Sammie's interaction with the sisters, her past faded into the cruel facts of the present. A cold chill crawled up Jac's spine. Sammie's smile, her animated voice, her southern charisma successfully camouflaged reality. A hard reality. A reality that the bruise by her eye validated. So did the drying bouquet of roses on the kitchen sink. Most abusers presented flowers and "I'll do betters" after a nasty scene. Looking back, Jac couldn't remember the last time Sammie's sparkling blue eyes held the glint of triumph so characteristic of their college years.

Jacquelyn wandered toward Brett's room and glanced inside. "Little carrot top," she said through a smile. The bundle of energy slept snugly under his Barney comforter as if he didn't have a care in the world. And Jac couldn't help but wonder, *How many times has Brett watched Adam hit Sammie? Is*

Adam also abusing his son? Her fingers tightened on the plastic tumbler, and she vowed to facilitate Sammie's timely departure. Since Jac never spent money on stuff she didn't need, she had a nice nest egg built up. Sometimes nest eggs were meant to be spent.

She stepped into the guest room, grabbed toiletry essentials from her suitcase, and moved toward the bathroom. Jac tuned out Sammie and Mel's chatting and wondered what the night might bring. She walked into the restroom and used the tip of her square-toed boot to nudge aside a small pile of building blocks. As with every other room in the house, the bright country decor sported a heavy curse of clutter. The few times Jacquelyn had frequented Sam's home, she never remembered it being such a mess. Perhaps the combination of career, motherhood, and an abusive husband had taken its toll.

Images of the amber-colored, long-necked bottles in the back of the refrigerator invaded her mind. Sammie didn't drink. That left only one option. Jacquelyn closed the door, locked it, and decided that if Adam came home drunk with plans for some action . . . She deposited her burden on the counter and thrust her right leg into midair in three consecutive kicks that had put more than one man on his back.

"I'm ready for you, you jerk," she snarled. Adam's mental form soon merged with that of the dragon to produce one foe — a foe Jacquelyn would stop in his tracks.

She stepped toward the shower and yanked off her jeans and shirt. The faint trace of Mel's laughter gave her pause. Her six friends were expecting her to interact in their sisterly phone chat — a supportive chat that usually ensued after one of them had endured some upheaval. Lawton's predicament certainly qualified as such. Melissa needed her friends now as through the years all of them had needed each other.

A knock on the door preceded Mel's voice. "Hey, Jac! The gang's asking about you."

She hesitated but a second, then removed her underclothes, stepped into the shower, and snapped the door shut. "Tell them I'm in the shower. I'll talk later — maybe on the internet."

Melissa's silence seemed an unspoken plea from all the sisters: pastor's wife Marilyn Langham; supermodel Kim Lan O'Donnel; homemaker extraordinaire

Victoria Roberts; veterinarian Sonsee Delaney; Sammie; and Mel.

"Are you sure?" Mel prompted. "I'm going to have to leave in a few minutes . . ."

Jac imagined the potential teasing about Lawton that the sisters just might slip into. She hardened her heart, turned on the water, and held her fingers under the tepid flow. "Yes," she called. "Just tell everyone I said hi, okay?"

"Okay, sure." Mel's dubiety oozed through the door, and Jac resisted a tinge of guilt.

Instead, she upped the level of hot water and turned on the spray. *You've always been the group maverick,* she reminded herself. *They'll just shrug and say, "That's just Jac."* Even though she loved her friends, she often found herself on the edge of their network. Like tonight.

No matter how good-hearted the sisters were, the subject of Lawton would undoubtedly arise. A subject Jac didn't even want to discuss with herself, much less with anyone else. A hot cleansing shower would better serve her needs. Jacquelyn figured they could just as easily speculate about Lawton without her as they could with her.

"Let 'em talk," Jac mumbled as she increased the hot water a fraction short of discomfort. Yet the stinging spray did little to wash away her thoughts of Lawton. Thoughts intertwined with longing. Longing and fear. Fear and uncertainty.

Eight

~

Maurice hovered in the hallway shadows —
shadows that embraced him like a familiar
lover. He reached for the doorknob, and his
fingers tightened around chilled metal. Behind him, four flights of emergency stairs
rose from the hospital's first floor. On the
other side of the door, the hallway stretched
past innumerable rooms. According to the
pink-clad receptionist, room 434 housed
Lawton Franklin.

And in room 434, Maurice would cata-
pult another soul across eternity's
threshold. "Only once more," he whispered as he turned the knob. The hallway
light struck him like a slap in the face,
urging him to leave the country without
the cache. *But that would only lead to more
crime,* Maurice reasoned. While he did

have enough money saved to support himself for a couple of years, the money would eventually run out. *Then what? I'd be forced to take a couple of jobs to fund my livelihood. Then when that money ran out, there'd be more killing and the cycle would never stop.*

However, if he went through with Fuat's orders and killed Lawton, the boss would think Maurice was falling in line like a good soldier. In reality, the murder would buy him enough time to go back to Ouray and find what he went there for in the first place. Gary Sellers had refused to produce them, and Maurice had prematurely ended the search. They had to be somewhere in the Sellers' home.

Maurice blinked as his eyes adjusted to the light. A furtive glimpse up and down the hallway proved that no one watched. In the distance, a couple of nurses in white uniforms stirred behind a desk. As Maurice had hoped, not much usually happened during the midnight hour.

He tugged the surgeon's cap closer to his brow and adjusted the drawstring on the scrubs. The string dangled inside the loose fitting pants he had stolen from the second floor linen closet. Tied to the string hung a slender leather pouch. Inside the pouch lay the syringe. A syringe filled with rust remover. A simple household liquid, the rust remover would enter Lawton's bloodstream and end his life. All Maurice needed was a few seconds. Just long enough to insert the needle into the IV tubing, plunge the liquid inside, and rush back to the stairway.

"Then it will all be over," Maurice whispered. He lowered his eyes and stepped into the hallway. The door sighed then closed with a final click.

The back door clapped shut, and Sammie jumped. She sat up in the twin bed and scrambled to the end. The midnight darkness played chase with moonbeams along the plush carpet in Brett's room. Midst the whispers of rustling sheets, Sammie's bare feet sank into the moon-touched carpet. She rushed to Brett's side and adjusted the covers. Her fingers flitted across his forehead, and she bestowed a gentle kiss on his temple. The child never stirred.

The sounds of heavy staggering on kitchen tile increased Sammie's pulse rate past the comfort level. A rush of sweat assaulted her fully clothed body, and she pushed forward with the mission of a protective mother. Without a backward glance, she exited Brett's room just as she had dozens of times in past months. Sammie closed his door without a sound and leaned against it.

"Oh, Jesus, protect my baby," she prayed.

So far He had. Not once had Adam struck Brett. *Not once.* But Sammie had taken enough blows during the last year for the both of them. Every time Adam came home late, Sammie stayed in Brett's room until her husband arrived. From there she emerged to divert the drunken beast away from her precious son.

As the footsteps neared, Sammie looked toward Jac's room. The two hadn't discussed Adam's problem. Jacquelyn had quietly moved from the shower to her bedroom even before Mel left an hour ago. Melissa had explained that Lawton and Jac had a disagreement and, as usual, when Jacquelyn was troubled she withdrew. Mel had struggled to understand Jacquelyn's need for privacy, and Sammie had decided to give her friend some space.

Adam's footfalls reverberated from the living room, up the hallway, and Sammie bolted toward the guest bedroom. A fearful part of her had hoped Adam would stay out all night, something that started happening as soon as school let out for the summer. Yet Sammie's reasonable side had wished he would come home and show Jacquelyn what Sam was afraid to tell her. Jac would know how to help her leave. Jac would take action against Adam — whatever action was needed. And maybe, just maybe, Sammie could escape without Adam killing her or harming Brett.

Sammie scurried into Jac's room, stepped to the side, leaned against the wall, and waited.

"He's home, isn't he?" Jac whispered beside her.

A shock surged through Sammie. She jumped and stifled a squeal. "You scared me," she hissed through clamped teeth as she covered her pounding heart.

Jacquelyn stood inches away, her dark eyes gleaming with a steel glint.

Adam entered the hallway, and a belch mingled with the noise of his unsteady gait. Sammie pressed her body against the wall, closed her eyes, and held her breath. Perhaps he wouldn't call her name. Perhaps he would stagger into bed. Her pajama-clad friend stepped around Sammie and edged toward the door's threshold. Sammie peered over the pintsized detective's head as Adam's tall, thin form meandered toward the bedroom they once shared. Now Sammie only frequented the room if Adam forced her.

Gulping for air, Sammie blinked against stinging tears and hugged herself in an attempt to stay the violent trembling. A flash of pain shot from the right side of her rib cage, and she winced. Three nights ago, she had wondered if her ribs were broken. She had since decided they were only sorely bruised. That same night, she had truly feared for her life and begged God to find her a way out. When Jac had asked to stay with her, Sammie had wondered if God were answering her prayer.

Muttering under his breath, Adam stumbled out of sight and into the bedroom. The bedding swished, and he produced a final belch. A distant horn pierced the night, silencing the screeching crickets. As the rancid smell of alcohol and body odor drifted up the hallway, a stifling pall cloaked the darkness.

Without a word, Jac closed the bedroom door and held Sammie's gaze. The two stared at each other while a wealth of silent communication floated across the lambency-laden shadows. As if the luminescent rays were carriers of truth, neither

Sammie nor Jac flipped on the light that would dispel them.

"How long has this been going on?" Jacquelyn whispered, an edge to her voice.

"The physical abuse started a little over a year ago," Sammie said candidly. "After . . . after his father's death. But he's been hateful and verbally abusive for quite a bit longer than that."

"Why didn't you tell us?"

"At first I thought it was just a phase in our marriage that we needed to work through. Then, when he started hitting me, he said he'd kill me if I told."

Jac nodded as if she expected that exact explanation, and her bobbed hair swung in sequence with her movement. With a jerk of her head she hissed, "Let's go to the kitchen. We need to talk."

Sammie followed her up the hallway and paused a second outside Adam's open door. The man lay face down, his arms and legs sprawled as if he were a skydiver. Whether he was asleep, unconscious, or just lying still until the room stopped spinning was anybody's call. Sammie never knew when he might rise and be on the prowl for action. She knitted her brows and couldn't conjure even a trace of the love that once glowed bright and strong.

The man who stood before God and promised to cherish her had annihilated her love, but he hadn't destroyed her self-worth — yet. A strong voice deep within insisted, *You don't deserve this. You do not. Get out. Get out any way you can. Get out before it's too late.*

With renewed bravado, Sammie reached for the knob, pulled the door shut, and followed Jacquelyn up the hallway.

His gaze downcast, Maurice strode up the hospital hallway as if he were a doctor on a mission. Without a glance to either side, he slowed and stopped in front of room 434. He opened the door, stepped inside, and shut it. The room's darkness enveloped him, and he paused to allow his eyes to adjust.

As Maurice tread ever deeper into Rantomi's dark world, he found himself repeatedly amazed at how easily he could find out nearly anything about anyone. A quick check on the internet that evening had confirmed what Maurice hoped. Lawton Franklin was a single man with no children. Had Maurice discovered that Lawton had children, he might have reconsidered the murder or most likely, he would have followed through and fought the excessive guilt later. Nevertheless, the lack of little ones had sealed the blind man's doom.

He tugged on the scrubs' drawstring, pulled out the attached pouch, opened it, and removed the capped syringe filled with the deadly acid. After the syringe, he pulled out a pencil-thin flashlight. His forehead beaded in cold sweat, and Maurice cursed his own weakness. The IV's perpetual clicking ushered in thoughts of the crucifix . . . the suffering servant . . . the thousands of prayers that Maurice had extended after each one of these nasty deeds — prayers that seemed to never reach beyond the ceiling. And the burden of guilt that attacked him after every murder exploded upon his soul.

Maurice's heart pounded as if *he* were the one facing eternity. A bead of sweat trickled down his spine. The syringe shook like an extension of his hand. The crucifix, indelibly ingrained upon his heart, beckoned Maurice to turn and run.

But Bangkok's call won. *Bangkok.* Where the women were beautiful. The city was magnificent. And he would be free — financially free for life. *But only if I obey Fuat and kill Lawton. Only Lawton's death will ensure Fuat's lack of suspicion.*

He raised the syringe and walked into the room. Maurice clicked on the penlight and scanned the IV setup. He had hoped for a heplock at the IV's point of entry into Lawton's hand. None existed. Maurice bit back an oath and trailed the IV tubing up to the port where a nurse would insert a piggyback. That would have to do, even though it would take longer for a lethal dose to invade Lawton's body.

Lawton's legs jerked, and he muttered an unintelligible stream of protests. Maurice placed the penlight between his teeth and pointed it toward the piggyback port. He gripped the port with one hand, inserted the poison-filled syringe, shoved the liquid into the tubing, removed the needle, and capped it. A band of tension uncoiled within Maurice. His final job was complete. Lawton Franklin would be dead within the next ten minutes.

Once in the kitchen, Jac settled at the breakfast bar and turned to her friend. The makeup that once partially covered the bruise had been washed away by the tears seeping from the corners of her eyes. The dark circles under her eyes appeared nearly as dark as the bruise. And for the first time Jacquelyn realized that Sam must have lost ten pounds since she last saw her.

"Want to leave tonight?" Jac snatched up the glass vase that held the wilting roses and slammed them into the trash can at the counter's end.

Sammie claimed a stool. Face contorted, she stared at the discarded blooms then covered her face with her hands. She propped her elbows on the bar and stifled a sob. "I w–wanted to leave — to leave a year ago when all this started," she stuttered. "But I've been s–so terrified."

Jacquelyn neared Sammie and placed an arm around her. She laid her head atop her friend's. A new sob rushed from Sammie, and Jac tightened her hug. She had never considered herself emotionally supportive since she usually maintained a strong reserve, no matter how she was feeling. That had worked until last spring when she began having that horrid nightmare. During an extended visit with Mel, she had collapsed on the floor, sobbing until she had no tears left. Mel had been there for her. She'd held Jac. She'd cried with her. She'd never judged. And for once, Melissa hadn't posed too many questions. Instead, she gave Jac the space to mourn the loss of her childhood innocence.

Unfortunately, Sammie didn't have the

luxury of that much time. Jacquelyn moved to the kitchen, opened a linen drawer, and scrounged through a jumble of dish towels until she found a small one. She dampened the towel with tap water and silently walked back to her shuddering friend.

"Has he ever hit Brett?" Jac asked as she sponged Sammie's face.

"N–no," Sammie gasped. She took the towel from Jac and pressed it against her closed eyelids. "I've — I've always been able to divert him."

Tears stung her own eyes, and Jac forced herself to deny showing the emotions. Nonetheless, they raged within her. Her fingers tightened on the edge of the bar as she imagined Sammie's cries for mercy at the hand of that savage. A sisterly instinct deep within Jac wished that Adam had lunged for them only minutes before. She would have liked to give the brute a kick or two he wouldn't ever forget.

"Why don't we get you and Brett packed?" she asked, glancing toward the hallway. Chances were, Adam wouldn't awaken until the morning, but Jac didn't want to play those odds. "Do you have any place you can go tonight? If not, I can rent a hotel room and you can stay with me."

"N–no," Sammie said. "That's fine. I — I think my boss would be glad for Brett and me to come stay with her. She guessed what's going on and wanted me to move in with her earlier this week, but I've been s–so, s–so scared."

"I know," Jac said. "I understand. I've felt exactly what you're feeling. That jerk who molested me when I was a kid had me terrified that if I told anyone he'd kill me."

Sammie sniffled and peered into Jac's soul with candid blue eyes that glowed with a hint of shattered naiveté. "Did you ever find out who did that to you, Jackie?"

"Nope. Still don't know." *Not sure I want to know,* she added to herself, then averted her gaze toward the stack of *Romantic Times* magazines lying near Sammie's elbow. The top issue featured a cover photo of Kim Lan's parents beside their glass greenhouse that was constructed from a collection of antique window frames. *This is really romantic times, isn't it,* she sneered to herself.

"This is not getting easier. You said it would!" the weasel croaked. "Even after five years, I still hate this. I hate all the killing! Gary Sellers had two children asleep in their rooms and while they slept I — I can't do this again. Do you hear me?"

The bear's hot body stretched across Lawton. The door handle clicked. The car door sighed open, and the humid night attacked Lawton's face. "Shove him out and shoot him or you'll be next!"

With a whimper, the weasel shoved Lawton out head first. The hard earth ate into his face and filled his mouth with grit. Lawton tried to scream. He tried . . . he tried. But his mouth refused to cooperate. Help! Oh, dear Jesus, help me!

The taste of dry earth filled his mouth, and Lawton held his breath as the weasel hesitated then uttered a stream of oaths. A gun exploded. The bullet seared an unforgiving path into Lawton's right shoulder. The car door slammed. The engine revved. The auto's tires hurled gravel that stung innumerable pinpoints into Lawton's face. And the dark beyond, all soft and peaceful and irresistible, covered him once more.

This time Lawton struggled against the dark. "No!" he yelled. "Not now! No . . .

no . . ." He turned from side to side and fought against the loose gauze that someone had wrapped around him. A fresh surge of panic consumed him as he continued to fight. *What if I'm in a casket! What if I'm being buried alive!*

"Noooooo!" Lawton screamed, and the darkness retreated past the horizon of his consciousness. His senses came to full alert. The whir of the air conditioner, the distant ringing of a phone, the faint sounds of traffic reminded him that he was in a hospital room. He wasn't in a casket. And the gauze was really sheets.

Yet something in this reality didn't feel right. Someone stood beside him. Someone who smelled of Cuban cigars.

"Excuse me, did you need something?" Kinkaide asked as his loafers tapped against the tile.

"I was just adding some medication to his IV," the man's voice, thick with a French accent, mingled with the sound of retreating footsteps. "Doctor's orders." The door closed with a clap.

The foreign accent rang false. Lawton sucked in a short stream of air as he tried to place the tenor of voice. Something in the subtlety of the tone was familiar . . . he had encountered it in the recent past.

134

Kinkaide laid a hand on his brother's shoulder.

"Are you okay?" he asked. "You were having a nasty nightmare, I guess." Kinkaide paused to yawn.

As the smell of cigars dissipated, Lawton's mind whirled with bits and pieces of the preceding seconds: the odor of expensive tobacco, the nasally tone, the man's mentioning the medication.

The immediate recall of his real-life nightmare swept a veil of cold sweat over his body. A frantic realization started as a pinpoint of light in his soul. The pinpoint expanded into a blinding beam. The blinding beam exploded into an eruption of terror.

"The weasel!" Lawton bellowed and sat straight up.

Nine

~

Sammie's phone rang, and both she and Jacquelyn jumped. "There's — there's a phone in Adam's room," Sammie whispered as she slid from the stool. Jac lunged toward the end of the bar and snatched the receiver in the middle of the second ring. She held the phone in midair, stopped breathing, and strained for any sound in the hallway.

Her hand shaking, Sammie took the receiver as Jac sneaked down the hallway. She paused outside Adam's room, twisted the doorknob, and peeked inside. The man hadn't budged. A tendril of relief mixed with disappointment. The more Jacquelyn talked to Sammie, the more she wanted to give Adam a taste of his own treatment. She gritted her teeth and shut the door. Retaliation wasn't supposed to be her mar-

136

tial arts motive. But instead of diminishing, the temptation posed itself ever stronger. Her dragon and Sammie's were much alike. Too much alike. An abusive husband's tactics usually encompassed a wide range of activities.

Sammie's shadow appeared at Jac's feet, and she looked up. A silent question flashed between them. "He's still down," Jac whispered.

Without a word, the redhead crooked her finger, and Jacquelyn followed her up the hall. "Mel's on the phone," she whispered, and Jac neared the receiver lying on a stack of strewn bills at the bar's end. "They've had an emergency at the hospital," Sammie continued.

Jac stopped. She stared at the phone as she considered her last encounter with Lawton. Her fingers trailed to her right wrist, and she recalled the sound of platinum slamming against a hospital wall. Then their words, stilted and resentful, reverberated through her mind.

I was crazy for even thinking about coming here.

I must have been crazy for calling you. I guess I'm just a glutton for punishment. . . .

Jacquelyn's bare toes rubbed against the cool linoleum. The various possibilities of this emergency presented themselves. In a flash, she wondered if Lawton had taken a turn for the worse or if someone had threatened him. A cold dread sprouted in her midsection. She snatched up the phone and bit out a habitual, "Lightfoot."

"Jac, it's Mel. Sorry to call so late, but there's been a big problem here at the hospital —"

"Let me talk to her," Lawton's demand filtered through Mel's words.

"Calm down, Lawton," Mel snapped. "Jac, we need you here," she continued.

"Let me have the phone!" Lawton said, and Jac frowned in an attempt to cover the slight smile. At least the emergency didn't involve a medical setback. Lawton was still as feisty as ever.

"Somebody tried to —"

A series of bumps and shuffles accosted Jac's ear. A muffled chorus of Mel's exasperated edicts floated over the line. Then Lawton's voice erupted.

"Listen, somebody came in here and injected some kind of acid into my IV," he barked. "We won't know exactly what until the lab report comes back. Meanwhile, the police have been here and they won't let me leave unless I have a bodyguard. My brother says the same thing. You've got the job. I'm going to Ouray."

Jacquelyn blinked as Sammie's Siamese skulked from behind the couch and dashed toward her water bowl. "What in the name of common sense are you talking about? If somebody put acid in your IV . . . some forms of acid will kill you quicker than you can say scat."

"So I've heard."

"You don't *sound* dead."

He snorted. "No joke, sister! That's because Kinkaide and I realized something was up and pinched off the IV tubing until a nurse could be notified. Somebody dressed up like a surgeon sneaked in here and injected a syringe full of that stuff into the piggyback port!" his volume rose a decibel with every word. "He told Kinkaide he was injecting medication, but I recognized his voice! He was one of the men who nabbed me at the airport."

"Holy smokes," Jacquelyn breathed.

"And in the middle of all that, I was having a dream about being shot and I remembered who they said they had murdered — *Gary Sellers!*"

Jacquelyn's brows drew together as her stressed mind tried to recall why that name sounded so familiar.

"You know — the real estate guy who

was killed in Ouray a few days ago!"

She gripped the back of her neck and squeezed. "You have really managed to get yourself into something big, haven't you, Lawton Franklin?"

"Now she blames *me!*" he groused.

"I'm not blaming you!"

A series of shuffles preceded Mel's voice. "Jacquelyn, he's being impossible. They've taken out his IV, and he's decided that if the doctor won't dismiss him, he's walking. He's got it in his head that he's going to Ouray to get to the bottom of why the Sellers were killed."

"I *am* going to Ouray," Lawton's voice floated over Mel's irritated outpour.

"Would you *please* come up here and try to talk some sense into him?" Mel continued. "I don't think he's strong enough to go flying off to Colorado!"

"What makes you think he'll listen to me?" Jac asked.

"Because he's halfway in love with you, for crying out loud!" Mel exclaimed. "When a man won't listen to anybody else, he'll listen to his woman."

Jac's face flashed hot, and her knees weakened. Silence permeated the line — no background commentary from Lawton this time. And Jac imagined him just as stunned as she was. The ticks of Sammie's ancient clock counted the seconds as embarrassment oozed across the line.

At last Mel mumbled, "Well, I've done it again. . . . I've stuck my foot in my mouth, haven't I? Jac, I am *so sorry!* We're so uptight, that we don't know what to do."

"I'll be there soon," Jacquelyn said and glanced down at her boxer-short pajamas. "Just give me time to get changed."

She hung up the phone and turned to address Sam, only to see an empty stool. A long shadow crept up the hallway accompanied by the staggering footfalls of an unsteady gait. Adam, disheveled and hunched over, appeared on the living room's threshold. Jacquelyn clutched the back of the bar stool and narrowed her eyes as an antagonistic bile, thick and bitter, erupted from the bottom of her spirit. Like a fox, she scanned the living room. No sign of Sam. Jac stiffened and waited as Adam glowered.

"Sammie!" he slurred out. "Where are — are ya?" He leaned against the hall wall then hung his head. "You've let that kid of ours spill somethin' all over the bed! It's wet!"

Jacquelyn glanced down at the angular man's jeans. A dank ring soiled the front of both legs. Jac's lips twisted and she strained to see traces of the groom she recalled from Sammie's wedding. That sandy-haired man had been hopeful, promising, and supportive. But this man appeared to be the antithesis of what he once was. Adam Jones had trudged through pits of sludge. Sludge that penetrated his soul. Sludge that splattered onto Sammie every time he lifted a hand against her.

Jac swallowed against the acid rising in her throat and stepped forward.

The movement snared his attention, and his gaze drifted toward her. Adam's bottom lip sagged. His stringy hair fell into glazed eyes. His shoulders slumped as if they were weighted with the contamination of sin.

"Who're you, woman? And what're you doing here?"

"Jacquelyn Lightfoot," she responded. "And I'm going to help Sammie leave."

"Leave!" he hollered then threw back his head to produce a series of disdainful guffaws. "She's not go—going anywhere." He released a belligerent belch and narrowed his eyes.

"Yes, I am leaving," Sammie said from behind him. With Brett on her hip and a large duffel bag in tow, she marched past her husband. Yet her quivering lips belied the bravado.

Adam's eyes flinched. He grabbed his wife's arm, yanked her toward him, and lowered his face to within inches of hers. "Listen, woman, you aren't going *anywhere!*"

Brett screamed and buried his face into Sammie's neck. Jac tensed. Sammie's cheeks blanched, a tear trickled down the side of her freckled nose, and she tried to twist away from the beast's unpardonable grip. He raised his fist and began the descent that would crash knuckles against nose.

Jac surged forward, hurled herself into the air, and slammed her bare heel against his ribcage . . . just short of hard enough to break a few ribs. A rush of air left Adam. He stumbled backward, tripped, and crashed into the sofa. The couch rammed into the end table, and the brass lamp toppled to the floor with a swoosh and clatter. The cat's surprised howl preceded her dash from the kitchen and up the hallway.

"Go get my suitcase and backpack and get out, Sammie," Jacquelyn bellowed as a disoriented Adam struggled to right himself.

"I'm not leaving you in here with him," Sammie protested. "I'd never forgive myself if —"

"Mommy! Mommy!" Brett howled. "Mommy make him stop!"

"Just do what I say!" Jacquelyn yelled as Adam staggered to his feet. *Now!*

Sammie dropped her purse and duffel bag and raced up the hallway with Brett wrapped around her like a terrified monkey.

Eyes blazing, Adam roared and lunged for Jac.

"Okay, you asked for it, you creep," she spat and slammed a solid kick smack in the middle of his solar plexus. A nasty voice inside tempted Jac to follow through with a fatal slam against his neck. But she bounced back to her feet and stopped.

Adam's eyes rounded. He produced a choked gasp and again tumbled onto the couch. A potted plant smashed and soil scattered near his feet. This time Adam didn't move.

A sobbing Sammie huffed up the hallway, dragging Jac's suitcase and backpack. Without a word, Jac took the luggage and stepped over a bag of cat food to usher Sammie toward the doorway. "Get your duffel, and let's get outta here," Jac said.

"I'll call the police on my cell phone and have them pick him up."

"Is Daddy dead?" Brett wailed.

"No. He isn't dead," Jac placated and glanced over her shoulder at his unconscious form. "He probably just wishes he were," she added under her breath.

"Where *are* you? It's two a.m." Lawton's voice erupted over Jac's cell phone as she guided Sammie's car through the sparse freeway traffic.

"We've been waiting for over an hour!" he continued.

"Thanks for your concern," she chided. "We've actually just left the police station." Jacquelyn glanced over her shoulder. Sammie cradled Brett to her chest and rested her head against the seat. "I had to take down Goliath," Jac said under her breath.

"What?"

"Never mind. It's a long story. I'll explain later. Meanwhile, you'd better sit tight. It's going to be awhile before I get there. I've got to get Sammie squared away at her boss' apartment. It might be three or four before I get back to the hospital." She stifled a yawn and widened her gritty eyes. This had turned into a nightmare of a day.

"Are you okay?" Lawton asked. This

time concern replaced the edge in his voice.

"Of course I'm okay." Jac slowed the Honda and merged south from Richardson to downtown Dallas. Sammie's boss leased a penthouse one floor up from the magazine's office. "Why wouldn't I be?"

"Okay . . ." Lawton hesitated. "I've messed up . . . once again, folks," he added like a circus announcer. "Something has gone really wrong with you, hasn't it?"

"Nothing that a few kicks and an arrest warrant didn't take care of."

"Are you hurt?" Lawton rushed. "Did someone try to —"

"Lawton, I haven't been hurt in years — except one broken arm in a wild chase." She quirked a brow. "In my business, you learn to defend yourself — and do it well or you don't make it."

"I guess I forgot." The smile in Lawton's voice spoke much more than mere approval.

Jac glanced over her shoulder again. Sammie's mouth lolled open. Brett, his head still on Sam's chest, softly snored. "Okay, Sam's asleep, I'll tell you," Jac continued as the car's air conditioner hummed forth with a steady stream of icy air. "Sammie's husband has been abusing her.

I didn't know until tonight. He came in drunk while I was there —"

"And you took him down and had him arrested," Lawton finished.

"Yep."

He chuckled. A low chuckle. An endearing chuckle. A chuckle that wove its way beyond Jac's exhaustion and unleashed a veil of expectation around her heart. She pictured his jocose grin, all charming and captivating. She imagined the daredevil tilt of his chin, dark with five o'clock shadow. She pondered his tenacity . . . his grit . . . his poetic spirit. And as the illuminated traffic signs merged into a green blur, Mel's words smacked Jac right between the eyes. *He's halfway in love with you, for crying out loud! When a man won't listen to anybody else, he'll listen to his woman.*

As the silence lengthened, Jacquelyn realized that the arrival of Lawton's latest emergency had momentarily swept aside their heated exchange. But now the memory was back. All she could think about was Lawton's coldly telling her to "get over it," the look on his face when she returned the bracelet, the fury that had catapulted the platinum memento against the wall. *If Lawton really is halfway in love with me . . .* Jacquelyn forced herself to dismiss the thought. Even if he fell all the way in love with her, the relationship would come to naught. Jac was fine on her own. Just fine. *And Lawton . . . Lawton is nothing to me. Nothing,* she reminded herself. *And he never will be.*

"Hey! Did you go to sleep on me?" Lawton asked, and the tender nuance of his voice suggested he'd just proposed.

Jacquelyn's hand tightened on the steering wheel. "Not quite," she said and tried to fend off the memories of a sea bathed in moonlight and of the man who wrote poems about stars as if he had the universe by the tail.

"Look, why don't you get a good night's sleep and come by in the morning?" Lawton continued as if he were her devoted subject. "There's a security guard here now. Kinkaide and Mel are still here, too. I can wait until tomorrow to leave. Actually, I seriously doubt there are any flights to Colorado at this hour in the morning anyway. So, if I just stay put, that oughta make everybody happy — including my parents and my bossy sister-in-law."

Jacquelyn eyed the nearing Dallas skyline, twinkling with a thousand lights glowing against a velvet sky. Lawton's parents. *The next step in every romantic relationship involved meeting the parents.* Jacquelyn gritted her teeth and dragged her attention to the road in front of her. A dull road. A predictable road. A road that wouldn't merge into the enigmatic unknown. If she were to introduce Lawton to *her* family, she just might introduce him to a dragon who consumed precious childhood dreams. Unlike Lawton's family, Jac's family hid nasty secrets.

A glacial resolve penetrated Jac's mind. *I'll help you with this case, Lawton,* she thought. *But that's it. Even if you do fall in love with me and want to get married, I don't ever want another man touching me. Ever! Not even you!*

"Helloooooo . . ." Lawton called.

"Yes, I'm here," she stated without inflection.

"So I guess I'll see you in the morning?" Lawton asked as if he were a schoolboy eager to find out if his favorite girl was going to be sitting nearby.

"Yes. Midmorning. That works. Maybe we can catch a noonish flight to Colorado."

"So you're going with me?"

"Of course." Jacquelyn paused and a

149

grin forced itself upon her, despite her intent to remain stoic. "I thought Mel made it clear. I didn't think I had a choice."

"Ah, and the lady has a sense of humor. So tell me, Jacquelyn Lightfoot, is Mel the only reason you're going?"

"No, she isn't." Jac pressed her lips together, checked her speedometer, and relaxed a bit of the pressure against the accelerator. "I want to know who killed Gary Sellers and why."

"So your going has nothing to do with me?" His silver-tongued challenge, subtle and laden with ardor, stroked her spine. A delicious rush, unexpected and breathtaking, hurled her into the land of longing.

Jacquelyn stiffened and raised her resolve. She slammed shut the door to her heart.

"Listen, I'm almost downtown," she said, eyeing the Texas skyscrapers now towering nearby. "I'll see you tomorrow." Without missing a beat, Jac disconnected the call and turned off the phone. Just as she had kicked Sammie's dragon flat on his back, so she annihilated all images of Lawton from her mind. Allowing her thoughts to center on him reminded her of how empty her life had become, how desolate her heart had grown, how desperately needy she really was.

A tear pooled at the corner of her eye. An unanticipated tear. A tear from the contaminated well of a long-imprisoned soul. Jacquelyn scrubbed at the damp despair as a spontaneous prayer began in her spirit and posed itself upon her lips. "Oh, Jesus," she breathed. "I don't know where to start. I don't even know what to say. I've locked the pain away so long, and I'm scared to know the whole truth. I'm really, really scared."

As she steered the vehicle between the towering skyscrapers, a verse, long held captive in her soul, resurrected from childhood Sunday school: *You will know the truth, and the truth will set you free.* Once more the shaft of radiant gold from the edge of her nightmare forest roved toward the center of her heart. She clamped her jaw and shrank from the enlightenment. *No . . . not yet. I'm not ready. The pain is too much.*

"I just can't," she breathed. "Oh, dear Lord, I can't."

Ten

~

"Lawton Franklin is not dead," Fuat's voice challenged over the receiver. "I thought you were going to take care of that last night."

"What are you talking about?" Maurice bit down on his slender cigar then dropped into a chair, whose cushion released a sigh. The candles, flickering on the mahogany coffee table, snared his attention. Bathed in wavering light, the crucifix whispered that the morning confessional was again for naught. And a chain-like bondage dropped from Maurice's spirit.

"How could he have survived?" Maurice asked as he deposited the smoldering cigar on the edge of the crystal ashtray. He slapped his hand against the leather-bound guest directory. "I injected rust remover into his IV tubing!" He raised his hand.

"How did he survive that?"

"They got suspicious and pinched off the tubing until the nurse confirmed that the guy wasn't due any medication," the words tumbled out like a machine gun's steady tattoo. "They tested the tubing's contents and found acid."

"You must be losing your touch!" Fuat accused. "I really thought you were going soft on me when you botched the shooting, but in retrospect, you also came away from the Sellers' killings empty handed. Now this! I'm beginning to wonder if you've outlived your usefulness."

Maurice gazed around the elegant room and glanced at the digital clock on the nightstand. Eight-thirty approached. Already, he had showered and was in the last stages of packing. He had expected the call from Fuat, setting up their meeting to explore a new tactic in the Ouray quest. But Fuat didn't know that Maurice was going to suggest he go back to Ouray, not for Fuat's interest, but for his own. Now, Maurice was no longer sure of Fuat's plan. Too many death threats had rolled off the boss' tongue in the last couple of days.

As the hair along the back of his neck prickled, an alarm descended upon Maurice. A wary voice. An irrefutable knowing. Animal instinct. *Fuat is my enemy.* Maurice had always known this day would come. Now that it had arrived, his drive for survival insisted he bolt. His gaze darted from the sleigh bed to the striped sofa to the claw-footed mahogany wardrobe. He could be packed and out of here in five minutes.

"I think we should meet this morning and try to plot our strategy from here," Fuat suggested in a softer tone. "Don't you?"

Maurice's toes dug into the thick-piled carpet, and he snatched the cigar from the ashtray. He didn't need an interpreter to decipher those words. He knew Fuat well enough to smell a trap. The boss would arrange their meeting in an isolated place and have one of his cronies kill Maurice. Just like that. The bottom line was that Fuat usually went with his gut, and his gut was telling him that Maurice's loyalty was waning. *And with good reason,* Maurice thought.

"Okay, sure," he said aloud and took a quick drag on the cigar. "Name the place." As Fuat gave the north Dallas street address, Maurice ground the half-smoked cigar into the ashtray and exhaled a stream of smoke. He didn't even bother to write down the address. He'd be on his way to Ouray by the time Fuat realized he wasn't going to show.

As soon as he hung up, Maurice dialed the travel agent's 800 number which he'd long ago memorized. In a matter of minutes, he had booked himself on the first available flight to Denver — the 11:35. A coordinating shuttle flight would carry him to Montrose. In Montrose, a rental car would await him. By that evening, he would be back in Ouray. Back at Gary Sellers' home. Back to the place where the cache must be hidden.

Gary wouldn't have offered them on the market if he didn't have them, Maurice thought as he blew out the candles and snatched up the crucifix. *They must be somewhere in his home. And if not in his home, perhaps there will be a clue to their location.*

Jacquelyn opened one eye and peered at the brass alarm clock on the nightstand. Nine o'clock was four minutes away. She closed her eye again and snuggled under the covers. The smell of freshly brewing coffee tantalized her senses, and her eyelids slid half open. She glanced around the ultra-modern room bathed in morning

155

shafts of sunlight spilling through elegant sheers. For her life, Jacquelyn couldn't remember where she was or how she got there. Then she recalled Sammie's boss graciously insisting that Jacquelyn take the room across from Sammie's. Colleen Butler and her husband, Tom, had opened their arms to Sammie as if she were their daughter. Then they had refused to allow Jac to leave their penthouse at such a wee hour. Instead, they ushered her into this plush guest room and stopped just short of tucking her in.

With a stretch and a yawn, Jac decided to go ahead and find the coffee. The day loomed before her — a day when she would be escorting a fascinating man to Ouray, Colorado.

"Heaven help me," she mumbled. "I need the whole pot."

Jac swung her legs out of bed and straightened her crumpled pajamas. When she left Sammie's last night, she drove all the way to the police station in her pajamas. Outside the station, she'd struggled in the front seat to slip her jeans and T-shirt on over the PJs. The jeans and shirt now lay at the end of the quilted comforter. She reached for them then decided to just find her robe. Jacquelyn rummaged through her

suitcase and slipped into the man's robe —
a hand-me-down from her grandfather.
Shortly after his death, she and her mother
had been going through his clothing when
they stumbled upon the new robe. No
male members of the family stepped forward to claim it, and Jac needed one
anyway. The robe had served her purposes
for over two years now, and Jacquelyn usually reached for it instead of the silky robes
her mother insisted upon buying for her.

With the sash tightly cinched, she
padded down the hallway, stopped in the
restroom, then pursued the smell of coffee.
She tried to go light on the caffeine-laden
extra, but nonetheless allowed herself an
occasional cup or two. A child's laughter
echoed through an open doorway and Jac
paused to peer across an expanse of mint
green carpet and cream-colored furniture
toward yet another entryway. She followed
her nose and meandered into the kitchen.

In the center stood a husky man who
held a smiling Brett. The man's hair was
short except for a thin braid that fell
halfway down his back. His black T-shirt
and jeans, while clean, looked to have been
washed and worn and washed more times
than most fabrics could survive. A heart-
shaped tattoo peeked from beneath the

sleeve of his T-shirt, and he looked as if he hadn't shaved in several days. Jacquelyn wondered if there were a Harley somewhere with his name on it. She also wondered if a street gang awaited him at some clandestine destination. A sharp glance at the lines around his eyes and the trace of gray in his beard suggested that he was too old to be out running the streets. Her gaze briefly met his sharp, brown eyes, and his grin hinted that he read her every thought.

"Do it again, R.J.," Brett squealed as he clapped his hands on the side of the man's face. "Do it again!"

Without a word R.J. spun around in circles and made airplane noises. Like a pre-programmed robot, Jac marched toward the coffeepot. R.J., whoever he was, must be loved by Brett. And the boy certainly needed healthy, adult attention from a balanced male. *That is if this R.J. is balanced,* she thought.

Jacquelyn found an oversized mug hanging beneath the cabinet and poured a cup full of coffee. She inhaled the essence of the steaming fluid, leaned against the marble-topped cabinet, and drank a mouthful. The taste, so mellow and smooth, reminded her of the man whose bathrobe she wore. When Jac was a child her grandfather always let her sip his coffee.

Sammie, her hair in a towel, appeared in the doorway. She stretched her hands toward the coffeepot and flexed her fingers as if she were a toddler reaching for candy. With a chuckle, Jacquelyn nabbed a cup from one of the hooks under the cabinet and extended it to Sammie. The night's sleep had certainly given her a more healthy demeanor. Already she was fully dressed, and her flawless makeup covered all signs of the bruise near her eye. Nevertheless, Jacquelyn wondered how many fading bruises were covered by Sam's clothing.

"Who is he?" Jac mumbled as R.J. turned Brett upside down and tickled him.

"Colleen's son. He occasionally pops into the office and here," Sammie said. "His name is Rhett James Butler," she continued under her breath as her thinly penciled brow quirked.

"No way," Jac hissed and stifled the threatening chortle. "So that's what R.J. stands for?"

"Yep."

"Are you going to introduce me, Sammie, or are you two going to stand over there and whisper all morning?" R.J.'s decided Texas drawl made Jac wonder if he rode a quarter horse rather than a Harley. *No, it has to be a Harley,* she thought.

As Brett squirmed from R.J.'s arms, Sammie filled her mug with coffee and blandly observed him with crystal-blue eyes that belied reading. Jacquelyn wasn't prepared for the loaded undercurrent that flashed between the two.

R.J. crossed his arms and rocked back on the heels of his worn riding boots as if he had the world by the tail. Yet the slight twitch of his lip suggested otherwise.

"R.J. Butler, meet my friend, Jacquelyn Lightfoot. Jac, meet R.J. He's Colleen and Tom's son," Sammie announced as if she couldn't care less. Brett ran toward his mother, and Sammie deposited her coffee on the counter then scooped up the freckle-faced child. "Have you had breakfast already, little carrot top?" she asked and ruffled his hair.

"Uh-huh," he said. "R.J. fixed me wassles!"

"Thanks," Sammie said in R.J.'s general direction, then she retrieved her mug and walked toward the living room with Brett riding her hip. As she stepped from green marble tile onto light-green carpet, she turned back to Jac. "I'm just going to dry my hair. What time are you planning on leaving?"

"Within an hour." Jacquelyn took a long sip of her coffee then grabbed the carafe and added more coffee to her mug.

"Okay. I'll be around. I'll wait on going to the office until you leave. I think Colleen will be okay with that."

"Sure thing," Jacquelyn said.

"She's already at the office," R.J. drawled as he walked toward the coffeepot. "She said to tell you ladies to make yourselves at home and that she'd be back up in a bit." He picked up a used mug from near the sink.

"So I guess you got the job of babysitting us?" Sammie asked, her words loaded with tension.

Jacquelyn blinked, narrowed her eyes, and waited for R.J.'s response.

He paused near the coffeepot and lifted a brow. "Yep, I guess you could say that." Without another glance at Sammie, he poured his coffee then reached for the dainty sugar bowl on a silver tray.

Sammie focused upon her child and padded toward the bedroom. Jac scooped up a banana from the crystal fruit bowl in the center of the kitchen table. "Nice to have met you," she called over her shoulder as she prepared to follow Sammie. R.J.'s presence presented a host of unanswered questions, and Jac had enough trouble without getting into more of Sammie's turmoils.

"I guess Sammie finally got tired of that husband of hers beating her," R.J. said so softly Jac barely heard him. "This morning Mom told me she filed charges."

Stopping in her tracks, Jac pivoted to face R.J., who casually examined his fingernails. Then he took a slow swig of his coffee and eyed Jac over the mug's rim. "She also said you took him down."

"I did what I had to do," Jac said, her gaze sliding toward the kitchen cabinets, the color of pristine pearls.

"Are all Sammie's friends as tough as you?"

Jacquelyn dashed a glance back at him, and his smile revealed sparkling white teeth. "Nope. Not by a long shot," she shot back through a smile of her own. Whatever problems R.J. and Sammie had, he didn't seem half bad. *Not half bad.* If his treatment of Brett were anything to go by, the Harley look probably hid a heart the size of the Colorado Rockies.

"I tried to tell Sam not to marry that moron five years ago, but she wouldn't listen to me," R.J. mused. Narrowing his eyes, he observed Jac. "How long has he been abusing her?"

Jac hesitated. She didn't know exactly how much Sammie wanted this guy to know. By Sammie's reaction to him, Jac estimated that the less he knew, the better Sammie would like it.

"Too long," R.J. muttered through gritted teeth. "Even if it was only once, it was too long." His massive fist tightened near his thigh.

"All I can say," Jac measured her words, "is that he definitely hit her on more than one occasion."

A hiss escaped him, and he turned his back on Jac. His broad shoulders hunched as if he were the one who had been abused. Intrigued, Jacquelyn stared at him for several seconds with only the refrigerator's steady hum breaking the silence. Sammie had never mentioned this man, but apparently she had known him for a number of years. Furthermore, he obviously cared for Sammie despite the questionable undercurrent between them.

Odd . . . very odd, Jac thought. *Or maybe Sam did mention him at some point but I missed it.* Jacquelyn was forever happening upon forgotten or initially unnoticed bits and pieces of her friends' lives. At times, she was sure she had exasperated every one of them by missing important details.

"Well, I guess I better go hit the shower," Jac said and glanced out the window at the bright August sunshine. The morning was marching forward. Lawton would be waiting. "I've got to catch a plane, hopefully by noon. Nice to meet you."

"Sure. Same here," R.J. said over his shoulder.

Jacquelyn turned and stepped upon mounds of mint carpet, only to stop as an idea, sudden and breathtaking, rushed upon her. She whirled back around. "You'd be perfect."

"Huh?" R.J. swiveled to face her, his brows drawn.

"Would you be willing to keep an eye on Sam while I'm gone? I'm a little worried about Adam posting bail and getting out. She really needs to be careful right now."

R.J.'s jaw muscles flexed, and Jac knew that he understood well — all too well. "Sure. I was planning on keeping her in focus anyway."

"Thanks," Jac said, and the shadows that had been plaguing her faded a bit. "Oh, and," she hesitated and smiled, "do you own a Harley?"

"Of course." R.J. crossed his arms and

tucked his fingers under his arms. His thumbs remained on his chest. "Actually, I own two of 'em." He grinned. "A Fat Boy and a Road King."

"Great. I'll let you give me a ride on one sometime."

"Sure thing."

With a wiggle of her fingers, Jac left the kitchen and couldn't deny the strong hunch that whispered of the future. Somewhere down the line, she and Rhett James Butler might be great friends. She walked past a room where Brett's singing mingled with the sound of Sammie's hair dryer. Coffee in hand, Jac stepped into the room where she'd slept. She closed the door, retrieved her leather backpack off the floor, and deposited it on the bed. After sipping her coffee, she plopped the cup on the nightstand with the banana and dug through her backpack. She pulled out her cell phone, turned it on, and punched the redial button. The hospital had been the last number she called.

At last, Mel's voice broke over the line.

"Hey, it's me," Jac said.

"Have you had your cell phone off?" Mel asked.

"Yes." Jac stood, dragged her suitcase onto the bed, opened it, and began gathering the toiletry items necessary for a shower.

"I've been trying to call you. As a matter of fact, I tried to call you last night after you hung up with Lawton."

"I turned my cell phone off then. I'm just now turning it back on." Jac had figured that Lawton might want to call her back after she'd abruptly ended the call, and last night she hadn't wanted to talk to him again.

"What's going on with Sammie?" Mel asked. "Lawton said you karate-chopped her husband, had him arrested, took Sammie down to press charges, then went to the Butlers' home."

"That's about the extent of it," Jac said.

"So, it's just all in a day's work. Is that it?"

"What's the deal with you people?" Jac asked. "I do this sort of stuff for a living. Hellooo?" Shampoo in hand, Jacquelyn snatched a fresh pair of jeans and an oxford shirt from her case.

"I guess we peace lovers are just a little dazzled by your prowess, that's all," Mel said dryly. "I told Sam last night before I left that she ought to leave Adam. Did you notice the bruise by her eye?"

"Yes."

"Did she say how long this has been going on?"

"She said the physical abuse started a little over a year ago when Adam's father died, but the verbal and emotional abuse have been going on much longer."

"Do you think she'll mind if I tell the sisters? I already e-mailed them from my laptop this morning, but I didn't go into the details."

"Might be better to let her tell the details," Jac said. "After all, it's her life and all."

"Okay, right. I understand. Anyway, all the sisters are praying."

"Send them an 'e' for me and tell them to pray really hard. Legally this is Adam's first offense. His bond will be set low, and he most likely will be able to get bailed out. He told her if she ever told anybody he was abusing her that he'd kill her." Jac flopped down the suitcase lid and shivered as if the dragon's breath had whispered in her ear. "He most likely means it. I don't know if you're aware of this, but many women who live on the streets with their kids are running from men who promised to kill them. I don't think Adam was kidding."

"Yes, I know."

"Reality stinks, Mel, it always has."

"Remind me to give you the Ms. Sunshine Award next time I see you."

"I'm just stating the truth," Jac said.

"So what are you going to do now?"

"I'm going to leave her here with her boss and some biker character I just met. I have a gut feeling that if anybody tries to hurt Sammie, he'll be all over him. I asked him to keep an eye on her. Have you ever met R.J. Butler? He's her boss's son."

"R.J.'s there?" Mel blurted out.

"Yes. How do you know him?"

"He's Sammie's former fiancé."

"What?" Jac's eyes bugged. "I didn't even know she'd ever been engaged before Adam. How did that get past me?"

"Jac," Mel said with a sigh, "where is your poster picture of the sisters?"

"What?"

"Right now. Where is it? You know, the big picture Kim Lan sent to all of us?"

"Uh . . ." Jacquelyn eyed a Monet print hanging above the bed. "Uh . . ." she hedged again and hated to admit the truth. "I think it's still in the box it came in, stuck in the back of my closet."

"And you ask me why you don't know about Sammie's ex-boyfriend?" Mel asked. "There are all sorts of things about the sisters you don't know because you wander off on your own and don't keep in touch like you should." Mel's voice rose in volume and sharpness. "I can't count the number of times in the last few years that I've left messages on your machine, and you never bothered to return them."

"I keep in touch!" Jac defended.

"But not nearly as much as the rest of us."

"What do you want from me?" She raised her hand. "Good grief! It's like you guys think my goal in life should be to sit around and chat or something!"

"That's not it at all, Jac," Mel said. "We just wish you'd keep in touch a little better, that's all. Look, if you must know," she continued, "R.J. and Sam were engaged briefly right after she finished high school. The breakup happened before we ever met Sam. He's about six years older than she is, but from what I understand he needed to do some serious growing up. He wound up riding off into the sunset, literally."

"On his Harley?" Jac asked.

"You got it. Sam doesn't mention him much and hasn't talked about him but once or twice that I can remember since I've known her."

"But she's working for his parents' magazine?" Jacquelyn shook her head. "This is just about the weirdest setup I've ever seen — and I thought I had a strange past."

"Here's the deal," Mel said. "Tom Butler and Sammie's dad have been best friends since they were teenagers. Sammie has known Tom her whole life. Of course, R.J.'s parents loved Sammie nearly as much as they loved their son. They hoped that marrying Sammie would somehow help R.J. settle down. Well, when he broke off the engagement they sided with her. You know Sam's mom deserted her family when she was a kid, and Colleen is like a second mother to her. R.J. never has bothered to show up much, so that left Sammie and the Butlers to continue their friendship. From what I understand, when Sammie needed a job a few years back, Colleen and Tom Butler made her a good offer."

"Does Adam know the Butlers were nearly her in-laws?"

"I . . . don't know," Mel said.

"You don't know?" Jac demanded as if she were scandalized then placed her hand on her hip. "How could you not know? Are you Sammie's friend or not? I mean . . . if you were *really interested* in all the sisters, you would have already framed your sister poster in gold and at least know how many fillings Sam's teeth have!"

"Very funny," Mel said dryly.

Jac grabbed yesterday's jeans and T-shirt and stuffed them into the suitcase's outer pocket. "You know," she said, shoving aside all banter, "Lawton's problems are less complicated than all this."

"Yes, but not less deadly," Mel said.

"Not in the least," Jac agreed, and a tense silence ushered in Lawton's grim reality. "I'm about to hop into the shower," she said and glanced at the clock once more. If they were going to catch a flight to Colorado today, she couldn't waste time. "Tell Lawton I should be there in an hour or so."

"Will do. Oh, just a minute. He wants to talk with you. I think he's gotten the tickets to Montrose and wants to give you the details. Kinkaide is at the door and needs to talk to me. Bye!"

Before Jac could protest, Lawton's voice came over the line.

"Hey!" he said.

"Hey!" Jac replied and sat on the edge of the bed.

"Just wanted to let you know that I've arranged two tickets to Denver for today at

11:35. I checked with several airlines and 11:35 was the soonest I could get us out. We'll also jump a puddlehopper to Montrose where we can rent a car. Is that okay?"

"Works." Jac darted a glance toward the alarm clock. "It's nearly 9:20," she said. "I guess if I'm going to make it, I need to hurry. I should be there in about an hour — make that 30 minutes. You'll have to be ready to leave when I get there."

"I'm ready to leave *now!*" Lawton said. "I want to get to the bottom of this so I can get on with my life."

"I understand." Jac toyed with the zipper on her backpack and caught a glimpse of the leather-covered bracelet box resting midst the backpack jumble. Not bothering to analyze her motive, she wrapped her fingers around the box and withdrew it.

"Listen, Jac, Mel just stepped out for a second, and I wanted to say . . ."

Lawton's words faded into the background as Jac flipped up the box's top. The hinges creaked with the effort; and the snowy velvet, void of the bracelet, blurred into the backdrop of pale carpet as Jacquelyn pondered the generosity of the man behind the gift. Even in the face of her Rome rebuttal, Lawton had still extended the symbol of his affection. Last night she had essentially thrown the platinum keepsake back into his face.

But he was beyond unreasonable in telling me to "get over it," she thought. *He doesn't even know what I'm dealing with!*

She bit her lip and tried to concentrate. The line was quiet.

When the pause had extended past the realm of comfort, Lawton prompted, "So, are you going to reply or not? All this silence makes me nervous."

"Uh . . . sorry. Wh–what was that you were saying?"

Following a heavy sigh, Lawton drawled, "Never mind. Mel and Kinkaide are coming back in the room now anyway. I don't exactly need an audience, here. We can talk on the flight."

"Sure. We'll talk on the flight," Jacquelyn concurred. After the proper adieus, she disconnected the call, snapped the box shut, and dropped it and the phone into her backpack. "Out of sight, out of mind," she quipped and wondered if the person who invented that cliché had ever met Lawton Franklin.

Eleven

~

"Leaving already?"

Sammie's fingers flexed against the front doorknob as R.J.'s voice sent a trail of resentment along her back.

Brett clung to Sammie's neck and began the mantra she had attempted to shush the whole time she was preparing to leave the penthouse. "I wanna stay with R.J., Mamma."

Pressing her lips together, Sammie picked up Brett and looked squarely into his crystal-blue eyes.

"No," she stated. "You need to go to the office with me today."

"Ah, come on, Sammie. Why not let him stay here?" R.J. asked as he neared.

Sammie sucked in a slow breath and kept her back to him. "Because —"

"I don't get to town often, and I might not get to see him for two or three months." He stopped mere inches from her.

Sammie closed her eyes and tried not to scream. "It's best for Brett to come with me today," she said. "He'll stay in the playroom off my office. I've got plenty of kids' videos in there. Besides, I want to be able to keep an eye on him."

"I'll keep an eye on him."

Brett reached for R.J. and lunged toward him. While her resolve weakened, Sammie tightened her hold on the child, as if a firmer grip could somehow help her maintain her stance. The last thing she needed was for her son to become more attached to R.J. than he already was. The big-hearted biker had been visiting his parents all week, and Brett had fallen in love with him . . . just as Sammie once had.

Stifling a scream, Sammie at last released her grip and allowed R.J. to embrace Brett. She turned to face him and shook her head. "You always did get your way, didn't you?"

"Not always." R.J.'s mouth settled into a stressed line. He walked past Sammie, opened the door, and checked the hallway. He stepped out and pressed the elevator button. "There have been many times in life that I didn't get anything I wanted . . ." his words trailed out as if they were a lethargic thunderhead above an expanse of lazy Texas prairie.

His freshly shaven jaw flinched, and Sammie's gaze traveled across a prominent nose to encounter a challenging brown gaze. For the first time since her arrival, she dared look deeply into his eyes. Eyes that stirred with innumerable emotions. Emotions and memories. Memories and compassion.

"I'm sorry," he said, and the words echoed around the corridor as if they were the faintest rumble of thunder.

"What for?" Sammie's frigid smile grew colder with every passing second.

"Let's play airplane!" Brett interrupted as he patted R.J. on the head. Sammie walked into the hallway. "I'll be back by lunch. By then you should be exhausted." The elevator arrived, and R.J. held the door as she stepped in. When the door shut, she took a deep, relieved breath. Adam wasn't lurking nearby, ready to expend his fury upon her tender flesh. She leaned against the wall, bit her lips, and closed her eyes against the stinging tears.

What a week for R.J. to show up, she

176

thought. She'd seen him only about a dozen times since that day before her marriage to Adam. The biker had begged her to reconcile and told her she would one day regret marrying Adam Jones. But Sammie had stubbornly clung to her belief that she was doing the right thing, that R.J. would never change his wanderlust habits. She believed Adam represented the Christian stability that R.J. would never aspire to.

"Oh, dear Jesus," Sammie whimpered and choked on a sob, "I think I trampled Your will for my life. I should have never married Adam. R.J. was right. You were right." Sammie would never forget the spiritual unease she had experienced the day of her wedding. Instead of heeding the heavenly warning, she had pushed forward, determined to have her own way.

By the same token, R.J. had left town and done exactly what Sammie told him he would do — wander all over the States. The man made a point of being as free as the wind. Sammie had long ago quit expecting him to change. *Yet he had vowed he would change, if only I'd take him back*, she remembered. Sammie eyed the elevator button. The man was a figure from her past. Nothing more. Sammie was married, and regardless of the tragedy of her life, re-gardless of her wrong choices, she was still married . . . if she survived.

An image of Adam's contorted face flashed through her mind. Months ago he had met her in the hallway and delivered a blow to her midsection. Astonished by the sudden attack, Sammie had doubled over then fallen to her knees.

"That's what you get for going to our pastor," Adam screamed. "If you ever tell anyone again, I'll kill you! Got it?"

Sammie, reduced to a trembling huddle, gasped for breath as scorching tears spilled down her cheeks.

"Got it?" he yelled again then drew his leg back as if to kick her.

"Got it!" she gasped out, and he placed his foot back onto the floor.

The elevator bell rang, and Sammie jumped. Jac hadn't minced any words when she told Sammie that Adam would probably be able to meet his bail and be released. If nothing else, Sammie figured their pastor would help him. Pastor Laurel was convinced that Sammie was a rebellious and undisciplined wife who re-fused to bow to her husband's authority. By the look of Pastor Laurel's wife, Sam figured that living with him probably wasn't much better than living with Adam. When Sammie stopped attending church with her husband, Pastor Laurel was even more convinced that she was in the wrong. He even called to set her straight. Sammie believed that Adam's public charm would continue to dupe this pastor who refused the biblical teachings of mutual submission and servanthood. Even though she had filed a restraining order against her husband, the pastor would no doubt believe the story Adam made up, the story that he told Pastor Laurel from the start — that Sammie was crazy.

With a hard swallow against a churning stomach, Sam waited for the elevator door to open on the magazine's editorial floor. She didn't for one second think she would get any work done today, but staring at a computer screen certainly beat sitting around an apartment with R.J.

"Okay, looks like these are our numbers," Jacquelyn said as she eyed the airline seats. She turned to Lawton, who trailed close behind, his left hand lightly gripping her upper arm. "Do you want to put your carry-on in the overhead or under the seat in front of you?"

"The overhead's fine," he said, and the

cabin's low lighting flickered across the surface of his dark glasses, "if that's okay with you."

Jacquelyn paused among the flurry of boarding passengers and tried to squelch the sensation that the man was looking right into her soul.

He produced a lopsided grin. "What?"

"Nothing," she said and plopped his small case next to her backpack.

"Do you prefer the window or the aisle?" she asked.

"I prefer whatever you don't want. Either is fine with me."

"Okay, then I'll take the window. I always like to see the Rockies when they come into view."

"Good choice. That way you can tell me what they look like," he said as the two of them jostled into their seats. "Maybe you'll say the mountains look like they're covered in powdered sugar or something equally creative."

Jacquelyn fished for her seat belt, connected the ends, and snapped them shut. "Or maybe that they look like they're covered in marshmallow cream."

"Now you're talkin'!" Lawton said with a chuckle as he searched for his seat belt.

"How 'bout clouds that look like great

mounds of cotton candy!" Jacquelyn added.

"Oh, baby, you *do* go on!"

Chortles erupted from the seat behind, and Jacquelyn realized they were attracting an audience. Meanwhile, Lawton managed to snare one side of his seat belt but continued to use his left hand to grope for the one on the right side. All the way to the airport, Lawton never once complained, but his right arm moved with little grace. Every activity most likely affected his injured shoulder.

"What does a guy have to do to get help around here?" he teased. "Are you going to offer to get my seat belt or am I going to have to holler for an attendant?"

She stretched her neck to peer past his denim shirt and pleated shorts, toward the vicinity of the seat belt's locale. No seat belt posed itself for easy access. In a flash, Jac pictured herself leaning over Lawton to find it. *That's probably exactly what he wants,* she thought, and wondered if perhaps he wasn't half as helpless as he was insinuating. She eyed his injured shoulder, where a bandage bulged beneath the shirt. Just about the time she decided to capitulate, a movement from up the aisle prompted her to raise a hand. "Excuse me," she called toward the tall flight attendant as she neared. "My friend needs help with his seat belt."

"Sure," the blonde said as she knelt beside Lawton. In a second, the metallic buckle clicked, and the attendant hesitated. "Is there anything else you need, Sir?" she asked, honey dripping from her alto voice as her concerned gaze roved Lawton's features.

Jac suppressed a groan.

"Oh, sure, if you don't mind," Lawton said with a smile that would charm the stripes off a zebra, "I'd enjoy a cola once we get into flight. Jac," he asked, turning toward her, "would you like one?"

The flight attendant's beguiling gaze barely flitted to Jac, who glanced toward the woman's ring finger. The decided absence of a gold band proclaimed the blonde's availability.

"No thanks," Jac mumbled.

"Ah, bring her one anyway," Lawton said.

"If you're going to insist," Jac said, "make it bottled water."

"Of course, no problem. Anything to make your flight better," the attendant said as she made her way up the aisle.

This is disgusting, Jac thought and

scooted down in her seat. She crossed her arms and glared out the window toward the long line of planes that were either unloading or boarding. She nibbled at the dry skin on her bottom lip and wondered if she had completely lost all traces of sanity. Without warning, Jac relived that moment when she lowered her face to Lawton's and told him that her past was none of his stinkin' business. She tugged harder on the tiny strip of skin, and a sharp burn accompanied the taste of blood. Her tension mounted — tension that just might not go away. Despite their undeniable attraction, a chasm separated them. A chasm filled with an infectious past that contaminated the present and future.

Lawton leaned into her space, and she held her breath. The alluring smell of his sporty cologne was the last thing she needed to encounter.

"You're a tough cookie, Jacquelyn Lightfoot," he muttered under his breath.

"What's that supposed to mean?" she asked, as the smell of his cologne invited her to move closer.

"You're the first woman who hasn't jumped to my rescue every chance she got."

"Is that what you like?" she snapped. "A

woman who stands around just wilting to wait on you?"

"Oooo." Lawton's brows raised from behind the glasses and a grin indented the laugh lines that spanned from his nose to mouth. "I think somebody might be jealous."

"Yeah, right." She rolled her eyes. "In your dreams."

He raised his chin and let out an uninhibited laugh. "I love it! I love it!"

"Oh . . . go to sleep or something. You've been injured. It's a long flight. You're going to need the rest."

"Go to sleep at a time like this?" he declared. "I'd surely miss my cola, *wouldn't I?*"

Jac glared at him, only to remember the expression was completely wasted on him. Despite her barbed rebuttal, he didn't move away. As his fragrance wove a delicious cloud around her, a TV aftershave advertisement assaulted her thoughts. A rugged man rode his stallion along the beach at sunset, straight toward a woman dressed in a gauzy dress the color of luminous pearls. The wind blew through her fair hair, and the folds of her attire danced around as if they were an extension of the white-capped waves rolling onto shore. The woman took on the profile of the accommodating flight attendant . . . and the man on the horse became Lawton.

Jac's toes curled. She repeated the thought that was quickly becoming a hollow chant: *Lawton is nothing to me.*

"I'm sorry about what I said last night," he said, his voice barely audible.

"What?" Jac asked, even though she understood his every word.

"That's what I was trying to tell you on the phone this morning," he said as the plane rolled backward and the pilot's voice crackled over the speaker. "I'm sorry I told you to 'get over it.' Kinkaide says I was about 18 different kinds of stupid. What do you think?"

"What does Kinkaide know about what I'm trying to get over?" Jac asked. A suspicion crept through her soul as she stared at the airline magazine tucked inside the back pocket of the seat in front of her. *If Mel told her husband about my past, and he told Lawton, then . . . I've had it with Mel! I've absolutely had it!*

"I have no idea," Lawton said, his words laced with regret. "He wouldn't tell me — said it would betray his word to Mel."

So she did tell Kinkaide! Jac fumed. *Mel, now you know why I keep my distance from the sisters at times. Sometimes you people are just big gossips.* Jacquelyn grabbed the mag-

185

azine and stared at the cover to see none other than one of the sisters smiling up at her from a backdrop of Hawaiian palms. The cover line promised that supermodel Kim Lan Lowery would share about all her favorite Hawaiian haunts. Jacquelyn sighed and shook her head as Kim's liquid-brown eyes seemed to accuse her for her bad attitude toward her dearest friends.

"Well, you're a fine one to talk," Jac muttered. "There you are, all the way in Hawaii, and I'm here having to deal with *them!*"

"Excuse me?" Lawton prompted as the plane began to taxi toward the runway.

"Oh, nothing," Jac mumbled, then stuffed the magazine into the seat pouch, back cover facing out.

"Do you have a mouse in your pocket?" Lawton quipped.

"Ha, ha," Jac said and leaned her head against the rest. "I just noticed a photo of one of my friends on the cover of that magazine, and I was talking to her."

"Hmmm. I guess we don't need to worry about this unless she answers you."

Jacquelyn scowled in an attempt to stop the grin that exploded all over her face.

"Let's see," Lawton mused and tapped his index finger against his chin, "Mel has mentioned that you two are part of a group of seven close friends and that one of them is a supermodel — Kim Lan Lowery, to be exact. Am I right?"

"Yep." Jac closed her eyes and prepared for the approaching takeoff.

"Is she the one on the cover?"

"Yes."

"Isn't she part Vietnamese?"

"Uh-huh."

"And what about you?" Lawton asked.

Jac's eyes popped open, and she lifted her head from the rest to stare at him. "I'm not Vietnamese," she said. "Whatever gave you that idea?"

He chuckled and his white teeth flashed against his deep gold complexion. Although he had shaven, the shadow of his whiskers darkened his skin. He had yet to back away from leaning so close, and Jac resisted the urge to shove him over into his own space. The man was far too appealing at a distance, but up close . . .

"I didn't necessarily think you were Vietnamese," Lawton said. "All I know is what Kinkaide has told me, and he says you're dark. So . . ." He shrugged. "I was just curious."

"Well, does it matter?" she snapped.

"Matter?" he asked as if he were thoroughly enjoying her vexation. "Matter, as in . . ." he raised his hand.

"Never mind," she bit out and plopped her head back on the headrest. "If you must know, my father is a full-blooded Alabama–Coushatta Indian. My mother is half African American and half Caucasian," she snapped as a suspicion, dismal and ugly, snaked through her. If Lawton Franklin had adopted any cultural prejudices, that would give her one more reason to keep her distance. Somehow, the thought did about as much to comfort her as the over-attentive stewardess. "You're dark too, for whatever it's worth," she added as an afterthought.

"So I've been told." At last Lawton leaned his head against his headrest. "My mom's mother and father migrated from Italy. People say that Kinkaide and I got their coloring."

As the pilot instructed the attendants to prepare for takeoff, Jac sneaked a peek at him out of the corner of her eye. Nothing in his demeanor suggested a hint of prejudice. Not one hint.

"I hope my curiosity didn't offend you," he said and tilted his head toward hers as if he sensed her scrutiny. "It's just that . . ." he shrugged and his bottom lip turned down a bit, "I'm interested in how you look. I guess, well, I guess you would be too, wouldn't you?"

"Yes," Jac said and smiled. "Yes, I would. No offense taken."

"And whatever color bronze is, according to Kinkaide it's done lovely things for your skin." A lazy grin followed the compliment.

The plane swished across the runway, the wheels lifted from earth, and Jac's weight shifted deeper into the cushioned seat.

"Does Mel know Kinkaide said all that?" she asked.

"Sure. She was standing right there when I asked."

"Oh? And when would that have been?"

"On the cruise, remember? We were on a Mediterranean cruise together a few months ago."

"Oh, so that was you?" Jac teased as the airplane's wheels bumped into place.

"Must have been really memorable," he mumbled, then grimaced.

"Memorable enough," Jac said and examined his blanching face. "You're looking a bit pale," she said. "Are you going to be okay?"

"So the lady *does* care whether I live or

die." Lawton touched the right side of his chest.

"Look, are you due a pain pill about now?"

"Probably," he said. "At least, that's what my shoulder is telling me. They're in my carry-on."

"Maybe the flight attendant will bring the cola shortly. I'm sure she'd also be *delighted* to retrieve your carry-on," she said with a twist of her lips.

"Ah, the flight attendant. Wanna tell me what *she* looks like?"

Jacquelyn's mouth fell open. "Not in a million years, Bucko!"

"Ha! You *slay* me!"

As Jac reached above her head to push the passenger request button, the snickers behind them reminded her that they were providing free entertainment for some other passengers. She purposed to remain silent. No telling what that couple behind them thought.

Jacquelyn stoically focused out the window. The receding Dallas skyline now seemed nothing more than a collection of childhood replicas. *Sammie's in one of those skyscrapers,* she thought. Pondering Sam's dilemma produced a band of tension around her heart as her gaze trailed to the miles and miles of land that surrounded Dallas. The green patches resembled a huge quilt made of squares and rectangles. The plane soon bumped through a thin layer of clouds that really did look like mounds of cotton candy.

Too bad my childhood couldn't have been as simple as cotton candy and dolls and trips to the park, Jacquelyn mused. She closed her eyes and swallowed as the dreadful memories erupted from the recesses of her tormented soul. The overhead vent's cool swish of air blew across her features as the icy reality of the past wafted upon her. A little girl's broken cries, deep in the night, erupted from the corridors of her heart, and Jacquelyn bit back a sob.

Oh, God, she prayed and gripped the seat's arms, *will I be in agony the rest of my life?*

As if in answer to her prayer, Lawton's hand covered hers. Jacquelyn opened her eyes and blinked as she stared at the long, sensitive fingers that rested atop her tensed hand. Mel's words sliced through her thoughts. *He's already halfway in love with you.* As if answering Mel, Jac posed a question she couldn't avoid, no matter how hard she might try: *If he is really falling for me, will his love be strong enough to overcome his aversion to my tainted past?*

"I wrote a new poem," Lawton said. "Remind me to recite it for you one day."

For once Jacquelyn didn't pull away. Instead, she obeyed the whimper of her wounded heart, turned her hand upward, and twined her fingers with Lawton's. The corner of his mouth twitched, and he tightened his grip. She thought of the lone, dried bloom in her desk at home.

"Thanks for the daisies," Jac whispered as the flight attendant approached. "I really enjoyed them."

"Ah, the daisies. I never heard from you. I expected to, but . . ."

As if he were her lifeline, Jac spontaneously clung to his touch and wondered what life would be like if only . . .

Twelve

~

The minute the pilot gave permission for the passengers to move about the airplane, Maurice unbuckled his seat belt and stood. He flexed his neck in an attempt to ease the tension headache that threatened to erupt across his skull. His gut tight, Maurice began the journey up the aisle, out of coach, through first class, toward the front of the plane. Once past the first row, Maurice pretended to check the lavatory occupancy then turned and began the trek that would give him the chance to inspect every passenger. His knees moved in sequence with the plane's airborne sway as he scanned the features of each traveler. Not one person looked even remotely familiar. Maurice relaxed a fraction as he passed from first class to coach. So far, every person was irrefutably an unknown.

With only about six aisles left before the bathroom, the ball of anxiety in Maurice's midsection significantly diminished. Then he caught sight of a pair of round sunglasses gleaming in the glow of sunshine that oozed into the cabin like an ethereal aura. His eyes widened as he encountered the image of Lawton Franklin, his head resting against the seat, his mouth in a tight line, his right arm cradled in the clasp of his left hand. Maurice's attention darted toward the woman next to Lawton. A woman with skin the color of rich copper. A woman whose finely chiseled features and hair of black satin defied racial identification. A woman who was vaguely familiar.

Jac shifted her focus from out the window and cast a cursory glance toward Maurice. He drew in a sharp breath and darted his gaze to the floor. After he passed their seats, Maurice glanced over his shoulder. The woman calmly resumed her observation of the clouds. Maurice released his breath and forced himself to scrutinize the remaining passengers — all strangers. He fumbled his way into the vacant lavatory, snapped the bar slide into place, closed his eyes, and inhaled.

While he had feared that Fuat somehow managed to send a tracker, he never dreamed that Lawton Franklin would be on this flight. *The man has never seen you,* Maurice reminded himself. *He has no idea what you look like. But what about the woman?* his mind insisted. *She might not even be with Lawton,* Maurice parried. *Nevertheless, she does look familiar.*

"But why?" Maurice whispered and pressed his fingertips against his aching forehead. His mind's frenzied racing accompanied the fervid need to assign the woman an identity. *Somewhere I've encountered that woman,* he mused with conviction, *and I'm sure it was not positive.*

As if his mind were a media screen, the image of a newspaper headline swam into focus: "Private Eye Busts Major Drug Ring." Featured beneath the caption was the photo of the petite detective, midstride, as she trotted down courthouse steps. The name "Jacquelyn Lightfoot" descended into Maurice's mind like a jolt of electricity. Within the last couple of years, she had stumbled upon a drug operation that had cost some of his acquaintances a significant avenue of income and presented them with time behind bars. Maurice's hands curled into tight balls. In the underworld the woman's reputation was about a hundred times bigger than her stature. Why somebody hadn't put a contract on her was beyond Maurice's understanding.

What if she's working with Lawton? Maurice thought. *And what if they're going to Ouray together?*

He had spoken the name Gary Sellers in the car when he presumed Lawton to be unconscious. *What if that idiot heard me?* The death of Gary and his wife had been plastered on the front of more than one newspaper. Anybody who even remotely stayed atop the news would know the couple had lived in Ouray, Colorado. The plausibility of Lawton traveling to Ouray with a private eye gained credence with every second. Furthermore, the boss's insistence that Lawton die posed itself more logically than ever before.

Maurice suppressed a groan and rubbed his face with his unsteady hand. *All I wanted to do was get the cache and leave for Bangkok. I don't want to kill anybody else; I'm sick of the killing . . . sick of it!*

He looked into the mirror, into deep-green eyes that once sparkled with joy. Years had passed since he had tasted happiness. All bliss had been consumed in hungry flames that ripped his family apart and left him so angry. Angry at himself for not being home when they needed him. Angry at life. Angry at God. The hardness that settled upon his soul had numbed any reaction to the tiny steps he took toward corruption. His cooperation with the Rantomis soon turned to a partnership. The resulting murders had initially provided a vent for his anger. But then, the guilt caught up. Now, instead of releasing the anger, his bloody hands ushered in condemnation.

"Oh, Jesus, Son of God, forgive me," he muttered, then habitually crossed himself. A recurring scene arose like a ghostly mist over a deserted graveyard. Maurice stood in a circle, holding hands with six others. They were part of the same family — except him. Fuat gave the nod, and they bowed their heads. Fuat's red-lipped daughter, Angelica, began the prayer for those in the circle who would be committing the latest murder. Maurice's blood turned to ice. He imagined those prayers falling to the floor and being trampled by the feet of that murderous family, just as they heartlessly overran the lives of those who got in their way.

A light tap sounded on the door. "Excuse me, sir, are you — are you okay?" a masculine voice queried.

"Yes, yes, I'm — I'm fine." Maurice's head pounded with no hope for release.

"There's quite a line," the flight attendant politely prompted.

"Okay, I'll be out shortly." Maurice lifted the sink's miniature lever and collected a handful of cool water. He closed his eyes, splashed his face, then sponged it dry with a stiff disposable towel. *If Lawton and that Lightfoot woman do show up in Ouray, the next few days might require murderous action. But if I can just get the loot, I won't ever have to kill again after that. I'll find peace in Bangkok. Peace . . . and maybe even another woman.*

Maurice snapped open the sliding lock and exited the lavatory. A line of four people, none of whom appeared at ease, stood awaiting their turn. Without acknowledging their presence, he slid past them and began the trek up the aisle. When he neared Lawton, Maurice stole a glimpse out of the corner of his eye. The detective had settled her head on the blind man's shoulder. Her eyes were closed; her mouth relaxed. Maurice swept along the narrow aisle and bit back a curse.

The two of them are together. Together! he

blasted to himself.

Lawton fitfully dosed during the rest of the flight. Just about the time he thought sleep would indeed overtake him, Jac would stir or he would remember that somehow her head had settled upon his shoulder. Then, despite the lull of medication, his mind would zing to alert status. Her close proximity was enough to disturb the sleep of a thousand men. The scent of her freshly shampooed hair, the sound of her steady breathing, the uncanny sense that she trusted him implicitly wove together to produce the stuff dreams are made of. And Lawton knew in the deepest recesses of his heart that he was gradually losing his ability to think clearly where she was concerned. This spunky woman had marched into his life and left an indelible imprint upon his heart.

Last night Mel had blurted that Lawton was halfway in love with Jac, and he had, for once, been speechless. And he wasn't so certain that his ornery brother hadn't swallowed a few chuckles. Jacquelyn never brought up Mel's claim, but Lawton couldn't help but wonder if she believed her friend. Nonetheless, the truth was that he was well on the road to irrevocably losing his heart.

Oh, Jac! he thought, *I hope you don't rip my heart right out and leave me half the man I once was.* Lawton shifted his position and adjusted the angle of his arm. Fortunately the pain medicine had kicked in and relieved much of the discomfort. *But they don't have pain medicine for broken hearts,* he thought as a sense of caution bade him take heed. Dealing with Jac was like dealing with a tide, forever approaching and receding. She had certainly enjoyed her time with him on the cruise, then told him to get lost in Rome. She kept the bracelet, flew all the way from Denver just because he needed her, then dropped the bracelet back in his hand and told him her past was none of his stinkin' business. She then proceeded to promptly hop the next flight to Denver and Montrose with him, place her head on his shoulder, and sleep like a baby.

But only after she clobbered Adam Jones, Lawton thought with a grin. If ever a woman could take care of herself, Jac could. *Yet she's scared.* He frowned. *She's scared to death to develop a close relationship with me. Something in her past . . .*

Lawton's former resolve to remain understanding diminished a bit in the face of his own experience in struggling to survive. The anger of his youth had driven his parents to near desperation. Lawton had systematically and irreverently lashed out at anyone who came close to him — including God. While the family attended church services, he spent most of his mental energies shaking his fist at the heavens and saying, "Why me? I don't want to be blind! Why did *You* do this to me?"

Yet the furor of his youth had grown into the strength of adulthood. Somewhere in the middle of all that struggling, Lawton had relaxed his fists and decided he was on God's side and God was on his side. Together, they would succeed. Mobility school had also been a gateway to accomplishments that, even now, took his breath away.

He gently rested his head atop Jac's and wondered why she couldn't get past this thing that kept them apart. His "get over it" edict, while admittedly harsh, had come from a life of experience, rather than a chair of judgment. After all, he, too, had to transcend a lot in life. *I could have sat down and had a pity party years ago, Jac,* he thought. *But I didn't. Instead, I decided to move forward and grow, despite life's hard-*

ships. You can do the same. You can! But only with God's help. Have you asked Him to take this from you? Really asked Him? The words he so wanted to express rotated through his mind like a chorus doomed to never be heard. And he wondered if she would ever give him the opportunity to communicate these truths to her.

The plane's gradual descent attested to their nearing Denver. Any minute now Lawton expected to hear the pilot's voice over the intercom announcing their proximity to their destination. Meanwhile, Jac's head ground into his shoulder and she began a series of agitated protests that escalated into the outcry of a victim's wail.

"No . . . no . . ." she mumbled as her head rolled from side to side. "Oh, no — no . . . I d–don't want to — want to know —" She choked on a sob.

"Jac," Lawton said and stiffly extended his right arm to nudge at her shoulder. Lawton eased away to give him enough distance to support her weight with his stronger arm.

"N–no, Grandpa! No!" she rasped as a cascade of weeping spilled from her inner being. "Oh, God, help me —"

"Jac!" His mind reeling, Lawton tapped her cheeks. "Wake up!"

Her unsteady gasping, her death-grip on his hand, the cessation of her cries revealed she had gained consciousness.

"Are you okay?" Lawton whispered.

Her elongated silence made him question her alertness.

"Jacquelyn?" He brushed the backs of his fingers against her damp, overheated cheek.

"Y–yes, I'm — I'm okay. I need to go to the ladies' room," she whispered. Before Lawton could utter another word, she jostled past him and strode up the aisle.

Lawton rested his head against the seat and frowned. Whatever troubled Jacquelyn obviously involved her grandfather. Lawton's mind whirled with possibilities. The most disgusting scenario posed itself as the most logical. Lawton ripped off the dark glasses and pressed his fingers against his gritty eyes.

Oh, Lord, please help her, he prayed and contemplated the atmosphere upon her return. When she settled into her seat, Lawton fully expected the tide of her emotions to recede like they had all during this relationship merry-go-round they were trapped on. Jacquelyn Lightfoot, independent, strong, invincible, would once again be unreachable, aloof, hiding in the inky abyss that forever isolated her from him. She would once again be so terrorized that she would shut him out.

"Ah, Jac," he whispered. "Please don't keep me out forever." Then his own words to Kinkaide slammed against his conscience: "You know I've always said that I wanted a woman who lived by the standards I've lived by." Lawton winced. *There's no need to jump to conclusions about Jac's past,* he chided himself. *If she's lived by biblical standards then that will make her the perfect woman for me.*

"There's no need to jump to conclusions!" he whispered, shoving aside the doubts that sprang upon him like thousands of gleeful demons ready to annihilate his dreams of an enchanting wedding night.

Thirteen

~

Laptop case in hand, Sammie opened the penthouse door and stepped into the shadowed haven. The afternoon sunshine squeezed through the lowered blinds to create razor-thin strips of light across the pale carpet. The faint hum of the air conditioner mingled with the sound of soft snoring, and Sammie scanned the living room. At last, her gaze rested upon a pair of partners stretched out in the leather recliner. Brett, his head snuggled against R.J.'s shoulder, slept in the crook of the biker's arm. The child's snoring mingled with R.J.'s steady breathing.

Sammie, her eyes pooling with warm tears, stood in the open doorway. The barely discernible tick of the cherry grandfather clock seemed to count the years that had lapsed since Sam and R.J. first fell in love. Years that almost stretched to an eternity. The man always had been rough around the edges, and Sammie attributed that to his mother's trying to make him into something he wasn't. But despite his insistence that his leather stayed, despite his ever-present need of a good shave, R.J. Butler would have made a dynamite father.

With a cringe, Sam glanced over her shoulder and spasmodically closed the door. Using double caution, she turned the deadbolt lock then tiptoed toward her bedroom. Sammie stared straight ahead and refused another glimpse toward Brett and R.J. After a late lunch, Colleen had insisted that she go back to the penthouse to get some rest. Contrary to her original assumption, she had indeed been able to accomplish much in the office. She had worked as if her safety depended upon it. But in reality, the drive to produce had come from a longing to close out the turmoil.

Sammie trudged up the hallway, entered her room, closed the door, and snapped on the light. In a flash, she dropped the laptop case in the center of the bed, removed the business suit Colleen lent her, then changed into pleated shorts and a printed T-shirt. The churning anxiety that spanned her chest and muddled her mind belied her heavy eyes. Sammie plopped onto the ancient sleigh bed, crossed her legs, opened her laptop, and turned it on. As the machine chugged through the usual routine, Sammie gazed around the room filled with meticulously chosen antiques. The highly polished mahogany and cherry pieces blended with the room's overall mood to create a melody of decor that soothed the nerves like a comforting poem.

With a frown, Sammie thought of her own cluttered domain. "Nothing soothing there," she whispered as her frown increased. "Nothing at all." Stifling a yawn, she dug the phone line out of the portable case. Within minutes she was connected to the internet and downloading her e-mail. She hadn't checked her mail in several days, but the past week had been like one huge emotional roller coaster — knowing she needed to leave Adam, but not seeing how. Among everything else in her life, her e-mail correspondence had suffered.

Fully expecting a basketful of e-mails from her six dearest friends, Sammie focused upon the screen and smiled at the witty interchange that had brightened her days more than once. Even in the midst of her darkest hours when she couldn't utter a hint of the agony she was experiencing, just interacting with her six sisters had always lifted her spirit. All six of them — Marilyn, Kim Lan, Sonsee, Melissa, Victoria, and Jackie — had each been there for each other when life got tough. Before opening one of the e-mails, Sammie skimmed down to see that Jac's address was missing. *Doesn't surprise me,* she thought. *You're not much for chitchat, are you? But you were the one who was there when I needed somebody the most.*

Sammie thought about the minute Jac's foot slammed into Adam's rib cage. Memories of his rounded eyes and telltale gasp sent a gurgle of laughter from her soul. Never had he expected a woman half his size to take him down. But Sam's mirthful release soon mingled with sobs.

"What am I going to do if he comes after me?" she choked out in a barely audible whisper. The fear multiplied tenfold, and her eyes darted around the room then rested on the closet. She stared at the doorknob until she was sure it rotated. Sammie sucked in a sharp breath and begged God's protection. When the door didn't open, she forced herself to stand and approach the closet.

Open the door! she demanded, yet her trembling arm refused to obey. *There's no one there. Open it!* Sammie held her breath, snatched the doorknob, twisted it, and flung open the door. The walk-in closet stood void of any human occupation. Instead of harboring a menace, the cavity held a neat array of boxes, odds and ends, and Colleen's winter wardrobe. The tiny room beckoned Sammie to step inside, close the door, and huddle in the farthest corner, behind a stack of boxes. She stepped forward, then remembered Brett.

She wrapped her fingers around the cold doorknob, clicked the door shut, and inhaled deep gulps of air. Sammie padded toward the window, draped in elegant sheers. Compulsively, she checked and double-checked the window locks. There was no way Adam could climb up the outside of a skyrise, but that fact did little to deter her paranoia.

Satisfied that the locks were sturdy, Sam plopped back on the quilted bedspread. The polished cotton, the color of creamy taupe and swirling garnets, offered a cooling comfort to her bare legs. With a shuddering breath, Sammie crossed her legs once more and forced herself to focus on the e-mails from her dearest friends. As she read the loop messages, she deleted them one by one until she came upon an exchange that halted her progress.

Melissa: Hi! I just want everyone to know that Lawton has been found. He's in a hospital in Dallas. He's been the victim of a shooting. This is all very scary. We're leaving on the next flight to Dallas.

Sonsee: You're in our prayers, Mel . . . you and Lawton and Kinkaide. Incidentally, has anyone heard what Jac's plans are?

Victoria: I just got off the phone with Sammie. She says that Jac is going to fly to Dallas to be with Lawton.

Marilyn: Okay, this is all starting to sound suspicious to me. I think Jac might be a little more taken with Lawton than she wants to admit.

Kim Lan: I'm praying that she is. It's time that woman gets in line with the rest of us and gets married. Then she will eventually know the joys of potty training — her inevitable child, not her husband that is. Tee hee!!

Sammie paused to chuckle. Kim Lan and her husband, Mick, had adopted a little boy from Vietnam earlier that year. As a result, the supermodel's meticulous appearance had certainly undergone a severe alteration the last time Sammie had seen her. She had been helping Melissa pack for her move from Oklahoma City to Nashville, where Kinkaide lived. Motherhood had left its mark on the model.

Like Kim Lan, Sam had been in the throes of potty training her son. But after almost conquering the process, Brett had experienced a severe setback. Sam squeezed her eyes shut and her fingers trembled against the keyboard. At last, she refocused on the sisterly interaction and began deleting the chatty messages as she read them until she came to a new series that required more direct attention.

Melissa: I am in Dallas. Lawton is fine. We don't know exactly what all is going on, but he's definitely on somebody's list. Someone sneaked into the room and inserted some kind of acid into his IV tubing. They caught it before it entered his body. Meanwhile, he and Jac are planning to go to Colorado. Seems like all this is somehow linked to the Gary and Rhonda Sellers murders — you know the real-estate tycoon who has been plastered all over the papers. On another note, please keep Sam in your prayers. She's going through a terrible time in her marriage right now.

Marilyn: Sam? Are you out there? Call me. Maybe I can help.

Victoria: Sam, what's up? Praying for you.

Kim Lan: Sammie, don't be a stranger, girlfriend. We need to know how to pray for you.

Sonsee: Sam, this is a private e-mail. I've sensed for awhile that you were having a tough time. I've just not really known what to say or if I should say anything. If you want to call me, I'll be happy to talk. You know, I've got all the free time in the world right now since the ob/gyn put me to bed.

"Yes, and you've also got a great marriage to a lifelong friend who fell head over heels in love with you and adores you," Sammie whispered and dashed at the hot tears that the sisterly concern inspired. "You're expecting a child that your husband is thrilled about." *And me? I've just been trying to stand in the way if my husband lunges for his son.* Even though she knew Sonsee meant well, Sam couldn't quite stretch her mind enough to believe that she could offer much advice. Certainly the young veterinarian would provide a sympathetic ear, but that would be as far as it went.

Likewise Kim Lan was married to her dream man — missions coordinator Mick O'Donnel. The two had met and fallen in love on a trip to Vietnam. Then both were so filled with a love for reaching out to others, they had returned to Kim Lan's land of origin and adopted a special-needs child, Khanh Anh. Kim's husband loved the Lord. He loved God's Word. And he was spending his life as a missions-minded man. *All my husband wants to do is use the Bible to prove he has a right to beat me,* she thought bitterly.

Sammie, longing for a friend to share with, continued to ponder the sisters one by one. Victoria Roberts, domestic genius extraordinaire, never said much about her marriage, but Sammie had also never seen any bruises marring her fine-boned face. Then there was Jacquelyn. *Jackie has been a huge help in getting me out. I probably owe her my life. But as far as her being someone who's been there . . . no way. She isn't even married. End of discussion. And Mel . . .* Sammie shook her head and rolled her eyes. Melissa Moore was still a star-struck newlywed. She went to Rome last spring a single woman and came back blissfully married. Sam wasn't sure she even remembered much bliss with Adam.

"That only leaves Marilyn," Sammie whispered. Marilyn's first husband, a pastor, had an affair and left her for another woman. As a minister's wife, Marilyn had doubly struggled with the implications of her husband abandoning her and her daughter. Then God gave her a second chance at ministry and marriage. Now Marilyn lived in Eureka Springs, Arkansas, with her new husband, Joshua Langham. They diligently served the Lord together. Marilyn had never mentioned if her first husband had physically abused her, but Sam sensed that she, better than all the sisters, would be able to offer the support of one who has survived a broken marriage. Even though Sam was still legally married,

Adam had so violated their vows that she had long ago quit feeling like a wife. *The Lord only knows how many women he's been with in the last two years,* she thought. Sammie had no proof of adultery, but Adam had spent enough nights away from home to make her question his constancy. As a result, every time he forced her into physical intimacy she was terrified that she might contract some dread disease.

Yes, Marilyn can help me. Marilyn and Josh. Josh has been through a lot himself, Sammie thought.

After typing a brief note to the sisters thanking them for their prayers, she briefly explained her situation. For the first time in years of verbal, emotional, spiritual, and physical abuse, Sammie shared her plight.

After sending the message, she prepared to exit then noticed a final e-mail she had overlooked. An e-mail titled: "Hello, Doll." Sammie's eyes widened as she recognized Adam's e-mail address. Her heart pounded. She panted. Her palms became clammy. As if she were under the power of his evil hypnosis, Sammie read the brief e-mail. "I'm out of jail. Just thought you might like to know. Love, Adam." A broken cry forced itself up her throat and Sammie deleted the e-mail before she had time to reread it. Her heart pounding hard, even beats in her temples, she exited the program, disconnected from the internet, and unplugged the computer.

The faint tap on the bedroom door zipped through her. Sammie dropped the phone line, stared at the unlocked door, and scooted toward the headboard.

"Sam?" R.J. called. "May I come in?"

She covered her face as a wave of nausea bulged against her throat. *Adam's going to kill me. He is. I know he is.* The thoughts, strong and unrelenting, silenced her.

"Sam?" R.J. called again. "Are you in there?"

"Yes," she croaked. "Come in."

The door opened and R.J.'s sensitive eyes observed her. "You woke me up when you walked through," he said. "I just wanted you to know that I'm stepping out for awhile. Dad's just come in. Brett's asleep in the room your friend stayed in last night."

"Okay, thanks," Sammie said, her cold face stiff. Her eye twitched, and she pressed the corner with her index finger.

"You don't look so hot."

"Would you?"

"No." He shook his head. "No, I wouldn't." His smile, laced with sympathy, heightened Sam's emotions. "Okay," he continued, "I should be home for dinner. Jac asked me to keep an eye on you for awhile."

"Oh?"

"Yes. Do you mind?" His southern drawl reminded Sammie of a golden-hearted cowboy from an old western.

"Do you have anything else to do?" she shot back as her irrational ire rose. Jac had been a godsend, but the last thing she needed was for Jac to assign R.J. as her guardian.

"No, not really," he said without acknowledging the barb. "I was just stopping through town to meet with my financial planner anyway," he said. "Keeping an eye on you for a few days won't alter my schedule too much." His gaze drifted toward the window. "Mom says she wants you to stay here for now. If you like, I can go to your home with you while you pack up some of your stuff."

"Adam's restraining order includes our home," Sammie stated, despite the fact that she wouldn't dare go back home alone. Restraining order or not, she didn't trust Adam. However, the thought of going anywhere with R.J. left her squirming.

After a pensive pause, his attention

shifted back to Sammie. "How do you know he won't violate the order?"

Sammie held his gaze as the horrid chant reverberated through her mind. *Adam's going to kill me. He is. I know he is.* She rubbed her foot and clenched her teeth.

"Sure, you can call the police if he shows up, but what's to stop him from breaking in before they get there or hiding inside until you get home one evening?"

"Stop it! Stop it! Stop it!" Sammie cried and slid from the bed to encounter the cotton-soft carpet against her chilled feet. "Just — just stop it!" With her hands clasped, she trembled so violently she thought she would collapse.

In seconds R.J. stood in front of her, gently gripping her upper arms. "Listen, I'm not trying to scare you, but you also need to understand —"

"I understand!" Sammie stumbled away from his touch. "I've lived — lived with him for f–five years! I under– understand!"

"Okay, okay." He held up his hands, palms facing Sammie. "I just wanted you to know that I'll be back by dinner. Until then, *please* don't go anywhere."

Sammie released a huff as the e-mail's implied threat snaked its way through her mind. "If you think I'm going anywhere,

Butler, you're nuts." She crossed her arms and hugged herself as she focused on the tufts of dark hair at his collar line.

"I'm sorry. I didn't mean to freak you out. I'm really worried here. Mom says that Adam threatened to kill you. I don't think you should take his threat lightly."

"What makes you think I do?" she snapped. "I'm not some idiot who —"

"Because you've stayed with him for five years for crying out loud!" R.J. raised his hand, then dropped it to his leg. The faint snap of skin against denim punctuated his words.

"The reason I stayed is because . . ." A rush of tears gushed past her lashes. Sammie hiccuped and covered her face. "Because I was afraid he *would* kill me. You don't know what it's like, R.J. I've been terrified!"

His arms draped around her shoulders, and he patted her back in an awkward tattoo. Sam, stiff with caution, rested her head against his chest.

"I am *so sorry*," R.J. breathed, and the rumble of his voice vibrated against her cheek. "I know you're scared. I'm worried about you, that's all, and — and I'm worried about Brett, too. That little guy could steal my heart in a New York minute."

As if the mention of his name jolted the child from slumber, his horrified wail erupted from across the hallway: "Mamma!"

Sam jumped then pushed R.J. aside and hastened from the room.

"Mamma!" Brett shrieked again then burst into a chorus of sobs. "Mamma! Where are you?!"

Rushing into the darkened room, Sammie collapsed onto a mound of rumpled covers and gathered the confused child into her arms. "I'm right here, Honey," she crooned and rested her cheek against hair the color of an acorn's heart. She stroked his temple and her fingers encountered a sticky substance. She pulled away and observed a glob of pudding plastered near his ear. Sam bit her bottom lip as a fond smile tugged at her mouth. Even in the center of turmoil, Brett would forever be a source of joy.

R.J. appeared in the doorway, and Sammie glanced at him then focused on comforting her whimpering son. "Brett has pudding in his hair," she said as he wrapped his arms around her neck and settled his head on her shoulder. "Do you?" Sam peered up at the giant of a man whose frame filled the doorway and whose shadow spanned the room.

He chuckled. "I'm not sure."

Sam bestowed a gentle kiss on Brett's forehead then looked back at R.J. "Thanks . . . for everything," she said.

Without a word, R.J. narrowed his eyes a fraction then pursed his lips. Finally, he mumbled under his breath, scrubbed his knuckles against his jaw, turned on his heel, and disappeared up the hallway.

Fourteen

"Where are we?" Lawton asked, his voice heavy with sleep.

"Just outside Ouray," Jac said as she steered the rented car along the winding road. In the near distance, the San Juan Mountains rose like mighty sentinels standing over the town.

Lawton rubbed his face, then reached for the bottle of water hanging in the door drink holder.

"Did you get a nice little nap?" Jac asked.

"Yes," he said after a long swallow of water.

"I'm surprised the new car odor didn't keep you awake. Whew! They must have just driven this one off the lot."

"What color is it?"

"The car?"

"Yeah."

"Red."

"Tell me what red looks like."

Jac rested her hand on the floor gear-shift and tried to describe the color without using another color. "Is this a pop quiz?"

He chuckled. "You can't do it, can you?"

"Nobody's ever asked me before. How's your shoulder?" she said, changing the subject to something a little less abstract.

He winced. "My medicine is wearing a tad thin, but I'm not in too much pain. Actually, that short nap really perked me up."

"Is that a warning?"

"Take it any way you like."

Jacquelyn eyed the San Juan Mountains against a sky that reach down in blue splendor to christen the snowy peaks.

"So, if you aren't going to tell me about red, then tell me what you see," Lawton said.

"This is like a long lazy trail, and we're coming upon mountains that would inspire poetry in the most staid soul. They've also got some kind of white stuff on 'em at the very top." Jacquelyn pressed the compact car's brake and twisted the steering wheel to maneuver a long curve. "And don't you dare tell me to describe white."

"I don't think I've ever been on this stretch of highway," Lawton said.

"From what I understand, it's much more tame than the road south of Ouray. That's called the Million Dollar Highway because it's got dirt and rocks in it that are supposed to have gold in them. Anyway, that road is supposed to be like a roller coaster."

With a chuckle, he rubbed his hands together. "Maybe we could drive south before heading home."

"And I guess you love roller coasters, too."

"Oh, yes. Doesn't everyone?"

"Nope."

"You mean you don't like them?" Lawton said as if he were scandalized.

"Hate 'em. And just for the record, I'm not really fond of the idea of taking that drive." Jac gazed ahead to finally see Ouray coming into view. The scenic town, nestled between a collection of imperial mountains, promised peace and presented a welcome reprieve from the day's travel. "Actually, I hate heights."

"But flying didn't seem to bother you."

"Doesn't bother me in the least."

"But that's inconsistent. If you hate heights —"

"So it's inconsistent. Deal with it!"

Lawton threw back his head. "Ha! I love it!"

"What's to love about it?" Jacquelyn growled.

"You knocked Sammie's husband to Timbuktu, but you're afraid of heights!"

"Oh, give it a break," Jac teased as they began the final stretch to the waiting town. "I'm sure you have your own set of fears." Jacquelyn eyed him and wondered exactly what those phobias would be. The man denied any hint of intimidation. "Nobody's perfect," she continued. "Everybody has a few fears, you know — even you, whether you'd ever admit it or not."

The words fell between them like tiny bombs. Even though developing a relationship with Lawton terrified her, some sort of understanding was nonetheless developing between them — and fast. Yet after the ordeal on the airplane, Jacquelyn had barely spoken to him. The embarrassment of having one of those nightmares in his presence had plunged her into stony silence. Several times, she felt as if Lawton wanted to speak, yet he remained silent. Then the upheaval of disembarking the plane, retrieving their luggage, and arranging for a rental car absorbed their attention. By the time the two of them had settled into the compact Ford, the awkward moment had passed. After Lawton went to sleep, Jac decided to pretend that nothing odd had happened. When he awoke she was thankful that he played along.

Despite the pretense, the nightmare on the plane trailed her. Jac had been bound in something that, even now, she couldn't identify. Instead of having the freedom to step into the shaft of light, glowing on the edge of the forest, she had been fettered by an unforgiving force. As the dream replayed itself in her mind, the sound of the dragon's satisfied chuckle reverberated through the corridors of her soul. A chuckle that was familiar. Too familiar. A tendril of nausea wove its way through her stomach. Jac gripped the steering wheel and fiercely focused on the small town streets before her.

"Airport curbsides at midnight," Lawton said.

"Excuse me?" She wrinkled her brow and peered at him.

Lawton produced a wry grin and turned his face toward her, the setting sun flashing on his dark glasses. Jacquelyn refocused on the task of driving. "I'm afraid of airport curbsides at midnight," he repeated.

Jac grunted. "Yes, and you'd be crazy not to be. As a matter of fact —" She stopped herself from verbalizing the thought that sprang forth: *You probably should think about arranging an escort. You really don't need to be traveling alone.* But Jac knew that the suggestion would deeply offend Lawton.

"Are you going to finish?"

"No, I'm not," she replied. "End of discussion." She braked and pulled into the parking lot of a small, affordable hotel that looked like a large, inviting bungalow. "Here's a hotel. I'm going to check to see if they have any vacancies."

"Were you going to suggest that I arrange some sort of chaperone for my traveling?" he challenged.

Jacquelyn drove under the brick portico and put the vehicle into park. The engine's purring seemed to reflect the churning of Lawton's thoughts. With his face turned to her, those ever-present glasses gleaming as if they had a life of their own, Jac reminded herself that he couldn't read her telltale expression. *Or can he?* The man had certainly developed his senses to an uncanny level — more than enough to overcome the blindness.

"I'm going in to check on the rooms," Jac said and turned off the engine.

"Nice sidestep, but it won't work."

"Well," Jac snapped, "it's nerve-wracking to think of you hopping all over the U.S., and you can't see a thing! Now, you've gone and stumbled into something that's almost taken your life and you act like you plan to just . . . just . . ." She waved her hand and groped for words.

"Get to the bottom of who tried to kill me then resume business as usual?" Lawton asked, a sarcastic twist to his words. "Yes, that's exactly what I plan to do."

"Aren't you the tiniest bit concerned about traveling alone? Maybe you should consider an alternate career."

"No." He raised his chin. "It's my calling."

Jacquelyn propped her elbow on the narrow window ledge and pinched the bridge of her nose.

"Who is going to encourage blind people to independence if I don't? There are some of these people who have been trapped their whole lives, Jac." His voice rose in volume. "I *refuse* to enter a cage just be-cause —"

"Because you were almost killed!" Jac exploded. The new-car odor suddenly seemed too thick to breathe. The dark emotions that engulfed her when she'd heard of Lawton's disappearance plagued her anew. Jac was beginning to suspect that his brush with death had touched her far more than she wanted to admit to him — or herself. "Do you have any idea how this has affected the people who know you?"

"You are now officially starting to sound like my mother." Lawton sat rigid, his head stubbornly facing forward.

"Okay, okay, drop the whole thing." Jacquelyn held up her hand. "This is the reason I cut my words off in the first place. I didn't want to get into all of this with you."

"I'm not quitting my job!" he growled.

"Drop it, Lawton. I'm not telling you to, okay?"

"And don't try to push some bodyguard off on me either!"

"Who said anything about that?"

"I know what you're thinking! I'm a grown man, Jac! I'm not some invalid who is defenseless. Just because I'm blind doesn't mean —"

Jacquelyn unfastened her seat belt and snapped open the door.

"Where are you going?" he queried.

"I told you, I'm going to see if they have a couple of vacancies. Go ahead and vent while I'm gone and get it all out of your system." Jac stepped onto the cement drive, stretched, and covered her mouth with the back of her hand as she yawned. The cool mountain air danced around her like a refreshing brook. "And don't start thinking for one minute that I in any way feel sorry for you because you're blind. You're more ornery than a junkyard dog, Lawton Franklin. You'll have to lose both legs and one arm before I start feeling sorry for you."

"Oh, yeah? And I guess you're the epitome of Little Red Riding Hood!" he shot back.

"No, I'm more in line with the big bad wolf." Jac slammed the compact car's door, and Lawton's raucous laughter still reached her ears. Shaking her head, she strode toward the glassed-in entryway and paused as she grasped the elongated handle. A new thought struck her. A thought that left her reeling. Her shoulders hunched, and she peered at the magnificent mountains as if she were seeing them for the first time. The evening sun bathed the east ridge, where majestic firs stretched toward the sapphire-blue sky. The sun's golden glow, like the breath of angels, warmed the heart and inspired dreams. Somehow she had managed to land herself in one of the most romantic spots on earth with one of the most fascinating men she had ever met. A thrill zipped through her midsection. An unexpected thrill. A thrill that defied all the reasons she shouldn't welcome Lawton's growing regard.

As she whisked open the door and stepped through the homey foyer toward the receptionist's desk, Jac reminded herself that a huge obstacle lay between her and Lawton. An obstacle greater than the mountains hovering over Ouray. Yet for the first time, Jac toyed with the idea of actually telling Lawton.

Might be best, she thought. *If he's going to have a problem with my past, then I'd be better off knowing now, before . . .* She stopped in front of the desk and stared at the applejack candle flickering near the computer and producing the aroma of a cozy welcome. *Before what?* she asked herself, and didn't quite know how to answer her own question. As the plump receptionist approached the desk, Jac faced another question that could not be ignored. *Even if Lawton completely understands, how will I ever want marital intimacy?* She gripped the protruding counter and the fragrant candle's flame blurred.

Somehow, Jacquelyn managed to state her request. As she went through the motions of arranging the two rooms, "real life" hung around her neck like the yoke of a barbaric taskmaster. As much as Jac liked Lawton, thoughts of physical intimacy with any man hurled her into a sphere where high emotions ruled and uncontrolled shaking threatened to consume her. Even though she was attracted to Lawton, that element alone did precious little to overcome her woundedness.

Okay, I'm not "just attracted" to him, she admitted as she signed the appropriate form. *It's more in the realms of a lot. As in, seriously,* Jac added while trying to focus on the receptionist's moving, pink lips. *Why else would I have almost dropped in a dead faint when I found out he was missing — then fly all the way to Dallas?* The brunette seemed to be giving her instructions on where the rooms were. Jac absently nodded and accepted the keys. *All right,* she continued as she turned to walk back to the car, *I think I could fall in love with the man. He makes me laugh. He's refreshing to be with. He's independent to a fault and would let me be independent to a fault right along with him. He knows Jesus. Umm, . . . he seems to know Him better than I do. He might even help me with a few things in that department.*

Jacquelyn stopped just inside the glass door and observed Lawton, who was climbing out of the car. His denim shirttail had come out of his pleated shorts, and he looked like he could use a few weeks sitting at her grandmother's high-calorie table. The woman's meals were just as intense in fat as they were in taste. Lawton rested his left hand on the back of his head, flexed his neck, then yawned. Jacquelyn crammed her hands into her jeans pockets and curled her toes, ensconced in short-topped leather boots.

Okay. She forced herself to breathe steadily. *I might already be falling in love.* Jac thought of the bracelet she had returned only last night. With a sigh, she shook her head. *Was it only last night? So much has happened in less than 24 hours.*

If Jac were completely honest with herself, she would have to admit that she regretted releasing the platinum piece. The man had somehow managed to perfectly fit her taste. But even if she hadn't cared for the design, she still would have lamented parting with those stars — stars that forever reminded her of a poetic man who sat beneath a Mediterranean moon and began the process of snaring her heart.

What in the world am I going to do? She frowned.

As if Lawton sensed someone watching him, he stiffened and raised his head like a vulnerable deer in a wide-open field.

She walked through the doorway and extended the key toward his hand. "Here's your room key."

"Great!" he replied as she placed the plastic card into his hand.

"How much was the room?"

"This one's on me," Jac said, rounding the car. "You refused to let me pay for my plane ticket. Now it's my turn to be hardheaded." The two of them had had a battle of wills that Lawton won simply because the cost of the ticket was already on his credit card. This time, Jac's credit card gave her the triumphant edge.

She opened the car door and plopped inside.

Lawton slid into his seat. "You got that one right," he mumbled and snapped his door shut.

Jacquelyn rolled her eyes, closed her door, and cranked the engine. "You of all people should recognize hardheaded when you see it." She drove to the end of the parking lot and parked.

Amidst a never-ending tide of banter, the two unloaded the car then settled into their rooms. As soon as Jac deposited her cases on the bed, she prepared for the next step in her mission. According to the bits and pieces she had gleaned from the variety of reports regarding the Sellers' murders, Gary Sellers had a brother named Austin who also lived in Ouray. Jac shoved her laptop case across the bed and plopped onto the paisley comforter. She fished through her leather backpack, grabbed her cell phone, then pulled out the nightstand's top drawer. As usual, an area phone book awaited her perusal. Jac flopped the pages open and ran her index finger down the "S" list. She stopped at "Sellers, Rev. Austin." Just as she turned on her cell phone, the room's phone rang.

Jac jumped, then frowned and snatched up the receiver. "Lightfoot."

"So does my being blind bother you?" Lawton's voice erupted over the line.

"Excuse me?" Jac asked, even though she knew full well what he said.

"Blind. I'm blind. I cannot see. Does that bother you?"

"As in . . ."

"I mean — do you think I'm somehow less . . ."

"Less what? Valuable?"

"Yes."

"No. N-O," she spelled. "As in, the opposite of yes. As in no way. Not even remotely. Why should I?"

"Just double-checking, I guess," he hedged.

Jacquelyn eyed the brass lamp attached to the wall and squinted. *Why in the name of common sense are you calling with this question now?* "So, does it bother you?"

"As a matter of fact, yes it does. Sometimes I get really tired of it."

"Do you feel less valuable because of it?" Jac queried.

"Not now. I used to — in my younger years. But now, no, I can't say I feel less valuable. I *do* get frustrated, though."

"I'd have never guessed it," Jac said. "As a matter of fact, on the plane you more or less milked it for all it was worth."

"Oooo, so we're back to the flight attendant. What *did* she look like?"

"Really ugly. Big green teeth. Huge zits. Stringy hair. Not your type at all."

His warm chortle did something delicious

to the pit of her stomach, and Jac didn't even try to fight it this time. "Look," she said, forcing a businesslike edge to her voice that did nothing to curb the flow of fondness that gained volume with every hour. "I was about to call Austin Sellers, Gary's brother, like we planned, to see if he will talk to us. Was there another reason for this call?"

"Yes, actually. I called to see if you would think I was the wimp of the century if I cried off on our dinner date and asked you to bring something to my room. As badly as I want to get to the bottom of all this and talk with Austin Sellers, I'm beat. I've taken my pain medicine and my shoulder is feeling somewhat better, but I'm about to go into a coma here, ya know?" His polite yawn floated over the line. "My nap has officially worn off, and my wild weekend is catching up with me. Honestly, it's eating my lunch not to go with you — if Sellers agrees to talk — but I got to thinking that he might agree to meet me tomorrow, even if you do talk with him tonight."

"Oh, sure. No problemo," Jacquelyn said and blinked against her gritty eyes. Her airplane snooze had likewise faded into a distant memory. "Look, let me call Austin and see what he says. It might be that he would want to meet with both of us tomorrow anyway." The idea of waiting until morning burned a trail of impatience through Jac. "Then I'll run and get us some chicken sandwiches. If he'll talk to me tonight, I'll head out to his house after I've dropped off your food."

"Sounds like a deal to me. I'm really sorry about this. I feel like a complete weakling here, but —"

"Look," Jac said, "you were shot this weekend. It's a miracle that you've gotten this far. You aren't superhuman, you know."

"The shot was more in line with a serious graze."

"Yes. But then there was the concussion."

He sighed. "I know. I know. This is frustrating, that's all. I'm used to jumping up and running off in all directions any time I want to. There's one more thing I've been meaning to say," he added. "Thank you for dropping everything and coming to the hospital and then coming here. This means more than you can ever know."

"I'd have done it for anybody," she said.

"That's *not* what I wanted to hear," Lawton drawled, his voice full of the ardor of a smitten schoolboy.

Jacquelyn's cell phone pealed forth a shrill ring, and she looked at it as if it had sprouted horns. "My cell phone's ringing, believe it or not. Wonder who is after me now."

"Me. I'm after you," Lawton drawled as if he were eyeing a delectable gourmet dish.

Gaping, Jac gripped the receiver and watched her cell phone as it persisted in the ringing. His claim spun through her mind like a whirlwind in a Colorado blizzard. She possessed no means to respond to his outrageous declaration.

"Answer your cell, Jac," Lawton said with a laugh. Then the phone clicked in her ear.

Jac pushed the green button on her tiny phone, pressed the receiver to her ear, and gave out her customary greeting.

"Jac, it's Sammie."

"Hey, girlfriend," she said through an encouraging smile, "whaz-up?" Jac refused to allow the tense moments with Lawton to color her speech. Nonetheless, his bold proclamation still rocked her.

"I wanted to tell you that I've been on the phone with Marilyn."

"Oh, good." Jac stood and paced toward the disposable water cups sitting on the oak dresser. Water. She needed a long drink of water. And maybe a tranquilizer.

Jac snatched one of the cellophane-wrapped cups, and tried to tune in to what Sam was saying.

". . . was a great help. She really gave me a lot of support and encouragement. She also asked me to come stay with her and Josh for awhile. I really think I should, Jac. It will get me out of Dallas and give me time to think."

"Great plan." Jac stopped in front of the sink and grappled with unwrapping the cellophane from around the cup while holding the diminutive phone between ear and shoulder. "I think some time with Marilyn and Josh will do you good. Didn't she say something on the internet a few weeks ago about her and Josh both getting certified for family counseling?"

"Yes. They are working toward that together. Aside from all that, Marilyn has major personal experience with a difficult husband."

Jac snorted. "I think Adam is a notch or two above difficult, don't you?"

"Yes," Sammie heartily agreed. "I just meant that Marilyn has been in a troubled marriage. And, well, I really think some time with them will be a big help."

Jac freed the plastic cup from its wrapper, turned on the faucet, and placed the container in the stream of water. While Sam continued her chatting, Jacquelyn tried to shove Lawton's brazen words from her mind, but they refused to leave. And with the cadence of his claim as a backdrop, Jacquelyn remembered his telling her on the plane that he had written a new poem. As the cup of water overflowed, Jac wondered if the poem were especially for her. She set the drenched cup on the sink top and turned off the water.

"One other reason I called, Jac, is because I got an e-mail from Adam."

Sammie's words barged into Jac's mind like a roaring hurricane, effectively clearing all other thoughts in their path. She stopped in the middle of reaching for the cup.

"What?" Jac snapped.

"I got an e-mail from Adam," Sammie repeated in a barely audible voice.

"He's not supposed to be contacting you for any reason, Sam. That's the whole gist of a restraining order. He's supposed to stay away from you. No personal contact. No phone calls. No e-mail. No nothin'!"

"Yes, that's what I thought." The tremor in Sammie's voice suggested she'd pondered much, much more.

"What did it say? Did you keep it? Can you print it out? This is a violation of the law. They could pick him up for this."

"I deleted the message before I knew what I was doing, Jackie," Sam said.

"Can you retrieve it from your deleted folder? What did it say?" she repeated.

"My deleted folder empties out every time I exit the program," Sammie said on a sniffle. "Oh, Jac, what am I going to do? It said something like, 'I'm out of jail. Just thought you might like to know. Love, Adam.'"

Jac tottered back on her heels and pressed her fingertips against her forehead as Sam's precarious situation exploded to the forefront of her mind. While the restraining order was certainly something Adam *should* abide by, there were no guarantees that he would. Jac had learned from experience that if a man would violate his wife, he would also violate a court order. And too many battered women lay in their graves because their husbands chose not to live by the rules.

"Okay, listen to me, Sammie. I want you to pack and get to Marilyn's *now*. Tonight! Start out tonight. But don't — *do not go alone*. Do you understand?" Jac shut her eyes and clenched her free hand.

"I don't have a choice in that. R.J. said that he's following me to Marilyn's on his Harley, whether I agree or not." Sammie paused, sniffed, then huffed. "Thanks a lot for appointing him my guardian."

"I don't think my suggestion made any difference to him. Do you?" Jac leaned against the edge of the mirrored closet behind her.

Sam sighed. "No, probably not. I'm sorry I snapped at you."

"Don't give it another thought." Jac crossed her legs at the ankles, then rubbed her heavy eyes and denied the yawn creeping up her throat. "I understand. It's okay."

"Where are you now, anyway?" Sammie asked.

"We just checked into our rooms in Ouray. I was about to call Austin Sellers to see if he'll talk with me."

"Okay. I won't keep you. But, Jac, listen, thanks — thanks for everything. Y–you saved my — my life." Sammie's voice broke.

"Hey, that's what friends are for, right?" Jac whispered and dashed at a tear seeping from the corner of her eye.

"Yes, but I'll never be able to repay you," Sam continued in watery regard.

"You just take care of yourself," Jacquelyn softly challenged. "And take care of Brett, too. You hear?"

"Yes, I will. Keep us in your prayers."

"You're there, girlfriend. Oh, and Sam?"

"Yes."

"Call me when you leave." Jac checked her watch. "It's nearly seven here."

"It's almost eight here. It might be ten before we pull out. We'll also have to get hotel rooms on the way and start out again in the morning. Brett's only three, and I'm exhausted."

"Good idea. Make sure R.J.'s room is next to yours. *Be careful!*"

"We will."

"And one other thing — make sure you call me when you get there."

"Of course."

After the usual adieus the two hung up. Jac gulped her water, then walked toward the phone book laying on the bed. As she repeated the task of spotting the designated number, Lawton's claim squirmed back into the folds of her jumbled thoughts: *I'm after you.* His blatant statement did nothing more than put words to his actions, but the words shimmered with a magical aura that hinted of ecru satin and soft music.

"Get out of here," she charged as if the

thought were from another person. "I've got business to take care of. Leave me alone."

She punched Austin Sellers' number into her cell phone and waited for him to answer.

Fifteen

~

At first Austin Sellers hesitated about talking with Jac. But when she stressed that she was a private eye and mentioned Lawton's contact with the probable killers, he agreed to speak with her in person. As soon as Jac got directions to his home, she went out and grabbed a couple of grilled chicken burgers. She left Lawton's dinner with the receptionist, who graciously agreed to take the meal to his room. *That way,* Jac thought, *I won't get sidetracked and flustered.* Facing Lawton after his bold proclamation would have thrown her into a tailspin. Jac determined that she needed to keep her wits if she was going to glean facts regarding this case. An encounter with Lawton might annihilate her concentration.

Focusing on the task at hand, Jac devoured her chicken sandwich on the way to Austin's home. She sipped the final traces of her large water and pulled the rental car into the driveway of a quaint, rock home. The parsonage was nestled next to a country church, replete with stained glass windows and a white steeple. With the backdrop of the mountains, the whole setup looked like a photo on a Swiss postcard. Jacquelyn vaguely remembered hearing somewhere that Ouray had been dubbed the "Switzerland of America."

Putting the vehicle into park, she turned off the engine and got out. The evening shadows, now long and hinting at sooty night, smudged the surrounding evergreens in strokes of gloom. The twittering of birds sailing overhead became a dirge. Foreboding cloaked Jac and the hair on the back of her neck prickled. As Lawton had snapped to alertness when she was watching him at the hotel, so Jac stiffened and peered over one shoulder then the other. Even though her perusal proved fruitless, the sensation of being watched never abated.

With renewed resolve, Jac snapped shut the car door and strode across the lawn. She halted outside the home's front door and pressed the doorbell that was stationed on gray trim. The inner knob immediately rattled, and the door swung open. A tall man with dark hair and a prominent, straight nose solemnly observed her through the glassed-in storm door. His rumpled oxford shirt and slacks looked to have been starched and pressed at some point. His eyes, the color of an indigo sky just after sunset, appeared suspiciously red.

"Jacquelyn Lightfoot?" he queried.

"Yes." She held up her ID and gave him several seconds to observe it. After he nodded, she dropped the wallet into her diminutive handbag. "You're Austin Sellers?"

The man nodded again and opened the outer door. "For some reason, your name rang a bell, and now I'm thinking you look familiar."

Jacquelyn stepped into the living room that was filled with the aroma of freshly baked cookies. "A few years back I stumbled into a major drug ring. I was looking for a missing person and wound up uncovering a big Cuban operation — replete with organized crime connections. The national press decided to make me into some kind of hero, I guess." She shrugged. "Really, the whole thing was an accident."

"I remember now," Austin said. "You were featured on national news."

"Guilty as charged," Jac said with a wry smile. "You know how those things go. Somebody in the media needs to get a life and decides to make a huge story out of someone who is just an ordinary —"

Austin held up his hand. "That *was* a huge story, Lady," he said. "Everybody talked about it for weeks."

Jacquelyn eyed the toes of her boots peeking from beneath her jeans. "Well, enough about me," she said.

"Actually, there were some things I didn't want to discuss with you on the phone," he responded before Jac had a chance to utter another word. "But I've decided to go ahead and tell you some recent discoveries." He led the way through the living room. The scatter of toys, an overflowing laundry basket, and mud-splattered canvass shoes hinted at the presence of children. The silence, broken only by the faint hum of a refrigerator, suggested that Austin was alone. He plopped onto the striped sofa and stared at a small leather bag atop a pine coffee table.

Jac paused by the table and scrutinized the bag. In the middle of it lay seven burnished silver coins that glistened in the lamp light.

"Gary and I found 14 of these in Mom's attic a month ago." Austin picked up one of the coins and extended it toward Jac, then waved her toward the cushion next to him.

She accepted the coin, joined him on the couch, held up the piece, and examined it. The peculiar looking coin, about the size of a quarter, was not perfectly round. A carving of a woman wearing a helmet was on one side and an owl on the other.

"When we asked Mom about them, she said they were passed down in the family, and we were next to receive them. At the time I thought it was strange she hadn't given them to us before now."

Jac rubbed her thumb across the cool coin and narrowed her eyes. The piece gradually warmed with her body heat as if it possessed a life of its own. "You are implying?"

"I think Gary and Rhonda's murders were somehow linked to these coins." Austin's words, thick with emotion, hung between them.

"Why do you think that?" Jacquelyn asked and scooped up the remaining six coins. One by one she began examining them.

"I didn't until this afternoon." Austin leaned forward, placed knees on elbows, and rested his head in his hands. His lean fingers dug into his springy hair as he continued. "Before you called, my mother and I had just finished a long discussion. She's beside herself. It would appear that my whole life has been based on a lie."

"Really?" Jac asked as she determined that all the coins were identical.

"She's here now," Austin listlessly continued. "She took a tranquilizer and went to bed. She has a bad heart, and we're all concerned about her."

"I see."

"Gary and I were twins. Did you know?"

"No, I didn't." Jac shifted in her seat as the surreal aura that surrounded the parsonage reached its fog-like fingers into the living room.

"I haven't known where to turn," Austin said, raising his head from his hands. "My wife just took the kids to McDonald's because I needed some time alone. She's so wonderful to know when to give me some space. I don't know how we're going to manage all these kids. The last few days have been like a zoo."

Jacquelyn blinked as she tried to piece

together the bits and pieces of unrelated information.

"We have four now. Our two, then Gary's — Gary's two." His voice caught, and he bit his lip. "The funerals were only yesterday."

Austin stood and paced toward the rock fireplace. He picked up a pair of glasses from the rustic mantel and slipped them on. The addition of the black frames lent him a scholarly, sensitive appeal, and Jacquelyn suspected that the man was using mammoth control on his emotions. He walked toward the patio door, surrounded by potted plants replete with sympathy decor. His back to Jac, he slipped his hands into his pockets and stared upon the never-ending stretch of mountains. His long shirttail sagged outside his beltline, and he hung his head.

"On the phone you said that you were investigating the case. My first response was to tell you to get lost. We've been covered by police and reporters, and I've never been so sick of publicity and questions in my life. It's bad enough to have this happen without — without —"

"I understand," Jacquelyn said.

"But then you said your friend was shot by the same people, and I don't know. . . .

I just had this gut feeling that I should talk to you." He pivoted and faced her. "Actually, it's more than a gut feeling. I've been praying since we talked, and I have peace about telling you some of this."

Jac observed a taper candle sitting on the edge of the cluttered coffee table. The fervid certainty in the minister's eyes was something she had seen in Marilyn's eyes . . . and even in Kim Lan's. They usually got that look when they were positive they had received an answer to prayer.

"Have you told anyone else about the coins . . . about your supposition?" Jacquelyn hoped that Austin would fill in some of the gaping holes in her present battery of information.

"No. No one. I didn't even suspect they were related until after my mother and I talked." He paced back to the couch and settled on the end. "That was about two hours ago."

"And?" Jac prompted.

Austin released a heavy sigh. "My mother and father adopted Gary and me — sort of — and they never told us. Today my mother broke down and told me the whole story. And it's a real doozy." Austin shook his head. "If all this weren't happening to me, I'm not sure I'd believe it."

"Try me," Jac prompted, her heavy eyes reminding her of her exhaustion. "In my business, I encounter all sorts of farfetched scenarios."

"Well, according to Mom, her old college friend, Amanda Hasgrove, came to her 35 years ago and begged her to take Gary and me. We were only three months old at the time. Mom said she hadn't seen Amanda in about a year when this happened. The two of them were really close, but they drifted apart after college when Mom got married. Anyway, when Amanda came to Mom, she was scared — really, really scared. She said that if Mom didn't agree to taking custody of Gary and me that she was afraid we would be killed. Amanda was terrified for her own life as well and thought that, even if she was killed, we wouldn't be if she placed us with Mom."

Austin removed his glasses and rubbed his eyes. "I can't believe all this," he mumbled.

"You're doing remarkably well," Jac said, "considering all you've been through." She turned toward him, propped her knee on the cushion then began methodically pinching the inside seam of her jeans.

"Have you ever had a time in your life

when you felt like everything you held dear had been ripped right out from under you?" Austin stared straight ahead as if he were talking to an unseen person.

Jacquelyn blinked. "Yes I have," she said while her mind wandered back to the spring when she had realized that something exceptionally horrid festered beneath the surface of her childhood memories. And she still had yet to gain her equilibrium. Next, Jac thought of Sammie's awful predicament. "Life certainly has a way of throwing curve balls."

"That's an understatement. Sometimes it's like you're hit smack in the teeth with a boulder."

"Been there; done that." Jac nodded.

Austin peered right into her soul then narrowed his eyes in speculation. "Do you believe in God, Jac?"

"Yes," she stated simply.

"Do you *know* Him?"

"I know Jesus as my Savior, if that's where this is heading," she replied then stared out the patio window. The shadows gradually claimed the countryside, and the end table lamps burned brighter than the remaining sunlight.

"I suspected so." Austin removed his

glasses and inserted an earpiece between his teeth. He stared across the room.

But I'm not as close to Him as I should be. The thought sprang upon Jac, and she stopped herself before it left her lips. Several of her six sisters certainly increased Jac's awareness of this issue every time she saw them. And the more time she spent with Lawton, the more Jac believed that he possessed a spiritual depth she had yet to plumb. Lawton didn't wear his religion on his sleeve, but during the time she had known him he occasionally spoke of the Lord as if they were the dearest of friends. Jacquelyn began to wonder if perhaps, in her attempts to shut others out, she had also distanced herself from the one person who could heal her wounded heart — Jesus.

"Anyway," Austin continued, "Mom naturally didn't want to agree to take us because she was suspicious of the whole situation. But Amanda was so urgent and frightened —"

"Why?"

"Mom said she was running from her husband — that would be my biological father, I guess."

Sam's predicament flooded Jac's mind. She groaned and covered her eyes. Silence permeated the room, and she sensed Austin's scrutiny.

Shaking her head, she returned his appraisal. "I have a friend doing the exact same thing right now. We filed charges against her husband last night for domestic violence. He's already posted bail and has broken the terms of his restraining order by e-mailing her."

"What in the world is being done for these women," Austin said as if he were swallowing bitter bile. "It just makes me sick!"

"Yes, and the fun part is that Sammie told me that their pastor has taken her husband's side. Her husband convinced their pastor that Sammie is trying to cause trouble in their marriage and is essentially crazy. The pastor diagnosed the whole problem and told Sammie she wasn't submissive enough."

"Oh, now that just makes about as much sense as a three-headed camel." Austin raised his hand. "Just submit a little more so your husband can beat you to death. Is that it?"

"You know, I like you," Jac said with a half smile. "I told Sammie almost the exact same thing."

Austin slumped back into the couch. He

rested his head against the back and closed his eyes. "I'm sick to death of people using the Bible to validate their sin."

"Okay, I *really* like you," Jac said. "Wanta come pastor in Denver?"

"Do you not care for your pastor?"

"I don't know. We got a new one a few months ago. I . . . haven't been to church in awhile."

Austin shot her a glance out of the corner of his eyes. Jac held her breath and awaited the inevitable condemnation, yet none came.

"Maybe you could commute here," he said with a chuckle.

"Maybe."

He closed his eyes again, breathed deeply, and exhaled on a huff.

"Where was I?"

"Let's see . . ." Jac observed the ceiling fan, lazily spinning overhead. "Amanda was running from her husband and trying to get your Mom to take you and Gary for keeps."

"Yes — yes — okay. Anyway, Amanda presented Mom with a notarized statement, saying that she gave Mom all custody rights. She also gave her our birth certificates. Mom took the paperwork and did agree to keep us for a few days. But she made Amanda promise to come back. Mom's straight, Jac. She hates duplicity of any form."

"Believe me, so do I," Jac asserted and tucked a wayward strand of hair behind her ear.

"But that was the last time Mom saw Amanda. She said that it was several days before she noticed the two leather pouches in the bottom of our diaper bags." He leaned forward and lifted the edge of the pouch that was laying on the coffee table. And when a few more days rocked by and Amanda didn't show, Mom was planning to report the whole thing to the police. She and my father were getting ready to move from New Jersey to Ouray because Dad had just accepted a teaching position here, and they didn't want to be part of anything illegal."

"What changed their minds?"

"Amanda was found." He placed his head in his hands once more.

"Dead?" Jacquelyn prompted.

"Yes." The whispered affirmation was so faint that Jac barely heard him.

Her throat tight, she stopped herself from whipping out her cell phone and making Sammie doubly promise that R.J.

was indeed following her to Arkansas.

"It was plastered all over the local TV, of course. By this time Mom and Dad were scared stiff. They didn't know what Amanda had gotten mixed up in, but they knew it was serious. Mom said she couldn't stand the thought of turning over two defenseless babies to the state. She was afraid they'd just give us to our father, whom she suspected was a murderer, whether it was ever proven or not. Needless to say, she was scared for our safety. And Amanda's frightened eyes kept haunting her. Amanda had wanted Mom to have her children — Gary and me — and Mom said she couldn't betray a dead woman's wishes. Mom and Dad couldn't have children, and they had prayed so long and so hard for children . . ."

Austin gulped and flopped back against the sofa. "Mom said they just decided to bundle us up and move to Ouray. Somehow, they managed to acquire some new birth certificates, and —"

"Do you think they were legally obtained?"

"I have no earthly idea!" Austin exploded. He raised his hand and flopped it against the couch's arm. "I've used it all these years for whatever I needed without a hitch!"

Shaking her head, Jac refocused on the coins. She hated to push the birth certificate issue, and there was really no need. Austin had endured a tragic loss and shock regarding his parents. The last thing he needed was her speculation that the birth certificates were most likely less than lawful. His faith in reality was shaken enough without her suggesting that his parents had stooped to such deception.

"And to think last week I was living a simple life in simple small town America," Austin mused. "What a hideous week."

"So," Jacquelyn picked up another coin, "why do you think these coins are linked to your brother's death?"

"Because Gary started running a check last week about their value."

"Define what you mean by 'running a check.'" A floppy-eared Basset Hound trotted up the hallway, settled at Austin's feet, and dropped his head on his front paws. His eyes rolled up as if he were begging for the slightest sign of affection.

"Gary's dog," Austin said. "The poor guy howled almost all night two nights ago. I might join him tonight." Austin bent to scratch the hound's ears. "By 'running a check,' I mean he placed a dozen or so calls to some antique coin dealers."

"And that's it?" Jacquelyn ran her thumb across the surface of the untarnished coin one last time then dropped it back into the pile with the faint ting of silver on silver.

Austin pulled away from the dog and propped his feet on the coffee table. "Yes. One dealer even put us in contact with a man who offered a quarter of a million for all 14."

"No way," Jac said.

"Here's what we thought — if somebody was willing to offer that kind of money fast, then perhaps we should do more research. Gary told the man we'd do some more checking. The man pushed to the point that Gary finally just turned him down. That was Thursday morning. Gary and Rhonda were killed Friday evening."

"Do you have that man's name? Where are Gary's coins now?"

"I don't have the man's name. It might be in Gary's records. And, presently, I don't know where Gary's coins are," Austin said. "I was thinking of going over to his house when you called. I haven't been over there since — since I found . . ." He pressed his knuckles against his mouth and turned his head from her.

"You're the one who found them?"

"Yes." His voice broke, and he choked on a sob. Austin rose, dashed toward the wide-open kitchen and began pacing. Several more wails burst from him, and the hound joined in. Just about the time Jacquelyn thought she was going to break down and cry with them, Austin got himself under control.

Standing, Jac decided that the time for her departure had arrived. She had uncovered more than she ever imagined on her first interview. Lawton wanted to meet Austin. If the minister agreed, she would bring Lawton in the morning, and they could decide which direction to go.

Austin sponged his eyes with a paper towel and paced across the open threshold from kitchen to living room. "I'm sorry," he said. "It just hits me at the oddest times, and I don't seem to have any control."

"Don't worry. I understand. Really. I did the same thing when my grandfather died a few years back. Grief is weird. That's all there is to it." She retrieved her tiny handbag and placed the strap over her shoulder. "Listen, I'm going to go now, but may I bring my friend back some time in the morning? He's the one I told you about on the phone — the one who was shot."

"Oh, good. I want to meet him. I'll be around all morning." He finished mopping at his face and replaced his glasses. "The church has been so gracious. They are giving me a month off. I need it," he finished with a sigh.

"Of course you do." Jacquelyn extended her hand and gently squeezed his forearm.

He patted her hand and smiled. "Thanks. You are a godsend. Really."

She shrugged. "I haven't done anything yet."

"Well, you let me talk." He scrutinized the coins, still on the pouch, and narrowed his eyes. "Maybe we can all go to Gary's house tomorrow morning and see if we can find his coins."

"That would be fine. Let's plan on it. The house is tightly locked, right?" Jac questioned.

"Right. I made sure of it. I checked the locks on Gary's house about three times. I don't even know why I did. There's nobody there." Austin bit his lips.

"Look," Jac asserted. "I have an idea. Do you have a copy machine or an instant camera?"

He raised his dark eyebrows in silent query.

"I brought my laptop with me. I'd like to do some searching on the internet sometime between tonight and in the morning. If I had some sort of picture or copy of the coin, it would help."

"Oh, sure." He stepped toward the coffee table, and the Basset Hound flopped his tail. "Just take a coin with you."

"No!" Jacquelyn pressed her lips together and held up her hands, palms out. "I *absolutely* refuse. Sounds to me like these things are worth a mint, and I don't want to be responsible for even one of them. As hectic as my life has been the last couple of days . . ." Jac paused for a yawn, "I just might accidentally get the thing mixed in with my change and leave it for a tip or something equally stupid."

"Okay. That will sit better with Tara — my wife — anyway. She's always telling me I'm too trusting." He smirked.

Jac nodded. "Maybe she's right."

"Oh! That's not to say that *you're* not trustworthy, it's just that —"

She held up her hands again. "I understand. And your wife is right. You need to hang on to those coins."

"Look, I have an instant camera in my bedroom."

"That works," Jac said with a nod and a

smile. "I'm no expert," she added as an afterthought. "But I did go to Greece last spring. If I'm not badly mistaken, I'd say that the woman on the coin resembles the Greek goddess of wisdom — Athena. She was the patron goddess of Athens according to Greek mythology. It would make perfect sense that she was the one on the coin because the owl is supposed to be her symbol." Jac shrugged and smiled. "Our tour guide said that's the reason why owls are traditionally considered wise."

"You know," Austin said, "Gary *did* mention last Thursday afternoon that these were called Athena owl coins. He had found out that much."

"So I guess I'm right then!" Jacquelyn rocked back on her heels. "That was kinda cool," she said with a triumphant grin.

A companionable smile brightened Austin's face, yet the dark circles under his eyes served as a steady reminder that all was not well.

"I'll be right back," he said as he turned toward the back of the home.

Shortly, he returned with the camera, took a few shots, then handed Jac the photos.

As the pictures touched her fingers, Jac scrutinized the silver images, small and yet so intriguing.

Sixteen

⌇

Maurice plastered himself against the side of
the massive log home. The argent moon,
blurred in the atmospheric mist, peeked
from behind long stretches of gauzy clouds.
The brisk breeze off the San Juan Mountains lifted the hair at Maurice's neckline
and cooled the sweat forming along his
collar. He ripped off the ebony jacket and
tied it around his waist. The heat of deception far outweighed the chill of nature. He
hated going back into the Sellers' home.
Even the sight of the massive house, nestled
next to the dramatic mountains, immersed
Maurice in more dread than he wanted to
wade through. But the coins had to be inside
this home. They had to be.

Maurice listened and waited, making
sure no one had followed. He had struck

out from the hotel on foot so that his rental car remained at the hotel, a little more than a mile away. So far, he had not perceived anyone tracking him, but he knew that Fuat probably had placed a tracer on him. Maurice wasn't stupid enough to think he could dodge the boss for long. His need for haste increased. He held his breath and listened. The distant rush of a river wove a rhythmic cadence among the swish of wind through symmetrical evergreens. An owl's forlorn hooting brought to mind the Greek goddess whose image claimed the coins.

"Athena, my patron goddess," Maurice whispered.

A path of renewed greed blazed through his soul. Maurice stepped toward the imposing back porch. The mild crunching of his canvass shoes barely registered upon the night. He crept up the wooden steps and paused outside the back door. The porch's roof obliterated even the tiniest sliver of light. Maurice fumbled for the jacket's pocket, now hanging near his knee. He unzipped the pocket, retrieved a pair of thin cotton gloves, and put them on. Next he pulled out a penlight and a razor-thin lock pick.

He tugged on the screen door; it opened

with ease. Maurice flipped on the penlight, inserted it between his teeth, and bent to pick the lock that had given him no problem mere nights ago. Before wielding the pick, he twisted the knob, frigid from the night. This time the knob turned without resistance. He wasted no time stepping into the shadows of the game room and closing the door in his wake. The smell of new carpet once again greeted him. He waved the light's beam around the room and regained his bearings. The oversized room sported an array of exercise equipment and even a child's indoor play facility.

Maurice had searched this room after his dark deed. He had also scoured the living room, dining room, and kitchen. He had been on his way to the bedrooms when he'd spotted the children, the two little girls asleep together in a brass bed. As if an invisible wall had erected itself in the center of that hallway, Maurice had stopped outside that room and couldn't take another step. Images of his own children bore upon him. A sight that swirled him into the land of what might have been. Most of the people Maurice had killed were so depraved that he had considered their deaths a favor to society. But Gary and Rhonda Sellers were innocent. So were their children. Abhorred by his own corruption, Maurice had run from the house and returned to Dallas empty handed. Even though he never told Fuat the whole story behind his failure, he sensed that the boss knew.

Maurice tried to expunge that night from his mind. *Will I ever forget that heinous crime?* His fingers curled into his palm, and he forced himself to momentarily shove aside the mental specters. *If I can just find the coins and get out of the U.S. it will all be okay,* he encouraged himself. He stepped toward the long hallway that led toward the bedrooms. *If I find the coins tonight, tomorrow I can book the next flight to L.A. From L.A. I'll fly to Hong Kong. From Hong Kong to Bangkok. Once in Bangkok, I'll contact the Swiss buyer. I'll make the sell — quick and simple. Then, I'll be set for life.* The recitation of his potential plans fueled his steps, and Maurice found himself on the threshold of an office located next to the children's room.

Holding his breath, he stepped inside and flashed the penlight across the room. A computer resided next to an expansive desk, behind which sat a button-tucked leather chair. Bookcases, in dark, rich wood, lined three of the office walls. The peaceful room was appealing and inviting. The chirping of crickets accompanied him as his shoes sank into thick carpeting. He approached the desk and lowered himself into the chair. After pulling out the center drawer, he flicked the light across the expected office paraphernalia: paper clips and staples, pens, erasers, tape, and pencils. Maurice laid aside the light and tugged on the drawer until it squeaked then was free of the cavity. He deposited the drawer atop the desk then slid from the chair to his knees. When he grabbed the penlight and prepared to direct the beam into the cavity a hand descended upon his shoulder. A hard hand. A hand that broached no compromise. The hand of a killer.

Maurice stiffened and stopped breathing. His heart pounded out hard, even beats in his temples. He recalled the back door, unlocked, and cursed himself for his lack of suspicion. A thousand possibilities flashed through his mind, none of them pleasant. Only one recourse remained. In a flash he stood, pivoted, and directed the light toward the invader.

"Looking for these?" Fuat asked, and held up a leather pouch. With a wicked grin, he shook the tiny bag, and the clink-clink of coins mocked Maurice. When Fuat reached toward his waistband, the flash of a weapon in moonlight promised more than mere ridicule.

Swallowing against a throat dry and tight, Maurice eyed the snub nosed .357 and stepped back, only to bump into the computer and stop.

Fuat's dark hair, swept away from a weathered face, reminded Maurice of Count Dracula. All Fuat needed was a defined widow's peak, the fangs, and the high-collared cape. He already possessed the sharp nose, heavy brows, and eyes of evil.

A chill dripped into Maurice's blood like the water running down an icicle, yet a burst of warmth coated his torso in a fine film of sweat.

"Did you honestly think you would get away from me?" Fuat asked, his voice as smooth as the hiss of a cunning cobra.

Maurice stepped to the side and edged around the end of the computer table.

"I suggest you stop," Fuat snarled. "And please tell me why you were such an imbecile that you couldn't find a simple leather pouch in a desk drawer?" He wadded the pouch and shoved it into his jacket pocket.

"You didn't even look, did you? You came in here and killed my son and his wife then, for some reason, you chickened out."

"Your son?" Maurice rasped.

"Yes." Fuat's right brow arched.

"But — but you t–told me to get the coins, no matter what, even if I had to kill the owners. How could you —"

"Gary Sellers carried my genes, not my name. My first wife, may she rest in peace," he jeered, "took the boys and the coins and, the best I can figure, just gave them away. That was over 35 years ago. I haven't been able to find them since," he said, as if he were talking about a pair of misplaced work shoes. "Until now. Only problem is, there's only seven here. Now, where's the other seven?"

Shaking his head, Maurice's lips curled away from his teeth. "You ordered the slaying of your own flesh and blood? You are despicable," he ground out while memories of his own kids tore at his soul.

"Well, now, isn't that an interesting accusation, considering you are the one who killed them. Where are the other seven coins?"

"I hate you," Maurice growled. "I hate what you've done to me. I hate everything about this operation!"

"Exactly." Fuat clicked back the revolver's hammer. "You have without doubt lost every degree of usefulness you ever had. I've seen the signs too many times. Your type is good to be used until you can't stand anymore, then you're of no worth and have to be disposed of. Now, do you know where the other coins are or don't you?"

"I have no idea," Maurice snarled. His torso stiffened, and he relived every murder he had ever committed. Each crime had been so easily orchestrated it was ridiculous. His death would be no exception. In desperation, Maurice determined that he could stand there and be shot like a buck in crosshairs, or he could do something to defend himself. He had nothing to lose.

Without another thought, he hurled himself at Fuat's feet. The elder man grunted as he crashed into the bookcase then flopped onto the floor. Maurice's elbow ground into the carpet, and Fuat's shoe bulged against his gut. With a whoosh and a stab of pain, air exploded from Maurice, and he paused in a second of deathly silence to regain his breath. He rolled to his side, scrambled to his knees, and fully expected to take the man on fist to fist. Yet the expected stream of expletives did not occur. Neither did the anticipated scurry for power. Instead, Fuat lay motionless in the shadows, his eyes closed, his arm limply lying at his side.

A shimmer started in Maurice's midsection and radiated out to his limbs. He placed hands on thighs and heaved for breath. Then he pivoted, spotted his flashlight near the computer, snatched it up, and pointed the beam at Fuat. A trickle of blood oozed from his temple, and Maurice felt as if he had been given a reprieve. Never did he expect to overtake one of the most powerful men in the underworld. He skimmed the narrow beam across the champagne-colored carpet until it crawled upon the revolver, several feet away. Wasting no time, Maurice dug into Fuat's pocket and retrieved the leather pouch. He picked up the cocked revolver, aimed it at the boss's head, and stopped. Child-sized apparitions danced into his soul. His children. The Sellers' children. Perhaps some of the sorry no-goods he had exterminated through the years even had children. Children as innocent as his own. The ghostly chants that erupted in his mind rang forth in glee, but glee turned to terror; terror to misery.

Maurice began to pant. The gun shook in his hands. His knees felt as if they would collapse beneath him. A faint groan escaped Fuat. Maurice maneuvered the hammer back into the safety position then stepped toward the door.

"The other seven aren't upstairs, Bo—," a deep voice stopped midsentence as a shadowed figure stepped into the room. In the stunned second that followed, Fuat's hand clasped Maurice's ankle, and jerked his foot from under him. A hard blow to his temple obliterated all but darkness.

Seventeen

The next morning, Lawton fumbled with the latch on the balcony door then shoved open the glass. The blast of fresh mountain air prompted a deep breath and a satisfied exhale. Lawton had slept hard; he slept long. His shoulder felt a thousand times better. So did he. This was going to be a good day. He just knew it. Lawton stepped back to the circular desk and grabbed the Styrofoam cup full of scorching black coffee. He scooped up his Braille Bible, laying near the cup, then stepped through the balcony door and closed it behind him. Yesterday evening he had explored enough to discover that a small table with two chairs resided out here. Lawton paced exactly three steps then felt in front of him. The iron table's lattice design met his sensitive fingers. He deposited the

Bible on the table, took two small steps to his right, and settled into the cold chair. As he sat down, his walking shorts rose up his thighs and the metal's damp chill pierced his skin with icy tingles.

Ah, the mountains in August, he thought. *I'd be melting by noon if I were still in Dallas or Oklahoma City.* He pushed the tiny button on his watch, and a rigid voice announced, "Seven-thirty a.m." Lawton turned his face toward the east and soaked up the warmth of the morning sun.

Before he began his prayer time, Lawton's mind turned to Jacquelyn. He would have given ten years of his life to see the look on her face when he had point blank told her he was after her. Surely by now she knew, yet Lawton had never once stated his intentions. He had only allowed her to pick up on the cues. Of course, Mel's blurting that Lawton was halfway in love with Jac didn't exactly resound with subtlety either. *Ah well, it's best she knows for sure,* Lawton thought. *Might as well get everything out in the open and move forward.* He had known from the start that they possessed a certain chemistry and that Jacquelyn liked him — even when they were in Rome and she was stubbornly telling him to get lost. But there was that awful thing between them — whatever it was that she couldn't seem to get around. *Well, whatever her past holds, I'm sure we can overcome it together.* He began listing possibilities, deliberately veering away from any sexual issues.

A breeze burst upon the balcony and danced around him like a fairy, ushering in memories of the last few days. As Lawton contemplated the origins of Jac's problems, he couldn't stop the persistent memory of the conversation he and Kinkaide shared during his hospital stay.

"She wasn't a prostitute or anything was she?" he had asked, voicing the worst scenario his imagination could conjure.

"No," Kinkaide said as if Lawton had just voiced the most ridiculous scenario possible. "I will tell you that it isn't that. But . . ." Kinkaide had hesitated. "Would that matter to you now? I mean, if she had —"

"Can't really say," Lawton had replied. "You know I've always said that I wanted a woman who had, well, lived by the standards I've lived by."

"That's honorable and right, and I'm glad Mel did," Kinkaide said. "But as you know, due to my own stroll down Asinine Avenue, I can't claim the same. Now, what kind of fix would I be in if Mel weren't willing to forgive me for my past?"

The memory of Kinkaide's hedging about sexual issues took on implications that Lawton, in his wounded state, had originally missed. During that disturbing dream on the plane, Jacquelyn had been overtaken with some fear regarding her grandfather. As predicted she had then distanced herself from him in a manner that loudly said, "No trespassing."

Maybe she was a victim of some corrupt man's lust. The supposition sprang upon him once more. When he told Jac to "get over it" her outraged reaction validated the possibility.

The pieces of this mysterious puzzle began to plop into place in a manner that left him ready to pummel the face of an unknown degenerate. *Wait a minute,* he cautioned himself as he had yesterday on the plane. A long sip of hot coffee helped steady his reeling thoughts. *I don't need to jump to conclusions.* But Lawton wasn't so certain that his hesitancy about the growing evidence sprang from a pure motive.

He had always dreamed his wife would have adhered to the same biblical constraints he had. Lawton was just like any other man. He had occasionally daydreamed about that first matrimonial night. And in all his conjecturing, he and his fantasy bride would pledge to one another that they had shared that secret ecstasy with no one else. When Lawton met Jacquelyn all those months ago, he had never questioned her purity. After all, she was a good friend of Mel's and, according to Mel, she was indeed a Christian. Therefore, Lawton had naturally projected Melissa's standards upon Jac. Kinkaide had implied on more than one occasion that his respect for Mel extended to her decision to remain sexually pure until marriage. Lawton assumed he should heap the same honor upon Jac.

But what if she didn't have a choice? The haunting question stabbed his soul, and Lawton ran his fingers across the Bible's textured cover. A crow's caw echoed from the distance like a rhythmic underscore of his thoughts. The hypothesis both infuriated him for Jac and simultaneously presented a whole new set of complications. A fresh realization, unexpected and disconcerting, sprang upon Lawton. If he continued to pursue Jacquelyn he just might have to give up his fantasy bride.

"Morning," Jac's husky greeting burst into his thoughts, and Lawton jumped. The hot coffee sloshed onto his hand and he bit back an exclamation.

"Sorry. Did I scare you?" The sound of a chair scooting against wood on the next balcony accompanied her question.

"A little." Lawton set his coffee on the table and stood. Her voice's enchanting rhythm floated across the morning and filtered into his spirit like honey from heaven. All his misgivings about his fantasy bride dissolved in the face of his growing fascination for Jacquelyn Lightfoot. Whatever her past, Lawton pursed his lips and decided they would work through it together — if only she would give him the chance.

"How long have you been there?" he asked and stepped toward her balcony.

"I've been out here about an hour." Jac's footsteps stopped near the edge of Lawton's balcony.

"Why didn't you say something before now?" Lawton neared the rail and estimated that she was only about a foot away.

"Oh, I don't know," she hedged. "You know, just one of those woman things, I guess."

"You were watching me, weren't you?" Lawton teased with melodramatic flair. "Like big brother — or, I guess, that would be big sister."

As she chuckled, Lawton's fingers trailed along the top of the metal barrier, and he remembered that he hadn't put on his dark glasses. Early in his youth, Lawton had forced Kinkaide to be brutally honest about the appearance of his eyes. Kinkaide had suggested that Lawton wear dark glasses, and he had readily agreed. Lawton wondered if his uncovered eyes bothered Jac, then he remembered she had seen him in the hospital without them. During that visit she hadn't seemed the least bit fazed by his unattractive eyes. But then again, she had returned the bracelet and they had both been overwrought. This morning, she was rested, more relaxed, and undoubtedly possessed the presence of mind to either be repulsed or decide she didn't care.

"I forgot to put on my glasses," he said with a faint grimace.

"So?" she quipped. "I don't have on my shoes, either."

"Do you have ugly toes?"

"I don't have the slightest idea. What constitutes ugly toes anyway? I've never seen a set that I just fainted over because they were so gorgeous or anything."

Lawton threw back his head and laughed out loud. "I love it!"

"Oh, you say that about everything I say," Jac said, and the swish of fabric suggested she was shifting positions.

"Maybe it's because I love everything you say," Lawton said before he realized the words popped out. The resulting silence, awkward and stretched, resonated with his recent claim that he was indeed after her. The air between them, tinged with the smell of her floral talc, crackled with an electric chemistry that tilted the balcony.

Lawton imagined Jac's lips upon his. The impulse to kiss her pressed upon him more severely than ever before. He had thought of kissing her on more than one occasion, but the desire had always been overshadowed by a heavy dose of constraint. This morning the constraint was wearing thin — extremely thin. He placed his elbow on the rail and shifted his weight. The action inadvertently resulted in his hands brushing hers.

Lawton paused and debated whether to take his chances on a kiss or make light of the moment. After a split second, he decided not to push his luck. Instead, he tapped the backs of her fingers and said, "So, how 'bout them Red Sox?"

She pulled away and her laugh, mellow and throaty, seemed to wrap him in a warm embrace that promised more than Lawton could ever hope. "You're a nut, Lawton Franklin," she said, *a hopeless nut.*

"Oh?" He paused and held his breath. "And how much do you like nuts, Jac?"

The words swirled between them like a tornado tangled in electric lines. The resulting impact almost took Lawton to his knees, and he forced himself to deny the craving to press his lips against hers.

Her retreating steps validated his choice. "I've got my laptop out here," she said, her voice firm. "I was able to stretch the phone to near the door then stretch my computer line from the door to the table. I'm on the internet right now. I've been reading about Athena Owl coins."

Lawton's legs stiffened. His teeth clenched. His fingers curled around the handrail. *Don't do this!* he wanted to insist. *I'm tired of this cat-and-mouse business. Give it a break. Give me a chance, will ya?* Instead, he gave a polite, "Excuse me?" and was certain his preoccupation with Jac had somehow stopped him from picking up some clue about coins.

"I didn't call you last night when I got back to the hotel because I figured you were asleep, and I didn't want to wake you," she said. "But my conversation with Austin Sellers last night was quite interesting." In the succinct voice of a professional, Jacquelyn detailed every fact pertaining to her new discoveries. "The weird part," she continued, "is that according to everything I'm picking up from the internet, these Athena Owl coins are supposed to be a dime a dozen. There are millions of ancient Greek and Roman coins still around in nice shape. And for some particular coins there are more coins than collectors, so they're considered to be in oversupply. Let's see . . ." she paused. "The terrain near the Mediterranean and the surrounding area isn't like it is here. Over there, every time a hard rain comes there are old coins and all sorts of other finds that are uncovered. Sometimes people even find royal tombs or magnificent artifacts." The measured meter of her voice suggested she had stopped summarizing and started reading. "These types of coins are found all over Europe, North Africa, and the Middle East. One of these old coins might bring 5 to 20 dollars. Well, whoopee," she derided. "And you can spend 100 to 500 dollars on a great coin. Oh, here's something else. According to Greek mythology, Athena was the patron goddess of Athens, so they made a bunch of coins with her on them. That's somewhat repetitive . . ."

"So why do you think that man offered Gary Sellers a quarter of a million for the coins if they really are a dime a dozen?"

"I have no earthly idea," Jac said. "Gary took a photo of the front and back of one of the coins while I was there. I'm sitting here looking at the photos and looking at a picture on the internet that's almost identical to the coin he took a picture of. According to this website, the coin probably dates from about 400 to 100 B.C."

"Mama mia," Lawton said as a mountain-chilled breeze ruffled the tufts of hair at his neckline. "Are you sure it isn't worth much?"

"Like I already said, there are thousands of coins like this out there. They made millions of them and you could probably buy a bucketful of them over there without ever blinking. Don't you remember when we were in Greece? There were coin shops on every corner it seemed like. Remember, Kinkaide even found a coin near Mars Hill and the tour guide got a laugh out of how impressed we all were?"

"I vaguely remember that," Lawton said. During that trip, there were many occasions when he had been so distracted by Jac that pertinent details faded into blurred recollections.

"I can't imagine why somebody would offer so much money for them," Jac continued. "I'm beginning to question whether or not they were linked to the Sellers' murders. Perhaps they were, but it just all seems so unlikely right now." The faint clicking of the keyboard mingled with her words. "One thing that is different about these is that they aren't tarnished in the least. There's something on here about how cleaning them reduces their value."

"So you think somebody must have polished them up?"

"Maybe."

"Or maybe they're in mint condition."

"I find it hard to believe that they'd be so clean after 1600 years, ya know."

"Good point. But still . . ." Lawton didn't push the issue. He didn't know that much about coins anyway.

"So, let's just say they aren't that valuable, but maybe the collector believes they are, or maybe there's something else involved here besides the coins," Jac mused.

Lawton lifted his chin and took full advantage of the persistent zephyr as it flowed across his features.

"But then again," she continued as if she were talking to herself, "if they weren't of much value, why would Austin's birth mother have hidden them in the diaper bags?"

"Good question, Sherlock," Lawton said.

"Thanks, Watson," she responded on a dry note.

"What time did you tell Austin we would be at his house this morning?" he asked.

" 'Bout nine."

Lawton pushed the button on his watch and the voice announced, "Eight-oh-three a.m."

"I guess we should go get some breakfast then head that way," Jac said. "I'm going to get off the internet. This is frustrating me anyway. It's all so general. I think it might make more sense to call those coin collectors Gary called last week, if we can find the numbers."

"Good thinking," Lawton said, then added, "Hey, before you get off the net, would you mind checking my e-mail? I haven't checked it in a few days."

"Sure," Jac said.

Lawton succinctly called out the internet address then gave her his password. In a matter of minutes, Jac had downloaded his messages. "Do you mind reading some of them to me?" Lawton asked. "My laptop has voice software that talks to me. I hate to ask you to do this, but right now I don't have much of a choice."

"No problem. Okay, you have 316 messages. *Whew!* We might be here awhile."

"It's bad, but not as bad as I thought."

"You do like to chat, don't you?"

"I've got friends all over the world. And, yes, I enjoy being able to keep in touch," Lawton said with a smile. He didn't bother to tell her that some days he could get as many as 200 messages. The internet had increased his interpersonal network to unbelievable proportions. "Tell you what, just scan down and see if you notice anything from my employer — Lighthouse for the Blind. Kinkaide called my boss for me and all is fine. She's giving me a couple of weeks off and is rescheduling my clients. But she's the main reason I wanted to check my messages, just in case something has come up."

"Okay," Jac said.

As the minutes ticked by, the scraping of tiny feet against wood indicated that perhaps a squirrel was busy at work. An offended bark erupted, confirming Lawton's suspicions. A blue jay's raucous jabbering mingled with the squirrel's protests and Lawton figured the furry critter had vexed the feathered foe.

"Well, I don't see anything from Lighthouse," Jac said, "but there are probably over 150 messages from people of the female persuasion. Let's see, somebody named Tiffany e-mailed about 12 times, I'd say." The possessive edge in Jac's voice brought back memories of the flight attendant.

You're jealous again! Lawton stopped the gleeful claim before it erupted. *You might run from me every time I get close, but don't tell me your heart isn't involved here, Jac. You're up to your ear lobes in this thing between us, whether you want to admit it or not.*

"And then this one is from some woman who is calling you hot lips!" Her tone changed from possessive to irritated.

The laugh exploded before Lawton had the chance to check himself. "Oh, that's Cindy! She's a married woman, and we're great friends. She gives me all sorts of grief. Once I wound up on the same flight with her — totally by accident. After the plane took off, she got the flight attendant to say, 'Is there anything I can get for you,

291

Mr. Hotlips?' I was sitting in the row right behind Cindy, and I thought she was going to *die* laughing. That woman is *crazy!*"

"Is that the way you like your women?" Jac asked. "Crazy and outrageous and —"

"Cindy isn't *my* woman," Lawton defended. "She's married, like I said. We're just good friends — like a brother and sister, maybe. She and her husband attend my church and live right up the road from me. Both of them often help run me around town when my mom can't."

Lawton strained for the slightest noise from Jac, but all he picked up was a distant woodpecker. The keyboard's telltale clicking finally accompanied her resolute silence, and Lawton figured she must be getting off the internet.

"I'm going to finish getting ready," she eventually stated, then the computer screen snapped closed. "Can you be ready in ten minutes?"

"Jac, Jac, Jac," Lawton crooned. "Come here. What's the matter?"

"Not one thing, *Hotlips,*" she shot back.

"I told you, Cindy's married."

"Okay, so what about the other 189 females you chitchat with all over the world? One of them mentioned that she was in Britain, for Pete's sake!"

"You are *really* jealous, aren't you?" Delight oozed from every syllable.

"This is not funny," she fumed.

The sound of the sliding glass door prompted Lawton to hurry along the balcony rail and stop at the hotel wall. "Don't go in, Jac, we need to talk. *Please?*" he added.

"So shoot. I'm listening."

Lawton sighed and rubbed his fingers across his mouth. The means to convincing Jacquelyn that she was the sole special lady in his life momentarily evaded him. Finally, only one solution posed itself. Maybe the reason for her insecure reaction lay in the fact that Lawton hadn't once told her exactly how he felt. Oh, he had given her the platinum stars, but that wasn't the same thing as speaking the words. Besides, she had returned the bracelet. Then Jac had indirectly heard about his love through Mel — once again not the same as his telling her. Last night, Lawton had indeed told her that he was after her, but right now she might be thinking that he was after anyone in a skirt. From what Lawton understood, women needed verbal assurance. And perhaps, just perhaps, the kiss he so wanted to exchange would seal an understanding between them and underscore everything he planned to say.

Eighteen

～

Fuat Rantomi raised the binoculars and adjusted them until Lawton's image came into sharp focus. As he suspected, Lawton Franklin stood on a hotel room balcony chatting with a woman who looked remarkably like Jacquelyn Lightfoot. Fuat moved the binoculars to the next balcony and adjusted the lenses so that he received a crisp image of a petite woman with black hair and dark skin.

"She *is* Lightfoot," Fuat said, then uttered an oath. He lowered the glasses and stepped away from the hotel window. His fingers ate into the binoculars, and he rued the day he had ever hired Maurice Stein. Fuat fingered the small bandage on his temple, narrowed his eyes, and observed Edwardo. He stood with his hands clasped behind his back, his face as stony as his eyes. Fuat held no reservations that the young Mexican would prove a valuable replacement for that imbecile Maurice.

"How did Lawton hook up with her?" Fuat asked.

"According to our contacts, the two have known each other since early in the year," Edwardo's words fired forth with a heavy Hispanic accent. "Apparently, when Lawton arrived in the hospital, he called her."

"Why Dino didn't arrange for her extermination when she destroyed his operation is beyond my comprehension," Fuat growled and paced toward an ornate table next to the poster bed.

"I think Dino got scared," Edwardo said. "He almost landed in prison himself."

"He could have bought his way out. He's done it for his people many times." Fuat picked up the ready firearm laying on a stack of newspapers. His daughter, Angelica, had picked up Edwardo and Fuat in Montrose. As always, she supplied the necessary equipment to complete the tasks at hand.

"Maybe and maybe not." Edwardo crossed his arms and his vinyl jacket whispered with the movement. "Things are changing. The buyouts are getting more and more difficult to cover. Dino had a brush with his own limitations, and I believe his choice to back off was probably a wise one for that particular situation." Fuat eyed the 38-year-old then picked up a slender cigar from the open box near the stack of newspapers. He stuck the cigar between his teeth and didn't bother to light it.

Fuat, gun in hand, walked back to the paneled window and released the latch. He shoved the twin glass panels in the middle and they squeaked open with the nuance of decades of use. Last night when they checked into the Victorian hotel, Fuat had estimated that it was the perfect locale for their needs. The inn was strategically situated near downtown, not far from Gary's massive log home. He never dreamed that the location would also serve as the perfect perch for two more necessary murders. Fuat held the scope to his eye and placed the center of the crosshairs on Lawton Franklin's temple.

"What are you doing?" Edwardo asked, his voice void of emotion.

"I'm going to kill that blind man like I told Maurice to. He knows too much. He has heard my voice. And I know he is here with that woman to try to find out about the murders."

"If you shoot him now, will you be able to get her as well?"

"Of course. She will be next." Fuat's finger hovered upon the trigger.

"Are you certain?" Edwardo's steady voice punctured Fuat's assurance, and he eased off the trigger.

He lowered the weapon and faced the Mexican who tugged aside the heavy drapes and observed the man and woman interacting across their balcony rails. "She is a professional. If you shoot him, and he drops, she will go to the floor and wait. She is a tough one, if the reports are anything to go by. If you aren't able to kill her, she will see where you are shooting from and come looking for you. Then you will not be able to stay and find the other coins, as you have planned. You will have to be happy with the ones you retrieved last night."

Fuat's eye twitched, and he observed Edwardo's attentive profile. Last night this new assistant had neatly taken care of Maurice with a skill Fuat hadn't witnessed in years. Perhaps the Mexican would offer a brilliant suggestion to the present problem as well.

"What do you suggest?" Fuat asked and squirmed inwardly. Never had he asked the input of an assistant.

"We could each get a gun now and shoot them simultaneously," Edwardo mused. "But even then, if one of us by chance misses . . ." He paused. "There is the distance to consider. This far out, I am afraid that perhaps accuracy might be compromised. I think a better method would be to isolate them and take care of them one at a time. Perhaps the woman first, then Lawton. If we drop her first, then she will not be available to hunt for us after his death. He will be extra vulnerable without her, due to his handicap. Once she learns we are watching, even in a short timeframe, she might be detrimental to your finding the coins."

"Don't you think it's only a matter of time before they find out we were in Gary's house?" Fuat said and made certain his voice held an authoritative edge.

"Of course, Boss." Edwardo removed his hand from the textured curtain, and it danced back to cover half the window. "That only increases our need for haste. Do you agree?" he added with a new dose of compliance in his voice.

"Of course. Let's get the other seven

coins first. Then we kill those two. Or perhaps . . ." The boss narrowed his eyes then shook his head. "Angelica and the others would probably take care of this for me," he schemed.

"Good idea," Edwardo said with reverence as he retrieved Fuat's double-breasted jacket from the end of the bed. "Then you won't be involved."

Fuat strutted back to the table, deposited the gun, then shrugged into the tailor-made jacket as Edwardo assisted him. Edwardo flipped open a silver-plated lighter and snapped a wisp of flame into being. Fuat stuck the tip of his cigar into the yellow flame and inhaled deeply, relishing the experience of quality tobacco. The room's antique motif blurred in the cloud of smoke that swirled from his mouth in a narrow shaft. "I could have her and the boys take care of them late this morning, then we will all be out of here shortly after noon."

The Mexican crossed his arms and smiled. "Of course."

With the deaths neatly taken care of, Fuat's mind raced on to the task at hand. According to the coin appraiser, Gary had reported that all 14 coins were still together. Since they didn't find 14 at Gary's house, Fuat could only assume that Austin must be in possession of the other 7. There was a slim possibility that he was wrong, but a thorough search should reveal the truth. If Austin *did* possess the other coins, all that remained was relieving him of the artifacts. As Fuat pondered Gary's death, a mild tinge annoyed his spirit. He hadn't seen the two since Amanda stole the coins and walked out on him. Those twins were nothing to Fuat now — nothing . . . except the bearers of property that rightfully belonged to him. His orders to Edwardo would be what they were for Maurice: "Do whatever you have to do, but get the coins from Austin."

"I've been thinking," Edwardo said as he paced back to the window. "My father used to say that the best place to hide something was out in the open."

Fuat arched a brow and stared at the Mexican. Edwardo turned from the window, reached toward his jacket's inside pocket, then flopped open a billfold. The name Sylvester D. Lancaster claimed the space below Edwardo's photo. Across the top of the ID were the letters FBI.

An alarm rang through Fuat. He squinted then ticked off the possibilities. Either the ID was fake or Edwardo really was FBI. *But if he were, why would he flash an ID now?* Edwardo reasoned.

"I arranged this false ID last year," the Mexican continued.

"Why didn't you tell me you had this before now?" Fuat demanded.

Edwardo's gaze faltered. "I am sorry. I did not think to tell you," he confessed.

Fuat's immediate irritation was assuaged by a tendril of relief. Any mistake, no matter how tiny, on Edwardo's part would underscore Fuat's superiority. He needed to keep the edge.

"I'm glad you finally remembered it," Fuat growled. "So, what are you suggesting? That you just go in and show Austin the badge then request the coins as some kind of evidence?"

"Exactly," Edwardo said. "You can even go with me, if you like." The assistant paused and looked Fuat in the eyes. "That way you don't have to worry about my taking the coins and running."

"Of course I'm going with you," Fuat snarled. "After that fiasco with Maurice . . ." He left the rest unsaid and hoped Edwardo grasped the implied threat.

Jac cradled the laptop to her chest and

stared at Lawton. To say she hated her petty behavior would be an understatement. Her jealousy was ugly. It was childlike. It screamed of insecurity and immaturity. Nonetheless, she couldn't deny that seeing all those e-mails from women had covered her with a revolting dose of a slimy emotion she couldn't shake. She wanted to go into her room and have a good cry. She had never been so torn in all her life. Everything inside whispered that she should draw ever nearer to Lawton, while another part of her screamed in alarm if he even touched her fingers.

"I think it's probably best to start with Tiffany," Lawton said.

"Yes, please do," Jac said, her words as hard as a glacier.

"She's 12." He rubbed his freshly shaven jaw and the smile lines from nose to mouth increased with every second.

Never in her life had Jac so wanted to dissolve into a mound of remorse. "How do I know that?" Her spirited demand successfully hid all chagrin.

"Feel free to go back and see. You know my password." He ran his fingers along the top of the rail. "She lives in Knoxville, Tennessee. She's blind — has been since birth. The last time I chatted with her, she had just gotten a new kitten."

Three consecutive e-mails flashed through Jac's mind. All of them were from Tiffany and each bore the subject title "kitten." "What about the others?"

"What about them? I'd have to see their names. Do you remember them? Did you see the text of the messages?"

"I didn't read them. I figured they were *your* business."

"Well, if they're my business then why are you interrogating me?" he teased.

She covered her forehead with her hand and pressed her fingers against her temple. There's no telling what Lawton thought. She narrowed her eyes and observed him. On the other hand, she just might be correct in assuming that he was relishing every second of her outburst. With a sigh, she willed herself to shove aside the negative behavior. She had no ties on Lawton Franklin. He was free to chat with any woman he so chose. But even if they were engaged, Jac didn't want to be the kind of woman who tried to control every word that left her man's mouth — or computer.

"I'm sorry," Jacquelyn rasped, feeling more foolish by the second. "I — I don't know what to say. I — I guess I'm acting like I'm 15 here, not 35."

"So you're an older woman," Lawton said with a satisfied smirk as he crossed his arms.

"Only by a couple of years," Jac defended.

"Come here, Jacquelyn Lightfoot," he said.

"What for?"

"I want to know what you look like."

"How are you going to do that?"

"May I feel your features?" he asked. "Would you mind?"

She clutched the computer and tore her gaze from him to encounter the fathomless mountains that inspired awe and evoked dreams. If Lawton touched her in such a personal fashion, he might try to kiss her. Mere minutes ago, Jac had sensed that he had something other than the Red Sox in mind . . . and the Red Sox still weren't on his mind.

Her bare toes gripped the cool wood, and Jac longed for the blanket still draped across the patio chair. Her feet had been toasty warm when tucked beneath her, but now they felt like icicles.

"Have you ever been to Ouray?" she asked.

"Uh, no."

"Did you know they call this the Switzerland of America?" she chattered. "Every time I take the time to really look at these mountains, I expect angels to break out in the 'Hallelujah Chorus.'"

"Right now, I couldn't care less."

A swift movement caught the corner of Jac's eye. A scuffing sound followed. Jac shifted her attention from the mountains, back to Lawton. The man teetered atop the balcony rails, one hand and foot on each ledge.

"You're crazy!" Jac yelled and stepped forward. "You're going to fall."

With a lunge he sprang onto her balcony. A thud accompanied his ungraceful landing. Gaping, Jac stumbled away from him as swiftly as she had moved toward him. "What in the name of common sense are you doing?" she croaked.

"I'm paying a visit," he said as if he were stating the most practical of concepts.

He stood, gained his equilibrium, and moved toward her. Jacquelyn continued to back away until the computer cord stretched tight and she bumped into the balcony rail behind her. "I don't — don't know exactly what — what you think you're up to, but —"

"But what?" He stopped only inches

away and gripped the rail on either side of her. "There. I gotcha!"

His undaunted declaration about being after her rang through Jac's mind. Despite her determination to keep her legs stiff, they quivered. She gripped the laptop tighter, as if it were her only defense.

"Now, let's talk," he said. *"Really talk."*

"About what?" Jac gulped and focused on his lips, despite her attempts to look across his shoulder.

"Us. About us."

"You mean about our — our, uh, friend-ship?" she babbled, not even certain if any-thing she said was making sense. She only knew that his face was centimeters away. She only knew that something within her, surprising and strong and sweet, longed to feel his arms tighten around her.

Lawton's mouth compressed into a tight line, and his brows drew together into an exasperated scowl. "So, we're just friends, is that it, Jac?" he asked.

Jac's heart raced, and the tension be-tween them grew with each hammer of the tireless woodpecker in the distance.

"How many *friends* do you have?" His voice rumbled in a deceptively soft manner that reminded her of a lion scouting out his prey.

The rail pressed into her back. "I —"

He leaned closer and his spicy aftershave filled her scattered senses. "So we've been circling each other like two teenagers because we're *friends?* Is that it? So the reason you flew to Dallas when I landed in the hospital is because you thought we could develop a better *friendship?* Now you've come all the way to Ouray with me because you thought I was a nice *friend.* You've been melting every time we're together because —"

"Who says —"

"*I* do. Because I have, too." The strain in his words eased as his voice softened. "And you've got to know it, Jac, you've got to," he whispered. Lawton raised a hand and stroked her cheek with the backs of his fingers. Then his fingertips touched the bridge of her nose and moved up to her brow.

Jac closed her eyes and swallowed as a luscious wash of shivers radiated from his touch like a shower of miniature meteors.

His other hand joined the first one as the exploration continued. Jac's heart felt as if it were running circles in her chest. And her spirit sang that this was the man who just might be able to hold her hand as she struggled from the mire of her past.

Finally, his hands stilled and cupped her chin. His thumb rested on her lips then stroked the outer edges. Gradually, Lawton's head inched closer to her own. Jac licked her lips and wondered if the flames in her stomach might overtake her.

"Lawton," she said, her voice husky.

"Yes?" he whispered.

"Don't you dare kiss me," she croaked, voicing the fear that insisted she maintain her boundaries. Yet her tone, full of longing, denied her words.

"Okay, I won't." His breath brushed her cheek like the hot winds off a dry, thirsty desert. "But tell me you don't want me to, Jac," he insisted.

"I don't want you to," she repeated like a mindless parrot. Yet her declaration sounded as ridiculous as if she had told him she didn't want air.

His hands traveled from her face to her neck, down to her shoulders then encircled her. Lawton buried his head against her neck and held her tight. Jac, still gripping the computer with one hand, clutched the front of his cotton shirt with the other hand.

"So, if you don't want me to kiss you, then why don't you pull a move or two out of that martial arts bag of yours?" he mumbled in her ear, and his forever present smile thickened his voice. "You could kick me off this balcony in a heartbeat, and we both know it."

She buried her face against his chest, closed her eyes, and absorbed his warmth. Somehow, if she could just move beyond her childhood, maybe this was the way it could be between them . . . always.

"Please," he prompted.

A rush of tears blurred her vision as the purity of his request drove Jacquelyn to her final decision. Lawton wouldn't kiss her, no matter what *he* wanted, unless she bestowed the final nod. On a reckless impulse Jacquelyn decided to give him more than a nod. She lifted her head, stood on her toes, and crushed her lips against his.

His sudden intake of air accompanied a grunt. A consuming heat sprang between them like an uncontrollable forest fire. Lawton's arms tightened around Jacquelyn, and she forced herself not to collapse. She moved her hand to behind his neck and drank in his nearness. In that second they were transported to a ship's deck, beneath a moon that rained phosphorous rays upon a beautiful ocean. The memory of the Aegean Sea's mild swishing whispered that Jacquelyn had begun to lose her heart last spring while sitting at the Brazil Coffee Verandah.

At last Lawton pulled away, and Jacquelyn wasn't so sure she wanted the moment to end.

"I need some space here," he said, his breathing far from steady.

Jacquelyn rested her head on his chest and wondered where they went from here. Something inside her suggested that things were moving too fast . . . until she reminded herself that she had known this man for months. She also found herself wondering what she had been so afraid of. Her mind wandered down the mystic path of matrimony and right into the realm of their first night together. The dragon's hiss sent a rash of gooseflesh along Jac's spine. She stiffened, lifted her head, and tightly gripped the laptop with both arms.

"Is something wrong?" Lawton's finger followed the crest of her eyebrow then traveled to her cheek.

Jacquelyn swallowed hard and fought against the riptide of vulnerability that threatened to take her under.

"What is it, my little tiger?" he prompted, and the words that were meant to be an endearment stabbed her in the heart.

"Don't call me that," she snapped, and her cold toes dug into the wood beneath them. "That's what the dragon called me — all the time. I hated it. Don't call me that!" she repeated. Eyes wide, Jacquelyn stared into Lawton's attentive face as another memory entered her consciousness.

"Who was the dragon?" he whispered, and Jac sensed that somehow he had figured out what plagued her.

"How — how did you know?" she whispered.

"What?" he hedged as if he were afraid of being wrong.

"About the dragon?" she queried, scared to state the truth, but at the same time scared not to state it. As she perceived yesterday, the time had come for Lawton to know. If after knowing, he discarded her like some piece of rubbish, then Jacquelyn would rather be discarded today, while she still had at least a trace of her dignity intact, than be discarded months later when her heart was hopelessly lost.

"Yesterday on the plane you had a dream. It was about the dragon, wasn't it?" he asked.

"Y–yes." Jacquelyn covered her lips with the tips of her fingers as hot tears dripped from her lashes. "He comes to me when I

311

sleep. It's awful. There's always this shaft of light. It's full of — it's like gold glitter — and when I step into it, the pain is worse. So I pull away, but the dragon is right there. I'm scared to death to know who he was. I don't want to know," she burst out on a sob. "I don't. I don't. I don't." Her hand curled into a fist and Jac rested it against Lawton's chest.

He pulled her closer and eased his cheek against the top of her head.

"And — and every time I step into the light, I come nearer to knowing. But if I find out —" A wave of nausea seized Jac as she recalled a childhood filled with the smiles of a doting father. John Lightfoot, strong, solemn, kind, had made his daughter proud of her Native American heritage. While they never lived on a reservation, he had taken great pains to expose her to the wisdom of his people. She had grown up knowing that a fierce and relentless fire burned in her gut. A fire full of determination and valor. Valor and love. Love and endurance. "I don't want my father to be the dragon," she wailed, and her knees gave way beneath her.

Lawton's strong arms stopped her from falling. "The dragon wasn't your father, Jac." His quiet assurance penetrated her confusion. "He was your *grandfather.*"

The air hissed out of Jac's lungs as she jerked away and stared into his face. The assurance draped across his countenance countered any argument. "My–my grandfather?" she sputtered. "H–How do you — do you know that?"

"Yesterday on the plane when you had that bad dream, you kept talking about a grandpa, and you kept saying no." Each of Lawton's words dripped out like bulging droplets of sympathy.

"Oh, no!" Jacquelyn groaned, closed her eyes, and hung onto Lawton. That shaft of light near the forest's edge widened and increased in intensity until the whole brier-infested terrain shimmered with the brilliance of truth. In her mind, Jacquelyn turned to face the dragon. And this time he had no fangs. No scaly skin. No fiery eyes. This time he observed her with the blue-eyed lust of a man whom her parents had trusted with their daughter's life. They trusted him because he was her mother's own father. The abstract blended with reality and the memories rushed upon Jac like the bilious tide of a putrescent sea. There had been camping excursions and sleepovers and trips to the zoo; Christmases and birthdays and fishing lessons.

Every memory, every paternal kiss, every touch was now tainted with the rancid truth that sent a blazing rage through Jacquelyn's veins.

She broke away from Lawton and unceremoniously dropped the laptop upon the patio table. Jac raced into her room and yanked the masculine robe from the end of the bed. Since his death she had worn it to remind her of the man who had taken such a "special interest" in her as a child.

"I hate you!" she screamed and tried to rip the housecoat in half. Yet the thick material refused to yield to her abuse. Jac slammed the robe against the taupe carpet and stomped it as if it were a venomous viper. "I hate you!" she wailed again. "Do you hear me?"

"Jac . . . Jac . . ." Lawton's unwavering voice broke into her tirade, and his steady hands settled upon her shoulders.

"No! No! Don't — don't touch me." Jacquelyn shoved at Lawton's hands and stumbled backward until she slammed into the far wall. A wave of nausea overtook her and a dizzying warmth flared from her churning stomach. Covered in a clammy sweat, Jacquelyn lurched for the restroom and collapsed beside the toilet. The acrid heaves could no longer be denied.

Nineteen

~

Lawton paced across the room, all the while feeling to his right. When his hand encountered the wall, he ran his fingers along it until he came to the bathroom entryway. Jac's groans radiated from within like the tortured moan of a soul trapped in a dungeon of despair. Lawton hesitated and debated exactly what to do. If he joined her, he might embarrass her. If he didn't join her, he might distance himself from her at a time when she needed him the most.

A faint ringing from within the room urged him to find her cell phone. Lawton, torn between assisting Jac and answering the phone, debated his choices. At last, he decided to allow Jac some space and answer the phone. The call just might be an emergency. He had no idea what the life of a private eye was like. The whole concept conjured images of secret messages, furtive hideouts, and unexpected callers. His head high, Lawton moved toward the peal until he bumped into the dresser. He fumbled across the top and discovered what felt like a cell phone. Lawton picked up the resounding slip of plastic and ran his fingers along the top. The presence of the antenna assured him the phone was right side up. He fingered the keypad, limited his selection to four buttons, and began pressing. The ringing stopped on the third button. He held the phone to his ear and produced a distracted, "Hello."

"Hello. I'm trying to reach Jacquelyn Lightfoot," a polite male voice said. "Do I have the right number?"

"Yes — yes, you do," Lawton replied as dread silence permeated the room. Lawton strained to hear any signs from Jac, but none came.

"Good. This is Austin Sellers. She gave me her cell phone number last night before she left and told me to call if anything came up. Well, something has come up," Austin said.

"Oh?" Lawton prompted.

"Yes. May I — may I speak with her?"

"She's . . . indisposed right now," Lawton hedged.

Unsteady footfalls exited the bathroom and stopped several feet away. "Who is it?" Jacquelyn asked.

"Just a minute," Lawton said then covered the receiver. "Austin Sellers," he whispered. "He says something has come up."

A faint squeak and shuffle of fabric indicated that Jacquelyn must have settled onto the bed. "Find out what he wants," she said, her voice unsteady.

Lawton placed the phone back against his ear. "Jacquelyn isn't feeling well right now. She's asked that I relay your message to her."

"And your name?" Austin requested, as if he didn't trust Lawton in the least. Considering the man's recent turn of events, Lawton couldn't say that he blamed him.

"I'm Lawton Franklin," he said. "We are — were coming over there this morning."

"Okay, yes. Please tell Jac that I've been at Gary's house this morning. I've just come back home. I had to get out of there or I was going to lose it. Somebody has been in Gary's office. The back door was unlocked. The desk's middle drawer was on top of the desk, and there's blood on the carpet. Also, Gary's coins are nowhere to be found."

Lawton covered the mouthpiece and repeated the message word for word.

"Tell him we'll be right over," Jac said, her voice void of emotion.

Frowning, Lawton weighed the situation. Jacquelyn didn't have any business out chasing a mystery right now. She needed time — time to regain a semblance of her equilibrium. "Can I call you back in 60 seconds?" Lawton asked. "Jac and I need to discuss this. She's really feeling ill right now. I might hire a taxi and come over to your place. We can go from there."

A click interrupted the connection for a second. "Wait. I've got another call," Austin said. "I'm going to put you on hold."

"Okay, okay," Lawton agreed, glad for the reprieve. "Jac, I really don't think you need to go anywhere right now," he said. "You don't sound so hot."

"This is the reason we came here," she insisted.

"How long are you going to keep pushing yourself like this?" Lawton asked and shook his head. "It's okay to take an hour or two to get yourself back together."

"Hello," Austin's voice came back over the line.

"Yes. Still here," Lawton answered.

"You're not going to believe this. That was the FBI. They were asking about the coins. Tell Jac that they are requesting that I turn them over to their custody. It would appear that they are the property of the Turkish government. We arranged a meeting today at noon."

Lawton whistled and settled against the edge of the dresser. "Okay, I'll tell her. So what do you think then? Will you turn everything over to them and let them handle it from here on out?"

"Yes, I guess." Austin paused. "I'm so confused at this point, I don't know what to think. Even if the FBI retrieves my coins, Gary's are still missing."

"Right." Lawton rubbed his forehead and tried to piece together indicative facts that contradicted Jac's internet findings.

"Would it be possible for you and Jac to be a part of the meeting?" Austin continued. "I don't know, I just don't feel quite right about all of this."

"And it's at noon?" Lawton confirmed.

"Yes. They wanted to come now but my wife and kids are here. I know I'm probably sounding paranoid, but I want them out of here before the FBI comes."

"I understand," Lawton said. "Just a minute." He covered the mouthpiece and stated the pertinent details to Jac. "Austin wants to know if we can be there. The meeting's at noon."

"Yes. Tell him yes," she said with a wobble in her voice and a telltale sniffle.

"Okay. We'll be there," Lawton said, and he hoped Jac would regain her footing enough by then to function as needed.

"What does she think I should do about the break-in at Gary's house?" Austin asked. "Should I go ahead and call the local authorities or wait until the FBI gets here?"

Lawton relayed the message.

"Tell him to call — call the local police now," Jac responded, "and let them begin investigating. The FBI will undoubtedly take over from there, but in every crime, time is of the essence. They might find a lead."

"Yes, call the police," Lawton affirmed. "Then you can expect us before noon."

Lawton disconnected the call to the accompaniment of a pent-up whimper that burst into a sob. He deposited the phone onto the dresser, walked toward Jac, then knelt beside her. "Hey," he crooned, "it's going to be all right."

As if his words opened another floodgate of emotions, she moaned and collapsed onto the floor beside him. Lawton wrapped his arms around her and rocked as a torrent of words flowed forth.

"I was — was a good — good girl," she wailed. "I didn't want to — I didn't! He — he made me! He said he would kill me if I told!"

Lawton's teeth clenched, and for the first time in his life he was tempted to kill somebody. As her weeping escalated into volcanic proportions, his earlier desire to cling to his fantasy bride made him feel like the selfish cad of the century. He re-lived the days when he had harbored a certain pride in his own self-control along with a definite demand that he would only respect his future bride if she, too, were sexually pure. Lawton's secret disdain for those who made wrong choices surfaced, and he blasted himself for his lack of insight. No, Jacquelyn wasn't a virgin, but that didn't reduce her worth — not one fraction. Nor did it reduce his escalating respect for her. And Lawton didn't care one flip about her past — even if he later learned that the dragon wasn't the only one. He simply wanted to be part of her future — if she would have him.

"Shh, there now," he whispered. As Jac's tremors subsided, he stroked her hair, slick as new-spun silk. "It's okay. You're going to be fine."

"You told me to get over it," she finally choked out. "And I c–can't just . . . just get over it. It doesn't *work* that way." The fury from their previous conversation laced her words, and Lawton knew on an even deeper dimension that he had royally blown it that night at the hospital.

He closed his eyes and sighed. "You have no idea how sorry I am that I said what I did. I know I've already apologized once, but well, like Kinkaide said, I was about 18 different kinds of stupid." Lawton paused and decided to continue, despite the daunting notion that he ought to remain silent. "And well, I don't have any answers right now, but I do know that there are people who say that the Lord has helped them heal in this area. I know He's been there for me — to help me get over the anger of never being able to see and to finally give me peace." Lawton carefully chose his next words. "Frankly, I've never experienced what you did, and I'm not even sure that my blindness is even as bad as living with the shame I know you must feel, but I *do* know that God is faithful, Jac. And that when He says He heals the brokenhearted, I believe that means every heart that's ever been broken for any reason." He held his breath and awaited Jac's response.

Minutes ticked by — minutes when nothing marred the silence except her intermittent sniffling. Lawton felt as if his words had tumbled onto her head and one by one were seeping into her soul.

"Oh, Lawton," she finally said, her voice muffled by the folds of his shirt, "what are we going to do? I can't — can't — I just can't ever again. It would be torture."

Lawton frowned as he approached this junction in their relationship. He had yet to propose, but he knew that Jac would be daft not to understand his intent. He also read between the lines of her honesty. Their cat-and-mouse game had been far from a game for Jacquelyn. It had been about survival. Lawton rested his cheek against the top of her head and took in the smell of her freshly shampooed hair.

"It's okay," he whispered. "I understand. *I understand.*"

Twenty

~

By 10:45, Sammie pulled into the driveway of a blue-trimmed frame home in the heart of Eureka Springs, Arkansas. By leaving Dallas ahead of schedule and starting again early that morning, they were able to expedite the journey. She put the car into park, turned off the engine, and gazed toward the mountains. The Ozarks surrounded the quaint village with winding roads and offered what felt like a barrier against Adam — wherever he might be. During the journey, Sam had kept close watch behind her, all the while wondering if Adam had somehow discovered where she was running to.

The sound of a rumbling motorcycle pulling into the driveway prompted Sammie's glance in the rearview mirror. R.J.'s Harley, with its chrome gleaming, rolled to a stop behind her. The motorcycle's roar abruptly halted, and R.J. nudged down the kickstand with the tip of his boot. He removed his shiny black helmet, and the silver fringe on the front of his vest glistened in the blinding sunshine. Sammie wondered if the man would wear leather until he was 80.

Sighing, she glanced into the back. Brett's head rested against the side of the car seat, his eyes blissfully closed. After miles of impatient chatter, temporary outbursts, and ultimately full-blown screaming the child had finally dozed. "Probably about the time we turned down Emporia Street," she mumbled.

Sam caught sight of R.J.'s approach in the side mirror. She opened the door and stepped out. The smell of grilling meat put her saliva glands into overdrive. Her stomach, empty from her light breakfast, grumbled enough to remind Sam that she had also skipped dinner last night.

"Everything okay?" R.J. peered into the backseat. "Looks like the champ has received a TKO."

She stifled a derisive snort. "Yes, after screaming like a wild man for an hour. He *hates* that car seat."

"Poor guy. I can't say that I blame him."

R.J. straightened and eyed Sammie. His red bandanna tied atop his head reminded Sam of another red bandanna tucked in the corner of a box of mementos somewhere in her attic. "Sorry I couldn't ride in the car with you," R.J. continued. "I could have entertained him."

"That's okay." Sammie rushed, then leaned into the car to retrieve her purse. "You've already done too much as it is."

"I guess this is my cue to keep on driving, is that it?" he asked.

His loaded words prompted Sammie's untimely retreat from the vehicle, and she bumped her head on her way out. "No, that's not what I meant," she snapped as she rubbed the aching spot on her head.

"Ouch. You okay?" R.J. gingerly touched her hair in the vicinity of the wound.

Sam shouldered her handbag, sidestepped him, and snapped the door shut. "Yes, okay," she mumbled and rounded the back of the car to retrieve her sleeping boy. Her hand rested on the door latch and she eyed R.J. who retrieved their luggage from beside Brett. A shroud of guilt draped across Sammie. R.J. had done so much for her, and she felt as if she'd appeared miles from grateful.

"Seriously, R.J., Marilyn and Josh are expecting you to stay for awhile. You should plan to rest up before you go." She tried to smile, but the attempt at good humor faltered in the face of her dark predicament.

The biker stood to his full height, deposited the suitcases on the driveway, then propped his elbow on the car top. His soft brown eyes conjured up fond memories that Sammie had successfully buried in the depths of her soul. While she had been thrilled to receive the protection R.J. offered, his constant presence behind her vehicle had served as a steady reminder of their former relationship. By the time they got into Arkansas, Sam was drowning in a sea of "what might have beens." *But "what might have been" isn't reality,* she reminded herself.

Sammie had married Adam instead, for better or worse. While their current situation was definitely the worse, she was still married. However, any love she once held for Adam had been annihilated. Last night on the phone, Marilyn had asked her if she planned to divorce him. In her humanity, Sammie wanted to never see the man again as long as she lived. A divorce proved a mild solution to the fury that spewed from the bottom of her being. Nonetheless, she kept reliving those five little words she had uttered on her wedding day: "till death do us part." She wondered what Adam would do without her. *But I really couldn't care less,* she reminded herself. Caught in a jumble of conflicting emotions, Sammie opened the back door, unfastened the car seat belts, and stroked a lock of pumpkin-colored hair from Brett's eyes. Right now, all she knew was that she and her child needed a haven from the man who had promised to cherish her. Furthermore, if Sam *did* choose to divorce Adam, she seriously doubted that she would ever remarry again — even if the prospect were R.J. Butler. She picked up Brett, cradled him to her chest, and winced as she tried to straighten. Her back hadn't been the same since Adam slammed her against their bedroom wall two months ago. A whimper escaped Brett as he propped his head on her shoulder and wrapped his arms around her neck.

The crunch of boots on concrete preceded R.J.'s offer by only seconds. "Want me to take him in?"

She glanced up at him and bit her bottom lip. An unexpected urge to burst into uncontrolled weeping surged upon her. Adam seldom ever offered to help with Brett. Conversely, Sam had released bucketfuls of maternal energies trying to keep Brett out of Adam's path. The man charmingly taught high school math to students who were total strangers and did such a wonderful job that he had been voted favorite teacher two years in a row. He attended church, sang in the choir, and volunteered to assist widows. But when he came home, Dr. Jekyl turned into Mr. Hyde and acted out the secret sins of his father. If he had just shown half as much interest in her and Brett as he did in trying to fool the rest of the world . . .

"Sam?" R.J. prompted.

With a silent nod, Sammie allowed him to take her son, and the relinquishment of her burden eased the pressure on her aching back.

"Mom! They're here!" a high-pitched voice rang from the quaint home. The screen door banged, and Marilyn's daughter, Brooke, raced across the front yard. Her blonde ponytail swinging, Brooke's bare feet slammed against the emerald-colored grass as she hurled headlong into Sammie's embrace.

"Aunt Sam! Aunt Sam!" Brooke exclaimed, and Brett lifted his head from R.J.'s shoulder to examine this new addition to their little group.

Everyone agreed Brooke was a miniature clone of her mother: the same blonde ponytail, the same doe-brown eyes, the same fair complexion. But Brooke possessed her father's long, straight nose. Marilyn's nose was the pug variety.

Marilyn appeared on the front porch, her ponytail swinging just as vivaciously as Brooke's.

"Sam!" Marilyn shrieked and raced toward her.

The two fell into a fond embrace, and R.J. lowered Brett to Brooke's level. After the girlfriend chatter diminished, Sam's attention was drawn to R.J., who was intent upon helping Brett get reacquainted with Brooke. The two hadn't seen each other since January. Every six months the seven close friends got together for a sisters reunion. In July, the sisters had forfeited their biannual reunion to assist Melissa in her move from Oklahoma to Tennessee. Sam had little choice but to bring Brett with her, but Marilyn had left her daughter with Joshua.

"Well, aren't you going to introduce us?" Marilyn asked.

"Oh, sure," Sam said. "This is a long-time . . . friend of mine, R.J. Butler," Sammie supplied. "R.J., Marilyn is one of my closest friends. There are seven of us who met in college, and we still keep in close touch."

"Yes, I think Mom has mentioned you guys a time or two." R.J. allowed Brett to slide off his leg and take Brooke's hand. He stood and produced the gentlemanly nod, so prevalent in the south. "Nice to meet you, Marilyn."

"Joshua is just starting the grilling now," Marilyn said as the two shook hands. "I planned an early lunch for about 11:30. Does that work for you guys?"

"Yes!" R.J. agreed. "We ate breakfast this morning at six. When I smelled the grill, I thought about eating my bike." R.J. rubbed his hands together. "Did he cook an extra, say, six or so?" A mischievous grin accompanied his words.

"Yes, I think so," Marilyn said through a delighted laugh. "And I think if you let him take your Harley for a run he'd probably offer to grill an extra 12."

"It's a deal!"

Sammie listened in silence as R.J. systematically charmed the socks off of Marilyn. All morning, she had tried to ignore the dull ache in the center of her forehead, but the pain began to throb with decided aggression. The added stress of R.J.'s presence did little to assuage her tension. Fleetingly, Sammie wondered if Marilyn would mind if she went straight to bed after lunch. R.J. could sit and chat all day — and he probably would. The man had always been a master at interpersonal interaction with total strangers. In the past he just couldn't seem to handle the up-close-and-personal relationships.

Her attention drifted to her son who attentively listened to Brooke's request. "Want to come inside and see him?" she asked, tugging on Brett's hand. "He's got his own water bowl and doggie bed even."

Brett cast a glance toward his mother, and Sammie bestowed an affirmative nod. "Come on. I'll go in with you," she said and snared her son's other hand. She welcomed any excuse to distance herself from R.J., even if for a few minutes.

The three of them entered the charming home, and Sam admired the way Marilyn had turned the nondescript cottage into a cozy haven. The warm array of country decor mingled blues with peach and taupe to make the room appear half again bigger than it was. Sam figured Marilyn probably got half the stuff at garage sales, right down to the glistening brass candlesticks. Even on a budget, Marilyn seemed to be able to do more with decor than Sam ever could.

A gray puppy ran from the kitchen and hurled itself at Brooke. With an ecstatic yap, it hopped upon her legs then wagged its furry body toward Brett. The dog jumped on his bare legs, and his claws trailed pink lines down the three-year-old's shins. Brett gasped, promptly went into hysterics, and raced for his mother.

"It's okay," Brooke said, picking up the dog. "He's nice, see." She shoved the mutt toward Brett who all but climbed Sammie's legs.

She scooped up her son and stood a little too swiftly for her back's pleasure. "The pup —" Sam stopped and winced while her back adjusted to the added weight. "The puppy didn't mean to hurt you, honey, he just wants to play, that's all."

With a wail, Brett buried his face against her neck, and Sam sighed. The poor child had been through enough trauma for a lifetime. "I'm sorry, Brooke." Sammie smiled down at the wide-eyed little girl. "He's used to our cat. She's a big ol' fat Siamese that's more lazy than anything else."

"Did you bring her with you?" Brooke asked. "I bet Frisky would play with her."

"No. I arranged for a neighbor to take care of her," Sammie said. R.J. had accompanied Sam to her home last night so she could take care of all the packing and arrange for the cat's care.

Her father had offered to drive in from New Mexico and assist Sam in her transition. He had even asked if she wanted to stay with him, but Sam had declined. She and her stepmother had never really gotten along. Nothing had been the same in her family since her mother abandoned them. Sammie had been ten, her sister, eight. Sammie hadn't heard from her sister in a year. Once again, she stifled the urge to burst into spontaneous tears. Her life had been far from any kind of fairy-tale existence. At times she wondered why in the world she ever started writing for a magazine like *Romantic Times* or how she ever broke into writing novels with happy endings. More often than not, Sam found herself fighting resentment toward some of the sisters with happy-ending lives — especially Kim Lan and Mel. Those two had something close to love-story existences as far as Sammie calculated. Sure, Mel complained about her manipulative mother, but Sammie often wanted to scream, "At least she didn't leave you!" And Kim

Lan . . . well, who wouldn't be tempted to be envious of her rags to riches life that culminated in marriage to a man who adored her.

The telephone's ringing broke into Sammie's musings. Brooke hollered, "I'll get it!" and raced toward a cordless phone sitting on a refinished end table.

Sammie shifted Brett's weight and eyed Marilyn and R.J. as they conversed near the front door. Marilyn laughed out loud at something the biker said, and Sam even resented Marilyn for laughing at a time like this. *Okay, I'm having an attitude here,* she thought. *And I've got to get a grip. These people are stretching long and hard to help me. The last thing I need to do is alienate them.*

"Yes, sir. This is the Thatcher residence." Brooke's prim voice rang over the adult small talk. "Yes. She's here. Would you like to speak with her?" Her brown eyes shining, Brooke extended the phone to Sam. "He wants to talk with you."

She looked at the phone as if it were a viper then turned her gaze to Marilyn whose eyes were as wide as Sam's. Her head throbbed anew. Her eyes filled with unshed tears. And a series of panicked thoughts stampeded her mind. *He found me, and he's going to kill me! He really is.*

335

There's no way I can get away from him. Not ever!

"Think it's your father?" R.J. asked, his soft voice assuring.

Sammie released her pent-up breath. "Must be," she said. "I gave him Marilyn's number last night and told him that I'd be here by mid-morning or a little later."

R.J. nodded then reached for Brett who gladly fell into his new buddy's arms. Sammie tried not to wince as she took the phone. All the hours in the car had certainly taken their toll. "Hello," she said into the receiver as she gazed out the picture window onto Marilyn's lawn.

"Hello, Doll," Adam's venomous voice dripped over the line. "Don't think I don't know where you are or who you're with."

"Where are you?" Sam gasped and slumped to the floor. The last year replayed itself in her mind, scene by scene, blow by blow, and she choked on a sob.

"I'm in Eureka Springs. Where else? Did you get my e-mail?" The alcoholic slur in his words grated upon her pounding head.

Whimpering, Sammie scooted toward the corner, as if he were towering over her, ready to wreak havoc with her soul.

"Did you think you would ever be able to get away from me? Did you? Oh, really,

Sam, you are so stupid!" The final words blasted out like the shriek of a fiend.

"What is it? Who is it?" R.J.'s troubled voice neared, and Sam helplessly peered into his churning eyes.

Without a word, he grabbed the phone. "Adam, is that you?" he yelled.

Sam jumped, knotted her fingers against her mouth, and scooted as far into the corner as possible. From the corner of her eye, she noticed Marilyn ushering the two children out the back door.

R.J., his face aflame, shook his fist at the ceiling. "I know it's you — you slime bag!"

"Mommy! Mommy! I want Mommy!" Brett's retreating cries tore at Sammie's heart.

"Listen, you pervert, this is a direct violation of your restraining order. If you even so much as show one speck of your rotten self around Sam, I'll have you slammed into jail so fast —" R.J. stopped shouting, pulled the phone away from his ear, and stared at it. "He hung up," he snarled. The vein in his forehead protruded as he slammed the phone into the cradle. With a roar, he held his hands in front of him in a claw-like gesture. "I could just . . ." He stopped himself then knelt on the floor beside Sam. The biker covered his face, took a deep breath, then rested his hands on his thighs. Only the puppy's faint yap and Brett's unharnessed bellowing intruded upon the heavy silence. Finally R.J. looked at Sam, and she didn't ever remember seeing so much compassion from another human being. "It's going to be okay," he soothed.

Hot tears burned Sam's cheeks and pooled at the corners of her mouth. "N–no, it's not okay," she blurted then launched into a fervid torrent of terror. "He's going to kill me! He will! I know he will! He said he would!" She pulled her knees to her chest, wrapped her arms around her legs, and started rocking. "Why did I leave? I was crazy to leave. He's going to kill me. He followed me here. He knows where I am. He'll kill me and take Brett and who knows what he'll do to Brett. He's crazy, R.J!" Sam cried and reached for his arm as if it were her only lifeline. "He's a devil who acts like a–a saint! He's going to kill me!"

"Trust me, Sam." R.J. gripped her hand in both of his. "I will not let that man ever hit you again. I don't care if I have to . . ." The bulging vein in his forehead throbbed, and his face contorted into the mask of a livid warrior ready to fight to the death.

"Sammie?" a masculine voice called from the back door. "I really hate to disturb you, but Marilyn needs your help with Brett. He's going haywire out here."

Scrubbing at her soaked face, Sammie stumbled to her feet. R.J. offered his hand then steadied her with his arm. She looked into the kitchen to see Marilyn's husband, Joshua, standing with one foot in the kitchen and one foot on the backdoor step. He held an oversized spatula dotted with barbecue sauce and wore a red-checked chef's apron that said "Kiss the cook." There was nothing spectacular about Joshua Langham's gray eyes, brown hair, and average features. When Marilyn first met him, she described him to the sisters as "fair looking until he smiles." Joshua bestowed one of his million-dollar grins upon Sam and R.J.

A reciprocal grin managed to wobble across Sam's lips, and she was grateful that Josh asked no probing questions. As soon as she quieted Brett, Sammie planned to consult Jac about what to do. Adam was obviously not going to abide by his restraining order. A new shiver gripped her.

Joshua glanced toward the tall biker, and at closer range Sam couldn't miss the current of concern stirring his eyes — an unequivocal alarm that even the smile couldn't mask. "I guess you're R.J.?"

"In the flesh," R.J. said, never leaving Sam's side as they neared the back door.

"I hear you struck up a deal with my wife," Josh continued, then eyed Sam with much the same male protectiveness that R.J. had bestowed. "Twelve hamburgers in exchange for a ride on your Harley."

"Right now, you can *have* my Harley," R.J. mumbled and tightened his grip on Sammie's arm.

Twenty-One

~

Jacquelyn awoke with a start and listened, her eyes wide. A foreign noise had penetrated her sleep. She gazed around the hotel room to make sure she was alone. Despite Jac's protest, Lawton had insisted she lie down and rest. Shortly after he went back to his room, a heavy slumber claimed her. A rap on her hotel room door revealed the reason for her sleep's disruption. Her immediate thought was that she had slept past the FBI meeting. She looked at the nightstand's digital clock and noted that she had only slept a couple of hours. It was not quite eleven o'clock.

She stumbled from her bed, approached the door, and paused long enough to look out the peephole. A dark-skinned, granite-faced man stood on the other side, his hands clasped in front of him, his gaze fixed forward. He appeared vaguely familiar, and Jacquelyn grappled with how she knew him.

"Who is it?" she called, her voice husky from sleep.

"FBI!" the man barked and held up an ID that validated his claim.

Ah, she thought. *I remember now. We crossed paths on the Dino Lambert case.* Nevertheless, his name continued to escape her.

The click and sigh of another door opening prompted the agent's glance toward Lawton's room.

As Jac stepped away from the peephole and fumbled with the lock, she shoved aside all thoughts about her traumatic morning. Even though her heart still ached, she had learned through the years to cover the pain and keep functioning. She would continue in that vein as long as was necessary. While she focused on the task at hand, only one fleeting realization penetrated her mind. Jacquelyn had rested this morning, really rested for the first time in months. For once no dragon had haunted her, either through a direct nightmare or by a shadowed presence. With determination, Jac turned the knob and opened her door.

"I heard the knocking," Lawton explained as Jac stepped across the threshold.

"I need to speak with both of you — privately," the agent said, his lips terse. "May I come into one of your rooms?"

Without a word, Jac nodded and glanced toward Lawton. The latest tidbits from CNN floated from the recesses of his room, and he looked as if he had just been broadsided with an outlandish news flash.

"Wanta come over here, Lawton?" she asked and hid her chuckle.

"Sure. Let me get my key."

Actually, the appearance of the agent didn't surprise Jacquelyn in the least. Even in her shattered state she had pieced together the clues that suggested they were most likely being watched by "powers" greater than she. When Austin mentioned an FBI meeting, she possessed little doubt that those involved already knew that she, too, was involved.

"Please make sure your drapes are closed," the agent requested, then glanced to his left and right.

"They are." Jac pointed toward the striped curtains as she opened the door for his entry. "I closed them earlier so I could catch up on some sleep."

Lawton stepped in after the agent, who

smelled of expensive tobacco. Jac closed the door with a click that seemed to underscore the gravity of the moment. She followed the man toward the room's center, stopped, and crossed her arms. Lawton's measured pacing halted nearby.

The agent wore casual slacks and pale silk shirt that screamed of quality. The slacks, the color of gunmetal, descended to a pair of woven loafers that probably cost a fortune. The agent strode directly toward the window and inched the curtain away a mere fraction. After seconds of silent observation, he released the drapes.

"My name is Norman Green," he said, and his words shot out with the rapidity of a New York inflection.

"Yes, Green — Norman," Jac replied. "We crossed paths a couple of years back, didn't we?"

"You do get around, don't you, Lightfoot?" He never blinked.

"Looks like we all do," she replied with a shrug.

"We are currently investigating the Rantomi family." He paused and eyed Jac. "Ever heard of the Rantomis?"

"Of course. Who hasn't in our business."

Lawton's firm grip just above her elbow hinted at his alarm, and Jac forced herself not to smile. Poor Lawton had already received more crime-related action this week than he'd probably had in his whole life.

"What about Fuat Rantomi?"

"Don't know," Jac mused. "But I have heard of that family."

"Fuat is one of their leaders. He knows how to cover his tracks with the best of them. He's up to his eyeballs in all sorts of stuff, but we can't ever pin anything on him."

"Sounds like Dino Lambert," Jacquelyn said. The lightweight sweats that had proven necessary that morning now provided too much warmth.

"Exactly." Green approached her and pulled several photos from his shirt pocket. "Fuat Rantomi," he said, and Jac peered at the photo of a man walking across an airport, briefcase in hand.

Jacquelyn's eyes widened. "He looks a little like Austin Sellers."

"That's because he's Sellers' biological father," Norman said on a grim note.

Lawton's fingers flexed against Jac's arm. Immediately, Austin's mysterious tale echoed through her mind. A distraught mother, certain she would die. Fourteen Greek coins. Amanda's ultimate death. Austin's shadowed adoption.

"He's also the person responsible for Gary and Rhonda Sellers' deaths." Norman's words fell out like jagged rocks.

"Mama mia," Lawton mumbled while Jac whistled.

"But you probably can't try him, am I right?" Jac asked.

"Right." The agent nodded as if he were checking off the necessities on a grocery list. "The hit man responsible is former police officer Maurice Stein." Green pulled another photo from the bottom of the short stack. Jac peered at a man getting out of a limo on a crowded city street. He had dark hair and eyes as hard as marble.

"He looks a little familiar," she mused.

"We nabbed him last night. Rantomi thinks I killed him." Green narrowed his eyes. "I loaded him into the trunk of the car and told Rantomi I shot him and dumped him over the side of a mountain. Right now Stein is residing behind bars in Colorado Springs. From the looks of things, he was cracking up and really botching everything he touched. He could have grabbed Gary's coins several nights ago when he killed the Sellers but he freaked out and left without them. He keeps talking about children. From all we can gather, he had a couple of kids that were killed in a fire." Green waved his hand as if he were shoving aside all unnecessary details. "Anyway, he's willing to talk, and that's good for our government. Problem is, the Turkish government also wants Rantomi."

"Oh?" Jac and Lawton said in unison.

"Hmm. What do you know about Greek coins?" Green flipped out another photo.

This time Jacquelyn peered at a picture of an Athena Owl coin, exactly like Austin's. "Not much," she said with a dry smile. "We tried to find out something on the internet but basically struck out."

Green snorted and shoved the photos back into his pocket. "It's no wonder. Some of these babies are nearly worthless."

"Wait, don't tell me." Lawton raised his hand. "These are worth 20 million apiece or something. Am I right?"

"Close," Green confirmed. "Try 10 million for all 14."

Jac narrowed her eyes and crossed her arms. "Okay, so how do you figure that?"

"They're in mint condition," Green stated. His close-set eyes and hooked nose gave him the appearance of a glittery-eyed eagle about to swoop upon its prey.

"That's what I was thinking," Lawton quipped as if he were some sleuth of the decade. Jac shot him a wry glance, only to realize it was lost on him.

"They date back to ancient Greece — 465 B.C.," Green said. "They're worth a fortune because of their flawless condition and because they're decadrachms. There are only 27 in existence. The 14 between Gary and Austin leaves only 13 others in the world. They're still the property of the Turkish government, but they will bring a fortune on the black market."

"And how did Rantomi get them in the first place?" Jac asked.

"The best we can tell, he illegally excavated them while visiting relatives in Turkey, about 35 years ago. They came from a farmer's field near the southeast border."

Jacquelyn nodded.

"That makes perfect sense after what you read on the internet this morning about how that sort of stuff can just show up after a rain," Lawton said.

"Right," the agent confirmed and rushed on. "Then, the best we can figure, Rantomi smuggled them back into the U.S., which is easier than you could ever imagine. From there, we have deduced that he and his wife weren't getting along and she took the coins and their sons.

That's when they disappeared — until now."

"Until now," Jac repeated. "So how did Rantomi find out about them?"

"Gary called one too many coin dealers," Green said with a tinge of remorse. "One of them had connections with a middleman who had connections with Rantomi. That phone call triggered the whole nasty mess."

"And how do we fit into all this?" Jac rubbed her eyes and figured by the feel of them that she looked about as swollen-eyed as an owl herself. "Why are you taking the time to tell us all this?"

"Because . . ." Green glowered and stepped past the bed toward the curtains. He pulled aside the striped fabric but a centimeter, peered out, then let it drop. "We advise you to leave Ouray as soon as you can — as in *now*."

"Why?" Lawton squeaked.

"I have been with Rantomi for days now. He thinks my name is Edwardo Juarez." Green's words took on the swirl and flourish of a Spanish accent. "One of Rantomi's present goals is to make sure each of you is dead." He raised his hand. "As a matter of fact, I talked Rantomi out of shooting you this morning, Lawton." He observed Lawton with a flicker of compassion. "And you." Norman eyed Jac.

Her shoulders stiffened.

"Rantomi thinks I hold a false FBI ID under the name Sylvester D. Lancaster. We are going to be meeting with Austin today to retrieve the coins. Fuat is talking about assigning his daughter, Angelica, and four of her cronies to your murders. In two days, we have a meeting with a coin dealer in Greece. When Rantomi actually sells the coins, the Turkish government will arrest him. The U.S. has decided that those charges will stick way better than anything we could prosecute for. Also, they will give him a heftier punishment than we ever could." Green's smile was far from kind.

"Austin Sellers asked us to join you at the meeting today," Jacquelyn said. "He's scared."

"And well he should be." Green nodded. "We are taking every precaution to ensure his safety."

"But how do you know for certain that Rantomi won't just go in shooting or —" Jac waved her hand.

"He almost never shoots," Green said. "That's part of the reason we can't create a substantial case against him. He would expect me to do any shooting."

With a sigh Jac rubbed her forehead. "But you just said that he came within a breath of shooting Lawton and me today," she said.

"Yes, that's true." Norman eyed Lawton. "From what we can gather, Mr. Franklin, you landed at the wrong place at the wrong time. You have heard Rantomi's voice and could possibly link him to the Sellers' murders. Rantomi is known for showing no mercy in such cases. He's also known for impatience when a murder has been botched. Stein blew yours twice."

"Well, that's really heartwarming." Lawton rubbed the top of his left hand where the IV had entered.

"So, what's to stop him from unloading on Austin?" Jac demanded.

"Like I said, there are no guarantees," Green said. "Nonetheless, chances are all will go well."

"But we promised Austin we'd be at the meeting," Lawton insisted.

"So break your promise," Green spat out. "The two of you need to get out of here and let us handle this. If Rantomi sees you two at this meeting, there's no telling what he might do. It will ruin the whole setup. Do you understand?"

"Yes," Lawton readily agreed, and Jacquelyn nodded.

"Good." Green strode toward the door. "I recommend that you get out within the hour."

"I'm as good as ready now," Lawton said.

Jacquelyn glanced around the room and noted her possessions scattered here and there. "I can be ready in about 15 minutes," she said.

At 11:30 Jac and Lawton placed their suitcases in the back of the rental car, and Jac closed the door.

"Ready?" she asked.

"I know we need to get out of here," Lawton said, "but I really need to make a trip to the necessary room."

"Okay, be quick," Jac agreed and glanced over her shoulder. "I don't have a good feeling about this at all."

"Believe me, you aren't the only one." He walked toward the passenger door, opened it, and felt across the floorboard until he came upon his cane.

"Do you remember where it is?" Jac asked.

"Yep."

"I'll walk with you."

"No!" he snapped then straightened. "I

don't need a mother here, Jac. I can go to the restroom by myself."

"I wasn't going to go in there with you, for Pete's sake," she blurted.

"I know that," he said. "But I can make it by myself, okay? Look, it's right through the front doors, 40 paces straight ahead. Hang a right, 6 paces, then another right takes me where I need to go. How difficult can that be? Unless I'm wrong, you can watch me almost the whole way there."

"You're right — and I will."

"So fine! Watch me, then!"

Head held high, he strode through the glass doors and straight into the entryway. Jacquelyn shook her head and did a few quick stretches. *The man is as stubborn as . . . as stubborn as . . . I am, I guess.* Jac chuckled and continued her vigil.

This time, Lawton relied upon the cane that she had seen him seldom use. A few times in unfamiliar territory he had gripped her arm and relied on her as guide. More often than not, if Lawton was on familiar ground, he functioned fine with no aid — if hopping over balconies was considered within the boundaries of functioning fine. Jac figured the cane served as much a tool of protection as a need for guidance.

When Lawton disappeared around the corner, a plethora of jumbled emotions tore at Jac. She no longer doubted that Lawton was in love with her — really in love. What started between them last spring had turned into more than she had ever imagined. And now that he knew her darkest secret, Jacquelyn was amazed that she ever believed he would allow her past to taint his regard. In one sense the authenticity of Lawton's love immersed Jacquelyn in a cloud of wonder. In another sense, the reality of his love created greater complications. If he had rejected her, all Jac's decisions would have been made for her. Their relationship would have ended. They would have each continued their separate lives. But as things now stood, she suspected he was on the brink of proposing. She also suspected that he grappled with the implications of her ever being able to maintain a healthy marital relationship.

Her discovery about her grandfather had indeed disentangled Jacquelyn from yet another link in the rusty chain holding her captive. Nonetheless, the chain was by no means broken. At least the monstrous mask had been ripped from the dragon. However, she hadn't even begun the journey of forgiving him — nor did she want to begin that journey.

An uncomfortable ache pierced her spirit, and she began drumming her fingers against the top of the car. Images of her grandfather, always smiling, left bitter tracks upon her heart. Ever since the spring, Jacquelyn had repeatedly vowed her hatred for the person who violated her. A few times she had even fantasized about ending the mysterious fiend's life. Ironically, her dragon was already dead. Yet he had killed a precious part of his granddaughter years before his demise.

Now Jac didn't know if she could even think about healthy sexuality without shriveling inside. True, there was a certain magnetism between her and Lawton — a magnetism she had never felt with any other man. The sparks *did* fly, and she was certain they would fly even after marriage. But she had no idea at what point she might freeze and not be able to move to full physical union. In her estimation, the bondage from the past might very well sour her marriage. Despite Lawton's understanding spirit, she wasn't naive enough to think that he wasn't analyzing every angle. Jac hoped he analyzed it for a long, long time. The very idea of turning down

Lawton's proposal left her aching with remorse, but neither could she envision accepting him in the near future.

"It just wouldn't be fair to him," she whispered. "He deserves a wife who can be all his." *If I ever do get married,* she continued inwardly, *I want something better than what Mom and Dad have.*

The thought bore upon Jac from nowhere, and she blinked against the shafts of sunlight bathing the village. She never remembered a time when she sat down and analyzed her parents' relationship. However, there had always been a spirit of unease between them — a certain friction that Jac had accepted but never defined. Her mother, a gracious lady by anybody's standards, never seemed to really connect with her father. For that matter, Jac herself had a closer relationship with her dad than she had ever enjoyed with her mother.

Her fingers' drumming stopped as a new beast emerged from the miasmic marsh of her past. *If Grandpa took advantage of me, did he do the same to Mom? And if he did, did Mom know and still let me go to his house?* Her hand clenched to a fist against the vehicle's top.

Jac rested her forehead upon her arm and observed the car's red paint, blurred by the close proximity. A new wave of dismay doused her, and she blinked against fresh tears. Her fingernails ate into her palms, and she reeled in a tidal wave of possibilities. *I've got to stop this now,* she admonished herself. *I cannot allow this to overtake me here. Mom probably had no idea. I cannot start imagining things that I have no proof of.*

Raising her head, she sucked in great gulps of air. One by one Jacquelyn stuffed the negative musings into a closet deep inside her spirit. The whole time she promised herself that she must make a trip to see her mother and father. Some answers awaited her there — answers that would hopefully help her gain some perspective and, perhaps, some peace. Jac stowed away the last "what if," closed the bulging closet door, and locked it. As she expunged the final moisture from her eyes, she fought the temptation to unlock the door inside and allow the contents to tumble forth in a jumble and rush. Instead, she shook her head and focused on the hotel lobby.

Her fingers began another rhythmic cadence on the Ford's top as she peered through the glass doors and toward the hallway from which Lawton should emerge. The mundane sounds of tires crunching on pavement, a crow's distant caw, and a snatch of country music belied the gravity of the hour. At every turn Jac wanted to glance over her shoulder, but every time she did all she encountered was the line of Colorado Rockies that extended into a blue haze on the horizon. The realization that they were in Fuat Rantomi's scope that very morning left her highly aware of her own mortality — and Lawton's. Her fingers increased their tattoo.

Jac checked her watch and noted that Austin's meeting with the supposed FBI agents loomed within the next 30 minutes. She breathed a prayer for the grief-stricken pastor and threw in a few phrases for Norman Green as well. Jac had promised that she'd be at this meeting, and she knew that her absence would trouble Austin. The agent had instructed them not to contact the pastor, but the man would not leave her mind. When interacting with fellow law enforcement agencies, Jac usually made it a habit to respect their suggestions and play by the rules. She could name dates and places that wise mode of operation had saved her life.

"But what's one phone call going to hurt?" she mumbled.

With an impatient huff, she settled into the front seat. The new car smell enveloped her as she shuffled through her backpack and pulled out the cell phone. Jacquelyn pressed the redial button and watched the numbers of her last phone call flash across the tiny screen. She held the phone to her ear.

The midday sun christened the snow-streaked mountains with a glowing kiss. Even though Jac had been in Denver for eight years, she had never traveled to this tourist town. Lawton said he'd never been here, either. *Too bad it's under such negative circumstances,* she thought. *And too bad we have to leave so soon.*

"Hello," Austin's cautious greeting floated over the line.

"Hi. It's Jac Lightfoot," she said and paused for his positive response. She and Austin Sellers could have struck up a solid friendship if given the opportunity. "I just wanted to tell you that my friend and I are having to . . . leave town on an emergency. We won't be able to make the meeting."

"I was about to call your cell phone, Jac," Austin said. "I had a feeling you weren't coming." He paused, and Jac gripped the bottom of the steering wheel. "There's something about this whole thing that strikes me wrong. I don't like it. Neither does my wife. I'm having trouble handing the coins over to these people. I mean, somebody offered Gary a quarter of a million for all 14. Now Gary's are gone, and these people just showed up and said they're federal agents. I don't know. I'm scared. I'm really scared."

"Listen," Jacquelyn said, glad she had heeded the inner prompting and made the call. "I know people who know people. I have learned more than I can tell you, okay?"

"Okay," he hedged.

"Trust me. The coins belong to the Turkish government. Give them to Lancaster, and don't make a scene. Understand?"

"What have you found out?" Austin demanded. "How do you know the FBI agent's name is Lancaster?"

"I . . . can't say more. Just do what I say. When the men come, hand over the coins and leave it at that."

"Okay, if you're sure," Austin said.

"I'm sure," Jacquelyn said. "I know this is all really hard, Austin, but you need to do what I say. Understand?"

"Y–yes," he stuttered, and an echo in the digital phone's reception reverberated his incertitude.

A tall individual exiting the lobby distracted Jac from the present conversation. At first, she wasn't sure if the person wearing a snug baseball cap was a man or a woman. The loose fitting men's shirt and baggy jeans hid any feminine curves that might be present. However, when the person dug a set of keys out of the jeans' pocket, the turn of her hand implied femininity. So did the tuft of curly hair that escaped the cap's confines. Jac frowned.

Green's warnings about Rantomi's daughter surged upon her. *Lawton has been in that bathroom far too long,* she thought. *We've got to get out of here.*

Austin discreetly cleared his throat, and Jac remembered that she was supposed to be in the midst of a conversation. "Oh, sorry. I got distracted. Listen, I'm going to have to go now," she continued without a breath. "I'll be praying."

"Thanks."

Jac disconnected the call and realized she had prayed more in the last few days than she had since she could remember. She dropped the cell phone into her backpack and eyed the nondescript sedan pulling out of the parking lot. The woman with the baseball cap was behind the wheel. The hair on the back of Jacquelyn's neck prickled. A sixth sense hinted at darkness and despair.

She got out of the car, slammed the door, and locked it. Jacquelyn rounded the back of the Ford and entered the hotel lobby. An overweight man with bulging red cheeks and bugged-out eyes trotted from the hallway.

"There's a dead body in the men's room!" he squawked.

Jac stopped and fought the childish urge to cover her ears. The homey lobby tilted, and she felt as if she were disconnected from her surroundings. Disconnected and swept away in a tide of terror.

A brunette darted from behind the receptionist's desk.

"Call the police!" the man screamed.

The woman turned in a circle and raced back to the phone.

Her heart in her throat, Jac surged in front of the man and hurled herself toward the restroom. She slammed open the door and halted as if she had run into an invisible wall. A limp hand extended from under a stall. A hand touching a white cane.

Twenty-Two

~

"Lightfoot," Jac said into the receiver.

"You're with Lawton Franklin?" a male voice queried.

"Yes." Jacquelyn lowered herself into the vacant chair near the desk in the hospital waiting room.

"This is Dr. Corley. I've got good news and bad news," he said.

The chair-lined room, void of other occupants, took on a surreal aura. "He is alive?" Jac prompted as the activities of the last two hours replayed in her mind like a dread nightmare. The paramedics. The cardiac shock. Lawton's regaining a faint pulse. The care flight into Montrose. The frantic rush into E.R. The helplessness. The panic. The desperation.

"Yes, but . . ."

Jac imagined the frantic face of the aging doctor as he raced into E.R., straight toward Lawton's room.

"We were able to remove the bullet," he said on a grim note. "But he hasn't yet stabilized. There's still a chance that he might not make it. Eighty-five to 90 percent of people who take a bullet so close to the heart don't survive. And if they do, there's a chance of severe brain damage."

"As in?" she prompted.

"It's too early to say, but he could lose control over all bodily functions and his mental faculties," the doctor stated. "We lost him twice in surgery."

Jacquelyn slumped across the desk and stifled the silent sob that threatened to burst into a cacophony of grief. "How — how soon will you know?" she coughed out and nearly gagged over the smell of freshly brewing coffee.

"The next few hours are critical, very critical. I'm staying close. We're hoping that his vital signs will stabilize soon. Once that happens, you can step in to see him briefly. He's a fighter, I already know that. Otherwise he wouldn't have made it this far. An encouraging word from a loved one may give him the extra spark he needs to pull out of this."

"Of course. I'll do whatever I can to help him." Jacquelyn raised her head, propped her elbow on the desk, and cradled her forehead in her hand.

"One more thing — do you believe in prayer?" Dr. Corley prompted.

"Yes. Yes, I do," Jac said as she fought a haze of gloom.

"I suggest you pray like you've never prayed in your life," the doctor said. "The fact that he's made it this far is a major miracle. We can only hope that there's another miracle around the corner."

"I will," Jac said.

"Stay close to the phone," he continued. "We'll try to update you often. And like I said, we might need you soon."

"Okay. At this point what chance do you give him, Dr. Corley? You — you know, to survive without brain damage and live a normal life?"

The physician's ominous silence heightened Jac's trembling. "I'd say five percent; ten percent is probably pushing it" he finally said, and sympathy dripped from his every word.

"Okay, thanks." Jac replaced the receiver and covered her face with her hands. This time the sob would not be silenced. Her trembling increased, and she relived the horror of those dire moments when she saw Lawton's body on the bathroom floor. *Oh, God,* she pleaded, *if you stopped him from being killed at the airport and prohibited the acid from entering his body, then please, please continue to do something now.*

Her cell phone, cradled in her denim shirt's pocket, pealed. Jac jumped then rubbed at her eyes. She pulled out the phone, pressed the appropriate button, and held it to her ear. "Lightfoot," she stated, then sniffled.

"Jacquelyn? Mel here. We got your voice mail and wondered —"

"Mel, it's Lawton." Jac paused as the Coke machine turned into a blur of lights. "He's been shot. They really got him this time," she choked out.

"What? Is he — is he —"

"Not now. But I don't know. The surgeon just called. He made it through the surgery, but they lost him twice. The paramedics had to shock him, too. The bullet lodged next to his heart. The prognosis is *really, really* bad. The doctor says he only has a five- or maybe a ten-percent chance of surviving without brain damage." Jacquelyn's fingers dug into her leg as a series of shuffles floated over the line.

"Jac, it's Kinkaide. What is it? Mel can't talk."

"Lawton. It's Lawton. Somebody shot him. And this time, they meant it for keeps, Kinkaide. I'm sure it's the Rantomi clan." With the image of that shabbily dressed woman marching through her mind, Jac wadded a handful of hair at the back of her head.

"Who?"

"Look, it's a — a long story," she said. "But the long and short of it is that Lawton has gotten himself tangled with a criminal on the rampage for some rare coins worth millions. The coins belong to the Turkish government." She waved her hand. "Like I said, it's a long story. Lawton is just out of surgery. It doesn't look good, Kinkaide. It really d–doesn't." Jacquelyn stood, bit her lips, and strode toward the vending machines.

A muffled exclamation echoed across the line. "Where are you?" Kinkaide demanded, his voice thick.

"I'm at the hospital in Montrose." She moved back to the nurse's desk, snatched up a hospital brochure, and rattled out the necessary contact information.

Jacquelyn dropped the brochure in the middle of the desk, and the constant hum of the vending machines became a dirge. "The doctor says they hope his vital signs stabilize within the next couple of hours. If they do, his chances increase. If they don't . . ." She left the rest unsaid.

"Yes. Okay. Let's just hope and pray he stabilizes."

"Right."

Kinkaide's broken moan ushered in an extended bout of silence. Then another series of shuffles floated across the line. "Jac, it's Mel again," she wobbled out. "Kinkaide can't talk right now."

Jacquelyn nodded then settled near her backpack in one of the padded chairs. "I'll call you back as soon as I know something. The doctor said the next few hours are critical. I'll call you as soon as I know more."

"I understand," Mel said in a dazed voice. "What will they do? Keep trying until they really get him?" she wailed.

"Looks like it." Closing her eyes, Jac frowned and clenched her teeth.

"So, if he makes it this time . . ."

"I don't know," Jac rasped. "There's a definite possibility that they will be nabbing Rantomi within the week."

"Who?"

While Jacquelyn briefed Mel on the pertinent details that she had just stated to Kinkaide, she walked toward the change-maker, turned on her heel, then settled back on the edge of her chair.

"Well, what about you?" Melissa asked. "Will they try to do something to you? You're in the middle of this, too."

"I don't know." Jacquelyn leaned back in the cushioned chair, extended her legs, and propped her head on the wall behind her. She closed her eyes and the room felt as if it were spinning. The tears streamed down her cheeks like rivulets of grief. "My dad says I live a charmed life."

"But how long can that last? I mean —"

"Let's not borrow trouble, here." Jac peered at the ceiling, and the glint in Norman Green's eyes left her shuddering. Both she *and* Lawton had been in Rantomi's gun scope that morning. A movement from the waiting room's doorway snared her attention, and she glanced toward the opening. A nurse, dressed in white, walked into the room. She spotted Jac and stepped forward, her abundance of ebony curls bouncing with every step. Her olive complexion, stylish hair, and polished makeup made Jacquelyn think of a shampoo advertisement in which Kim Lan had been featured.

"Just a minute, Mel." Jac covered the phone's mouthpiece and stood.

The nurse stopped a few feet away. "You are with Lawton Franklin?" she asked, her thin brows arched in query.

"Yes."

"There's been a . . . negative turn of events." The nurse's dark gaze faltered. "The surgeon wishes to see you now."

The room tilted, and Jac clutched the phone tighter. A wave of heat started at her feet and rushed to her hairline. Cool sweat followed in its wake. "I've — I've g–gotta go, Mel," Jac stuttered.

"Wait! What's going on? Is everything okay?"

"Hurry!" the nurse urged as if Jac were daft.

Jac deliberated whether she should explain to Mel, then decided against it — not until she had all the details herself. Mel and Kinkaide were already distraught, no sense making matters worse with mere suppositions. "I'll call you right back." She disconnected the call, snatched up her backpack and handbag, and hastened after the nurse.

The telephone rang, and Sammie jumped. She stopped the rocking chair and tightened her hold on Brett as Adam's prelunch phone call resonated through her mind.

Marilyn looked up from her book, stared at Sam, then eyed the phone. Brooke's faint giggles from the driveway mingled with the Harley's rev that preceded the phone's next peal.

"You've got to get it," Sam whispered. Brett stirred then whimpered.

With a nod, Marilyn stretched to the end table and picked up the receiver. Cringing, Sammie awaited Marilyn's reaction.

"Oh, hi, Mel!" she softly said and gave Sam the thumbs-up sign.

Sammie loosened her grip on Brett. She resumed her rocking and bestowed a gentle kiss on the child's forehead. He frowned, then his breathing resumed a regular cadence. Sam settled her head against the back of the padded rocker as the after-lunch drowse began, despite the fact that she had eaten little. Adam's slurred threat had poisoned every bite and created a knot of nausea that left no room for food. Before they ate, R.J. insisted upon calling the police and giving them Adam's description, along with the details of his recent violation. The local authorities promised to patrol the area. They claimed they had no way of tracking Adam's location or his phone call. Jacquelyn's warning about the effectiveness of the restraining order was proving valid. As Adam's murderous intent reverberated through her mind, Sam resisted the urge to bolt from the rocker and run for her life.

"I see," Marilyn said. "Yes, we will. *This is just awful!*"

Sammie lifted her head and watched Marilyn. Her blonde ponytail shifted around her shoulders as she shook her head from side to side then pressed her fingertips against her chin.

"And how is Jac taking all of this?" There was a pause, and Marilyn, her troubled eyes filling with unshed tears, peered toward Sam. "We will certainly pray." Her firm voice only hinted at her emotions. "Okay, I'll be glad to call the rest of the sisters. Sam's here now, so that just leaves Kim Lan, Victoria, and Sonsee."

A needle-thin stab of pain radiated from Sam's lower back. With a grimace she shifted in the rocker.

"Yes, Sam's fine." Marilyn pleated the hem of her walking shorts. "Sonsee's fine, too, Mel. I talked with her this morning before Sam got here. Her doctor's appointment went well today. He just told her to stay in bed. But you need to quit worrying about Sonsee and Sam and focus on your family right now. Kinkaide will really need you if —" Marilyn snagged her lower lip between her teeth, and Sammie leaned forward in an attempt to solve the message's meaning.

"No, let's not," Marilyn agreed. "Let's hope for the best." After affectionate goodbyes, Marilyn hung up and stared at Sam.

"It's Lawton," she said. "They shot him again. This time —"

Sammie stopped rocking. "Is he —"

"No. He's had emergency surgery, but it looks really bad. The bullet lodged near his heart. The surgeon says he's got a five- to ten-percent chance to make it without brain damage. Mel says this all has something to do with a criminal family by the name of Rantomi."

"We certainly are living interesting lives of late, aren't we?" Sammie whispered.

"This is just awful." Marilyn laid her book on the knotty-pine coffee table and leaned forward.

"Do they think Lawton will make it?" Sammie asked. Her head resumed its pounding, despite the aspirin R.J. had insisted she take.

"They don't know." Marilyn placed her

elbows on her knees and rested her face in her hands.

"And what about Jac? Is she okay?"

"Right now, yes. She's really upset."

"Do they think the bad guys will come after her?"

"I didn't ask. I was afraid to." Marilyn stood and crossed her arms. "If they shot Lawton, then they know that he and Jac went to Ouray together. They will also know that Jac knows what Lawton knows." She shrugged. "Whatever that is."

"Don't you worry about Jac at times? She can get herself into some really tight fixes," Sammie said. "It's only been a couple of years ago that she uncovered that big drug ring. Frankly, I wondered if somebody would retaliate then." Sammie stroked a lock of red hair from Brett's forehead, and her fingers lingered on his chubby cheek.

"I mentioned something of that effect to her, and she laughed out loud. She said she could kill two grown men in three seconds if she wanted to."

"But what if they shoot her from a distance?" Sam insisted. "All that karate-chop business is meaningless if they're 30 feet away and pull the trigger."

"I know. I started to tell her that, but I

hated to sound like the pessimist of the South, ya know?" Marilyn whispered. "She gets aggravated when we start sounding like mother hens."

Sam nodded her agreement.

The motorcycle's engine revved once more then rumbled to a stop as Marilyn eyed Brett. "But I guess Jac *did* come through for you, didn't she?"

Sammie widened her eyes and nodded as Brooke's giggles neared. The door opened and Joshua entered with the little girl riding his back. R.J. was close behind. After lunch Josh had opted for a look at the Harley, since he and R.J. decided they shouldn't leave the ladies alone.

"Shh," Marilyn said and pointed toward Brett.

Josh turned down the corners of his mouth. "Sorry," he whispered and whisked Brooke toward the kitchen.

"How long has he been asleep?" R.J. whispered as he knelt beside Sam.

"Not long," Sammie said.

"Want me to take him?" R.J.'s brown eyes poured out buckets of empathy.

Sam's traitorous mind flashed to the week before her wedding. Out of nowhere R.J. had rolled up to her duplex, parked his Harley, and proceeded to beg her to marry him instead of Adam. His mother had leaked information about Sammie's wedding to him, and he couldn't stand the thought of Sam marrying somebody else. Looking back, Sam couldn't even remember praying about R.J.'s offer. Instead she had declared that he was too late. He had his chance and blew it. Now, she once again fought the urge to burst into uncontrolled weeping.

"I'll be glad to put him on the bed," R.J. continued.

"Yes, why don't you?" Marilyn agreed from just behind him. "I think Sam's having trouble with her back."

R.J.'s eyes clouded. He opened his mouth to speak, then snapped it shut. And Sam knew he knew. Just like that. He understood the source of her aching spine. A flash of fury sparked his eyes like a pop of lightning that crackles then disappears. He schooled his features and focused upon the child. "Come here, Champ," he whispered, then gathered Brett close.

"It's the second door on the left," Marilyn directed as she stood.

Sammie watched the sway of R.J.'s leather vest as he walked up the hallway. The sound of his riding boots barely registered upon the hardwood floor, and his spindly braid tapped against the center of his back with every step.

"He's still in love with you," Marilyn stated, without a hint of doubt.

"I know," Samantha responded. "But I'm married. I should have never —" Sam stopped the claim from tumbling out as R.J.'s form disappeared. "But if I hadn't married Adam, I wouldn't have Brett." She turned to her friend and gripped her hands. "And I love my son so much it hurts. This is all such a mixed-up mess, Marilyn. I'm so confused. I abhor what Adam has become, and I keep wondering how long he can fool all these people. Everyone thinks he's the most wonderful man on earth," Sam's words dripped with the disenchantment that spewed from her wounded soul. "He's got his pastor believing that *I'm* the one who is crazy. Since his drinking has increased, I keep thinking that they'll eventually see the truth. How long can he hide it? And now — now I just don't know what to do — or — or —"

"I know. I know." Marilyn wrapped her arms around her friend and began to pat her back. In turn, Sammie hung onto Marilyn as if she were her only link to sanity. The smell of Marilyn's jasmine perfume induced thoughts of carefree summer days . . . days long past.

"I have felt *exactly* the way you feel," Marilyn continued. "When Gregory had his affair and decided to leave me, I was nothing more than a crumpled heap. And you can only imagine whose side his parents took — some of our friends, too. By the time Greg got through, I was the most horrible wife on the planet. And I will admit . . ." Marilyn pulled away and her candid brown gaze never flinched from Sam's, "I did some things wrong. But then again, I was the one who wanted to go to counseling, forgive him for the affair, and move on. He just wouldn't give up his other woman."

"I guess Adam's other woman is alcohol." Sammie dashed at the tears, hot and stinging.

"Yes, and maybe the rage."

"And then, there really *are* the other women," Sam blurted, then shrugged. "I have no proof, but I can't help but wonder. He's drinking too much and staying gone too many nights."

"And his pastor suspects nothing?" Marilyn asked, her eyes wide. "At the level he's been drinking, how long can he hide it?"

Sammie stared at the blue plaid sofa and tried to gain the presence of mind to sketch in all the details. "In the first place, his behavior is getting worse and worse. This summer, the drinking escalated to the point that even *I* wonder how he's hiding it from the pastor. As far as the — the physical stuff —" She waved her hand and gulped for air. "I'll get to that in a minute. But this drinking business . . . he has missed some Sundays this summer." She paused and twined her fingers together. "But I quit going to church with him several months ago — unless he forced me. I haven't actually seen how he's been acting at church."

Pausing, Sam awaited Marilyn's reaction. After all she was a pastor's wife, and Sam figured she would have some negative remark regarding Sam's lack of church attendance. Instead, Marilyn nodded and never even blinked.

"Now the drinking has gotten so bad that *I* even wonder how he's going to do when school starts. Up until this summer, he has been drinking but not to this level. Frankly, I'm with you, I don't know how much longer he can hide it. But as far as the abuse goes, he has been a master of deception."

"Like Dr. Jekyl and Mr. Hyde?" Marilyn asked.

"Exactly." Sam nodded, crossed her arms, and hunched her shoulders. "I've thought of that exact analogy over and over. You would be shocked at the number of times he blasted me in the car before church on Sunday morning, after hitting me the night before. Then the second he walks into the sanctuary, he turns into this smooth-talking nice guy who drips humility and affection on everyone he sees. I'm left seething the rest of the service, and *I* come out looking like the sour one!" She pointed to her chest then turned and approached the picture window that overlooked the splash of emerald grass out front.

"Joshua and I have been taking a joint course in family counseling." Marilyn's steps neared from behind. "It would appear that that's the usual tactic of the wife abuser. Out in the world, he's the most charming man alive and might even be a respected leader at church. But when he goes home, he's like the devil himself."

Sammie shuddered. "It's a horrible way to live." She turned and observed her friend's fresh, girl-next-door appearance. If not for the knowledge of Marilyn's tragic first marriage, Sam would have assumed that she had never experienced anything but the good life. However, a whisper of wisdom stirred the depths of Marilyn's eyes that revealed her former hardships.

Sammie gripped Marilyn's hand and swallowed hard. "And one of the worst things about all this is the fact that my church wouldn't back me. Our pastor essentially told me I was lying. Up until that point, I *really respected* that man, Marilyn. And — and — I thought he respected me as well."

Sammie spun back toward the window and swallowed against the building fury. Two mockingbirds flitted across the yard and perched on an oak limb as if they didn't have a care in the world. On a whim, Sam wished she were a bird — free as the wind, free to sing, free to fly.

"I went to our pastor in his office and poured out my heart to him. All he did was look at me like I was a stupid child. He told me I had the most wonderful husband in the world and that if I would just submit like I was supposed to there wouldn't be any problems at home." The words tumbled forth in an unending stream. She turned back to Marilyn and squeezed her forearm. "Marilyn, you and Josh are in the ministry. Don't *ever* do that to anybody. You have *no idea* how devastating that is for a woman. I felt like a nobody — that not even God cared about what was happening to me." Sammie's voice broke over the final words.

Marilyn, her eyes brimming, focused past Sammie's shoulder. "I have a terrible admission to make to you, Sam." She sniffled then continued, her words stilted as if each were bitter to her taste. "The reason Josh and I decided we needed to take this course in family counseling is because there was a woman in our church who came to us and claimed that her husband was physically abusing her. Josh and I had a really hard time believing her because her husband was our Sunday school director and just about the strongest Christian you could ever meet — or so we thought. Even in the face of my negative experience with Greg, even after he fooled me and a whole congregation, I was ignorant enough to still doubt this lady." Tears seeped out of the corners of Marilyn's eyes. "And she knew it." Her tormented gaze encountered Sam's once more.

"What changed your mind?" the whisper trickled out of Sam on a note of incredulity.

"They live one street over. One Sunday morning at two a.m. she landed on our doorstep and begged us to please believe her and help her. Her eye was swollen. Her mouth was bleeding. She had two broken ribs."

"I have — have been almost exactly there," Sam said.

Marilyn swallowed, took a deep breath, and winced. "I — I took her to the hospital. We didn't know that her husband didn't know where she was. Josh had to stay here with Brooke until time for church. And Emily made us promise not to call her husband. She was scared to death. She said he said he would kill her."

"It's the same story over and over again, isn't it?" Sammie commented, shaking her head.

Nodding, Marilyn moved to the window, tugged aside the cornflower blue curtain, and gazed outside as if the whole scenario were playing before her.

"The next morning Josh went to church, and Emily's husband — his name is Caleb — showed up, wearing a smile and making polite excuses for his wife. Joshua couldn't stand it. He cornered Caleb, but the man denied everything. Then Josh told him that I was at the hospital with Emily. And with all the charm you could ever imagine, he told Josh that Emily was having an affair and that her lover must have beaten her."

Sammie covered her trembling lips as she eyed Marilyn from the side. Her self-disdain cloaked her features in a crumpled mask. "I helped Emily press charges. The police found evidence of violence, including blood, in their house. I have never been so disgusted with myself in my whole life," she said in a small voice.

"Don't — don't . . ." Sam searched for more words but found none.

"Emily could have been killed while I folded my arms, sat back, and doubted her."

R.J. cleared his throat from the hallway, and Sam wondered how long he had been standing there. She mopped at her tear-stained face and observed him.

"Brett woke up. He wants you."

"All right," Sammie said and stepped toward R.J. Yet before she had traveled three strides, the phone rang again. She stopped and shared a fixed gaze with R.J., then pivoted toward Marilyn who hesitated then picked up the receiver and gave a cautious greeting.

"Yes, she's still here," Marilyn said and eyed her friend. "Of course. Just a minute."

Joshua ambled in from the kitchen with Brooke at his side. Both nibbled frozen Fudgesicles. He looked at Marilyn and raised his brows.

She covered the mouthpiece and stared at Sam. "It's the police," she whispered. "They want to talk with you."

Twenty-Three

~

Her mind whirling with worst case scenarios, Jacquelyn followed the tall, slender nurse up the hospital hallway. As they passed the doors marked Critical Care Unit she expected the nurse to halt and ask Jacquelyn to either wait outside or usher her inside. Instead, she marched right to the elevator and pushed the down button.

"He's in ICU now. Next floor down," she explained without making eye contact.

The door whisked open, a knot of women stepped off, leaving two husky orderlies, dressed in blue scrubs, standing on either side of an empty gurney. Like the nurse, each man had dark skin, hair, and eyes. Both made brief eye contact with the nurse then focused on the floor. She stepped into the elevator and politely held the door for Jac's entry. Jacquelyn moved forward. Yet an unexpected warning started as a whisper in her spirit and erupted into the forefront of her mind.

Don't go!

She stopped and coldly evaluated the situation — a situation that screamed of duplicity. An image flicked through her mind — the image of a tall, thin person dressed in baggy clothing walking from the hotel, a tuft of dark hair hanging from the back of her baseball cap. Her slender, graceful fingers, void of any polish, had been the only indication of her gender. Jacquelyn glanced at the woman's hand pressed against the elevator door. A slender hand. A graceful hand. A hand whose fingernails bore no polish. Jacquelyn glanced into the woman's ebony, beguiling eyes, made up to perfection. The lady before her didn't even favor the person leaving the hotel. However, the individual at the hotel hadn't worn a hint of makeup. Jacquelyn had seen the transformation that professional makeup had wrought in her friend Kim Lan. Without it Kim was simply an attractive lady of Asian descent who might show up in any grocery store checkout. But with makeup, Kim Lan was transformed into one of the most gorgeous faces in America.

An orderly cleared his throat, and Jacquelyn focused upon him. The well-built man appeared a bit too polished for Jac's peace of mind. His hair, meticulously styled, glistened in the elevator's light. His freshly shaven face and manicured nails repudiated any hint of long hours or harried hospital activity. The empty gurney snatched Jac's attention, and she wondered who they planned to place on it. Next she stared at the wing-tipped shoe peeking from beneath the other orderly's scrubs.

Jac's spine stiffened. The surgeon's last words shot through her mind: *I'll have a nurse call you the minute we know something. Remember, no news is good news at this point.* This nurse's claims in no way paralleled the surgeon's remarks. Green's warning that Rantomi's daughter and her morons were assigned to her and Lawton's murders splashed upon Jac like a dash of ice water.

Two dark-complected men, dressed in business suits, and talking fast, neared from the side. As they approached, they fell in behind Jac and began jostling her forward. An image of herself lying unconscious upon that gurney set her in motion. She attempted to sidestep the men behind her, but the feel of a steel shaft against her ribs insisted that she move forward. The woman smiled — a wicked smile that might have emerged from the pits of Hades. The gurney seemed to hiss her name. The men shoved her. As her toes touched the elevator's entry, she knew beyond doubt that if she allowed herself to be forced into that elevator she would never see light again. A command, relentless and irrepressible, raged through her being.

Fight! Fight now or die!

Jacquelyn orchestrated a deceptively casual turn then snapped one of the well-dressed men's wrist in a wrist lock he wouldn't soon forget. She grabbed the gun. In the next second, she slammed her foot against the side of his knee. With a groan and a howl, he toppled to the floor as Jac shot a kick against his companion's groin. His grunt coincided with her elbow smacking his nose. When he doubled over, Jacquelyn delivered the same treatment to his knee that his companion now writhed over.

By the time his hulking form rumbled to the floor, she was sprinting up the hallway. In one hand Jac clutched her purse and backpack; in the other, she gripped the Glock 18. Jac skidded around the corner and paused long enough to gain her equilibrium, set the pistol on safety, then stuff it into her jeans waistband, beneath her oversized denim shirt. Her gaze darted up and down the hallway then landed on a door marked "Stairs." The nearing click of quickened footsteps mingled with masculine groans and spurred her forward. Jac bore down on two oncoming women, dressed in teal lab coats, each carrying a tray of glass vials. They stumbled from her path and bumped into the wall. The clink of shattering glass and a round of oaths accompanied Jac as she slipped into the stairwell and halted. She debated whether to go up or down, then recalled the security guard standing near the front entryway. Her palms moist, Jac grabbed the handrail and sailed down two flights of steps. At last the final flight loomed forth.

The sound of a door banging open two floors up preceded a male voice, thick with a New York accent. "Langley, you go up. I'll go down. Angelica, you take the hallway. If you don't see her, then come downstairs. She can't be far."

"Done." The woman's affirmation echoed down the stairwell.

Gasping for every breath, Jacquelyn hurled herself down the remaining flight and burst into the first-floor hallway, near the elevators. Once more she halted and skimmed the area, bustling with guests and professionals on a mission. The gift shop was 20 feet away. After that, the receptionist's desk. The waiting room lay just beyond the main entry hall. Rounding a corner near the elevators, she made brief eye contact with a couple who peered at her as if she had just dropped from Mars. Without another glance their way, she trotted behind them and turned into the main entrance, only to run headlong into a dark-complected man wearing a business suit.

Sammie took the cordless receiver from Marilyn and swallowed against a throat, dry and tight. A surreal fear, dismal and unyielding, descended upon her as she placed the receiver to her ear. All the while, she never took her gaze from R.J.'s concerned observation. He stood on the edge of the hallway, and Brett's faint whimpers seeped from around him.

"Hello," she said into the phone, her voice wooden.

"Hello. This is Mrs. Jones?" an emotionless male queried.

"Yes." Samantha licked her lips and the

air gradually flowed from her lungs.

"Mrs. Jones, this is Officer Victor Sanders with the Eureka Springs Police Department."

Sam's fingers ate into the phone, and the room began a slow spin.

"Earlier today a man by the name of R.J. Butler called, reporting that your husband had violated a restraining order placed in the state of Texas. He gave your husband's name as Adam Jones. Is this information correct?"

"Y–yes." Sammie closed her eyes, and her stomach's nauseous twist ushered in the officer's next words.

"Mrs. Jones, your husband has been involved in a two-vehicle accident just on the outskirts of Eureka Springs. He . . . was pronounced dead at the scene."

Without a word, Sammie sank to the floor and the braided rug met her knees with a muffled thud. The past six years spun through her head. Years that included her first meeting with Adam — his indubitable charm, his seeming commitment to Christ, his ultimately winning her heart. Then there were the years that followed their wedding. The early verbal abuse that escalated into threats — threats that he finally put punch behind. The drinking. The other women. The forever-spewing rage. And bit by bit the man who had promised to cherish Sam began systematically destroying everything she ever was. A sob swelled from Samantha and burst upon the room like an emotional bomb held long at bay.

Brett's whimpering escalated into wails. A man wearing leather knelt nearby. Marilyn retreated up the hallway to Brett's room. R.J.'s arm, strong and comforting, settled upon Sammie's shoulders. She leaned into his embrace.

"While we won't know for sure until after the blood tests," the officer continued, "there is every indication that Mr. Jones was intoxicated."

Sammie closed her eyes and nodded as a numbness began in the center of her heart then encompassed her whole being. "Yes," she affirmed, "when — when he called me — called me earlier today he sounded — sounded as if he . . ."

"I'm terribly sorry," the officer concluded, a strand of sympathy entering his otherwise sterile tones. "And just so you'll know, the other driver sustained only minor injuries."

Closing her eyes, Sammie nodded. She extended the receiver to R.J., who took it and mumbled a gruff "hello," then listened for the remaining details.

Marilyn padded down the hallway, Brett in her arms. When he saw his mother, he lurched forward and Marilyn almost lost her grip. She deposited the squirming child on the floor and allowed him to race to Sam. As Brett hurled himself against her, Marilyn came to a gradual halt near her husband and daughter. Sam wrapped her arms around her son, buried her face against R.J.'s vest, and reeled in the aftermath of this news.

In the middle of all the sorrow, an undeniable relief twined its way through her spirit. Sammie caught her breath and imagined her home without the death threats, without the violence, without the alcohol. Then she thought of Adam, the man who had wooed her. The charm he once bestowed. The promise he had vowed. She thought of the man he had become and the man he could have become, if only . . .

Relief was swept away by the whirlwind of grief.

A set of masculine hands gripped Jacquelyn's upper arms. Her heart pounding, she prepared to throw another series of punches and kicks until a familiar voice transcended her battle plans.

"Jac Lightfoot! I was coming here to see you!"

The tenor of that voice crashed upon her and stopped her in the middle of another well-placed kick. Panting, she peered at Austin Sellers. From around the corner a door banged open. Jacquelyn's frenzied gaze spanned the front entryway. No security guard. The dismayed howl of a startled visitor echoed from up the hallway.

"Excuse me, Sir," a matronly voice called.

Jac glanced over her shoulder. A steamroller grandmother, dressed in pink, plowed from behind the visitor's greeting center and headed toward them. Jac debated what to do about Austin. If the gurus of death got a good look at him they just might decide to do him in for the sake of it. The Rantomis had already killed his twin brother and maybe Lawton. A flash of desperation pierced Jac. *Lawton . . . Lawton . . . oh, Lawton . . .*

"Stop now or I'm calling security!" the steamroller grandmother's invasive bark echoed down the hall and flung Jac back to the present dilemma.

She saw no other option for Austin. He was safer with her. She eyed the wall to her right and noticed a door marked "Ladies." Jacquelyn grabbed his hand and yanked him with her.

"Hey! What are you doing?" he yelped as she pulled him inside.

Jac shoved against the closing door, and it popped against the frame. She rounded the tiled wall and glanced across the chamber, containing three stalls. Jacquelyn dropped to her knees and verified the room was vacant. "Come on," she demanded and pushed Austin into a stall with her.

The smells of soap and antiseptic enveloped them as the stall door snapped shut. Jac debated whether to lock it, but decided that the door might very well become an effective weapon if needed.

She turned toward Austin. Eyes rounded he peered at her as if she had lost her mind.

"Don't ask any questions. Just stand on the toilet," she commanded. "And leave room for me."

"Why?" he said.

"Someone is trying to kill me," Jac ground out and gave him a firm shove.

He crawled onto the back of the toilet, and Jac balanced on the front. "Keep your head down," she hissed then pivoted to extend him her backpack. "Here, hold this. I need to get my cell phone out."

He mutely obeyed and extended the backpack to the side as Jac used one hand to balance against the side of the stall and the other to forage through the jumble until her fingers wrapped around the phone. Only minutes ago, she had stated the hospital number to Kinkaide. She closed her eyes, wrinkled her brow, and tried to remember the number. Finally, she dialed the sequence that floated to the top of her mind. A shrill tone and a prerecorded message announced that she had misdialed her number.

"Who are you calling?" Austin hissed.

"This hospital," Jac whispered over her shoulder, and the faint scent of spicy aftershave testified that Austin's face was inches from hers. "I'm trying to alert security."

"I know the number. I call it all the time." He rattled off a series of numbers, and Jac punched them in.

"Community Hospital," a female cooed over the line.

"Hello. My name is Jacquelyn Lightfoot," she said. Austin shifted his weight. The toilet seat budged, and Jacquelyn gripped the top of the stall to keep from toppling to the floor. "Be still," she hissed over her shoulder.

"I can't help it!" he shot back.

"Okay, okay," she said then continued into the phone. "I am a private detective. I am currently in the ladies restroom in the hospital lobby. There are three people chasing me. I need you to connect me with somebody from security *immediately!*"

"I see," the lady said on an irritated huff, "and I guess that if we've got Prince Albert in a can then we better let him out. Right?"

"No, no, no!" Jac stated emphatically. "This is *not* a prank call. I am serious! This is a matter of life and death. Listen to me!" Her lips stretched tight against her teeth. "Can you see the front lobby at all?"

"Uh, yes," the woman answered, a new dubiety lacing her words.

"Do you see a woman in a nurse's uniform with lots of black curls?" Jac transferred her hand from the top of the stall to press against the cool metal partition. "Or maybe two dark-complected men dressed in scrubs?"

"As a matter of fact, there *is* a nurse with black hair talking to an orderly."

"They are with the Rantomi clan," Jac hissed. "Call security and tell them to detain them. *They are trying to kill me!*"

"Are you sure? They look harmless."

"Am I *sure?*" Jac stopped herself just short of a shriek.

Austin snatched the phone from her. "Hello," he snapped, and Jac glowered over her shoulder. "Who is this?" he continued.

"Sabrina. This is Reverend Austin Sellers." A faucet's slow drip punctuated the pause. "Yes. I'm in the ladies bathroom with Detective Jac Lightfoot. The Rantomi clan *really is* chasing her — us. Do whatever she says. This is *not* a prank call. Alert security *now!*"

Shaking her head, Jacquelyn looked toward the ceiling and forced herself to take several slow breaths.

"What?" Austin whispered. "Oh great! Okay — just call security *now!*" The bathroom door snapped open, and Austin's rapid breathing assaulted Jac's ear. "Sabrina says the nurse is coming in here. She has her hand in a purse, as if —"

"She's got a weapon," Jac barely whispered. Austin nodded.

Jacquelyn held her breath as the swish of thick-soled shoes neared. Finally, the white shoes came into view and approached the neighboring stalls. The nurse tarried outside the other two doors, pulled open the swinging panels, then allowed them to shut. After the second door slammed into place, the shoes appeared in front of her prey's stall.

Jac extended her hands to the sides of the stall, gripped the top with all her might, sucked in a great gulp of air, swung her feet outward, and released a war cry as she slammed her short-topped boots against the stall door. A hard thud accompanied the woman's startled bellow. While the nurse tumbled to the floor, Jac attempted a graceful landing in front of the toilet. But Austin's weight pressed from behind. Her grip slipped, and she crashed into the toilet then bounced onto the tile. The stall door slammed shut then bumped back open, and Austin's arms and legs appeared before Jac seconds before he collided with the door and sprawled in front of her. The door blasted open again then bounced back to wham Austin's head. Jac's knee and backside protested as she scrambled over him and crawled from the stall. The groaning woman lay propped against the wall, holding her bleeding nose.

The restroom door banged open. Jac yanked the Glock from her waistband, stumbled to her feet, and leveled the weapon toward the newcomer. A fresh-faced security guard held up his hands and halted in wide-eyed scrutiny.

Jacquelyn expelled a pent-up breath and raised the gun toward the ceiling. "It's okay," she breathed. "I'm the good guy." Jac peered over her shoulder toward the woman on the floor. "She's the one you want." An awkward scuffing sound accompanied the nurse's flailing attempts to stand. "Austin, throw her purse across the room and just *sit* on her," Jac barked out. "We'll be back."

Jacquelyn rounded the security guard and approached the doorway. "Did you catch the other guys? There were two of them dressed like orderlies," she shot over her shoulder.

"No. No we didn't — not yet," the guard explained. "We lost track of them. We *did* call the police. They should be here any minute."

"Good. There are two more by the fourth-floor elevators. They're going to have to make a trip through the emergency room before they head to the police station. One has a broken wrist and they both have broken legs."

The guard's brows shot up.

"I took them down," Jac said with a shrug. "But I went easy on them — on all of them." She eased open the door and peered upon a glassed-in entryway, now nearly vacant. A few onlookers huddled in a corner, their faces ashen, as two security guards sprinted out the front doors.

The guard with Jac eased into the entryway and nodded toward the grandmother in pink.

"Two men just ran out the front door!" the grandmother squawked. "The security guards are after them!" The lady in pink hurled her hulking frame toward Jac and the guard. Her eyes bugging, her cheeks flaming, she pointed toward the sliding glass doors. The telltale screeching of tires in the dim distance confirmed that the two dressed as orderlies had abandoned the other three.

From the restroom a chorus of female screeches mingled with Austin's yelling, "I need some help here! She's turned into a wildcat!"

"Coming," the security guard answered and whirled from his post beside Jac.

Jac stampeded toward the front door and halted on the sidewalk just outside. As the mountainous air, balmy and fresh, engulfed her, a dark sedan darted from the parking lot and revved up the road. Two security guards jogged to a halt near the lot's exit. She strained to obtain the license plate, but the numbers blurred in the distance.

With a frown and a growl, Jac whirled and began to retrace her steps. Her right knee protested. Opting for a limp, Jac hobbled back into the hospital, and memories of Lawton's still form on a gurney plagued her anew. She checked her watch to see that only 15 minutes had lapsed since the woman had led her from the waiting room.

She paused inside the cool lobby and pressed her forefinger and thumb against her eyes. A woman's heated objections erupted from the ladies' room as the door snapped open then closed. The door whipped open once more. This time, Austin's firm foot stopped it from reclosing. He and the security guard jostled the nurse imposter into the foyer. An undeniable conviction descended upon Jac — a conviction that this woman was indeed Angelica Rantomi and that she had tried to end Lawton's life. Jac's fingers flexed against the Glock's unyielding steel. She looked up to see one of the security guards stepping into the hospital. Jac suppressed the boiling urge to interrogate the woman. Instead, she extended the gun, butt first, toward the security guard. "This belongs to one of two men you'll find by the fourth-floor elevators. They both have broken legs, and one has a broken wrist," she said. "They're going to need immediate care." Jac pointed toward the nurse. "I believe her name is Angelica Rantomi. I think she tried to kill my friend, Lawton Franklin, earlier today. He just had emergency surgery. I'll be in the O.R. waiting room when the police come."

"Shut up you witch!" the woman howled, her glassy eyes filled with hatred.

Jacquelyn narrowed her eyes and scrutinized the overmade dame. The blood oozing from her swelling nose did little to distract from the definite similarities she possessed with the lady exiting the hotel. "I'm almost sure she's the one," Jacquelyn continued.

A hot wave of disdain washed across Jacquelyn. A quiver, persistent and unnerving, began in her aching knee, traveled to her throbbing hips, and assaulted her torso. With a scowl, she trudged toward the stairway.

"Wait a minute!" Austin called.

Jac pivoted to face him as he relinquished his grip on the woman to the second security guard. "Would you get my backpack and purse?" she asked.

"Yes. Of course. Then I'm coming with you!"

A third guard entered the hospital, and Jac motioned for his attention then explained again about the two men on the fourth floor. At last Austin stepped in beside her and extended her belongings. The two of them rounded the corner and headed toward the stairs. Jac's thoughts trotted ahead of her, and she pondered the waiting room, the long vigil spanning into the evening, and the reality of Lawton's possible future.

Twenty-Four

A pensive reticence enveloped Jacquelyn and Austin as they journeyed into the waiting room. Jac, regaining her equilibrium, plopped her backpack and handbag in the exact spot they had occupied minutes before. She descended into a chair herself. Austin remained respectfully silent as he sat in the chair next to Jac's. However, he rubbed his hands against his knees, sat back, crossed his arms, uncrossed his arms, then leaned forward.

Jac cast him a sideways glance. "Nervous?"

"You act like that whole chase didn't faze you in the least," he said. "Aren't you even a little bit wigged out?"

She extended her feet in front of her, rested her head against the wall behind the chair, and closed her eyes. The annoying quivering had almost ceased. However, her knee still insisted that it did not enjoy being slammed into a tile floor, and she figured her hip would sport a bruise by bedtime. The letdown that always followed such a surge of adrenaline began to creep through her veins.

"I am affected," she said.

"Nice to hear that," Austin snorted. "I'm blasted. We could have been killed!"

"Yep. Or I could have killed them." Jac relived those seconds outside the elevator. As with Sam's husband, she had chosen to allow the men to continue breathing. To date she had never been forced to kill, although the right blow to either man's neck would have ended his life.

"What happened before you ran into me?" Austin continued.

Jacquelyn briefed him on the details. "I think the woman chasing me was the person who shot Lawton," she concluded. "It would appear that Rantomi has decided we're too much in the way." Green's warning from that morning stomped through her mind, and Jac could only pray they would back off. Now that Rantomi had the coins, she hoped he would shift his focus to selling them.

"Do you think we're safe here and now?" Austin's suit rustled, and his shoes tapped against the tile.

Jac's eyes slid open and she observed the minister limping toward the doorway. "Best I can figure, there were four men and a woman. The woman is downstairs. Two men escaped. The other two are in E.R. That just leaves you and me."

"But how do you know there's not somebody else lurking around a corner?"

"The Rantomis don't work that way. They are more systematic than that. If anybody else was here, I figure they're gone. They don't like getting caught, so they take every precaution to keep themselves covered." Jac shifted in the chair and grimaced against the pain that shot from her buttocks.

"Are you sure?"

"I guess nothing is certain when you're dealing with criminals. But I'm sure enough to stay here right now. I don't want to miss the surgeon's call." Jac sat up and propped her elbow on the chair's arm. Lawton's unconscious form, still and pale, blazoned itself upon her mind and a nauseous twist invaded her stomach.

Austin pivoted and strode toward the vending machines. "Want a Coke?" he asked as he dug through his pockets for change.

"Sure."

"What kind?" He raised his brows and peered at her with considerate blue eyes.

"Whatever you're having is fine. As long as it's got fizz."

"I'm having two." He produced a half grin. "Maybe three . . . and a tranquilizer with them."

Jacquelyn chuckled. "Don't stroke out on me now."

"Really, I thought we were goners in that bathroom. Never once did I expect you to do what you did." Austin's quarters clanked through the slot, he pressed a button, and a bottle tumbled out. "Then I lost my balance and was afraid I was going to squash you flat." He retrieved the soda and repeated the steps until another soda plopped out. "I'm assuming by the shape of those two men by the elevator that you must have a black belt in something."

"You're assuming right. A fourth-degree black belt in tae kwon do. I could have killed all three of them, but I don't do that."

He limped toward her and extended the cola. The icy bottle connected with her palm and promised the boost she so needed.

"Remind me not to cross you," he teased.

"Are you hurting badly?" she asked, ignoring the quip.

"Not really." Austin shook his head and twisted the soda lid. A mild hiss escaped the drink. "My elbow feels like somebody has scoured it with sandpaper and my head is killing me. I'm not sure my ankle will ever be the same again. Other than that," he shrugged, "I'm in *great* shape."

Jacquelyn opened her drink and gulped several swallows. The tingling liquid burned the back of her throat. Her strict diet allowed the luxury of a soda only on rare occasions, and she relished the feel. "I'm assuming the meeting with Lancaster went as scheduled?"

Austin lowered himself into the chair next to her. "Yes. It went *fine* — just fine!" He waved his hand. "Before nearly getting myself blasted in the hospital ladies' room, I just handed over a fortune in coins to two total strangers. Sure. It went great! Not a hitch. They took the coins, smiled like two possums, and left!"

An unexpected grin pushed upon her lips, and Jac eyed the minister. "Please believe me when I tell you — you did the right thing." Jacquelyn hesitated and debated exactly how much information to leak to Austin. She scrutinized him as he focused on his opened soda. The dark circles under his eyes were the only indicator of his recent loss. The slight twitch at the corner of his mouth suggested that perhaps his stress level was at a high. Jacquelyn squinted and observed the vending machines. *No. I won't tell him all the details,* she thought with finality. *He doesn't need to know more.*

"I know the FBI agent who got those coins." Jac carefully chose her next words. "He came to our hotel room this morning. Everything is fine, Austin, *believe me.*" Jac laid her hand on his forearm. "Those coins belong to the Turkish government. Lancaster will make sure they get where they belong."

"And what about the other man?" Austin asked. "He didn't look like any FBI agent I've *ever* seen!" Austin raised his hand and produced a guttural sound, deep in his throat. "I've never even *seen* an FBI agent! What am I saying?" He shook his head. "I guess he just didn't look . . . *honest* somehow." Austin turned and scrutinized her. "You know more than you're telling

411

me, don't you?" he demanded.

Jacquelyn blinked, snagged her lower lip between her teeth, and peered into her cola bottle. A woman's monotone voice erupted over the speaker with a routine page.

"That older man looked somehow familiar, and I can't figure out why," he said.

"How did you know I was at the hospital?" Jac asked, hoping to alter their current conversational vein.

"Shortly after the FBI agent and that other man left, I received a call from a church member, telling me that a man had been shot at the hotel where you two were staying. I called the hotel, and they confirmed what had happened. Ouray is a small town. You can't keep something like that a secret for long. My wife came home with the kids by one o'clock, so I got here as soon as I could. Your friend's being shot is all related to those coins, isn't it — to those coins and that man with the FBI agent. I don't know who he was, but . . ." He gripped her upper arm with one hand, and the fingers of his other tightened on the cola then grew white. "You know, don't you? Tell me who he was!"

She peered into his desperate eyes, the color of an indigo sky, as the truth of her knowledge posed itself between them and refused to be denied. "He is your biological father," Jac said in a barely audible voice, then she proceeded to reveal the remaining details. She concluded with the identity of Angelica Rantomi, his half-sister.

His eyes wide, Austin maintained his grip on Jac and sat spellbound until the last words left her lips. "The reason why I dragged you into the ladies' room with me," she said, "is because if Rantomi ordered Gary's death, then he very likely wouldn't blink if they killed you. They might even have orders to kill you if you got in the way." She shrugged. "I figured you were safer with me than you would be on your own."

The color slowly drained from Austin's face. He relinquished his grip on Jac, propped his head against the wall behind him, and closed his eyes. Jacquelyn shifted her cola to the other hand, rubbed her damp, chilled palm against her jeans, and took a long swallow of the effervescent liquid. A grave silence, taut and heavy, descended upon them, and Jac inspected the pastor's face. The twitch near his lips grew in frequency, and she wondered how well she would have handled the upheavals he had endured.

The silence stretched forth, broken only by the hum of the vending machines. Jac finished her soda, rose, and walked toward the waste can near the door. She stepped into the hallway, gazed one way, then the other. Nothing out of the ordinary. Just the buzz of a janitor's floor polisher as he buffed the floor. Jacquelyn pursed her lips and checked her watch. *The police should be up here soon,* she thought and turned back into the room. She peered at the phone and imagined Lawton, lying motionless and weak in the recovery room. *Please, God,* she prayed. *Please.*

Austin stirred. Jac slowly neared him and examined his impassive face. The man was showing remarkable control. While Jacquelyn could take down a criminal with great assurance, she wasn't so sure she would have faired as well emotionally under Austin's circumstances.

His gaze, intense and fixed, focused upon a point beyond earthly realms. "The Lord gives and the Lord takes away. Blessed be the name of the Lord," he muttered.

Jac dropped back into her chair and pondered his serene features, void of any bitterness. She contemplated her year, the virulence that daily oozed forth, the gradual unfolding of her wounded past that pointed to her grandfather as the dragon due her abhorrence. Instead of the unwavering peace now cloaking Austin's countenance, Jacquelyn had been trapped in a whirlwind of revenge.

"I hope this whole thing is over now," Austin finally said.

"Aren't you the least bit angry with God for allowing your brother and sister-in-law to be murdered?" Jac blurted.

Austin turned to her as if he had forgotten she were present. He blinked, peered at the floor, then sipped his soda. "Well, I've asked 'why' enough, but I can't say I'm *angry* with God. Kinda hard to be angry with someone who holds you up and stops you from falling flat on your face." His smile, tight and sad, created twin creases from nose to mouth.

"Actually, I think I'm able to persevere now because of what I went through after my father died six years ago. I loved my father." He hesitated. "And he wasn't even my father."

Jac shifted. "I didn't mean to —"

He raised his hand. "No. It's okay." He stroked the side of his face. "It doesn't end there. I couldn't get past my anger. The fury was so intense I couldn't let it go. Every night before I went to sleep, I railed at God." A humorless chuckle escaped him. "What a horrible place to be in for a pastor who has told his congregation to trust the Lord in all life's circumstances." He shook his head. "Man oh man did I have a lot to learn.

"I fell so low that Gary even offered me a position in his real estate ventures. I almost took it. I'm glad I didn't because I finally realized I had no right to be angry at God." He hesitated and glanced at the ceiling. "I realized I'd been happy to serve God as long as the forecast was sunny. When the clouds came, I wanted to pack up camp and quit. You've heard people mention how God uses bad things to bring about something good. Well, I learned a lot through Father's death. So when all this came up with Gary, I'd already taken care of any anger I might've harbored. And instead of blasting God, I've been able to draw from His strength. I've been able to go to Him for support instead of shaking my fist at Him. Don't get me wrong. I'm not superhuman. I still hurt." Austin swallowed hard. "I cried myself to sleep last night. And the night before that . . . and the — the night before that," his voice grew thick, and he stood then strode back to the doorway. His shoulders trembled, and he repeatedly blotted his eyes.

At last Jacquelyn stared at the clock on the far wall. The second hand ticked around as if counting off the number of times that Jacquelyn had lain awake at night, so furious she lost all sense of reason. She hunched forward, placed elbows on knees, clasped her hands, then stared at the cream-colored tile until it blurred. Austin's claims of God's sustaining strength pierced her soul like the pinpoints of light on the edge of her dreamscape forest. In that nightmare Jac had forever cringed from the light because she had been so scared of the truth. The more truth the light revealed, the greater her wounds pulsated. But Jac now suspected that the only pathway to healing lay in the truths of Austin's claims. Perhaps only by allowing God's miraculous light to reveal the festering wounds, only by fully embracing the Savior, only by releasing her fury and revenge would she ever be able to move forward in her life. Jacquelyn saw with unrelenting clarity that until that day came, she would forever be trapped by the atrocity committed against her.

The memories she had locked away

mere hours ago burst forth. They danced around her mind like demons of her past, bent on haunting her for the rest of her life. Like Austin, Jac had been ravaged with death. The death of her innocence. The demise of any hope of a healthy childhood. From the time she was 9 until she was 12, Jac had been the victim of wanton selfishness.

She rested her face in her hands, and tried to recall why the abuse had stopped when she was 12. Last spring when the memories began, Jac realized the abuse ended before her thirteenth birthday. She never connected with *why* she knew. She just knew. *Yet Grandfather lived until a few years ago,* she mused. Another memory scampered from the cellar of her past. A memory that grew in detail as the seconds slipped by. A memory of the day she decided she would take no more.

Her father had insisted upon Jac's martial arts training from the time she was six. Jac always had been smaller than everyone, and John Lightfoot wanted to make certain his daughter could take care of herself. By the time she was 12, Jacquelyn had far exceeded her instructor's expectations. Upon the heels of her mother's parental talk about the birds and the bees and the necessity of Jac's protecting herself from any unreasonable advances, Jacquelyn had realized with unquestionable horror why her grandfather had threatened to kill her if she told. A seething resentment began in her gut that day — a resentment that she spontaneously unleashed upon her dragon. In short, the kick she delivered to that man at the elevator paled in comparison to the blow her grandfather had received. Jacquelyn remembered now. She recalled that she left him in the horse barn, writhing in pain.

Jacquelyn fought back that day. She fought and won. "And I've been fighting ever since," she whispered. "I'm still fighting him, even now." The pent-up anger stirred from the mire in her heart and lifted its head like a midnight monster dripping with hatred. A monster that roared with glee every time Jacquelyn had to fight. A monster that propelled her forward with the motivation of an unrelenting taskmaster. Over the years, Jac had been responsible for innumerable criminals landing behind bars. Now each criminal's features took on the lines of her grandfather's face. The kick that ended her tenure of abuse emblazoned upon Jac's heart the necessity of fighting. Fighting for life.

After bringing down her grandfather, she remembered marching into her grandmother's kitchen, where that dark-skinned beauty had turned and smiled as if there weren't a problem in the world. "I'm going home," Jac had blurted. She then stomped out of the house, mounted her bicycle, and pedaled like the wind until she reached her parents' abode. For weeks she checked her window locks at night and dreaded the possibility of her grandfather telling what she had done. Soon Jacquelyn understood that he wouldn't tell. He wouldn't because in telling he would reveal his detestable deeds.

After that day, Jac refused to go to her grandfather's house. She avoided him at all family functions. Her parents had laughed and said that Jac was a teenager now, more interested in friends than in grandparents.

And they said it so often, I believed them, she thought. *Because I wanted it to be true.*

Somehow she merged into adulthood and developed a new relationship with her grandfather. A relationship void of those excruciating memories. Eventually, he became so senile that Jacquelyn read to him at his bedside. And when he died, she mourned his death with her mother. She mourned just like Austin was mourning his brother's demise.

Now this minister insisted that he harbored no anger toward God. No anger. Instead, he clung to the Lord, who held him in strong arms. Jacquelyn tapped the toe of her short-topped boot against the tile and admitted that her teenage commitment to Jesus Christ, while authentic, had never matured into the depth that shone in Austin's eyes . . . that radiated from Lawton's very being. The final lines of Lawton's star poem trickled through the muck like a pure stream from the heart of a holy God. And the words, haunting yet profound, presented a sacred invitation to release all the anger. Release it. And embrace the Giver of light.

Come with me. Come with me.
We'll fly to the stars.
We'll embrace them
and soak up their splendor.
We'll embrace them
and forever blaze with His love.
Yes, I love the stars. I love them.
We are stars. We are stars.
We are the carriers of light.
The light of the universe.
We twinkle forth with a message
the world longs to hear.

Yes, He loves you. He loves all.
Come with me. Come with me.
Embrace this Giver of Light.
His jewel-like flame
will transform dark night.
Yes, I love the stars. I love them.

As the final line echoed upon the horizon of Jac's mind, a heavenly whisper beckoned to her soul, *Give Me your anger. Give Me your pain. I can heal you. I can teach you to forgive, if you will only let Me.*

Jacquelyn blinked. The lines of the tile snapped into clear view. A band of gooseflesh broke out along her spine. She clenched her fingers until they ached. Her pulse thudded in her temples. The dragon's roar invaded her soul. Jac imagined herself kicking him into a pulverized heap. And the revenge felt good. Oh, so good.

Abruptly, she stood, clenched her fists, and huffed out several short breaths. The idea of releasing the anger, of forgiving, of relinquishing her pain to God left a bitter taste in her mouth.

Jacquelyn had clutched the anger for so many years it defined who she was. She didn't want to release the fury. She preferred to nurture it; to increase its voracious need for her energies; to demand that she had every right to a life of rage.

God, if You really loved me, she railed, *You would have stopped him from doing that to me in the first place. You let me down! How do You expect me to ever really trust You?*

The telephone's demanding peal jolted through Jac. She jumped and glanced around the room. Austin sat in a chair on the other side now. He observed her as if he could see her struggle. A young couple sat in the chairs near Austin, and Jacquelyn wondered how they had entered without her knowledge. The phone rang again, and she stared at the black receiver, afraid to answer, afraid not to. Either the surgeon would tell her that Lawton was stabilizing, or . . .

She dashed aside every emotion except the desperate longing that Lawton would survive then dared to picked up the phone. "Lightfoot," she said on a snatch of breath.

"Yes, Ms. Lightfoot, this is Dr. Corley," a buoyant male voice chimed. "I just wanted to let you know that Lawton Franklin has indeed stabilized! While the next 24 hours are critical, things are looking up."

Jac closed her eyes, released her pent-up breath, and gripped the edge of the desk. "When can I see him?" she choked out and scrubbed at the rush of tears clouding her vision.

"Now, if you like. I can arrange for you to step in with him for a few minutes. He's unconscious, of course, but the sound of your voice might register with him on some level. I'm a firm believer in human contact — especially from those who care," the doctor continued.

A movement from the doorway distracted her. A gray-haired policeman strode past the vending machines and scanned the room. He observed Jac, then Austin approached him, and the two men fell into tense conversation.

"Of course. Yes, I'd — I'd like to see him," Jacquelyn agreed. "But the police are here — it's a long story. I need to speak with them briefly."

"I'll tell the CCU to expect you soon."

"And Dr. Corley?"

"Hmm?" the aging doctor answered as if his mind were already moving to the next case.

"Thanks. Thanks so much," Jacquelyn breathed. She tried to stay the gush of tears that threatened to take her under. "If he comes out of this, you have no idea how much — how much —"

"It's all in a day's work," he said softly.

"All in a day's work."

Jacquelyn breathed her thanks again then dropped the receiver into the cradle and directed a watery smile toward Austin. "He's stabilizing!" she exclaimed. "Things are looking up!"

"God is good," Austin said, and embraced her in a companionable hug. "So good."

Twenty-Five

~

After briefing the police, Jacquelyn was ushered into CCU by a plump blonde R.N. who
insisted Jac limit her visit to five minutes.
"That's all I can give you," she added as
Jacquelyn stepped into the curtained cubicle
where Lawton's stiff form lay.

"Okay, thanks," Jac said and neared the
head of the bed. The nurse swished past
the curtain's opening, and Jacquelyn's
heart swelled as she observed the man who
had been so full of life only hours ago.
Now his skin stretched pale across high
cheekbones. His lips lacked their usual
healthy blush. And the smile lines were
barely noticeable. The array of tubes and
monitors hooked to him spawned all sorts
of doubts about whether or not he would
pull through without brain damage. Yet

she gave herself a firm inward shake and recalled the surgeon's buoyant voice.

"Lawton?" Jacquelyn whispered and stroked his cool forehead. "I — I don't know if you can hear me or if you even know I'm here. But I want you to know I'm rooting for you. I'm praying for you and . . . and . . ." a hot tear trickled down the side of her nose and pooled at the corner of her mouth, "and I love you." The final words squeaked out before Jac could stop them. His latest brush with death had opened her eyes to the truth that sneaked up from behind. She had been falling in love with Lawton Franklin ever since the cruise. She'd thought about him almost nonstop since their trip. Several times she had even stopped herself from snatching up the phone and calling Mel to request his phone number. Then, when she got the report that he disappeared, she almost collapsed on the spot.

Jac bent and brushed her lips against his cheek. His whiskers tickled her lower lip, and she recalled the kiss they had exchanged only that morning — a kiss that tilted the balcony. Jac understood then that he was on the brink of proposing. With a sigh she pulled away and clasped his fingers.

She shifted her hand back to his face and gently stroked the dark lock of hair that insisted upon falling onto his forehead. Aimlessly she wondered if he ever made regular trips to the barber. The first time she saw Lawton, standing outside Melissa's front door, he needed a haircut. The memory of that initial encounter circled her, then finally settled within like a reminiscent ache. She had cooked Mexican food at Mel's place, and Lawton had eaten until he was miserable.

"Even then I knew there was something between us," Jacquelyn whispered and continued to stroke his thick hair.

"Excuse me, but your time is up." The nurse's crisp voice invited no argument.

Jacquelyn glanced toward the steely eyed blonde, then drank in Lawton's image. She pressed her lips against his forehead, backed away, and caressed his cheek with trembling fingertips. Her eyes blurred, and Jac shook her head. On the plane yesterday, Lawton had mentioned that he had a new poem. "Remind me to share it with you," he said before Jac clung to his hand. Now she wondered if this beautiful soul would ever compose again.

The nurse cleared her throat, and Jacquelyn backed farther away. She turned and strode from recovery. A wash of tears threatened to explode, but she suppressed them. Stoically, she determined to save the explosion until after she called Mel and Kinkaide. Then Jac would find an isolated alcove and release her agony.

Lawton struggled between the resplendent shimmer on the distant horizon and the darkness that tugged him from the promise of peace. The glowing eternal loomed afar, and Lawton pined for the radiance, all sparkling and pure and holy. Soon the glimmer expanded into a dazzling expanse of light that stretched into forever. Three times he trudged to the brink of the ebony shadows. Three times he placed one foot into the golden breadth. Three times he resigned to forever release the dark present. But each time his other foot remained firmly planted within the realms of his former existence.

A captive to his humanity, he teetered on the edge of eternity, only to hear a feminine voice spurring him to life, to feel taut fingers mingled with his hair, to smell the floral scent, delightful and familiar. With each encouragement, with each touch, with each press of lips against his hand, his face, Lawton slid farther away from the heavenly glow.

An inner voice, undeniable and unavoidable, insisted he fight. Fight to live. Fight for the feminine being who persisted in tugging him back into the dark present.

"Hello, Lawton, it's Jac again."

The number of times those words sprang upon Lawton tumbled together. And with every splash of that rhythmic voice like summer waves upon a thirsty beach, his humanity yearned for the companionship only she could offer. The greater his yearning, the farther the joyous serenity receded. Finally the glister diminished from a breathtaking golden glow back to a starlike glitter on the horizon. At last Lawton was yanked, wholly and irrevocably, from the promise. The resplendent shimmer that began as a pinpoint of light was extinguished, and nothing remained but inky sky.

With a protesting cry trapped in his soul, Lawton groped in the throes of raven night. Disoriented and alone. Unnerved and panting. A ship caught in a violent storm. He crashed into the present, enveloped by a clanging bell that accompanied his arrival. The bell halted. A round of clipped comments ensued. And that same feminine voice rippled across the dry wasteland of his heart like a mountain stream gurgling from the depths of a hidden cave.

"That was my new partner Eric on my cell," Jacquelyn said. "He's hit a major stump on this missing person case. He hated to call, but —"

"Do you think you should at least go home long enough to take care of some business details, Jac?" a maternal voice asked. "You've been here five days. We don't expect you to stay forever."

"I know." Her fingers encountered Lawton's, and his toes twitched. The smells of clean sheets and antiseptic mingled with a faint whirring. "But I just kept hoping that if I stayed maybe he'd come around. I just kept hoping . . ."

Lawton strained to speak, but he couldn't break free of the annoying bonds that demanded his silence.

"I guess I really don't have much of a choice," Jac continued. "Eric needs help. He sounds like he's about to pull his hair out." An impatient huff punctuated her next words. "And I've *got* to wrap up my income taxes. I filed an extension, and the new deadline is too close for comfort."

"You've been here almost day and night since this happened," Rosa Franklin continued. "Go ahead and take care of your business, Dear. We'll call you the minute he awakens." His mother's voice dubiously quivered over the final words.

"I am awake!" Lawton tried to yell, but his mouth refused to cooperate.

"Go on, Jac, you look beat," Melissa's voice chimed in with Rosa's.

"I *am* beat," she responded on a yawn.

A wisp of Melissa's discreet whispering floated above the slow hum of the air conditioner.

"Oh, of course," Rosa agreed. "Mel and I are going for some coffee, Jac. Want us to bring you something back?"

"No — no thank you," Jacquelyn said.

The shuffle of feet against tile preceded the door's snap, and the room fell into an elongated silence burdened with longing. Jac's fingers tightened on Lawton's hand and an urgent whisper tickled his ear. "Lawton Franklin, you'd better wake up soon, you hear? I'm rooting for you. I'm going home for a few days, but I expect you to be in full form the next time I see you." He relished the smell of wild flowers — as free as the woman who sported their fragrance. Then a pair of soft lips brushed his cheek.

And a corridor of memories crashed into

Lawton's mind. One of the last things he recalled was the balcony . . . the cool mountain air . . . the feel of Jac in his arms. They had shared a few laughs . . . an embrace . . . a kiss.

Lawton's fingers flexed against hers. A faint yelp erupted in his ear.

And the annoying bonds claimed him no more. "Mmm. You're a great kisser," he slurred.

Twenty-Six

~

Jacquelyn gasped and studied Lawton — not certain whether he had really spoken or if her overwrought mind conjured her most ardent hope. His fingers moved against hers once more, and a crooked grin tugged at his lips. His eyes slid open for a brief glimpse of cloudy irises then fanned shut. His legs stirred. Then his droopy lids opened — and focused on her.

Her knees buckling, Jac clutched the siderail and stopped herself just short of sinking to the floor.

"You're awake," she croaked.

"Oh, really?"

"You're actually talking," she blurted.

"Hmm," he responded and his eyelids flitted shut. "So are you."

"Can — can you move?" Jacquelyn stuttered. Mere seconds ago her five-day vigil had seemed like five years. Five years in which she urged Lawton to survive. Five years in which she begged for divine intervention. Now the five days diminished to a wrinkle in time in the face of the blazing wonder of this unfolding miracle.

Lawton wiggled his fingers. The covers trembled near his toes. He slowly tilted his head to one side then shifted his right hand to rest against his abdomen. "How's — how's that for moving?" he asked, his eyes again sagging.

Jac's vision blurred.

"My chest hurts," he muttered with a grimace.

"You took a bullet and almost died." She sniffed, then a delighted gurgle of laughter broke through the tears. "You look great," she said and stroked his face, dark with stubble. "I can't believe this."

"Yes, I remember," Lawton whispered. "I was in the — the bathroom at the hotel . . . then there was the light." He swallowed. "It was peaceful . . . so peaceful. But I came back for you . . . for — for your heart only," he rasped on an enigmatic note. "You called me — called me back."

"Yes, yes, I did," she whispered. "I

couldn't let you leave. Not now." Jacquelyn shook her head, and myriad possibilities tumbled through her. During all the hours she stood beside him, Jac had relived their every moment together. She had cherished his every word. She had refused to allow him to give up on life. But she had never once pretended that her past no longer existed. Feeling as if she were spinning in a tornado of conflicting emotions, she wondered where they would go from here. Jac hadn't prayed far past her desperate plea for Lawton's recovery. Now that the Lord was miraculously answering that request, she wondered what she was going to do with Lawton now that she had him.

"So what do you think, Jac Lightfoot?" He yawned and his eyes fluttered to a close.

"About?" Jac wrapped both her hands around his.

"You know . . ." he yawned again, ". . . about me . . . you . . ." his forehead creased, "the 'I do' thing."

Jacquelyn's eyes bugged.

"I came back for you . . . for your heart only," he repeated, and his final words ushered in a steady cadence of rhythmic breathing.

She blinked. His relaxed features settled

into a mask of sleep. Jac caught her breath, and the room, lined with plants, tipped into a dizzy blur of foliage.

The door clicked open and heavy footfalls approached from behind. Jacquelyn turned to encounter Kinkaide's listless gaze. She straightened to her full height and stopped herself from leaping into the air.

"He just woke up!" she exclaimed. "He talked to me!"

"What?" Kinkaide rushed to Lawton's side and scrutinized his features. "He really spoke to you?" he squeaked out. His dark eyes, smudged by circles beneath, sparkled like a kid's on Christmas morning.

"Yes!" Jac yelled.

Lawton started and his eyes popped open.

"You're awake!" Kinkaide exclaimed and grabbed his brother's arm.

"So are you," Lawton slurred out through a sleepy smile.

"What's going on?" Mel asked.

Jacquelyn pivoted toward her friend and Lawton's mother, who both halted at the bed's foot and observed Lawton as if they were afraid to believe what they hoped.

"He's awake!" Kinkaide hollered.

Lawton winced. "Re–remind me to tell you you've got a big mouth. Not so loud, m–man."

With a joyous roar, Kinkaide stretched both fists into the air and hollered, "Yes! Yes! Yes!"

Jacquelyn could no longer contain the leap. She sailed straight up. When she came down, Mel's arms wrapped around her. The two shared a tight hug then started jumping together. When Jacquelyn almost toppled an IV, the ecstasy subsided. Melissa broke away from Jac and joined her husband at Lawton's side, while Kinkaide Sr. rushed into the room. He clutched a rumpled newspaper, and his haggard eyes darted as if he feared the worst.

"I heard the yelling out in the waiting area," he said. "What's going —"

"He's awake," Rosa exclaimed from her post at Lawton's side. "Our son is awake! And moving!"

Kinkaide Sr. dropped the newspaper, fell to his knees, and a garbled sob spilled forth. "Thank You, Jesus!" he exclaimed. His eyes closed tight. His face tilted upward, and a lone tear trickled down the side of his nose.

A nurse hustled into the room, and Jacquelyn backed into the wall beneath the TV as the ecstatic family reported the miracle. Soon the doctor was summoned. The room's occupancy swelled past the level of comfort, and Jacquelyn moved farther and farther from the excited nucleus. Yet with every increase in ecstasy, Jacquelyn felt as if she were more and more out of place. Finally she decided that the close-knit family needed time together — time without an outsider. She approached Melissa and whispered she was taking off. Then she edged toward the doorway.

As she stepped across the paper Kinkaide Sr. had dropped, she glanced at the headlines. She stopped to once again relish the front-page story that claimed the lead spot. Beside a photo of Fuat Rantomi, shackled in handcuffs, a bold-lettered caption read, "Noted leader of the notorious Rantomis nabbed in Greece for smuggling a fortune in ancient coins while daughter faces charges of attempted murder. Incriminating evidence also links him to recent murder of real estate tycoon, Gary Sellers and his wife."

Jac smiled. A satisfied smile. A relieved smile. A smile that sent a rewarding warmth through her soul. Her eyes misted and she gazed upon the bubbly group still focused upon Lawton. For the first time in her life, Jac's fledgling faith soared to gigantic proportions. And she realized on a deeper dimension than ever before that

God really saw. He really cared. He really worked in answer to earnest prayer.

She observed Lawton as the physician turned to family members and shook his head in amazement. Lawton's eyes slid shut again, and his breathing regained the rhythmic cadence of a dozing patient. Jacquelyn resisted the urge to crowd back to his side as his recent question teased her into a state of quandary, *So what do you think . . . about me . . . you . . . the "I do" thing?* Jac covered her lips with a trembling hand and wondered where they went from here.

A need for some space pressed itself upon her, and she retrieved her handbag from near the sink, then slipped out the doorway. No one would miss her. They were too focused upon their miracle.

Within 15 minutes, Jac had maneuvered her rental car through intermittent traffic and arrived at the economy hotel where she had spent the last five nights. She stepped into her room, snapped the door shut, switched on the lights, and a spontaneous gush of glee bubbled through her veins. *Lawton's going to make it!*

"Yes!" she exclaimed and hoisted her fist toward the ceiling. The room's cool air sent a rush of gooseflesh along her arms, and Jac pranced to the air conditioner to adjust the manual control.

She noticed the flashing red glow on the telephone and lost no time retrieving her voice mail. "Hi, Jac, this is Donna," a decisive voice rang out. "I left a voice mail on your cell phone yesterday but you haven't gotten back to me. Your accountant just called and says he needs your figures in two days. What do you want me to tell him?"

"Great," Jac groused and plopped onto the bed. Right before Lawton awoke, Jac had been considering the necessity of a trip back home. She had reluctantly realized that she couldn't indefinitely continue her vigil. And now that Lawton was indeed showing signs of recovery, Jac was all the more drawn to be at his bedside. Then his "I do" question raced into her thoughts. No doubts remained. As far as Lawton was concerned, he had finished the chase and was ready to reel in the catch.

"I'm just not sure I'm ready to be caught," Jac whispered and covered her face. *I love him. There's no doubt about that.* She relived the gut-wrenching agony of the last few days. The fear that he would slip into eternity. The panic of losing him. The fervent prayers that would not be subdued. But even during those dark hours, Jac had never once duped herself into believing that his brush with death would somehow blot out her past. And even in the face of this miracle, Jac still grappled with demons. *There's no way I can function in a healthy marriage,* she thought. *No way. And despite the fact that I know he loves me, my problems are going to get old for him. Really old. Really fast.*

Jacquelyn plopped back onto the bed, and the mattress bounced with her weight. She stared at the textured ceiling and listened to the honks and bustle of city traffic. A new thought, laced with compassion, began in the most injured recesses of her soul and rippled its way to the surface of her mind. *If I could deliver Lawton from the grips of physical death, nothing but you can stop Me from delivering you from the grips of emotional death.*

A fresh surge of goose bumps prickled Jac's spine, and she squeezed shut her gritty eyes then rubbed her lids. Jac rested the back of her arm against her eyes and the bed's soft folds invited her to relax. Yet the thought that both challenged and promised still bore upon her. Jacquelyn yawned and her five-day vigil weighed heavy upon her sleep-deprived mind.

As she teetered on the brink of slumber and reality, the resplendent shimmer from the edge of her dreamscape forest erupted on the horizon of her mind. This time the light sparkled with greater intensity than ever before. The radiance hastened upon her, gaining splendor and force. The promise of peace beckoned her to release her anger, her hatred, her bitterness. *Release . . . forgive . . . live. For the first time since childhood, live — really live.*

Jacquelyn, gasping with the moment's fervor, backed away from the sacred luminance that offered a purifying deliverance to her vengeful heart. Yet the farther she shrank from the jewel-like splendor, the more she sensed the dragon's hideous presence. At last his odious snarl blew against her neck, shrouding her in a cloud of disdain. Jacquelyn whirled upon the scaled menace and delivered the fatal kick to his neck that she had yet to unleash on any human being. The dragon screeched and fell into a gagging heap. As soon as his last breath faded upon his lips, the scales fell off bit by bit and Jacquelyn's grandfather lay at her feet.

The radiance, all sparkling and pure and holy, spilled upon her grandfather's lifeless form then began a gradual retreat that allowed an inky darkness to creep upon his form and wrap its spindly fingers around Jac. As the ebony shadows gained intensity,

Jacquelyn glanced toward the golden breadth, now receding as swiftly as it had arrived. A still, small voice urged Jacquelyn to race for the dazzling splendor and jump into the sanctity of the blessed beams — beams that would deliver and heal. Heal and empower. Empower and purify.

Jacquelyn tried to take a step toward the promise of peace, whose diamond-like glister now glowed as a distant star, but she couldn't move her feet. With every step she attempted a needle-like jab shot up her leg. She peered downward. Her ankles were shackled by a chain made from the dragon's yellowed teeth.

Fury flamed from the teeth, licked Jacquelyn's legs, then raced through her veins — a fury fed by the need for revenge. With every increase of the cancerous need, the blaze roared until its inferno far exceeded the heat of the dragon's tainted breath.

A key, as translucent as a sea's limpid waters, appeared beside the barbed shackles, and Jac understood at once that freedom could be hers. Hers to embrace. Hers to relish. But not hers as long as she harbored malice. In order for the key to work, Jac would have to let God extinguish the flames that consumed her ravaged soul — extinguish them with the healing presence of His Holy Spirit.

Yet a rancid well, filled by pulsing childhood wounds, spewed forth a poisoned stream tainted with spite and aversion and revenge. The vicious fire fed upon the poison and grew in intensity. Jacquelyn, consumed in a whirl of fire, lifted her fists and screamed, *I hate you! I hate you for what you did to me! Do you hear me? I hate you!*

Jac sat straight up and gazed around the simple room as if she were a wild animal, cornered and terrified. A hot wad of sweat dampened her neck, and a cool droplet trickled down her back. Her breath puffed in and out in short bursts. She looked down. No dragon's teeth chain claimed her ankles. Her breath's intensity diminished, and she checked her watch. Ten o'clock in the morning. Only 12 minutes had lapsed since she walked through the doorway.

The tormented dream raced upon her once more, and Jacquelyn jerked to a stand. "Income tax," she said, determined to block the dismal images from further consideration. She approached the laptop lying open on the dresser and called up her e-mail. Eric and Donna's urgent requests proved a viable option to veil the distress. In seconds, Jac was typing quick e-mails to them, telling them the latest news of Lawton and that she

445

would take the first shuttle flight from Montrose to Denver that afternoon.

While online, she scanned the plethora of e-mails from her six closest friends. With a sigh she read the posts concerning Adam Jones' funeral, two days ago. A faint memory of Mel's mentioning that event presented itself in the recesses of Jac's mind. She had affirmed Mel's suggestion that both of them remain with Lawton and his family. An e-mail from Melissa briefly stated that she and Jacquelyn had decided to stay put. Sonsee, heavy with child, also e-mailed that her doctor had strictly forbidden her to get out of bed for any reason. However, the three friends had contributed to a mammoth potted plant for their college sister.

"But still, that only left Marilyn, Kim Lan, and Victoria there for Sammie." Jac shook her head as a wave of pity engulfed her. "Poor Sam," she muttered then gripped the back of her neck, still damp with perspiration. *But in one sense, it must be a relief,* she admitted, then thought of those dying roses near Sam's sink. "Poor Sam," Jac repeated and shook her head.

She continued skimming numerous other e-mails then came upon one from Kim Lan dated yesterday, titled "Money for Sam." With an affirmative nod, Jac imagined the lanky supermodel who had redirected her spending patterns from storing up more wealth than she would ever use to funding world missions.

Kim Lan: Hi! I wanted us to take up a little something for Sammie. She says her husband had a decent life insurance policy, but still, she's going to need extra. I talked with her on the phone today, and she's talking about selling her house. I don't know where she's going to move. Marilyn would like for her to rent the house across the street from her and start over in a new town, but Sam says she will probably keep her job in Dallas. As we all know, the Butlers have been really good to her. Anyway, direct all contributions to me here at my Boston address. Also, wherever Sam settles, I think we should all accommodate her and have the next sister reunion wherever she is. Let's plan to stay in a hotel and rent suites. That way she won't have to travel and won't have to put any of us up. I'll help cover the costs. No arguments!

Incidentally, Mick and I are in the process of selling my penthouse. Somehow, it doesn't jive with child-rearing. :-)

With a responsive smile, Jac hit the reply button and typed in her agreement to mail 500 dollars to Kim Lan. While Jac's nest egg didn't compare to Kim's wealth, she was willing and able to help Sam as much as possible. After completing that personal note, Jac started a new message:

Hi! I'm sorry I haven't been in the loop lately. As I see, Mel has kept you all posted on the situation with Lawton. I have great news! He just woke up and is showing signs of recovery. Given the fact that he only had a five-, maybe ten-percent chance to make it without being a vegetable, we are all pretty much blown away. I just left the hospital room, and everyone was still in orbit. Please continue to pray for Lawton — that his recovery will be complete. While you're at it, check the headlines. The Rantomis are the ones who tried to kill Lawton!

Jac paused, reviewed her message, and added one more sentence: "Also, pray for me. I've got a big decision to make. More details later." She copied in the addresses then hit "send."

Twenty-Seven

Jac tapped on the hospital room door then waited. When no response came, she pushed it open and stepped into the room, void of all occupants except the man in the bed tangled in sleep's snare. Mel had called Jac's hotel room an hour ago and announced that Lawton was asking for her. She also mentioned that they were all going to lunch and wondered if Jac might like to go with them. Jacquelyn had explained that she was scheduled on the 217 shuttle flight to Denver, and while she would be by to visit Lawton, she'd grab lunch in transit.

The smell of fresh roses heralded the presence of a bouquet that had arrived since Jacquelyn left. She eyed the copious red blooms and wondered if they were addressed to "hotlips." Their dynamite kiss danced into the present, and Jac smiled. *Well, if the shoe fits,* she thought and resisted the urge to look at the bouquet's tag. She eased around the side of the bed and reached to touch Lawton's hand, lying across his abdomen. She stopped. A row of platinum links was interwoven within his sensitive fingers. Jac took in a quick breath, gripped the siderail, and closed her eyes.

"Hi." Lawton's faint greeting came out over a yawn. "Who's there? Jac?"

She opened her eyes and nodded. "Yep, it's me," she affirmed softly and ached with the love that spilled forth. *Why does this have to be so complicated and hard?* she wondered.

"Mel says you've got to go back to Denver for awhile." He stirred against the bed, and the sheet rustled with his movement.

Jacquelyn reached to stroke his hair, then halted and propped her fingers back against the rail. "Yes. I've got to finish my income taxes and Eric needs me."

"Eric?"

"My new partner. He started in the spring. He's my secretary's nephew."

"Married?"

"No."

"Do I need to be jealous?" His mouth

450

tilted in a lazy grin.

Jacquelyn chuckled. "I don't know, *hotlips*," she taunted. "What do you think?"

"I think I better quit while I'm ahead." He extended the bracelet. "Here. I got Mel to retrieve it from my suitcase."

She bit her bottom lip and stared at the symbol of Lawton's affection. A breathless moment grew into an unspoken question, and one of the stars teetered back and forth as if dancing just for her. Jac looked into the face of a man she had rooted for and prayed for. A face she had grown to love. A face that revealed his own love. Love and adoration. Adoration and respect.

"Jac?" he whispered.

She reached forth and snagged the cool links with the tips of her fingers.

Lawton's chin lifted a fraction and he smiled.

With a sad grin of her own, Jac shook her head. "Nothing's going to keep you down for long, is it?" she asked.

"Not as long as you're at my side," he said. His hand felt along the rail until he bumped her hand then covered it with his fingers. "You never answered me today," he softly challenged.

She propped her other hand on top of his and the bracelet dropped to one side, falling limply across their entwined fingers. The room swelled with emotion that refused to be contained.

"I really think that we could make it, girl," he sang, and his weak voice cracked over the final note.

Her face crumpled; her eyes stung. Jac spun away then marched to the window. Shoulders hunched she gazed upon the parking lot, dazzled by a sun that celebrated its August existence. The platinum stars rested in her hand, and Jacquelyn groped for words. Any words. Words that would convey the mixed-up mess she doubted she'd ever be free of. And the dragon's wicked chuckle exploded into the silence.

"You love me," he assured her. "I know you do. I remember you telling me that while I was — was away. And I came back for you because I love you, Jac. I love everything about you."

"But don't you see," she said and spun to face him. "The question isn't whether or not we love each other. Just because — just because we're in love doesn't mean my past has been obliterated. I still have a lot to work through, Lawton. *Big problems!* I —"

"So what if we get married and let's say I

don't pressure you to be anything but companions for as long as you need."

Struck with the purity of his love, Jacquelyn remained dumbfounded until he spoke once more.

"Whatcha say?" he asked, and the loving plea snaked its way to the center of her heart.

"You deserve better than that, Lawton," she protested and eyed the twinkling stars. "You deserve a woman who can be a *real* wife. A platonic marriage isn't a good existence for a man."

"There's more to marriage than the physical side, Jac. I love being with you. Now . . ." the corners of his mouth turned down, "I'm not going to pretend that the physical side doesn't cross my mind. Believe me, I'm highly interested. But I love you more than I love the idea of having those needs met."

Jacquelyn felt as if she were dissolving into a heap of tears. Tears and awe. Awe and shock. "You are an incredible man, Lawton Franklin," she said, shaking her head.

"So whatcha say?" he repeated.

"I need to do some serious thinking." She crossed her arms.

"You're not saying yes?" the disappointed words limped out.

"No," Jac whispered, "but neither am I saying no."

"Ah." He reached for her. "Come back over here, will ya?"

Jacquelyn took a step toward the bed, then halted as raw fear coursed through her body. She found resisting his request much easier at a distance then up close. Nevertheless, her unrequited love pushed her to his side, and she once again reached to stroke his hair. This time she didn't stop herself. This time she followed through with a kiss on his forehead. Her lips lingered as Lawton's hand tightened around her forearm.

"Don't think for one minute that you're going to get away from me, Jac Lightfoot," he said.

She pulled back and chuckled. A chuckle laced in pain. "I've got to go," she said. "The plane won't wait."

"When are you coming back?"

"I — I don't know."

"There are plans for me to go to my mother's from here. She's determined to make me stay at her house for a month. The doctor says my recovery will be long." A yawn, slow and languid, crept upon him.

"Do what the doctor says."

"I will, I will."

Jacquelyn stepped away from the bed, out of his reach. His lips settled into a melancholic droop, and she steeled herself against falling upon the rail and accepting his offer. *I can't!* she reminded herself. *Not now. Not until I get rid of the dragon.* Wondering if she would ever be free of the fiend, she said a hurried goodbye then bolted. With every tap of her boots against the tile, her troubled soul yearned for the free expression of a husband who would cherish her. Yet Jac began to suspect that she was irrevocably incapable of giving the same. She opened the door and stepped into the hall.

"I love you, Jac! *I love you!*" Lawton's voice floated to her like winged messengers from an agonized heart.

Jacquelyn snapped the door shut and sprinted up the hallway. She ran straight from Lawton's room to her rental car, drove to the airport, and boarded the shuttle flight. When she arrived home, Jac hurled herself headlong into the details of her life. For the next several weeks, she felt as if she were an emotional refugee — hiding from anyone or anything that could remind her of her horrid past. She didn't return calls from her six sisters. She left two letters from Lawton unopened and didn't reply to his message left on her home answering machine. She didn't even check her personal e-mail. Instead, Jac hid from the world under mounds of work coupled with a fervid physical workout that pushed her body to the limit.

None of them understand, she kept telling herself. *They don't know what it's like. They have no idea about the pain I've endured. This is not something you can just get over and be done with. It might take years — or I might never get over it. Ever.*

At the end of all her running, Jacquelyn found herself sprawled face down on her bed one Friday afternoon. Physically expended. Unnerved. Emotionally tired. Tired of running. Tired of hiding. Tired of being dominated by a past that constantly shadowed her. Exhaustion forced her into a dreamless sleep.

She opened one eye and looked at the bedside clock that proclaimed six o'clock. Even after three hours of sleep, she felt as if she had run 30 miles. She stirred and her legs, clad in light sweats, felt as heavy as bricks.

"Oh, God, help me," Jac breathed into the covers. And this time she really meant it. She had so pushed herself past the limits of endurance that hanging on to the hatred proved too taxing. She pushed herself up and stumbled into her kitchen for ice water. The coffeepot, still on from the afternoon, emitted a bitter odor that proclaimed her over-indulgence of caffeine. Filled with abhorrence for her dietary weakness, she flipped off the pot, and extinguished the only light in the rarely used kitchen.

The evening shadows engulfed her, and Jac imagined what it would be like to forever be trapped in darkness. "Lawton never even sees a glimpse of light," she whispered. *Yet he did talk about seeing light when he almost died. But he came back for me. For me. For me. And I don't even have what it takes to receive his gift.*

The words fell like drops of acid upon her tormented mind, and a new obsession began stirring from the pits of her spirit — an obsession to reach and then fling herself into the arms of the resplendent shimmer from the edge of her dreamscape forest. A new path was before her. A path that led to her past. A path that a holy voice, loving and gentle, bade her trod.

Jacquelyn grabbed a bottled water from her ill-stocked refrigerator and dashed a mouthful down her dry throat. She hurried to her functional bedroom, and threw a collection of necessities into her worn suitcase. She didn't even question her instincts until she steered her new Jeep south, past the outskirts of Denver. By then, the light on the horizon of her mind was sparkling with such intensity, with such magnetism, that she couldn't have turned back for anyone — even for her carnal need for revenge. As Jac drove through the night, she hastened ever closer to the radiance that gained in splendor and force. The promise of peace beckoned her to release her anger, her hatred, her bitterness. *Release . . . forgive . . . live. For the first time since childhood, live — really live.*

"I want to live. I really do," Jacquelyn cried as she crossed the border between New Mexico and Texas. And the rising sun, spilling straight into her rig, encouraged her tormented soul to keep stretching for the sacred luminance that offered purifying deliverance to her vengeful heart.

She stopped once in her journey — just long enough to give in to her physical needs, including sleep and food. Even then, Jac only allowed herself a two-hour break. By noon, she was back in her Jeep, back into the throes of her quest. As the smell of the Jeep's new interior engulfed her, Jac's tattered heart prayed to be renewed. Yet the closer she came to east Texas, the more she struggled to suppress the dragon's satisfied chuckle. *You can't be new,* the fiend taunted. *I've got you for life. You will be trapped for the rest of your life. Don't even try to reach for the light. Turn around. Go back home.*

In response, Jacquelyn gripped the steering wheel, stared straight ahead, and pressed forward. The closer she grew to the jewel-like splendor the less frequently the dragon's voice interrupted her quest. At last, Jac found herself dropping beside a grave in a country cemetery near Livingston, Texas. Overhead, the lanky pines, stretching toward a sapphire sky, swished in the tepid autumn breeze and seemed to say, "Jump into the light. Jump into it. And be free!"

Jacquelyn fell atop her grandfather's grave and pummeled the grass-covered plot until the blades of dry grass were completely flat. "How could you have done that to me?" she wailed. But with every pound of her fists, a puff of the dragon's odious breath shrouded her in a cloud of disdain. Jacquelyn reached toward the tombstone and gripped each side as if she were choking the person whose name was etched in stone. The cool marble scraped her palms.

Only the radiance, sparkling and pure and blessed, spilling from the heart of God promised release from the torture. Jacquelyn's taut fingers relaxed against the tombstone, and her exhausted body draped across the top. "Oh, Jesus, Son of God, heal me," she sobbed forth. "Deliver me. Make me whole."

This time the golden breadth engulfed Jacquelyn. The dazzling light permeated the very base of her festering wounds. The balm of holy love from a holy God began the healing.

As the evening shadows stretched long arms across the graveyard, Jacquelyn found herself on all-fours. With tears and courage, she spoke her own declaration of independence. "I renounce everything this man did to me. I renounce the effects of this upon my life. I pray that Jesus Christ, through His mercy and love, will remove all effects of this horrible abuse from me. I claim that I can and will live a normal life and have a normal marriage. I plead the blood of Jesus upon my past, present, and future. Through the power of God, I *refuse* to live in defeat over my past." The words tumbled out from a soul ready to rise victoriously from the ashes of despair.

At last Jac opened her eyes and stared at the ground before her as an inexplicable serenity transcended the threshold from promise to reality. Her gaze journeyed to her right wrist, to the platinum stars she had donned that very morning. The lines of Lawton's poem floated forth as if to underscore the magnitude of her decision: "Come with me. Come with me. Embrace this Giver of Light. His jewel-like flame will transform dark night."

She rocked back on her heels and wiped her face with the corner of her cotton shirt. On the edge of the horizon lined with plenteous pines the first evening star glittered — a diamond against blue velvet, splendid and hopeful. The cooing doves on distant hills wafted upon a breeze that smelled of earth and new beginnings. A cricket's shrill chirp reverberated in sequence with the dove and seemed to announce that Jacquelyn Lightfoot had just fought the most strenuous battle of her life. She fought it and won.

Twenty-Eight

Jac decided not to visit her parents, who lived ten minutes from the cemetery. Her previous desire to discuss her past paled in comparison to her need to see Lawton. She decided to wait until the time was right to discuss her grandfather with her parents. And perhaps, just perhaps, her honesty would bring some healing to her mother as well. Jacquelyn's previous suspicion that murmured her grandfather had violated more than just her was growing to huge proportions. She also suspected that her mother, a master at masking her feelings, had most likely stuffed her own abominable memories into the crevices of her soul. For now, Jac was determined to pursue another mission — a mission that involved her future.

She drove north that evening and stopped in a lazy East Texas town to spend the night. Before going to bed, Jac phoned Mel and asked for directions to Lawton's home. Mel reminded Jac that Lawton was still recuperating under his mother and father's care.

"Why not call Lawton?"

"I want to talk to him in person. I need to talk to him face to face." Jac feared that if she called Lawton to announce her arrival she wouldn't be able to stop herself from blurting the message that threatened to gush forth like an open spillway.

The next afternoon, Jacquelyn drove down Windsor Drive in Nichol's Hills, a suburb of Oklahoma City. Nichol's Hills featured a classic, aging neighborhood, lined by majestic oaks with drooping arms laden with lavish leaves. The two-story frame home with a circular driveway appeared to the left just as Mel said it would. Jacquelyn flipped on her turn signal and stepped on the brakes. As she pulled to a stop in front of the stately home, she admired the well-kept lawn. Near a group of towering oaks resided a stone birdbath nestled in tender grass. Lavish ferns filled flowerbeds, while mums claimed a decorative plant stand. Only the faint sounds of sparse traffic suggested that Jac hadn't driven into an exclusive, horticulturist's haven. She eyed the front door, painted a bright red, put her Jeep into park, turned off the engine, and unfastened her seat belt.

As she slid from the vehicle, a movement from a varnished bench beside the house caught her attention. Lawton stood, his chin lifted, his face attentive. His leather jacket and worn jeans lent him a daredevil aura, and Jac was spurred to embrace a new life with this incredible man.

"Jac?" he called, and the autumn breeze shifted his dark hair around a face that glowed with health.

Immediately Jac knew Melissa had been up to her usual antics. The last thing Jac had thought before drifting into sleep the night before was that Mel would probably call Lawton and tell him she was coming. But for once she didn't care. Right now there were more important things on her mind.

Jacquelyn stuffed her keys into the front pocket of her sweatshirt and strode forward. Without a word, she stopped in front of Lawton, extended her hand, and stroked the face that she had grown to adore. The feel of freshly shaven masculine skin met her palm with warmth and promise.

"Hi, handsome," she whispered through a wobbly smile.

"Jac, oh, Jac," he breathed and reached for her. "I was praying you'd come."

"So, when can we pull off the 'I do' thing?" she asked as his hand settled upon her shoulder.

With an unrestrained whoop, Lawton grabbed Jacquelyn and the two toppled upon the bench. She landed in his lap, and the chair reared back on iron legs. Lawton's laughter echoed off the canopy of trees as the bench plopped back to a standstill. The splatter of sun and shadows danced around them while a chilled breeze hinted at cooler days ahead. Jacquelyn, reeling in Lawton's fervid embrace, leveled a kiss upon him that assured a true marriage in every measure of the word. At last, Jac was home — really home. She had traveled to the end of herself. And there she found Lawton waiting — patiently waiting — like the man of honor he would always be.

When their lips parted, Lawton thrust his hand into the air and yelled, "Yes! Now that's what I call a kiss!"

Midst a round of giggles, a haze of triumph, and a glow of attraction, Jac slid to the park bench, settled into the half circle of his arm, and leaned her head upon his shoulder.

"I'm sorry for not returning your letters or your call," she squeaked out on a guilty note. "I've just been all torn up, and —"

"It's okay, *really*," he assured her, and his joyous voice cast aside any doubts. "I knew you were struggling, and I didn't want to push you, but I *did* want you to know that I was still here."

The scamper and play of a trio of squirrels sent a peppering of leaves and bark onto the lawn. "Those guys are as wild as March hares," Lawton said on a laugh. "If you sit here long enough, one of them will start barking at you."

As if on cue, a squirrel's harassed yap resounded from the limb, and the beady-eyed critter furiously flapped his tail.

"See what I mean?"

"I think he's talking to you," Jac said.

"Yep. I've been putting pecans out for them, but I forgot today. When Mel called this morning before church and mentioned you might be here by one or so, I ditched the squirrels."

"I think that one's wounded for life." Jac looked at the pointy-faced creature who examined Lawton as if it were awaiting the

466

usual treat. Then the squirrel sat back on its haunches and began another round of vociferous complaints.

"Who cares!" Lawton blurted. "I've got you! I don't need those squirrels anymore! Get outta here!" he yelled toward the rodents. "Can't you see we need some privacy, for pity's sake?"

A burst of laughter exploded from Jac.

"You guys are worse than a bunch of little brothers!" Lawton accused. "Give us a break, will ya?"

"You're a nut, Lawton Franklin," Jac said.

"Maybe that's why I'm so popular with the squirrels," he quipped. His voice grew serious and the squirrels were forgotten, "And what about with you? I hope I stay popular with you."

Jac peered up into eyes framed by dark glasses, and she would have sworn the man could see squarely into her soul. "You're tops with me," she said as she clasped both her hands around his free hand. In a flash she relived all those hours she'd stood beside his bed and encouraged him to life. "The absolute tops . . . the most fascinating man I've ever met," she confirmed. "And don't you *ever* try to die on me again. Understand?"

"Yes ma'am," he said as if she were an overbearing drill sergeant. "I won't as long as you don't take me on more criminal chases."

"Hey! I didn't have a choice in that. You were going, thank you very much, and I could either go with you or let you roam off on your own." Jac waved her hand, and the smell of the nearby mums wafted upon a snatch of breeze.

"I'm just glad that Fuat and his daughter are under raps." Lawton shook his head.

"Me too."

"Austin Sellers came to see me before I got out of the hospital. He said you and he had a nasty encounter with a few of them after my surgery."

"We did."

"And that you essentially beat the living daylights out of 'em."

"Well, I didn't have much of a choice. It was either me or them." A distant honk preempted another round of squirrel complaints.

"Remind me not to cross you."

"Okay — don't cross me."

"Ah, you don't scare me," he said and leveled a pretend blow to her chin. "I could take you on any day." Yet when his hand met her chin, his fingers caressed the length of her jaw, and Jacquelyn reveled in the glow of being cherished.

"Does — does it matter at all to you?" she asked, voicing the one question that had shadowed her since she'd met Lawton so long ago.

"What? Nothing about you bothers me," he rushed before giving her a chance to speak.

"I mean, about what happened — when I was a kid." She rubbed her palm on her jeans.

"Yes, it bothers me," he answered on a steely note. "I've always been a peace lover, but when I realized what happened to you, I wanted to really let that man have it." His voice rumbled with the fury Jac herself had experienced, and she marveled that she'd ever doubted his acceptance.

"I was really worried that when you found out you'd somehow lose interest in me," she admitted, her voice tight with honesty.

"Not on your life," he said and shook his head. Then he paused, tilted his face skyward, then sighed. "Okay, I guess since we're baring all here, I should be totally honest."

Jac inched away, peered into his face, and waited.

"I *did* always dream that my future wife would share that part of herself with no one but me. After all, I waited," he uttered.

"But some of us weren't given much of a choice," she snapped, her back rigid.

"Now just hang onto your horses, li'l lady," he drawled and reached for her hand. "I know that. That's what I was about to say." His thumb caressed her tightened fist, and Jac's tension eased a fraction. "During this whole business, I had to reevaluate my preconceived ideas — and, I must admit, my pride. And somewhere along the line, I decided that the thing I wanted was you — regardless. I understand that this was something you had no control over. You were a kid who some *creep* took advantage of," he snarled. "But I also decided that even if that wasn't the case — even if . . . if . . ."

Jac's fist relaxed. She snagged her bottom lip between her teeth, and Lawton's hand slipped into hers.

"I still want you because I love you — just like you are — even with that quick temper of yours," he chided.

"Oh? And you don't have a temper at all, I take it?" she teased, and his previous offer of a marriage for companionship

470

posed itself as the natural reaction of a heart of gold.

"Nope." He raised his chin and his lips turned down. "Not in the least."

Jacquelyn settled back into the circle of his embrace. "Aside from my father, I have never respected a man as much as I respect you," she said, shaking her head. "I'm afraid there aren't many men like you anymore."

"Now that's what a man will die to hear!" Lawton said. "But I think there's plenty more good guys out there. The world hasn't *completely* gone to the dogs, you know."

One of the squirrels scampered to the end of a limb, peered upon them, and restated a round of accusations.

"But maybe it *has* gone to the squirrels," Jac quipped.

"Scat!" Lawton yelled, but the rodent never missed a beat.

A companionable silence settled upon them. A silence mingled with love. Love and tranquility. Tranquility and the unfathomable regard of two souls soon to be one.

"So tell me about the last few weeks, Jac," Lawton finally encouraged. "I've prayed for you like you cannot believe."

A robin landed on the side of the birdbath and Jacquelyn absently eyed it as she explained her journey — a journey that had culminated the evening before. "I'm not going to pretend that there won't be times when . . . that I'm through with all struggles," Jac finished. "I know that full healing will take time. But I'm finally to a point where I'm willing to sit alone with God every day and allow Him to complete what He started last night."

"I guess you prayed me back to life, and I did the same for you," he mused.

"Maybe that's the way it's supposed to be." Jac stirred in the warmth of his embrace and faced him. "You for me, and me for you."

"Hmm . . . I love that, Jac." Rays of light danced upon the surface of his dark glasses. On an impulse Jacquelyn pulled them off, folded them, and slipped them into the pocket of his oxford shirt.

"And I love you," she whispered then trailed her thumbs along his prominent brows and cupped his face in her hands.

"I think you started taking me under the night you told me the sea was like a sponge soaking up phosphorous."

"Oh, but it was," she said and laid her head back on his shoulder. "And I loved your star poem. I can't seem to get away from it."

"I have a new one, you know — just for you," he said, and his voice's vibration rumbled against her cheek.

"You mentioned one on the plane."

"Actually, after I came home from the hospital I rewrote that one. Want to hear it?" he asked like a little boy eager to please.

"What do *you* think?" Jac teased.

The poetic cadence of his next words drifted between them, deepening the bond that promised to last forever and calling to mind the moments when Lawton first gained consciousness.

I have walked the sable darkness.
I have seen eternity.
I know the joys that await us on
the other side.
But I came back for you,
In the here and now.
You.
For your heart only,
   I strained through the night.
For your heart only,
   I embrace this gift of life.
For you, and you alone,
   my champion, my friend, my
love.
For your heart only.

473

Lawton's gentle fingers trailed through Jac's hair, and she closed her eyes as the trees swished and swayed as if they were applauding the moment. "My offer still stands, you know," Lawton said. "I won't push you. I'll wait until you're ready."

Jacquelyn trapped his hand in hers, and pressed his palm against her lips. "I–I think I'm ready," she said. "And it's all going to be okay. We're going to be just fine."

Twenty-Nine

"With the powers vested to me by the state of Arkansas, I now pronounce you husband and wife." Joshua Langham looked up from his text and directed a smile straight at Jac and Lawton. "Lawton, you may kiss your bride."

Jacquelyn, captured by the flood of sunlight that invaded the glass chapel, leaned into her husband's arms for the classic seal of their lifelong vows. Lawton released a mild whoop, grabbed Jac, and smacked her with a kiss she wouldn't soon forget. Her narrow-brimmed bridal hat toppled to the base of her ankle-length satin gown. But, lost in the essence of Lawton's embrace, Jac barely noticed. As the kiss lengthened, the smells of her fresh bouquet mingled with Lawton's spicy aftershave and her floral perfume to heighten the ecstatic moment.

A long and low wolf whistle sounded from the sparse audience, and Jacquelyn suspected one of her six sisters was responsible. As the kiss came to an abrupt halt, the crowd burst into a round of joyous applause. Laughing, Jac glanced down, snatched her veiled hat with trembling fingers, and scrunched it back onto her silken hair.

"What happened?" Lawton whispered.

"You knocked my hat off!" Jac said out of the corner of her mouth.

"Well, you knock my socks off!" Lawton responded. His comment, meant as a private innuendo, bounced off the glass walls of the exotic chapel that thousands of tourists annually admired.

"You go, man!" Kinkaide called, and the group broke into spontaneous laughter.

Jacquelyn wiggled her fingers at her six sisters who sat in a cluster on the bride's side: Marilyn and Kim Lan both gave the thumbs-up sign. Sonsee, cradling her newborn boy, produced a tired, although triumphant grin. Victoria and Melissa both returned the finger-wiggles. Sammie, however, didn't notice Jac's greeting. Sam placed a calming hand upon her squirming son then glanced over her shoulder as a motorcycle's rev neared from the highway.

In that brief second, Jac relived the conversation she and Sam had shared when she was helping Jac zip her simple ecru wedding dress. "R.J. wants to get married," Sam had confided. "But I don't think I'm ready."

Jacquelyn glanced over her shoulder and into Sam's corn-flower-blue eyes. "Don't you think it's too soon?"

"Yes, I really do," Sam replied, her lips in a firm line. "And he has accepted that for now. The problem is that his mother is turning the magazine over to him, so he'll be my new boss."

"Has she gone daft?" Jac blurted and whirled to face her friend. "He looks about as literary as a caveman."

Sam laughed outright. "Actually, he's quite a writer. His parents even made him get a degree in journalism before he rode off into the sunset."

"Well, wonders never cease."

Now, standing on the brink of her own new life, Jac caught a glimpse of a Harley through the trees and wondered exactly what Sam's future held. She hadn't mentioned that R.J. would be at the wedding. Perhaps he just tracked Sam down on a whim.

The keyboard player burst into the customary music that announced the two were now one and on their way to a life together. Jac dashed aside all musings, and she and Lawton turned to face the beaming faces of their immediate family and a few close friends.

"I joyfully present to you Lawton and Jacquelyn Franklin," Joshua exclaimed.

Jacquelyn grabbed the arm of her tuxedoed groom, and the two marched down the short aisle. As they neared the back door, Jac glanced up, through the transparent roof, to the cascade of foliage tinged in autumn's gold. She extended her left hand to admire the wide gold band gleaming against bronze skin.

Lawton draped his arm around her waist and gave her a quick hug. "Happy?" he asked.

Jac stroked his face and once again felt that the dark glasses covered eyes that saw more than she might ever see.

"Happier than I've ever been in my whole life," she responded, feeling as if all of heaven were christening the moment.

Author's Note

~

Dear Reader,

I wrote of Jacquelyn's battle with the aftermath of sexual abuse from my own experience. I, too, have struggled with the painful reality of being victimized at the hand of a selfish man who cared for nothing but his own gratification.

According to statistics, about half or more of everyone in America has been sexually abused at some point in their childhoods. This widespread tragedy can be equated with a death and, at times, will make the victim wish she were really dead.

I have been there, right down the same pathway that Jacquelyn travels. During my late twenties, I would have gladly embraced death. I decided that if the rest of my life was going to be as painful as the previous years then frankly, I would rather just not go forward. During those dark days of depression, I was sorely tempted to end my own life. And I firmly believe that the only thing that saved me was God's ever-present grace. Not only did He preserve my life, He began a healing miracle within me. A miracle that Jac herself begins to experience. A miracle that took time but resulted in my eventual wholeness.

I don't know where you have been or what tragedies you have faced, but I will testify that the healing God offers is far from fictitious. It is real. It is lasting. It is truly awesome. Have you embraced Him for healing from your past? Truly embraced Him?

Have you taken the time to plug in the worship music, sit in His presence, and soak up His healing for a chunk of time every day? Have you committed to daily reading the Word of God and allowing it to speak to your injured spirit? Only when I began to regularly devote serious time to the healing process did I give the Lord the opportunity to orchestrate the deep, deep healing that He so desperately desires to extend to all who ask. Such healing doesn't come quick, and, frankly, I'm still in the final stages. Such healing doesn't come easy; I still struggle at times. But the healing does come to those who take the time to seek Him.

Are you seeking? God is waiting.

In His Service,
Debra White Smith

Debra White Smith

Debra enjoys writing both fiction and non-fiction and, since 1997, has nearly 500,000 books in print. Her fiction books include: *Second Chances, The Awakening, A Shelter in the Storm,* and *To Rome with Love.* Her non-fiction books include: *Romancing Your Husband* and *The Harder I Laugh, the Deeper I Hurt.*

Debra is often featured on radio programs throughout North America. She speaks across the nation and particularly enjoys stopping in at airport ice-cream parlors — especially if they serve German chocolate. Debra lives in small-town America with her wonderful husband of 19-plus years and two adorable children.

To write to Debra or contact her for

speaking engagements, check out her website at:

www.debrawhitesmith.com

or send mail to:

Debra White Smith
PO Box 1482
Jacksonville, TX 75766

The employees of Thorndike Press hope you have enjoyed this Large Print book. All our Thorndike and Wheeler Large Print titles are designed for easy reading, and all our books are made to last. Other Thorndike Press Large Print books are available at your library, through selected bookstores, or directly from us.

For information about titles, please call:

(800) 223-1244

or visit our Web site at:

www.gale.com/thorndike
www.gale.com/wheeler

To share your comments, please write:

Publisher
Thorndike Press
295 Kennedy Memorial Drive
Waterville, ME   04901